Killigrew Clay

Rowena Summers
Killigrew Clay

CANELO

First published in Great Britain in 1986 by Severn House Publishers Ltd

This edition published in the United Kingdom in 2020 by

Canelo Digital Publishing Limited
Third Floor, 20 Mortimer Street
London W1T 3JW
United Kingdom

A CIP catalogue record for this book is available from the British Library.

Print ISBN 978 1 78863 848 7
Ebook ISBN 978 1 78863 467 0

Look for more great books at www.canelo.co

Printed and bound in Great Britain by Clays Ltd, Elcograf S.p.A.

To Geoff and all our family, with love

Chapter One

The thunder and clatter of iron-shod wheels were heard well in advance of the china clay waggons careering down the narrow cobbled streets of St Austell town on the first of their twice-yearly arrivals from the pits.

Morwen Tremayne's blue eyes sparkled as she emerged from the warm spicy interior of Nott's bakery into the spring sunlight. It was her seventeenth birthday, and she had been sent to town to buy a bag of fruit buns for the family tea.

Her excitement grew, knowing she would be in the steep-sided town when the clay waggons came through, on their way to Charlestown port from the works, up on the moors. When the waggons reached here, they would be crawling, inching carefully to avoid damage to people and property. The waggons would be piled pyramid-high with the great white blocks Morwen had helped to stack, and on the precarious descent to the port they would need three good horses to pull them down the hills, and six to drag them back up.

Morwen's family all worked for Killigrew Clay. She felt a tingle of pride at her father's new position. Pit captain for Mr Charles Killigrew! And they were Killigrew waggons coming through St Austell town that afternoon...

'Dear heaven preserve us! These dreadful vehicles!' a townslady near Morwen exclaimed angrily, pulling her fine skirt above her ankles, regardless of dignity as the first lumbering waggon wove its way to lessen the gradient of the hill. Horse harnesses creaked and strained, chains rattled, waggoners roared to everyone to keep clear.

The streets were constantly white with clay traffic from various pits, and this new arrival sent flurries of white powder spinning from wheels and clay blocks. The waggoners, bare arms corded with taut muscles as they strove to control horses and load, were stippled ghost-like from the dust as they hollered like demons for the townspeople to mind themselves.

Morwen watched their weaving progress. The clay waggons were part of her life, and she didn't often see them from this vantage point. Usually, she was cheering the waggons away from the pits with the other bal maidens like herself, with the kiddley boys who made the tea and did the menial jobs, the clayworkers and the captains themselves. Sometimes, the owners would be at the works, away from their big houses and offices.

It was a great day, after months of allowing the china clay to dry until it was ready for cutting and blocking, loading and despatching, for use in industries far removed from its humble beginnings in the earth. For paper-manufacture and medicinal items, and fine china to grace society tables...

Morwen's mother had once said lyrically that on a day like this, the china clay was no longer their own, but belonged to the world. The comment was met by hoots of laughter from her brawny husband and three strapping sons. Even small Freddie had chuckled, without really understanding why. Only Morwen had smiled dreamily, liking the poetry of the words, and sharing a moment of pleasure with her mother, when there was normally little time for such sentiments.

In the dust-filled streets of St Austell town on that sunlit spring afternoon, Morwen knew exactly what Bess Tremayne had meant. She heard a quick bellow from one of the waggoners.

'Fastest time yet, Morwen,' Thomas Penry roared above the din of the wheels. 'Did 'ee have a wager on us?'

She shook her head, her long dark hair dancing beneath her white bonnet as she laughed. Her Daddy didn't allow wagers from his own, though most clay-workers took bets on the time the loaded clay waggons took to get from Killigrew pits to St Austell. It added a bit more spice to the thrills of the day...

Morwen stopped laughing, suddenly aware that the two townsladies beside her had realised that the comely young girl outside the bakery, with the flushed face and jewel-bright eyes, must be one of the common bal maidens from the clay works. In her best yellow dress and her boots polished for the walk to town, in defiance of the clay dust, Morwen could easily pass for town-bred. Her features were delicate, and not weathered by the winds of the moors.

'If you know these men, young woman, you might tell them they'll be the ruin of this lovely town!' the lady snapped, needling Morwen into a quick retort.

'If you'll tell Mr Charles Killigrew to build a railway track from his works to the port, the waggons needn't come through the town at all! No waggoner enjoys risking his life on every journey!' she flashed back.

But Morwen knew that they enjoyed it immensely, calling it the finest paid sport in the county. She smiled at the thought, which the good dames saw as insolence.

'You young women are as bad as you're painted,' the other lady said coldly, noting every bit of Morwen's dew-fresh appearance. 'Wild and unruly—'

Morwen tossed her head. She might have stalked away with head held high, when a familiar voice sounded right behind her, deep and masculine, and as thickly-textured as lemon-curd. It could be harsh, but right now it was jovial, and it addressed one of the tight-corseted ladies.

'Now then, Hannah! Gossiping with Morwen Tremayne, are you?' Charles Killigrew chuckled.

Morwen's face turned scarlet, and she hardly noticed the ladies' affront at Killigrew's assumption. She faced the thick-set man with the curling whiskers, the shock of grey hair still abundant, the portly stomach covered by a tweed waistcoat and a heavy watch-chain inside his country suit.

'I'm on my way home, Mr Killigrew.' Morwen was furious to find herself stammering, and the man laughed genially.

The girl was a welcome sight to any man. More so than his disapproving sister Hannah and her scratchy friend.

'No need to explain, m'dear. Your father tells me it's your birthday—'

A second waggon came thundering through, clay blocks rocking, and scattering the townsfolk quicker than a swarm of bees. Charles Killigrew smiled with satisfaction. Each waggon-load for the waiting ships at Charlestown meant more money in Killigrew's pocket.

He was a self-made man, with a little help from a rich wife, now departed, and he relished both facts.

His eyes shone as brightly as Morwen Tremayne's as he waved the waggon through. In the flurry of activity, Morwen had slipped away. As Charles turned to speak to her, he saw her collide with a tall young man, whose arms reached out to steady her, his grasp firm on Morwen's shoulders.

She felt the warm pressure of his fingers through the gauzy fabric of her dress, and her face flamed anew at this contact with a young gentleman. Barely glancing at him, she twisted away, picking up her skirts with far less fuss than the St Austell dames, and sped into the crowd.

The young man stared after her, intrigued by the pleasant sensation of holding her so briefly. The fresh clean scent of her hair had swung across his face for an instant. There was something about her... an elusive memory... he frowned slightly as he caught sight of the yellow swirl of her skirts, and the frown enhanced his good-looking face. He was healthily tanned, his features well drawn and very strong. More than one of his contemporaries at his fancy London college had respected the fists of Ben Killigrew when the sons of dukes and lords had sneered at his Cornish accent.

The girl was vaguely familiar, Ben thought, but he couldn't think why. He would certainly remember again those wide blue eyes and that creamy skin that had flushed so alluringly. Her cheeks were heart-shaped, shadowed charmingly by the white bonnet... and that very soft pink mouth had been parted in momentary confusion. She had made a surprising impact on him...

He leapt back hastily as the next clay waggon strained its way down the steep hills of the town, and a hand clapped him on the shoulder. Charles Killigrew smiled at his son, seeing in him the fine cut of the sprig he had once been. Young, virile, handsome... and Ben had all the advantages too. Ben's legacy was all there waiting for him, and the evidence was rolling through St Austell streets today. Charles beamed at his son, elegant in frock coat and tight white breeches, the fashionable neck-cloth at his throat caught by a pearl pin, and was well pleased with the results of the London college, despite the small fortune it had cost.

'Father, who was that girl?' Ben asked at once. His eyes still roamed after Morwen's straight, retreating figure, long since gone out of sight.

'What girl? Oh, Morwen Tremayne, d'you mean?' Charles spoke carelessly. The girl was the daughter of his newest clay captain, no more.

'Good God! That's it. Morwen Tremayne!' Ben said, his dark eyes gleaming. 'The last time we met, she was ten years old, and fighting like a whirling dervish with a group of bal maidens twice her size. You'd taken me to the clay pits to explain the workings to me after Mother died—'

'And you were bored silly,' Charles grunted. 'You'll find a good many changes now, boy.'

And Morwen Tremayne was one of them, and still in Ben's thoughts as they were joined by his Aunt Hannah and her friend, Miss Emily Ford. Ben saw that his aunt was still ruffled about the gathering at the house that evening, and looked even more put out than usual.

Hannah Pascoe was her brother's housekeeper, which meant that she and her son, Jude, had a permanent home at Killigrew House. Most of the time, the household was harmonious enough... but when Charles made one of his spontaneous decisions to hold a supper party, as he had done for this evening, Hannah had no choice but to deal with it. Even when he invited the most impossible people, as he often did, Hannah was reminded in no uncertain terms that if she objected, there were plenty more widows willing to keep house for Charles Killigrew!

And where would that leave Hannah? With no husband to support her, and a dissolute son who had gone through what little money Ned Pascoe had left her like sand through a sieve. Jude was a constant thorn in her side. She alternately loved him and hated him, and she more than resented the fact that Ben would inherit all the Killigrew pits and prosperity, while Jude seemed destined to live by his wits and his uncle's hand-outs.

–

Morwen was glad to leave the town and continue the steep climb to the moors above St Austell. The last of the day's waggons from Killigrew pit number one had passed her now, making relatively easy work of it in the fine spring weather. It was very different later in the year, when the tracks became quagmires, and waggon wheels dug inches deep in mud. St Austell dames really did have a complaint then, with fine wool dresses all mud-spattered as the vehicles wove through the narrow winding streets.

She paused for breath on the short moorland turf, drinking in the clean, furze-scented air, filled with whispering bracken and nodding pink clover, and the aromatic white blooms of yarrow. Above her were the huddles of the clayworkers' cottages, built in short rows of fours, all adjoining one another and set at angles to give a higgle-piggledly appearance.

The inner cottages were more snug and insulated by the walls of the others, but the outer ones had more yard space, in which to keep pigs or chickens. The Tremaynes lived in an outside cottage, and rightly so now, since Hal had been made captain of number one pit, working up from being a lowly kiddley boy, as his youngest son, Freddie, was now.

Beyond and around the clayworkers' cottages, rose the pale mounds of the spoil heaps, made eerily beautiful by moonlight, and as much a landmark for a returning clay-worker in his cups as any standing stone on the moor. In sunlight, the spoil heaps glinted with the discarded small mineral deposits. By then, the more valuable china clay had been washed clean of such impurities, leaving in its wake the milky-green pool that typified every clay pit working.

The exhilaration of the day had whipped up more colour in Morwen's cheeks. She untied her bonnet, letting the breeze spin through her hair, and loved the wild freedom of it. Far below her, beyond the town, the sea glittered.

Calmed and mirrored by distance, it belied the way it could thresh and churn into mountainous waves that made the Cornish coastline so magnificent and so treacherous.

The harbour and port of Charlestown, where the clay waggons were bound, was in the lee of the town. Down there, Charles Killigrew had his fine big house. Morwen drew in her breath as a warm gust of wind stung her cheek where a thorn or a pin had scratched her flesh…

A pin! She remembered instantly! A pearl pin in a gentleman's neck-cloth. From the moment she had stumbled into a strong pair of arms and felt her breasts flatten against a broad male chest, she had puzzled over his identity. Now, she remembered… and felt the old antagonism…

'Ben Killigrew!' she said to the breeze. 'That snot-nosed owner's son, too scared of dirtying his fine leather boots at his father's pit. And when he did come, it was to catch us scrapping, and to look down his nose—'

She heard running feet, and a child's laughing voice.

'You know what they say about folks talking to themselves, our Morwen. They'll call 'ee as batty as old Zillah! I'm sent to find you. Mammie's asking for the fruit buns, though we won't be needing 'em today now—'

'What are you drivelling on about, Freddie?' Morwen said crossly, annoyed that her small brother should have caught her talking to the air. Freddie was eight years old, and quite likely to go crowing to the older ones that his sister was turning as moon-struck as the old crone who lived with her cats in the hovel across the moor. Zillah the wise one, Zillah the witch – or just plain old crazy woman, depending on each private opinion.

'Why shouldn't Mammie want the buns for my birthday tea?' Morwen demanded, since Freddie had lost interest in her now, and was busily chasing butterflies instead. His blue eyes, as candid as all the Tremaynes', glowed with excitement.

'We're all invited to the big house tonight, that's why! Mammie says the buns can keep till tomorrow, and 'tis a shame she didn't know about Mr Killigrew's supper before she spent the pennies on buns—'

'Mr Killigrew's supper!' Morwen taunted. 'Why would he want to invite us to supper, you ninny? You're gaming with me, aren't you, Freddie?'

Her heart was jumping in her chest. It couldn't be true, and if it was, she wouldn't go to be inspected like a fly on the wall. None of the Tremaynes had been inside the big house, which to Morwen was as large and palatial as a mansion, and only emphasised the meanness of the humble cottage where she and her family lived.

Morwen felt no resentment about that. The Tremaynes and the Killigrews lived in two different worlds, which was as it should be. Owners in the mansion, workers in the cottage, and the two should never mix socially. Freddie must be mistaken. She willed it to be so.

'Mr Killigrew's son has come home to stay,' Freddie said importantly, glaring at his sister. 'Mr Killigrew told us so when he came to the works. You'd gone off to town by then. He came in a fine carriage, all for one person, and went off to S'n Austell faster'n flying! You missed un, Morwen, and Daddy told un you'd be dawdling because it was your birthday. And Mr Killigrew said if that were so, then we must all go to supper tonight, because he were so pleased with the clay-loading!'

He paused for breath. It must be true then. She had wondered how Charles Killigrew had known it was her birthday. Owners didn't keep account of such things. Now she felt doubly embarrassed – because of her Daddy telling him about her birthday, and because she would be seeing Ben Killigrew for the second time that day. And her Sunday best dress was already rumpled and dusty, and her cheek was scratched, and she didn't know why she should care, but she did!

She got to her feet, the precious bag of buns already tacky. She felt the same. She grabbed Freddie's hand.

'Let's get home then. I want to find out some more about this posh supper. What do the boys say to it?'

'Sam says he don't fancy poncing about in some big house. Matthew don't mind, but Jack's saying he won't go. Mammie says he will, and there's an end to it.'

He sounded so like his mother that Morwen smiled in spite of herself. The tide would stop ebbing and flowing before Bess Tremayne changed her mind about a thing. But Morwen didn't want to go to Killigrew House either. It wouldn't be a comfortable evening. Perhaps the Tremaynes would be the only guests, she thought hopefully, and doubted it. Just as though Charles Killigrew would arrange a supper for a handful of employees and nobody else. There would be fine ladies and gentlemen, and Morwen would be all fingers and thumbs, conspicuous with her country manners and her dusty dress, and ashamed of her family's shortcomings, when she loved them fiercely, every one.

She stopped so quickly that Freddie almost fell over her. What was wrong with her? She was seventeen years old, and as good as anyone, even Mr High-and-Mighty Ben Killigrew with his new city ways and smart clothes. She needn't even speak to him. He probably wouldn't notice her among all the more important folk invited that night. Her chin tilted.

'You nearly had me down,' Freddie raged. 'You were dreaming again, just like old Zillah, with that daft look in your eyes. Daft old Zillah. Daft old Morwen!'

He began chanting, racing away from her on nimble feet that gripped the turf better for not having boots to impede them. Morwen raced after him towards Killigrew pit number one, where their father was now pit captain, and top man.

Hal Tremayne worked the main day shift, from seven in the morning until half-past three in the afternoon. There were two other shifts, and he had worked them all in his time, but he now had the more regular hours, and would be free for tonight's social gathering at Killigrew House.

The clogging clay dust rose in their nostrils as Morwen and Freddie neared the pit, humming with activity at mid-afternoon. The dust was irritating to the throat, yet many clayworkers swore by the clay water to relieve an over-flatulent stomach. It was cheaper than a doctor's visit to take a quick hand-scoop of the slurry, and the dry-tasting stuff quickly cured the bile.

The ground in the pit was often likened to a river of milk, as the greenish-white liquid seeped and squelched underfoot. Standing in the clay for hours on end was hard on the feet. The men wore long leather boots with wooden soles, and packed them with straw in winter to keep their feet snug and warm. The local cobbler had lasts with every man's name painted on them, and prided himself on knowing individual footprints and peculiarity of tread.

It was a familiar scene to Morwen; the constant drone of the beam engine, pumping and winding and removing the coarse sand and stone to what Charles Killigrew affectionately called his sky-tips. There were the settling tanks, the fire-hole and pan-kilns; the linhay where Morwen worked with the other bal maidens, scraping sand and dirt, from the clay blocks beneath a reed-roofed, open-sided structure where the air assisted in drying the blocks already stacked for transporting. It was as familiar to her as the new pit captain in his hard hat and dark jacket, mark of his new status, striding towards her and Freddie at the end of the main day's shift.

Hal Tremayne had the good looks of all his family. He was strong as an ox, and well respected by his fellow workers. Pit captain of number one pit carried a special prestige. He smiled at his youngest son and his pretty daughter.

'You'll have heard the news from our Freddie, then, Morwen. We're to go to the big house tonight—'

He spoke as if it were a great honour. So it was, but Morwen wasn't prepared to see it that way. She frowned.

'I've nothing tidy to wear, Daddy—' she began heatedly.

'You've the pretty dress you're wearing now, me dear, and a pretty sight you be an' all. Aside from the scowl on your bonnie face!' His eyes suddenly twinkled. 'Your Mammie was expecting as much, and she has a surprise for you, Morwen—'

'A surprise?' Her eyes glowed like sapphires, and Hal realised that his girl-child was fast becoming a woman, with a rare beauty like her mother. In Hal's eyes, Bess was beautiful still, but Morwen had something more. It was that odd little air of self-assurance that added to the delicate colouring of her skin and the richness of her smile, and the rippling blue-black sheen of her hair.

'I'll see the surprise before you do, our Morwen!' Freddie shouted. With a squeal of laughter, Morwen grabbed up her skirts and raced after him, a child again.

A mile away from the pit, they arrived at the Tremayne cottage, both panting, the bag of buns a sticky mess in Morwen's grasp.

Inside the cottage, warm and cosy, Bess Tremayne smiled. This was her favourite time, when the family came home, and they were all together again. The two elder boys, Sam and Matthew, worked the early shift, and were already scrubbed clean for the evening. Jack, at thirteen, and overly conscious about himself, still grumbled about going to the big house for supper, but knew he'd find no compromise in his mother. Charles Killigrew was actually sending a conveyance to take the Tremaynes to town and bring them back again, and Bess intended seeing that her brood was well turned out for the occasion.

'Daddy said there was a surprise for me, Mammie,' Morwen said, out of breath. Another surprise for her birthday…

Bess asked for the buns first, and Morwen burned with impatience as she handed them over. Freddie hopped from foot to foot and was ordered to go outside to the privy at once, or he'd be left at home that night.

'Mammie, don't tease me!' Morwen pleaded. Bess relented at once, and told Morwen to follow her upstairs to the room she and Hal shared, with the curtained-off portion for Freddie. The three older boys shared a second upstairs room, while Morwen had one corner of the one big downstairs room for herself. It meant waiting for everyone to go to bed before she had complete privacy, but at least she could pretend it was a room of her own in a big house, like the one where the Killigrews lived.

Upstairs, Bess took out Morwen's white muslin dress from the clothes recess. It was Morwen's second best, and she was lucky to have two good dresses. Her Mammie did sewing for the townsladies at times, and had been given the discarded dress for Morwen. It was fresh and neat, but far too plain to wear tonight… at least, it had been.

Now, there were ribbons sewn across the bodice, swathed and crossed, and looped around the hemline too. The ribbons transformed the plain muslin into a frivolous affair of blues and mauves, and Morwen gasped with pleasure at her mother's handiwork.

'Mrs Pollancy gave me the ribbons, and when Mr Killigrew asked us to supper, I knew just what to do with them,' Bess smiled. 'You'll be the prettiest girl there, our Morwen!'

'It's beautiful, Mammie! The best birthday gift ever!'

Morwen held the dress against her. The silk ribbons were soft and shiny, smoothly sensual. How must it feel to wear a dress made entirely of silk… she couldn't imagine it. It must be wonderful, but no more wonderful than the way she felt at that moment. She wouldn't disgrace the company at the Killigrews!

And following hard on that thought was another one, sliding sweetly into her mind before she could stop it. Ben Killigrew would see that not only could Morwen Tremayne look like a lady in company, but that she could behave like one too.

Chapter Two

Hannah Pascoe's face darkened as she studied the guest list her brother had just handed her. A deep suspicion sharpened her tongue even more than usual.

'There are seven guests here called Tremayne, Charles. Wasn't that the name of the common girl on East Hill today?'

'Quite right, Hannah,' Charles Killigrew said, watching the satisfying spiral of smoke from his best Havana cigar curl around his elegant drawing-room. 'Morwen is the daughter of my new pit captain, Hal Tremayne—'

'And this – this Morwen person – is coming here—?'

Charles looked directly at his sister. She recognised the edge in his voice.

'Are you going deaf, Hannah? Yes, this Morwen person, who happens to brighten up my day whenever I see her, will be coming here this evening, with her entire family. And as my housekeeper, I shall expect you to give them every courtesy, the same as you give the Carricks and the Gorrans and that whey-faced friend of yours. Is that clear enough?'

Hannah's lips tightened. She understood Charles very well indeed. He was generous and affable, but his moods could change quickly, as his clayworkers knew full well.

He was fair, but sometimes unpredictable, and at home and in business, his word was law. Hannah knew at once when she had gone too far.

'I've never given you cause to complain, Charles,' she said stiffly, swallowing her fury. 'But you don't give me much time to cater for seven extra people—'

'This house can cater for seventy extra if I wish it,' he retorted. 'There's food and plenty. If not, then send out for more, and don't bother me with trifling details. And tell that old hag of a friend of yours to get that sourpuss expression off her face if she's coming here tonight. She's enough to turn the wine to vinegar.'

Hannah counted to ten, trying not to betray her mounting rage. She knew she had provoked her brother's aggressive mood. But really... inviting a common bal maiden and her family to Killigrew House, along with the prosperous Carricks from Truro, and the digni-fied Gorrans. Couldn't Charles see that these Tremaynes would be out of place? Sometimes she thought Charles was going daft in the head.

Ben joined them while the harangue continued, which annoyed her even more, especially since he seemed to find their verbal battles so amusing. Hannah could be quite fond of Ben, if she wasn't always comparing his lot with her son's. Ben had everything, while Jude...

Where was Jude, anyway? Hannah's thoughts went off at a tangent as she stormed away to the kitchen to vent her anger on the housemaids. She hadn't seen her son since early morning when he'd left the house. Hannah had her suspicions as to where he went. There was too often a whiff of the sea on his clothes, a reckless gleam in his eyes, a simmering excitement...

Hannah would like to come up a bit in the town. If only she could meet a well set up widower with a bit of money, so that she wasn't dependent on Charles... and so that she could stop fretting that Jude might be hob-nobbing with those wretched, infamous wreckers, the scum of the Cornish coasts.

She had no real proof, aside from the unexplained amounts of money Jude sported from time to time, and a feeling in her bones. She should demand to know, but something held her back. If she knew for certain, then she would have to tell her brother, and Jude would be sent packing. Charles would have no truck with such activities, and Hannah couldn't bear the disgrace of it all.

So she said nothing, to her own self-disgust. Only to her dear friend, Emily, did she hint that Jude's movements were a constant worry.

–

'Why didn't you tell me you'd invited the Tremaynes to supper tonight, when I was asking about Morwen earlier, Father?' Ben exclaimed, still grinning at the sight of his aunt marching from the room, broom-pole stiff.

Charles laughed. 'I wanted to surprise you, m'boy. Thought you'd enjoy having two pretty girls in the house. Which reminds me. The Carricks will be here soon. You'll enjoy seeing Jane again—'

Ben sighed. 'You're not still trying to marry me off to Jane Carrick, are you? I like her well enough – as a sister—'

Charles moved to the crystal decanter on the side table and poured a drink for them both. He eyed his son lazily as he settled into a deep leather chair.

'But you don't love her – is that it?'

'Good God, I hardly know her!' Ben exclaimed.

'You've known her for years. I've always thought it would be a good match, and her parents certainly think so, Ben. It would bind us together more strongly, with Richard Carrick being my partner in the clay works, for all that he likes to keep it a silent partnership. You and Jane—'

'*No!*' Ben said harshly. 'You may manipulate other peoples' lives, Father, but you won't manipulate mine!'

Charles looked at him in genuine surprise.

'Manipulate? That's an odd word between father and son, when I only want the best for you, boy. As for the love business – I didn't love your mother when we were wed, but that can come later. We had you, didn't we? All that romantic nonsense soon passes, and Jane's a comely young woman now, you'll see.'

Ben gave a muffled oath. His father wore blinkers on this topic, but he could argue until the moon turned blue. Ben would marry whom he chose, and when he chose. He wasn't ready yet. He was only twenty-one years old and had plenty of time, and he was determined to stand up to Charles in this.

He glanced at his father, knowing he was well able to take care of himself. He'd had to, in the fancy London college that Charles thought so elite.

Ben had believed that only girls fought for their honour, but he'd had to fight for his too. He'd proved his masculinity and virility to his own satisfaction in the London bawdy-houses along with the college rowdies. He'd also proved himself on the gaming tables, amassing more money, shrewdly invested, than his father ever guessed about. He liked the feeling of independence it gave him.

Ben Killigrew was a fine fellow now, with his modulated Cornish accent spiced up with plummier vowel sounds, to his father's pleasure. But Ben had seen plenty of low life in London, enough to be sickened by it. He had decided that fornicating merely to spin the broadest, lewdest tale to a group of roaring, table-thumping college students, wasn't what he wanted out of life. There must also be love…

And love was not what he felt for Jane Carrick. Ben had no intention of making her his life's partner to fulfil some dream of their parents. He hadn't seen Jane for a year. To him, she would always be – just Jane. They had begun to make a game of their supposed fondness for each other. Now he wondered uneasily if it had been wise. He pushed the thoughts away from him for the moment.

He drained his brandy glass, feeling the warm sting of it in his throat, and thought of the other girl he would see that evening. A vaguely pleasurable memory of holding Morwen Tremayne against him filled his senses. It wasn't the first time he had recalled it. She had felt soft, rounded and feminine, gazing up at him for a moment with those extraordinary blue eyes, like a startled fawn. He wished the moment had been longer…

'Have you seen your cousin today, Ben?' Charles said abruptly, preparing to leave the room.

Ben shook his head. 'He keeps out of my way. We don't have a lot to say to each other when I first come home.'

'He'd best get used to seeing you about the place then,' Charles snapped. 'I'll not see you two bickering as though you were children. You're young men now—'

'Remember that, Father, when you're wanting to choose me a bride. I'm old enough to choose my own, wouldn't you say?'

For a second, the older man said nothing, then he roared with laughter and clapped his son on the back. The brief irritation changed to good humour. Charles Killigrew liked what he saw in his son, despite the clashes he guessed would have to come between two strong-willed men.

–

While the Killigrew men conversed, Jude Pascoe stole up the back stairs of the house, concealing the bottle of French brandy beneath his jacket until he reached his own room. It was fair produce of the sea… though he doubted that his mother would agree, and the brandy must be well hidden from her eagle eyes. He placed it beneath the loose board in his closet, the small spoil of a recent wrecking.

Jude's blood ran faster at the excitement of it. There was little else to do here. He had no fortune to expect like his cousin, Ben, whom he resented bitterly. Not so much Ben himself, as what he represented. The pit owner's son, well educated, and slipping easily into boots already well heeled. While Jude had the legacy of a drunken father and a caustic-tongued mother who expected him to be grateful for his uncle's patronage. Grateful was his mother's word, but her tone was brimful of her own humiliation, and not surprisingly Jude felt exactly the same.

He thrust the brandy beside others stacked in his closet for selling at a profit to a kiddleywink inland, where the landlord didn't question its source. He had just finished when his door opened, and Jude's head spun as he stood up quickly to face his mother, on his guard as always.

'So you're back,' she snapped, her eyes scanning the room. 'And not before time. You're to tidy yourself for this evening. We're having guests for supper, and you'll not disgrace me. A scrub with a yard broom wouldn't come amiss, and a rake through that tangle of thatch you call hair. Have you no pride in yourself? Look in the mirror, and how you appear. You're a fine contrast to your cousin!'

Jude's dark eyes flashed. He was roguishly handsome, without the refinements of his cousin, and he didn't need reminding of Ben's advantages.

'Then you'd best get out of here and let me attend to it, Mother dear,' he growled sarcastically. 'Unless you're offering to scrub my neck for me?'

Hannah swept from the room, slamming the door after her. He was her son, and for that she tolerated him, but there were times when she cursed the day she had let Ned Pascoe sweet-talk her into marrying him. If she'd known that Jude would be the result, she would have sent Ned packing without a second thought.

–

A dozen miles away in Truro, Jane Garrick put the finishing touches to her toilet. It was a while since she had seen Ben Killigrew. She liked him very much, though not in the way her mother thought. Liking wasn't loving, and Jane didn't love Ben, despite the fact that Mary Carrick hoped that her one ewe-lamb and the Killigrew boy would make a match of it. She'd dreamed of it since the children were babies, even though her husband teased her for indulging in romantic fantasy and assured her that people in this Victorian age had sense enough to choose their own life partners. Mary thought that sense didn't come into it where the emotions were concerned.

Jane smiled as her mother entered her bedroom, twirling around in her shot-green taffeta gown with the deep neckline and puffed sleeves, a matching fan hanging from a cord at her wrist.

'Will I do to meet the Killigrews, Mama?' Jane smiled, knowing the answer. 'I'm not too fine for this evening?'

Mary kissed her, handsome in her own rustling grey gown.

'You look beautiful, dear. Ben won't be able to take his eyes off you tonight—'

'Oh, Mama,' Jane said in exasperation. 'It's not only Ben we're going to see—'

'I hope you won't bother giving the time of day to that ruffian cousin of his,' Mary said, deliberately misunderstanding, knowing that Jane disliked Jude Pascoe intensely. She saw the expected frown on Jane's finely arched brows.

'Poor Mr Killigrew, having that lout in the house,' Jane said with feeling. 'No, Mama, that's not what I meant—'

The chimes of the grandfather clock made Mary exclaim at the time, and curtail her daughter's attempts to explain.

'It will have to wait, dear. We must leave in five minutes precisely, or your father will be cross.'

Richard Carrick's laborious lawyer's manners had rubbed off on his wife. There were times when Jane found the two of them stifling. She was normally dutiful, but wondered how it would feel to break away from all the conventions. To be free and unfettered, like the wild ponies of the moors... and knew that her parents would be shocked if she ever voiced such a thing.

She tucked a wisp of her red-gold hair into the ornate comb she wore that evening, her tresses upswept to reveal the swan-like neck her mother admired so much. The mark of a lady... as though all those poor girls with shorter stems to their heads were somehow lacking. Jane smiled at the thought, and prepared to enjoy the evening.

Why shouldn't she? She and Ben Killigrew were good friends. They had an understanding, though not the kind her mother fondly imagined it to be. Mary Carrick just wouldn't listen to things she didn't want to hear, though Jane had tried to tell her often enough. It was Mary's own fault if she continued happily in her dream-world...

–

As the time drew near for the Tremaynes to leave for Killigrew House that evening, the more nervous Morwen became, and more annoyed with herself for feeling that way. They were only people, like themselves... but *not* like themselves, and that was the trouble.

She didn't like to feel inferior. She wasn't inferior, except in some folks' eyes. She remembered the townslady that Charles Killigrew had called Hannah that afternoon, and felt a smile curve her mouth. Did the woman think Morwen was touched by the plague, because she worked at the clay pit?

'You look a real picture, Morwen, don't she, Bess? A real beauty!' Hal said, as he came downstairs.

He was resplendent in his best shirt and breeches, his neck-cloth tied formally at his throat, and threatening to strangle him as he shrugged into his jacket. Bess nodded, her critical eyes noting how the bright ribbons enhanced the muslin dress, but it was Morwen who enhanced it more.

Their family was a credit to them, but Morwen was her only daughter, and to Bess, Morwen was the icing on the Tremayne cake. Morwen glowed with a mixture of excitement and nervousness, and Bess knew it. But she would surely not be outshone by anyone at the Killigrews tonight.

The boys were more curious than excited, though Sam, the eldest, could think of better ways of spending the evening. At twenty, he was courting a girl from Penwithick, a couple of miles away, and going down to St Austell that night would take him that much farther away from his Dora.

Jack had come round from his sulks, and Bess gave a final tweak to his hair as the Killigrew carriage-wheels sounded outside. Matthew had met the Killigrew nephew once or twice, and said carelessly he'd find something to jaw about with him. Freddie just found it hard to keep still, as always.

'Look to your manners now,' Bess warned them all as Hal ushered them outside, grand as royalty, knowing that they were watched and envied by their neighbours.

The Killigrew manservant held open the carriage door as they all climbed inside.

'Drive on, please.' Hal called out when they were all seated, which reduced the younger ones to helpless giggling.

'Daddy, you sound so fine!' Jack said. 'And he's so stiff and starchy—'

'And employed by Charles Killigrew, same as you and me, boy,' Hal said. 'I reckon that makes us level, no matter that he looks as though there's a bad smell under his nose.'

'It puts you up a peg, Father,' Sam put in. 'You're a pit captain. Any fool can drive a carriage if he can hold a pair of reins. 'Tis a skilled man who can coax the clay from the ground and see it through 'til 'tis loaded on the waggons for the port. Don't sell yourself short, Father.'

'Our Sam wants to be a pit captain,' Freddie taunted.

'Why shouldn't he, you little mudlark?' Bess asked, holding on in the swaying carriage as it went over ruts and dips in the track down to St Austell. 'Ambition's fine and healthy, so long as it doesn't become an obsession—'

'What's an obsession?' Freddie said at once.

Jack ruffled his hair, to Freddie's fury after being slicked down for the evening. ''Tis what you have with butterflies and grasshoppers, ninny!' Jack laughed.

'Don't make fun of the boy, Jack,' Hal frowned, smoothing down the curling dark hair into Freddie's nape again. 'If you and Matthew had more of Sam's application to work, you'd both mebbe enjoy it more.'

'Enjoying grubbing about in wet clay from morning to night?' Matthew said sceptically. His mother's eyes glinted.

'It's good enough for your father, and puts food in your bellies and clothes on your backs—'

'Leave it, Bess,' Hal said lazily. 'Don't get all steamed up before we get to the Killigrews'. Matthew has a right to his say, and 'twon't make no difference in the long run. He'll be up for his shift tomorrow, same as the rest on us, so we'll stop arguing right now. I'll not have us arriving at the big house snapping like a pack of curs.'

When Hal used that deceptively idle tone of voice they all knew it was time to stay silent. He was the most easygoing of men until he was riled. His family and his workmates knew that the soft, complacent tone often marked the calm before the storm. His sons had learned to be wary of its warning sign.

The conversation became more general, but Morwen's thoughts weren't on the little trivialities among them. She tried not to think about Ben Killigrew either, because she didn't want to admit that the snot-nosed owner's son she remembered was vastly different from the handsome young man who'd caught her in his arms that afternoon. She didn't want to think of him, nor of the fine folk they would meet soon, that could turn her stomach inside-out. With every turn of the carriage-wheels, they got nearer, and her hands got clammier.

She thought of what her mother had said about ambition. Had her father had ambitions to become a pit captain? It had just seemed like a natural progression to Morwen, moving up from one job to the next until he had mastered them all, and earned his new status. And Sam... yes, Sam would have ambitions to be a pit captain. Sam always strove to be the best in anything he did.

Morwen began playing a private game, assessing her family. She presumed Bess had achieved her ambition, of being a wife and mother. There was rarely any discontent in her mother. Matthew... Morwen frowned. Sometimes it was hard to know Matthew. He was the secretive one of the family. He might have ambitions too, though Morwen couldn't guess what they were.

Jack merely wanted to be like Sam, who was his idol. Freddie was the joker, too young to bother his head about the future. That was all of them... except herself. Morwen examined her square-cut fingernails. What ambition did she have? It had never entered her head before. To be like her mother? Was that such a bad ambition? To love and marry and have children...

She thought of John Penry, the son of one of her father's waggoners, who made no secret of his fancy for her. John's sister, Celia, was Morwen's best friend, and worked beside her at the pit. The two of them had jested over John's red-faced attentions to Morwen, making jokes over how they'd be related if John ever married Morwen.

Was that the sum total of her ambition? To wed a nice enough clayworker's son, whose smiles and yarns didn't stir her blood one jot? Was that the meaning of wedded bliss that some of the older bal maidens whispered about so coarsely? It had to be more than that. Her Mammie and Daddy didn't coarsen the physical side of love the way those old biddies did, teasing her and Celia and the younger ones unmercifully at times with their wild talk.

Bess had calmly explained it all to Morwen one day, in simple, loving terms, and Morwen had accepted the facts as naturally as breathing. Even to finishing off Celia's sketchy education on the subject. Celia's mother had died long ago from a fever, and it wasn't something a girl learned from her father.

Morwen's thoughts ended as she realised the carriage was trundling through the cobbled streets of St Austell town now, the movement enough to break every bone in her body. She had been thinking about ambition, and thought that one of Freddie's names for her was the most apt. She was a dreamer… as for marriage being an ambition, she supposed it all depended on whom you married.

-

'We're here,' Hal said tersely, his voice telling Morwen that he too was uneasy. Rightly so, she thought, gaping at the sudden blaze of lights from the windows of the big house. So many windows, with criss-crossed panes and gleaming facets of glass. Behind them would be the Killigrews… Morwen ran the tip of her tongue around her dry lips. Once out of the carriage, she followed her father to the great oak door of the house, her legs as wobbly as jelly. No matter how many times she told herself the Tremaynes were invited guests, it all seemed totally unreal.

A maid showed them inside. They entered a large drawing-room filled with heavy, solid furniture and deep carpets, and what seemed like a host of people. All were elegantly and beautifully dressed, the men in finest wool cloth, the women in shimmering taffetas and silks, and every one a lady, born and bred. Morwen took one horrified look around, and wanted to die.

Charles Killigrew stepped forward at once, his greeting a shade too hearty in the small silence in the room. The earlier guests looked a trifle startled at this sudden influx of visitors. Hal nodded briefly to a middle-aged man and his wife, recognising the man as the Killigrew accountant Charles had brought to the pit on several occasions. Charles introduced them as the Gorrans.

Next, they were introduced to a handsome-looking trio, the parents clearly wealthy, the girl pale and lovely with hair like spun gold above the beautiful green gown that bared the soft milky flesh above her small breasts. These were the Carricks from Truro.

Across the room was a young man with a look of Ben Killigrew about him, just as dark, just as handsome, but swarthier and a little shifty about the eyes. Morwen saw her brother Matthew nod to him as if he knew him well. Her heart thudded as she recognised the townslady she'd brushed with that afternoon, with her thin-lipped companion, and discovered who they were. She could hardly have made a worse impression on Ben's aunt, Morwen thought desperately.

She suddenly realised that Ben Killigrew was moving towards the Tremayne family now, and everyone began talking at once, as though to impress on each other that if Charles wanted to invite these strange people to his home, then it must be the right thing to do, and they must be made to feel welcome. Morwen's cheeks burned. They didn't belong here…

Ben squeezed her hand, and his eyes laughed down into hers. She felt strange, not knowing how to react, all her confidence gone. His fingers curled around hers for a moment and then released them.

'Forgive me for not recognising you this afternoon, Morwen,' he grinned. 'I hadn't expected a little firecracker to turn into such a lovely young lady!'

He was making fun of her, she thought furiously.

'Why should you have known me? We hardly live in the same world, Mr Killigrew!' Humiliation made her voice husky. It was normally soft, and he found it immensely attractive. She lowered her eyes to hide her fury. Not knowing the reason, to Ben it was perfectly charming.

He didn't dare tip his finger beneath her chin to make her look at him with those fabulous blue eyes, although he dearly wished he could. He wanted more, he realised with a stab of desire. He wanted to know if Morwen Tremayne was as prim as she looked right now, standing as stiff as board. He wanted to feel her bend, to yield to him as she had done so accidentally that afternoon. The sudden need of her startled him.

'My name is Ben,' he said gravely. 'We have no need to be so formal, especially when I have your blood on my shirt, if only a tiny spot. Surely that fact is of some significance!'

He patronised her, Morwen thought, as his eyes lingered on the small graze on Morwen's cheek where his neck-cloth pin had scratched her. Yet she had the ridiculous feeling that if convention had allowed it, he would have leaned across and kissed the mark. She flinched as though he had, as though she captured the imaginary touch of his lips and held the memory close.

'I apologise for branding you, Morwen,' he went on when she said nothing. 'I don't normally treat young ladies so—'

'It's nothing. It will soon fade. It was my fault for not looking where I was going.'

She stopped, hearing the agitation in her voice, and knowing that although the mark would fade, Ben Killigrew's words might be more prophetic than he intended. Branded... it was just how she felt, and how she had been feeling from the moment she fell into his arms.

As though she were blessed, or cursed, with old Zillah's second sight, she knew as surely as the sun rose and set, that hers and Ben Killigrew's paths were destined to cross. What she didn't yet know, was whether the shivery, almost intoxicating feeling inside her, was due to apprehension or delight.

Chapter Three

Charles felt expansive, telling the young folk to get to know one another, while the older ones did the same. Ben offered a plate of canapés, which Morwen was relieved to see were only tiny biscuit bites. She saw how the other young lady smiled up at him, as though they shared secrets. She felt the answering, irritating prickle of jealousy at the glance...

She wasn't jealous of Ben Killigrew's attentions to Miss finelady Jane Carrick, she told herself furiously. It was something more basic than even that sensation. A feeling that however fine Morwen had thought herself in the beribboned muslin dress, she knew she didn't really fit in here in these grand surroundings.

None of her family looked easy, except perhaps Freddie, and he was too young to sense the hostility from Ben's aunt, or the heartiness with which Charles Killigrew tried to make his unlikely guests mingle. Matthew seemed able to converse with the unruly cousin, but as for Morwen herself...

She found the contrast between Jane Carrick and herself taking on ridiculous proportions in her mind. Jane was small and genteel in her beautiful gown, while Morwen felt herself to be all shapes, her dark hair slipping and sliding from the pins with which she'd tried to tame it that evening.

Miss Carrick might be very nice, but Morwen knew they had absolutely nothing in common. They had nothing to say to one another, no point of contact…

'Mr Killigrew tells me you're a bal maiden,' Jane said suddenly to the strange, beautiful girl in the extraordinarily decorated dress.

'I work for Mr Killigrew, like the rest of my family.'

Morwen was unsure if the girl was being condescending or not, but made sure that Miss finelady knew she wasn't ashamed of an honest day's work.

'I've never met a bal maiden before—' Jane was just being curious, and if Morwen hadn't seen Ben's grinning face behind Jane right then, she might not have been quite so tart.

'I assure you we're quite normal. We don't have two heads or anything!'

Jane reddened, sipping her drink before answering evenly, refusing to be provoked.

'I can see that. You're very pretty, Morwen. I thought what a charming name it was, that's all. Where does bal maiden come from?'

'I don't know, miss. It may be a charming name, but the work's often far from charming. It ruins your hands.' Morwen stopped, biting her lips. What would this girl care about ruined hands, when her own were soft and white, and didn't know the meaning of work? The gap between them yawned wider.

'Please don't call me miss,' Jane said quietly. 'My name is Jane. We're all equal here.'

Until the instant they stepped outside Killigrew House and went their separate ways! The Carricks in their own carriage, home to Truro; the Tremaynes to the humble moorland cottage in the borrowed carriage.

What was wrong with her tonight? She had never thought her circumstances lacking before. The Tremaynes had a sound roof, enough food, and love to spare. She saw her mother across the room, and felt a fierce renewal of family pride. Bess had dignity of her own, even beside the snooty Hannah Pascoe and her friend.

Morwen's resentment seemed directed toward Ben Killigrew and his Miss finelady Jane. By now, Jane had turned from the sullen bal maiden, and was chatting with the Tremayne boys. Sam knew his manners, and Jack was quite sweet, like the baby, Freddie, Jane thought. If Matthew and Jude Pascoe were getting their heads together, then she didn't mind too much if Matthew ignored her.

'I've known Jane since we were children,' Ben told Morwen, as though he thought it necessary to explain.

'Really?' She tried to sound disinterested.

'She's pretty, isn't she?'

His tone should have alerted her. She should have sensed that he was baiting her to see her reaction, but she didn't.

'Very!' She was heavily sarcastic. 'I've never seen such a lovely, well-dressed, prettily-mannered young lady—'

'Aren't you overdoing it a little?' Ben was laughing at her now, and it suddenly struck Morwen that they seemed to be holding a private little conversation in a roomful of people. 'I only said Jane was pretty. So are you, in a different way—'

'A more common way, you mean!' Her voice might have frozen anyone else, but not Ben Killigrew. He was enjoying these spirited replies.

'Are you always so touchy?' he teased her.

'That's how your aunt sees it,' Morwen retorted. 'She said I was every bit as bad as the bal maidens are painted. Wild and unruly – and what she meant was common!'

Ben leaned forward to fill her glass with more sparkling fruit cup, cool and refreshing.

'I don't give a damn what my Aunt Hannah thinks,' he said arrogantly. Morwen was about to answer just as imperiously, when his aunt's voice seemed to float across the room towards her.

'Your daughter thinks a railway track from the pits is a necessity, Mr Tremayne.' Hannah's voice was amused, as though a young girl's views could be discounted.

Morwen's cheeks felt scorched. Were they all discussing the works to patronise her parents? Did they think the Tremaynes incapable of talking about anything else?

'Morwen talks sense, Ma'am,' Hal replied. ''Tis not the first time the notion's been thrashed out—'

'Nor the last,' Charles agreed. 'But there's pennies to be counted before we rush in with new-fangled ideas. We've worked well enough without rail tracks until now. The men do well enough with two shillings and more a day. There's always the prospect of an increase, Hal. With rail tracks to finance, such a prospect might be impossible. What say you, Daniel?'

Daniel Gorran was his respected accountant, and was nodding now, but with some caution. Charles kept his outgoings to a minimum, but rail tracks would be an undoubted advantage over other clay works, and Killigrew could be sticking his head in the sand by not seeing the fact.

Dangling the bait of a wage increase before Hal Tremayne was a trifle underhand in Gorran's opinion. He hated anything underhand. It wasn't the way he conducted his business.

'A major construction like a railway needs to be considered from all angles. I'm sure the townsfolk of St Austell would appreciate it, but the important issue is the advantage to Killigrew Clay itself. I can only offer facts and figures and give advice, and it's too important a matter to discuss over a glass of fruit cup!'

'How right you are, Mr Gorran!' Mary Carrick exclaimed. 'Can we not talk about something other than china clay?'

'I agree with you,' Gorran's wife said. 'Shall you be going to Truro Fair next week, Mary?'

Morwen didn't hear the answer. She spoke in a low, indignant mutter to no one in particular.

'Since Mrs Pascoe was complaining about our clay waggons, she should be the first to welcome the idea of rail tracks!'

'Well said,' Ben said dryly. 'But even Killigrew wealth is not a bottomless pit, Morwen!'

She glowered at him, forgetting where she was.

'When he pays his workers such a pittance that some of them can see the stars between the slates of their cottages because the repairs aren't done, and they're too poor to move elsewhere! Who gets the benefit of all that wealth, Mr Killigrew? Not the clayworkers' children who are lucky to get an hour's schooling a week, and don't get sent to fancy colleges in London to be educated—'

'Well, well,' Ben said quietly. 'So the workers have a champion, do they? I'd say your education is fairly wide—'

Morwen suddenly heard her brother Sam speak furiously.

'Apologise for being so free with your words, Morwen,' he snapped at her.

'Oh, leave her be,' Jude Pascoe said lazily. It was a change to hear a clash of temperaments that wasn't his own and his mother's, and a change from the usual dreary suppers he was forced to attend in his uncle's house. 'She speaks her mind, which is more than most wenches do.'

Morwen's hands clenched until the fingernails bit into her palms. Wench, indeed. She hated Jude Pascoe for putting her in her place while seeming to defend her. Would he call Jane Carrick a wench? She raged inside.

Ben gave a short laugh. 'It's different,' he agreed. 'Don't fret, Sam. The Tremaynes won't get a black mark because of your sister's freedom with words. It's always best to know where you stand. As for cottages needing repairs – I suggest you tell my father. He can't do repairs he doesn't know about.'

He turned away as though tired of the bothersome Tremaynes, but in reality incensed by his cousin Jude's crudeness. Anyone with half an eye could see Morwen wasn't a wench… anyone with two good eyes could see that she was very comely. And wasn't it her birthday? Ben felt suddenly reckless.

He went across to his father, and whispered in his ear. Next minute, Charles called for silence.

'If everyone has a glass, then let's drink to the birthday girl among us. To Morwen, the prettiest girl this side of Truro!'

Morwen flushed with pleasure and embarrassment, but Charles was obviously sincere. He strode towards her and put his great bear arms around her.

'I'm also claiming a birthday kiss,' he chuckled, and tickled her cheek with his whiskers for a moment as he kissed her soundly. He grinned at Hal. 'But since I'm sure any pretty girl would prefer to be kissed by a young buck, do we have your permission, Hal, for my son to give her a birthday kiss too?'

Morwen's heart leapt at his words, a mingling of horror and mortification. Would Ben really kiss her in front of all these people, including his Miss finelady...? She was left in no doubt as Charles let her go, and she was held in an embrace she already knew. The pleasing male scent of him was in her nostrils as his face blotted out the rest of the room. His mouth touched hers, strong and sensual. It was all she had imagined it to be, without ever being aware that she had imagined its touch. The nearness of him was warm, excitingly so...

It was a light kiss, no more than a brush of his lips against hers, which was all that etiquette allowed. Ben moved away from her smilingly, as though as embarrassed as Morwen. Yet, just for a moment, she thought his breathing was as ragged as her own from the contact between them. That he had turned from her to the little cheering group of young people because he couldn't look into Morwen Tremayne's eyes without giving away the secret yearning in his own.

Was she mad? Letting such dreams get the better of her? All the madder, because she didn't want to dream of herself and Ben Killigrew. Their names could never be coupled together. They were from different worlds.

An owner could kiss a clayworker's daughter on this sort of occasion, and it meant nothing. Morwen's throat felt oddly thick. She heard her brother Freddie start his chanting about being kissed by Ben Killigrew, and snapped at him to behave himself or he'd get a wallop, company or no company.

–

Celia Penry pushed her bonnet back from her hot brow and took the mug of tea Freddie Tremayne had brought her for her tea-break, and stared in disbelief at her friend, Morwen. Freddie had told her a tale, and she still didn't believe it.

'Your Freddie's turning into a little liar, Morwen,' she said baldly. 'Telling me Ben Killigrew kissed you in front of everybody at the Killigrew House last night! If I hadn't seen you going off as smart as paint, I'd never have believed you went there at all!'

'Well, it's true, so there!' Morwen's nose went up in the air as Celia's tone said more than words her opinion of folk who hob-nobbed with bosses. It was bad for the rest of them. But you didn't turn an owner down flat when he issued an invitation, either! The Penrys might understand that, if they weren't so knee-deep in thinking themselves a race apart from the Killigrews. Morwen forgot that it had been her opinion too...

'Now you're the liar,' Celia said rudely. 'Why should he kiss you? And why would you want him to, when you always said what a snot-face he was!'

Morwen's blood began to boil. Celia was her best friend, but sometimes she was as blind as a bat in sunlight.

'People change, dumb-bell,' she snorted. 'Ben Killigrew's not as gormless as he used to be. He's – all right—'

'But did he kiss you?' Celia squealed. It was the only important bit to know. 'The truth now, Morwen, on your crossed fingers and toes.'

'Cross them all, eyes as well,' Morwen said, putting it to effect. She felt the mischief dancing inside her. She twirled away from Celia. 'Catch me if you want to know any more!'

She whirled away, racing over the uneven ground and away from the constant hum of noise from the little trucks shunting between the settling tank and the kilns, the drone and beat of the beam engine, the shouts of the men and the scrape of shovels and picks. Together with the rush of water, it was an unending symphony, receding into the background as the two girls scrambled up, up, up, to where the small shining hills of the spoil heaps glinted in the sunlight. Celia finally caught up with Morwen, and they both fell in a laughing heap on the dusty clay waste.

'Tell me!' Celia demanded. 'I don't believe Ben Killigrew kissed you at all! Why should he?'

Morwen's eyes seemed bluer than ever. Blue as the sky, and the endless distant sea beyond St Austell. She relived the moment as she related it to Celia.

'It was because it was my birthday! Mr Killigrew kissed me first, and said he thought I'd prefer a young buck to kiss me instead. And then – then Ben kissed me. That's all!'

Neither spoke for a few seconds. Morwen was caught up in the wonder and glory of it all once more, because whatever the reason, Ben Killigrew had kissed her, and it was the first time in her life that a young gentleman had done such a thing. She heard the caw-cawing of the sea-birds overhead, as though they were laughing at her for imagining for an instant that Ben might be remembering it too.

'*Ben*, is it?' Celia said caustically. 'Watch out, Morwen. Posh folk only have one reason for kissing girls like us. He'll be wanting to lift your skirts next—'

Morwen hated her for spoiling the moment.

'He's not like that—'

'They're *all* like that! What was the posh supper like? Did you have to act all hoity-toity?'

Morwen tossed her head. 'No, I didn't. It was funny, anyway. Even posh folks have arguments, it seems, and Ben's cousin Jude upset his uncle at the table for not minding his manners, and Mr Killigrew swallowed the wrong way, and cursed Jude even more for making him spill his wine.'

Morwen giggled at the memory. It had been better than fireworks to sit back and see how that miserable Mrs Pascoe had tried to calm her brother down, and how Charles Killigrew had roared at her to mind her business and see to her son's antics.

One argument had spawned another, and she had been absurdly pleased to see how Ben was able to cope with an awkward situation without losing his dignity like his blustering father, and that stupid red-faced Jude.

'Ben's going to come to the works soon—'

'What?' Celia looked sceptical. 'Don't tell me he's going to soil those fine gentleman's hands by working alongside us!'

'Of course not,' Morwen said crossly. 'But he wants to see it all for himself, and his father seemed well pleased.'

'I bet he was! But can't you see, it's *you* he wants to see, ninny! He only ever looked down his nose at the clay pit before, didn't he? He means to sport with 'ee, Morwen, and only bad can come of it. You keep un at arms'–length before he does you a mischief—'

'Shut up about un, can't you?' Morwen was suddenly hot and upset. 'He wouldn't bother with me! He's got a lady-friend, name of Miss finelady Jane Carrick from over Truro way. She was there last night—'

'Don't mean nothing,' Celia said doggedly. 'Many a young buck has one girl for marryin' and another for sportin', and you mind you're not taken for a fool, Morwen.'

A bellow from below reminded them that their break from work was over, and they slithered down the shining spoil heap. Celia ran ahead, and Morwen felt the soft warm breeze sting on her lashes, and dashed away the stupid dampness there. Of course Celia was right. She wouldn't consider Ben Killigrew for one more minute. It was madness. It was courting heartbreak to admit to the sudden rush of warmth inside whenever she thought of him, or know that her heart raced erratically whenever she remembered the touch of his mouth on hers.

She ran down the slope towards the pit, and thought how illogical it was to look down on the town of St Austell from the summit of a spoil heap, to where the Killigrew house had existed for several generations of lordly folk.

Looking down… when Morwen and the human ants scurrying about in the clay works were of the lower order, and the bosses lived in the beautiful houses near to the sea, where the land was lush and green. It was hopeless to think that one of them could truly love a clayworker's daughter.

The Tremaynes had left the Killigrew House before the finer folk last evening. Bess had remarked dryly that they had probably all sighed with relief at the fact. Had they known it, the arguments that Jude had provoked continued long after the Gorrans had departed. The Carricks were old friends, and Charles Kiliigrew felt free to speak his mind in front of them.

'If Ben's prepared to spend some time at the works, then so can you, my lad. One day a week for both of you for a start, until I decide what's to do with you both.'

'You've no need to lump me with Jude Pascoe, Father,' Ben said angrily. 'I've said I'm willing to go, to learn about the business from all angles—'

'Especially if they're covered up by soft wenches' clothes,' Jude said slyly. 'But you don't really expect me to use a pick and shovel and fill those dirty little wagons with clay, do you, Uncle?'

Charles rounded on him at once. 'If you don't like the arrangement, Jude, I'm sure you can find some other place to live and sleep. And when you can explain the workings of the clay pits that provide the food in your belly and the clothes on your back, then I may reverse my idea of you as a parasite in my house.'

He turned away from Jude's glowering face, and the mortification on Hannah's. He turned to Jane, and asked her to lift the mood of the evening, and play them all something light and frivolous on the pianoforte. She agreed with a smile, too used to these Killigrew outbursts to be embarrassed by them.

As Ben stood beside her, ready to turn the music, their parents thought what a handsome couple they made, and

Jude Pascoe slumped back and drank as much of his uncle's brandy as he dared, knowing he'd be in for another head-rocking later from his mother. If it wasn't such a soft life, he'd cut and run. He'd get right out of here and across the sea, to that land of golden dreams across the Atlantic Ocean... but he was weak enough to enjoy the soft life... as long as it lasted.

—

'Can I be excused now, Mr Killigrew?' Jane asked, when she had played half a dozen pieces. 'It's warm in here, and I'd like a turn in the garden.'

'Of course, my love,' Charles beamed. 'I'm sure Ben feels the same. Go along, the pair of you.'

They could hardly contain their laughter until they were out of sight in the shubbery. Charles was so obvious in throwing them together.

'What an evening!' Jane giggled at last. 'Heaven knows what that poor family thought of us all!'

'You're not patronising, are you, by calling them poor?' Ben grinned, remembering how Morwen bristled on that score.

'No, and well you know it. Why do they always take offence so quickly, do you suppose?'

'Perhaps it all goes with being poor,' Ben said dryly.

'Are we talking about the same person?' Jane asked. 'You were very taken with Morwen Tremayne, weren't you, Ben? She's very beautiful, but please be careful—' she stopped in embarrassment as he laughed and asked why he should be careful of a pit captain's daughter!

'Careful that you don't break her heart,' Jane said, to his surprise. 'You're quite capable of it, Ben. If I was as enamoured of you as your parents think I am, I'd be quite jealous of the way you looked at her tonight. And certainly jealous that you kissed her!'

'One meaningless kiss!' he mocked her. But it hadn't been as meaningless as all that, he realised. It had been more pleasurable than he had expected it to be, and had filled him with a sudden powerful longing to keep her in his arms. He had wanted to bend her to his embrace and make her soften to him. The feeling had been so strong he had ended the kiss quickly, afraid that he might betray his sudden desire to everyone there.

Had Jane sensed it, or been upset by it? He felt a sudden concern, and asked if she had really minded. She leaned up and pressed her lips to his cheek as naturally as a sister.

'Dear Ben, of course I wasn't upset. Just be sure of what you're doing, that's all. And if I can help in any way by diverting attention from the lovely Morwen, just tell me how and when. Just as I shall expect you to help me when you come to Truro Fair.'

Ben looked at her sharply, seeing the quick colour in her cheeks. 'In what way? Have you found someone special, Jane?'

'Very special,' she said softly. 'And just as impossible for my parents to accept as your father accepting Morwen Tremayne as a wife for you! I won't say any more at the moment, Ben.'

Her mouth shook slightly. She could still hardly believe the way love had come to her, swiftly and spectacularly.

Even to speak of it might diminish its glow...

'You know you have a trusted friend in me, Jane.' Ben assured her. 'Let's walk around the gardens, and let the parents think we're billing and cooing, since it pleases them.'

She agreed, mischief in her eyes at the game they played. She took his arm, and he teased her, and wondered if she guessed how her soft words had stirred a new and intriguing thought inside him. An impossible thought, of course. Marry Morwen Tremayne? Yet it was a thought he couldn't quite get out of his head, enticing and heady.

Chapter Four

The two girls stood at a distance from the cottage on the moor. Even though the spring weather was warm, the customary curl of smoke rose from the chimney. They knew that the air inside would be thick and cloying, with the mixtures of peat and the old woman's evil-smelling pipe, and the herbs and potions she boiled. Old Zillah's hovel.

Celia licked her lips. She had teased Morwen into visiting the old woman, against their parents' wishes. Zillah could tell them their marriage prospects, Celia had coaxed...

'We don't need a crystal ball to tell us that!' Morwen had scoffed. 'We'll marry clayworkers, same as our mothers did.'

Celia gave a sly grin. 'Don't you have better plans now, Morwen? Now you've been kissed by Ben Killigrew, don't you have a fancy to lie between silken sheets of a night?'

'Fat chance! And don't go prattling on about that, Celia. I've had to bribe our Freddie to keep his trap shut, to stop folks baiting me!'

'Bribe me too then,' Celia taunted. 'Sounds to me you're already goin' up in the world to do such a thing! Anyway, I'm goin' to see old Zillah, so you can come or not, as you please.'

'All right,' Morwen had been nettled into agreeing. 'At the end of the day's shift, but don't go telling anyone. If my Daddy gets to hear, he'll have my hide for breakfast.'

She felt a thrill of anticipation, all the same. Zillah scared and excited her, and Morwen was a true daughter of Cornwall. She believed in magic...

Celia's words ran through her mind all afternoon. Going up in the world, was she? It didn't feel like it. She still lived in a crowded cottage, when others had space to breathe, and great houses with tiny windows that glowed and shimmered in the sunlight...

Did such folks lie between silken sheets? Silk sheets... how must that feel? She tried to imagine herself lying between them, the slippery fabric cool and sensual against her skin. Enveloped in silk, and warmed by a lover's arms. A lover whose imaginary face was uncannily like Ben Killigrew's, and her mouth was dry, knowing it.

She bent to her task in the linhay, scraping the dirt from the clay block and scattering the fine powder over her hands. Miss finelady's hands were naturally white, not whitened by clay dust like her own. The depressing thought made the sweet fantasies vanish at once. Celia was right. Young gentlemen only looked at working girls for one thing. They married Miss fineladies, and sported with the rest.

-

She tried to forget it as she and Celia neared old Zillah's hovel. She wondered what their reception would be. It varied, according to Zillah's mood. Visitors could be just in time to see one of the old woman's mangy cats hurtle out of the door, squawking and screeching, with old

Zillah's boot up its backside. It was wiser, then, to creep away unseen.

Today, they were in luck. Zillah emerged from the hovel as they approached. Her blackened clay pipe hung from one corner of her mouth. Her hair, like grey wisps of fern, was caught by the breeze in comical strands. Her wizened face creased into a cackling smile as she saw them.

'Been waiting for you, my pretties,' she wheezed, as two cats wound about her legs like encroaching vines. 'Come to jaw with old Zillah, have 'ee?'

Celia giggled nervously, nudging Morwen's arm to go inside as Zillah stood back for them to enter. It was like stepping into a strange murky world, as the mixture of smells clogged their nostrils, and they tried not to breathe too deeply.

'What do 'ee want of old Zillah, my pretties?' The old woman said keenly, eyeing them both as she bade them sit on the edge of a dark settle.

'We want to know who we're going to marry,' Celia said boldly, since Morwen seemed temporarily struck dumb.

Zillah cackled again, her black eyes boring into them both, one after the other.

'Old Zillah never needed a man in wedlock, and mebbe 'twill be the same for you—' she taunted.

'Of course it won't,' Celia said crossly. 'Don't talk to us in riddles—'

'Can you tell us, Zillah?' Morwen's voice had a small catch in it. Celia was doing this all wrong... Zillah turned to her at once.

'There'll be a man for you, my pretty,' she slurred, and Celia snapped angrily, annoyed at the inference.

'What kind of man? Tall, dark and handsome and well connected?' she said sarcastically.

Zillah's old eyes flashed. 'I'm in no mood for fortune-telling today. You can make your own destinies and get what you deserve. I might just tell 'ee how to foresee a certain important man in your lives, if you've the nerve to follow instructions,' she challenged them.

Morwen's spine prickled. 'What sort of instructions?'

'Do 'ee dare to go to the Larnie Stone at midnight? If you go there and drink the potion I give 'ee, then walk slowly round the stone twelve times before 'ee look through the hole towards the sea, you might see the face of a certain man—'

Celia sniffed. 'You mean we'll be tipsy by then, from your evil mixture and circling the stone, and we'll imagine anything!'

Zillah fixed her cold eyes on her.

'Why did 'ee come here with such doubts in your mind, miss? 'Tis all I can tell 'ee for today. Suit yourselves if you want the potion.'

She stared at them unblinkingly, like her cats. She was tired of them now, and Morwen knew they'd get nothing more from her. She shivered, unsure whether she would want to visit the Larnie Stone at midnight. It was a great granite mass of stone, halfway down the moor between the clay works and St Austell. Its middle was a great gaping hole, through which the sea could be seen. It was reputed to have mystical powers, and many a poor child was said to have been cured of the rickets by passing him through the stone at sunset.

Why midnight for this particular experiment? Morwen dreaded the thought, and knew how Celia hated the dark.

It was the only thing she feared. She was steeped in super-
stition, since her mother had died in darkness, and two
relatives had perished in a collapsing tin-mine several years
back. To die alone and in the dark was Celia's worst fear.
But since Celia had goaded Morwen into coming here,
she suddenly found a new strength.

'We'll take the potion, Zillah,' she announced, 'if you'll
tell us the charm will still work on a moonlit night, and
that we can choose the date.'

Zillah croaked triumphantly. 'I knew 'ee for a brave un,
my pretty! Aye, the potion can be safely kept until needed.
Depends on how soon 'ee wants to know your fate. And
you'll have some pennies to pass into old Zillah's hand, I
trust?'

She never asked a proper fee for her services, then no
one could say they didn't get value for their pennies. She
was usually overpaid, by folk who wanted the most potent
of her charms. It was only a pittance from the two girls,
but the potion was handed over gravely.

'Don't waste too much time, pretties. You'm ripe for
the loving, and there'll be many a young sprig ready for a
bit o' cuddling. Remember now. Twelve times round the
Larnie stone. Not one more nor less, or the charm will be
wasted. Take half the potion each, before you begin your
circling. There's magic in the circle, pretties. Remember
old Zillah's words.'

They got to their feet as the old crone's voice grew
heavy, and the atmosphere of the hovel seemed suddenly
charged with a force they didn't understand. It was a relief
to them both to be outside in the clean fresh air, and only
then did they manage a hesitant laugh. If it hadn't been

for the small green bottle Morwen clutched in her hand, they might have thought they had imagined it all.

With one thought in mind, they grabbed at their skirts and raced over the moors, and as far as possible from the old mystic. There was one comfort. The moon was on the wane right now, so they had several weeks before they need do anything about Zillah's potion. They had time to find their courage.

—

The group of men walked determinedly towards the largest of Killigrew's clay workings. Grim-faced, white with dust from their shift, they intended to waylay Hal Tremayne before he went home. The group was led by their own pit captain, Gilbert Dark.

John Penry was among them. He was in total agreement with the grievances of his fellow workers, but thinking privately that he was sorrier to have missed seeing Morwen Tremayne that afternoon. He hadn't seen her for a while. He'd dearly like to work here, but his mother's death-bed wish was that the family shouldn't all work in the same pit, because of the disaster that had befallen his two cousins in the tin-mine. And since his sister Celia worked alongside Morwen, John continued working in number two pit.

He was too indecisive to change things. In his heart, he knew he'd never win a girl like Morwen. Even coming here today, staunchly behind his pit captain, was no personal decision. He swam with the tide, and despised himself because of it. He saw the tall figure of Hal Tremayne ahead of him, and heard Gilbert Dark greet him, shaking Hal's hand to show that this was no disorderly arrival.

'Now then, Hal Tremayne. The men of Clay Two would have words with 'ee, and with your men.'

Hal saw the glints in the clayworkers' eyes, and the set of their chins.

'There's few of my shift left here now, and the rest are about their work. If there's words to be said, say them to me. Is there trouble?'

Murmurs of discontent rumbled among the men.

Gilbert Dark stood with feet spread apart and arms folded, an implacable bull of a man. 'There will be, man,' he said grimly. 'Fact is, we've heard that several pits over Hendra way are paying their men twopence a day more than Killigrew pays, and their bal maidens a penny a day more. Since most of us have got whole families working for Killigrew, that makes a goodly reduction in overall income!'

The muttering grew, and some of Clay One's workers stopped work to listen as Hal called sharply for quiet.

'If this is true, and not just kiddleywink gossip, what's to do about it, Gil Dark? Why this deputation to Clay One?'

''Tis bloody obvious, man,' Dark snapped. 'Clay One's the biggest pit, shipping near to seven hundred tons of china clay to put silver in Charles Killigrew's pockets. Clay Two ships less than half that much, with Three and Four lagging behind, but still healthy enough to make Killigrew Clay a powerful concern—'

Roars of assent stopped his flow for a minute, and he shouted louder as he continued.

'If 'tis the likes of us, working our guts to make Killigrew's fortune, then the likes of us should get some of the rewards from the bugger, in line with other pits.'

'I'll not incite my men to strike!' Hal bellowed.

'Boss's man!' Some of the Clay Two workers chanted. 'Bloody boss's man taking supper at the big house—'

'Which of you bastards said that?' Hal roared. Normally slow to anger, he felt his blood boil, and his blue eyes blazed like fire as he glowered at the men.

There was a scuffle among them as some resented their fellow workers' baiting, and Gilbert Dark hollered at them.

'We came here with a proposition,' he snarled. 'If you buggers will be silent, let's put it to the man.'

'What proposition? I've said my piece. No strikes from Clay One,' Hal snapped back.

'I ain't mentioned no strike, dammit!' Dark roared. 'I'm proposing a march down through St Austell town to Killigrew's fancy office to put our case to him, all above board. What's your thought on that, Hal Tremayne?'

Their eyes clashed, but Hal knew it made sense. He resented upsets like this being thrust on him without warning, but he had the wits to know that his own men would be disgruntled if some action wasn't taken. The news of the wage rise in other pits would spread like wildfire. He cursed the gossip-mongers who'd brought the tale to the Killigrew workers. And cursed even more the owners who hadn't put their heads together to keep the clay wages on a par with one another. He nodded shortly.

'I'll agree to a march, if 'tis organised right. We've had few complaints about the boss before now, and 'tis best that we keep calm and sensible until we hear him out. Have you talked to the captains of Three and Four yet?'

'Not yet. We came to you first,' Dark's voice had altered now, looking to Hal Tremayne as their natural leader.

'Then see them next.' Hal took command. 'We'll set a day, then after the main shift, each pit captain and half a dozen selected men will make the march. 'Twill be near to thirty men in all, and enough of a crowd to be marching through St Austell streets. No more would get into Killigrew's office. Do you approve, Dark?'

'Sounds fair enough. But make it soon. Next Monday would be a good day—'

'All right.' Hal felt angry at being pushed into this. There were ways of settling things without strikes and force, and he considered a march only just short of either method.

'We'll have the new young workers to add to the march, to make up the numbers,' Dark went on relentlessly, and Hal's eyes narrowed.

'New workers? We're not taking on more at present—'

''Tain't what my men heard at the kiddleywink, then,' Dark was full of resentment now. 'Seems that Killigrew's putting his son and nephew to work at Clay One for a day a week to learn the ropes. I suppose Killigrew thinks a boy wi' brains enough for college can learn in a day what it takes a man a lifetime to learn. And as for t'other one—' He spat noisily.

'The nephew's brains be all in his breeches, be all accounts,' one of the men sniggered.

'You're mad, the lot of you,' Hal said angrily. 'I've heard nothing of this, and Killigrew would have told me—'

'Oh aye, we know you're in his pocket wi' your invitations, Hal Tremayne, but mark my words, 'tis true. So do we have your word on it that the two new apprentices will be included in Monday's march?'

Hal felt cornered, and knew there was only one answer he could give to the grim-faced Clay Two men. He laughed harshly.

'Aye,' he said sarcastically. 'If young Ben Killigrew and his cousin appear here on Monday morning, which I reckon is as likely as seeing pigs fly, I'll see to it that they're included in the march, though I fancy an extra twopence a day to either on 'em will be laughable. How did you come by the tale?'

One of the men spoke up.

'I seen the nephew in the kiddleywink late last night. He were well away wi' the drink, and cussin' like no gennulman ever should because he and his cuz had to show their faces at Hal Tremayne's pit on Monday morning. Heard it from his own mouth I did, and I'll fight any man who calls me liar!'

'Clear off to your home instead,' Hal said, more incensed than he let on at hearing the tale third hand, instead of from Charles Killigrew himself. 'You've had my say-so on it, Gil Dark, and that's my last word.'

He strode through the Clay Two men, who opened out and scattered to let him pass, respectful towards Hal Tremayne, no matter how much jawing there was between them. Hal walked at a good pace, his fury hardly abated by the time he reached his own cottage and banged the door shut behind him. Only then did he let out his rage in a great hammer blow of his fist against the wall.

Bess had left the pit long ago. She should be here. Hal needed her, and raged at her absence. No one was at home. The boys and Morwen were off on their own pursuits. Hal was as prickly as gorse when Bess arrived home minutes after him, her eyes shining, and oblivious to her man's mood.

'I've taken Mrs Pollancy's sewing to her, Hal, and she gave me afternoon tea and introduced me to two of her friends, real ladies with nice ways! She's been showing them my work, and they want to employ me as a seamstress, and say they'll get me more work if I want it. They said my work's of a high standard, and 'tis criminal for me to be working at the clay pit, Hal, and I should be using my skills properly. 'Tis a wonderful chance for me, dar, and I'd be here all day for when you came home. It's whatever you say to it, Hal, and if you think 'tis being disloyal to Mr Killigrew to leave the works, then I'll abide by your say-so—'

The bubbling words died away as she saw that Hal was saying nothing, nor sharing in her excitement. They had always shared everything, joys and tears. She touched his arm and felt it rock hard. He relaxed at her touch and hugged her to his broad chest, smoothing the dark hair back from her forehead. His Bess looked as young and eager as Morwen at that moment, and his voice was thick as he answered, annoyed that he'd been so caught up in Gil Dark's revelations that he hadn't captured his wife's joyous moment.

'When did I ever hog-tie you to doing what you didn't want to do, Bess? If 'tis your pleasure to sew fine fabrics for others, then so be it. As for disloyalty to Charles Killigrew, 'tis no one's business but our own. He'll not miss one of his minions, when there's always more to replace them—'

Bess was startled. This was so unlike Hal. Especially now that he was an important cog in Killigrew's wheel.

'What's happened, dar?' she said quietly. They didn't often use endearments, but the shortened form of darling was their own special word when private moments were shared.

Hal felt the tension creep back. He told her quickly what had happened at the works, and that he was probably making too much of it.

'No, you're not!' Bess exclaimed. 'It's demeaning that Clay Two workers should march to Clay One like that. If they've a wish to try for more wages, then let them. And it's quite wrong for young Ben and that Jude boy to report for work on Monday without your knowing of it first. You've a right to feel angry.'

His face softened at her indignant look. She calmed him, as she had always done.

'What would I do without 'ee, dar?' Hal asked her softly.

Bess smiled, thankful enough to see the cloud lifting from his brow. She kissed him lightly on the mouth.

'Don't even think of it, Hal. So do I take it I'm the first of the Tremaynes to cut the Killigrew cord?'

He laughed. 'I like the sound of the words, Bess! Aye, you'll be first, and no doubt the last. I'll tell the boss on Monday.' The fact gave him an odd feeling of satisfaction. Whole families worked for the same boss until they died, and saw no shame in it. But for his Bess to retire voluntarily, gave him as much pleasure as his own raised status to pit captain.

'You'll have to finish out the week, of course,' Hal said.

'I can give him one more week!' Bess was jubilant. 'It'll be almost like living the soft life, to be home all day long, just like a lady, Hal!'

He held her around the waist, and spoke with mock anger.

'You've always been a lady to me, woman, and don't you ever forget it!'

—

Morwen was unaware of the coming changes in the Tremayne household, more concerned with carrying the green bottle of precious liquid she held so tightly. She was feeling light-headed at the thought of taking the potion, and the consequences that Zillah promised, and giggled nervously as she and Celia raced over the turf towards home.

'What's tickling your fancy now?' Celia's eyes danced with shared excitement. 'Wondering if it'll be Ben Killigrew you spy through the Larnie stone, or our John?'

'It'll be your John, with my luck,' Morwen groaned, and then blushed. 'Oh, I didn't mean it like that, Celia—'

'I know.' Celia forgave her. 'No one could call our John very bright. And you and me both want summat more than a country lummock! Your Ben just fills the bill from what you tell me—'

'He's not *my* Ben!' Morwen was charmed by the sound of the words, all the same. 'His cousin might suit you, Celia, if you like a rougher cut—'

'Stuck up like college Ben, is he? No thank you—'

60

'He's not a bit like Ben. He's got an eye for the girls, I reckon, so you mind yourself if you see his face through the stone—'

'Well, as I've never laid eyes on un, I'll never know, will I? 'Twill just be a face in the mist to me.' A tingling thrill ran through her. 'Do we dare, Morwen? 'Tis tempting fate, and your Mammie wouldn't approve.'

'My Mammie won't know!' The more Celia voiced her doubts, the stronger Morwen became. 'If you want to change your mind, I'll do it alone—'

'You wouldn't, would you? Promise me you wouldn't go alone in the dark.' Celia was pale at the thought.

'All right, ninny!' It didn't take much persuasion. Being alone on the moors after dark with a mist rising was utter madness. A person could be driven crazy, becoming disorientated in the dark, losing the footing and breaking a leg. Or worse, falling prey to any villains on business of their own. Even the wreckers, if they chanced to be crossing the moors with their spoils from a broken ship floundering along the coast.

Morwen shivered. They certainly wouldn't venture out on a bad night. It must be a night bright and shining with moonlight. It would be less unnerving to take the walk to the standing stone, and it would make any ghostly lover's face float that much more clearly in front of them. The uncertainty passed. They had the potion, and they would use it. And if necessary, Morwen thought, somehow she would find the courage for both of them.

Chapter Five

Morwen arrived home from her walk on the moors with Celia, and quickly hid the small green bottle among her possessions, amid the uproar among her normally harmonious brothers. They argued the toss with their father, while Bess tried to keep the peace.

'You're a lily-livered, whining babby!' Sam blazed at his brother. Matthew glared at him murderously, the cords on his neck rigid as reeds. His voice rose furiously.

'Where's the sense in it? What good will it do if Killigrew turns against us, tell me that! You're a fanatical strike-monger, and I'll have none on it. March to hell and back again if you must, but I'll not be with you!'

Hal crashed his fist between them. The table creaked ominously, and Bess snatched up a platter before it hit the floor. She knew better than to intervene for the moment.

'Stop slandering one another, and listen to me,' Hal thundered. 'I'll have one of 'ee marching to town wi' me, and it'll be Sam, since our Matt's averse to putting one foot in front of the other for a cause—'

'Not because I'm afraid, Father, and I'll fight any man who says it—' Matt flared up at once.

'All right, dammit!' Hal snapped. 'If you'd both listened to me, I'd have told 'ee I'm in agreement with Matt over this. I don't want the men to think we Tremaynes are the only ones involved. It's to be a fair representation from the works—'

Morwen managed to get a word in, as she looked from one angry face to another.

'What's happening? Will somebody tell me?'

Jack spoke from his curled-up position on the settle, his eyes round with excitement as he babbled out the information.

'Our Sam and Matt are fighting over who's to march wi' Daddy to the clay office on Monday, and Matt don't want to go, and Sam's calling un a coward. Daddy's to take seven men from the works, same as the other pit captains, and Ben Killigrew and Jude Pascoe's to march wi' em and all, if they show up at the works on Monday morning—'

Hal gave Jack a friendly cuff about the ears and told him to leave mens' talk to the men. It was all startling news, but the most startling to Morwen was that Ben and his cousin were to be at the works on Monday morning. Her heartbeat drummed at the thought. She saw Sam turn quickly, and stamp out of the cottage, presumably to walk off his anger.

'Why would Ben Killigrew and his cousin be at the works, Daddy?' she asked Hal.

He snorted. 'Seems we're to be honoured by their presence,' he said sourly. 'The nephew was bandying it about in the kiddleywink, and Gil Dark informed me I'm to have two new apprentices for one day a week. Just as if the young bucks can learn all there is to know in so short a time—'

'We had to start somewhere, dar,' Bess said gently. 'Give the boys a chance, even if 'tisn't right that you weren't properly informed. Now, if you've all finished trying to split the table in two, Morwen can help me set it, and I'll tell her my own news.'

'What news, Mammie?' She tried to sound interested, but there was only one piece of important news spinning in her head. She would see Ben at the works on Monday. She would see him again, so soon… but her mouth opened in astonishment as Bess told her of Mrs Pollancy's offer.

'You'd stop working for Killigrew Clay?'

Bess laughed, handing her daughter a pile of dishes for the table, and a loaf to slice.

'Did you think we were all fixtures there, Morwen? This is a golden chance for me. I love to sew, and to be paid for it too, and to be at home all day – well, I feel as if I should pay the ladies for the privilege!'

Morwen gave her mother a quick hug.

'No, you shouldn't. They're the lucky ones to have you, and so are we. Is this what you really want, Mammie?'

Bess looked thoughtful. 'I didn't know it until it was offered to me. It's even lovelier to realise an ambition without even having to strive for it!'

Was it? To Morwen, an ambition fulfilled without striving and working for it seemed like no ambition at all, but she wouldn't dim her mother's elation by saying so. Instead she got on with preparing the family meal, and tried not to think too much about Ben Killigrew.

–

On Sunday afternoon Ben Killigrew was visiting the Carricks in Truro for tea. Jane's blood ran fast at the thought, but not in the way her mother might have imagined. She and Ben would stroll through the cobbled town,

64

and make for a narrow, tucked-away street, there to climb some rickety stairs to the attic rooms of a tall terraced house. The home of someone very dear to Jane, someone she wanted Ben to meet. Tom Askhew.

Even thinking of his name made Jane warm inside. She was in love, and it was a glorious feeling, however much her parents would throw up their hands in horror at her choice. Tom would be condemned at once. He was not only a northerner, speaking with flat, nasal Yorkshire tones. He was also a newspaperman.

Tom Askhew boasted that he had printer's ink in his veins, and it was the very trade that Richard Carrick detested, dealing as he said in garbled muck-raking gossip. Jane knew very well that her scrupulously honourable father would never understand some of Tom's methods of extracting information for his paper. Far from hating them, they exhilarated Jane, adding a spice of drama to a mundane world.

Today, Ben had agreed to meet Tom for the first time. She dearly wanted the two men to like each other. There was no need for rivalry between them, nor ever had been. She felt a shivery delight. Tom was earthy and virile and spoke his mind without frills. When he held her he smelled faintly of that printer's ink that he loved, sweet and tangy and alive. There was power in his work, and matching power in his body.

Tom did double duties in his work, like every other man on the vigorous new paper, the *Informer*. The paper was dedicated to exposing all that was bad in society, giving opinions and comments without fear of reprisal, and all reported in short, pithy sentences that were easy to read, far removed from the wordy coverage of the established press. The *Informer* was hated or applauded, but never ignored.

–

'Ben, this is Tom Askhew,' Jane said, as the two men eyed each other. 'Tom, this is my good friend, Ben Killigrew.'

She made the distinction carefully. Tom was sensitive about her long friendship with Ben, but she needn't have worried.

'It's good to meet you, Tom,' Ben said easily. 'I began to wonder if Jane had invented this wonderful man of hers.'

Tom laughed, visibly relaxing. 'Aye, I'm real enough,' he spoke in the Yorkshire twang Jane found novel and attractive rather than tiresome. 'So you and Jane intend to prolong the myth of your courtship, do you? It seems a wise move for the present.'

'It does, Tom,' Jane said quickly. 'You know Mama wouldn't approve – she means well, and wants the best for me—'

'So do I, and we both know what that is, lass,' Tom said slyly, without taking offence.

Ben gave a short laugh. 'I see you're a man of plain speaking, Tom.'

Askhew's eyes were suddenly keen. 'Happen you'd best be the same come Monday, lad, if all I've heard is true. Jane says you're to report to the clay pit, and there's other tales doing the rounds. There's dissent among the Killigrew workers and other pits and rumours of a march to your father's office to demand like payment for all. How do you fancy choosing sides, Ben?'

Ben was angry to hear it from a newspaperman, whom he had no doubt had got the gist of the matter. Tom's reputation assured him of that. He was angry at being told of private matters in so casual a way, and if it hadn't been for Jane's anxious look he might have demanded to know more. As it was, he shrugged stiffly.

'I'll decide that when I'm good and ready,' he said coolly. He looked at Jane. 'I don't think we should stay out much longer. Your mother will be expecting us for tea.'

'Give us a moment or two, Ben,' Jane pleaded.

He nodded, leaving the two of them together, his thoughts racing. If there was trouble at the works, then perhaps it was as well that he was home for good. He still resented being thrown into the thick of it with Jude by his father's irritating insistence that they should be properly employed, but something basic in Ben began to assert itself. Family pride was involved if there was dissent among the clayworkers. That Tom Askhew's nose for a story had discovered it first was really of no consequence.

Jane appeared a few minutes later, tucking her hand in his arm and looking anxiously into his face.

'Do you like him, Ben?'

He noted that her mouth looked well and truly kissed, her cheeks flushed, her eyes bright, and he hid his irritation.

'I'd say his goose is cooked,' he said irreverently. 'You're as determined a woman as your mother, and a mere man doesn't stand a chance—'

'You like him,' she stated. 'And you'll tell Mama you're taking me to Truro Fair, won't you, Ben? And if I disappear for an hour or so until you take me home again, you'll understand, won't you?' Her cheeks coloured more, knowing he would understand exactly what she meant.

'I suppose you know what you're doing?' Ben looked directly into her eyes.

'I know perfectly well,' she said calmly.

She knew more than she would say, even to Ben. Tom was putting everything into the *Informer*, and there were influential northerners with an eye on the ambitious young man. He had already been half promised their backing on a similar newspaper in Yorkshire if this one showed continued promise. When he left Cornwall to begin that new venture, as Jane was confident he would, she had every intention of going with him. But that was a secret known only to herself and Tom.

–

By the time Morwen went to bed on Sunday night, she knew it was impossible to put Ben Killigrew out of her thoughts. She would see him tomorrow... and from the moment she had heard the news, he had seemed to fill every corner of her mind. She had thought she would rarely see him, because the fine folks didn't mix with the workers very often. She could pretend that all Celia's teasings about her dreaming of marrying Ben Killigrew were like will o' the wisp...

She could forget that his pearl pin had scratched her cheek, leaving a tiny indentation in her skin, as if he really had branded her, reminding her of his words every time she touched the mark. Every single time...

While she believed she would rarely see him, it had been easy. Now she knew she had only been deluding herself. She had such feelings about Ben Killigrew... akin to the thrill of turning a sixpence at the sight of a new moon and guessing at its luck. They muddled her senses and fired her blood. She didn't understand them, but she knew their power. They excited her and angered her, because she knew they could lead nowhere.

Morwen's throat tightened with a bittersweet pain, knowing she wanted a man who was destined for someone else. She told herself she wouldn't think of him… but she couldn't stop him filling her dreaming hours. Foolish, impossible dreams, where Ben Killigrew marched right up to her and took her in his arms, and told her he loved her… sweet, wonderful dreams that made her sigh gently in her sleep, and let the soft trickle of tears dampen her pillow.

–

Ben had marching of a different kind on his mind on Monday morning. He still bristled over last evening, when he'd gone to his cousin's room. He'd looked at Jude's sprawling shape on the bed with disgust, noting the smell of drink and the dulled eyes and flushed face of his cousin.

'You know we're to go to the clay works tomorrow?' he said abruptly. 'Do you know anything of a march to the town?'

'Why should I?' Jude slurred.

Ben glowered at him. 'With the kind of company you keep in the kiddleywinks, I thought you might have known. It seems there's dissent over payment between the pits. Father seems in the thick of it—'

Jude began to laugh, swinging his legs over the edge of the bed and sitting up so fast his head swam.

'We'd best keep away, then. We'd be an embarrassment—'

'No we won't,' Ben snapped. He'd had no plan until a short while ago, but now he knew exactly what to do. 'We'll show our faces, dressed for work and not as gentry, which won't be difficult for you. We'll go on horseback, and we'll apply ourselves to whatever's asked of us. And since my father wants our full co-operation with the clayworkers, we'll join this march and show him and the clayworkers that we sympathise with their cause and are not just play-acting with them.'

Jude's eyes flickered with surprise. 'Defy your father, Ben?' he said mockingly. 'You'd march with men demanding more pay from him and cut your own throat? 'Tis your money in the end—'

'If Father wants me to be one of them, we back them all the way,' he said curtly. 'Are you with me?'

'That I am!' Jude wouldn't miss this chance of getting one over on his uncle, which was just what Ben expected.

'For once we're in agreement. Be ready to leave the house soon after seven o'clock in the morning.'

He strode from the room, not wanting to prolong this conversation with Jude. They had acknowledged their mutual dislike long ago, and only the blood ties made them tolerate each other.

The march had begun to appeal to Ben. He had no thought of toadying up to the clayworkers, and he knew there would be plenty who resented the owner's son amongst them, and would suspect him of spying on them. But if he was to be one of them, however briefly, then he'd abide by their rules, and by God so would that toe-rag Jude Pascoe as well.

The two of them left Killigrew House next day, while the mist still hung about the moors above the town, and the good dames of St Austell were barely stirring in their beds. Jude hated the dampness, but Ben found the early morning ride exhilarating, and sharpened his wits. He realised he looked forward to the day, and also to seeing Morwen Tremayne again.

She figured in his thoughts a great deal. Seeing Jane and Tom together in Truro, and their shared closeness, he'd realised the lack in his own life, and he'd thought of Morwen. And known it was as unlikely a match as that of Jane Carrick and Tom Askhew. Jane was right. If ever her parents found out…

'Well, look at that, cousin! There's a sight to see on a Monday morning, like a gift from heaven.' Jude's sly voice broke into his thoughts.

Ben looked ahead and saw the group of bal maidens laughing and gossiping on their way to Clay One pit, and found himself searching for a dark-haired girl with the bluest eyes…

'She ain't among 'em,' Jude jeered, guessing at his thoughts. 'But there's a pert little maid if I ever did see one.'

He made an exaggerated bow from his horse as the bal maidens went giggling by. Some glanced shyly at the two handsome young men on Killigrew horses; others were more bold, smiling freely, and it was Celia Penry smiling at the admiring leer of Jude Pascoe.

'Looks like he fancies 'ee, Celia,' one of the other bal maidens giggled. 'You want to watch the likes of 'ee!'

Jude heard her laugh and glance his way again. He liked the sound of her name. Celia. A pretty name for a pretty maid. And looking as though she knew her way about too. His practised eyes took in the swinging hips beneath the flouncing skirt, and the way her waist nipped in to accommodate a man's grasp. He liked the way her dark hair rippled down the straightness of her spine, and felt a quickening interest. Perhaps working one day a week at Killigrew Clay would have its compensations after all.

'Let's find Hal Tremayne,' Ben said shortly, irked at not seeing Morwen, and feeling even more annoyed to know it. What ailed him lately? He acted like a love-sick swain at times, which was galling to a young man with the world at his feet.

—

A couple of hours later, Ben wondered about that partic- ular world he was to inherit. Hal Tremayne had thrust him and Jude into the thick of it, deciding to give no favours to owner's kin. The two new apprentices found aching muscles they never knew they had.

The rhythmic beat of beam engine, the constant whine of machinery and swish of water made their heads throb. Ben gritted his teeth and swore to drop dead before he'd complain. Too many here expected that. He could see it in their eyes. Jude had been put to work outside. Ben was in the kiln, where it was unbearably hot. The men worked almost naked, with sweat pouring off them, and the stink was acrid and unbelievable.

He was used to bathing and clean clothes whenever he wanted them, and Ben's nostrils rebelled against the stench. The man with him, Eric Leeman, clearly resented his presence, and growlingly told him what to do as the hatch boards between the settling tank and the kiln were removed, and a quantity of semi-solid clay flowed into the kiln to commence drying.

From the far side of the tank, the clay was shovelled into wheel-barrows and brought by hand to the kiln, where Leeman and Ben used the long-handled shovels to distribute it evenly. As he worked, the sweat poured off him in rivers. He quickly discarded his shirt, and worked only in trousers and boots.

The kiln was long and narrow, no more than the width a man could reach with a shovel. It was searingly hot and humid. Ben wondered grimly how Jude fared, hauling waste into the little trolleys up to the sky-tips. At least he breathed fresh air...

After what seemed like days, a whistle sounded, and Eric grunted that they could take a tea-break. Ben hated him, but he eased his aching limbs and smiled as he saw the cheeky young Freddie Tremayne, loaded down with a tray of tea mugs.

'Daddy said you'd be wanting this, Mr – uh – Mr Ben—' Freddie floundered a little, then his face brightened. 'Our Morwen was asking after you—'

Ben towelled off his glistening back with his own shirt, and laughed at Freddie's perky face.

'Was she now? Where is our Morwen then?'

'Not so far away. Over in the linhay, o' course, stacking the clay!' He pointed.

The kiln shed was on a higher level than the linhay, so that the dried clay, scored and cut, could be heaved over to the air-dry below. The bal maidens could then begin stacking and scraping, allowing the natural movement of air to complete the drying process, and the kiln would be ready to receive the next load. He had been close to Morwen all this time without knowing it. He walked across and looked over.

As though she sensed it, Morwen looked up at the same moment. Her heart leapt at the sight of Ben Killigrew; as unlike the elegant young man at Killigrew House as she could imagine. This Ben was stripped to the waist like any kilnworker, his broad chest bronzed and glistening, even the virile growth of hair upon it. Although that, and the hair on his head, was dusted white from the drying clay. The sight of him was so startling, so oddly exciting, that Morwen began to laugh.

'Do you find me so funny, Morwen Tremayne?' Ben mocked her. 'Do you not fancy me as a clayworker?'

The girl Ben and Jude had seen earlier sidled up to Morwen, her eyes laughing and daring.

'I'd fancy 'ee, Mr Ben, if Morwen don't!'

Morwen dug her in the ribs. It wasn't the way to speak to the owner's son, however different he looked without his posh clothes.

'You'll have to stand second in line, Celia,' Ben called back teasingly. 'Ask Morwen about the brand!'

Morwen went scarlet as Celia demanded to know what he meant by that. She spoke as boldly as Celia now.

'You mean third in line, don't you, sir?' she said quickly. 'Don't forget a certain Miss finelady from Truro!'

'Are you mad, to put ideas in his head that may not be there?' Celia hissed, as Eric Leeman called Ben back to his work with a surly glare at the two bal maidens below.

'You two maids stop gossiping and get about your work,' a sharp female voice called to them, and Morwen went back to the clay thankfully. The sight of Ben Killigrew had disturbed her more than she had expected it to, and she knew Celia wouldn't let the little matter of the brand rest until she knew what it was all about.

A while later, Hal Tremayne came to the kiln with a small group of men and told Leeman and Ben to come outside a moment. Thank God, Ben thought. He breathed in great gulps of air, clear as wine after the steaming atmosphere of the kiln. He'd dearly like to sit down, or lie down… but these men stood with folded arms and he had no choice but to do the same. He saw Jude, ghostly white from head to foot from the clay dust, and as weary as himself.

'You know what we're about,' Hal said. 'If the two new men aren't aware of it by now, we march to the clay office this afternoon to demand wages on a par with other pits hereabouts.'

One of the men spoke up angrily. 'We don't want 'em marching wi' us. 'Tain't their place to be included, no more than 'tis their place to be working alongside us.'

One and another growled their assent, heads nodding and showering those next to them with dust. Another spoke loudly.

'The pit be the place for the likes of we, cap'n, not for boss's spawn.'

Ben saw Jude throw the man a look of pure gratitude, and Ben couldn't argue with the sentiment. Not now, when every muscle cried out for rest at the unaccustomed punishment it was getting. He had new respect for the workers, but he no longer wanted to work beside them…

Hal quietened them with a loud bellow.

'Fact is, we've got to include 'em on the march, boys. I gave Gil Dark my word on it. But if 'tis your wish that we tell Charles Killigrew we find their presence here unwelcome, then so be it. Do I have a show of hands?'

All hands went up at once, and Hal looked at Ben.

'You've heard the general feeling, boy,' he said, not unkindly. 'What's your say on it? 'Tis nothing personal, and if you refuse to march with us, then 'tis your right to say so.'

Ben knew everyone watched him, and expected him to back down. But he'd be damned if he'd go scuttling away from here with his tail between his legs. He spoke in language they'd understand.

'I understand the mens' feelings. My cousin and myself are unused to this work, but I trust there's no man here will say we haven't worked our guts out this morning.' He waited for any argument, but there was none. 'Since you don't want us here, it's up to you to tell my father so. It's your right, but it's his right to make the final decision. As to the march, God knows my feet wouldn't carry me that far,' he said honestly, 'but I believe in fair payment for all, and we'll come with you if you'll have us. If you've no objection, we'll ride, or our horses will be left up here on the moors—'

'And 'twill save your poor soft feet—' a man jeered.

'You're damn right it will,' Ben snapped. 'Take it or leave it. Your pit captain wants us along. We'll go, and we'll ride, and we'll back up every demand for wages that you make.'

The men grunted approval, and Hal brought the meeting to an end, while Ben was unsure if he had won a victory or not. Hal called him as the men dispersed.

'Your working here is a bad idea, Ben,' Hal said bluntly. 'The men don't like it, and I'm going to ask your father to reconsider. I want no disharmony at Clay One. I hope you understand—'

Ben gave a short laugh. 'It's the best thing I've heard today. You'll get no arguments from either one of us, I'm sure.'

He refused to despise himself for agreeing so readily. He was strong and fit, but he simply wasn't used to this kind of work. It became more evident as a string of blasphemies left Eric Leeman's throat a few minutes later as he bawled at Ben to come and do the work he was sent to do or get back to his afternoon tea parties and leave men to do mens' jobs.

Ben moved quickly towards the inferno of the kiln shed and picked up his long-handled shovel. At that moment, he would dearly like to crash it over the glowering Leeman's head. It did nothing for his self-respect to hear the tittering laughter of the bal maidens in the linhay below. They had probably heard every word, and that meant Morwen would have heard it too.

Chapter Six

Charles Killigrew smiled with satisfaction as his accountant, Daniel Gorran, gave the monthly accounting figures to the pit owner, in Killigrew's office in Greeley Street.

'It's looking healthy enough,' Charles grunted. 'I'm obliged to you, Daniel, so take that disapproving look off your face, man. I'm aware you don't like the thought of my sending Ben to work at the pit—'

'I don't recall you working with the wet clay yourself,' Gorran said drily. 'It's not right—'

'It'll do the boy no harm to sweat it out awhile, and I don't intend it to be a permanent arrangement,' Charles agreed. He looked sharply towards the open window.

'What's all that rumpus?' He strode across the room and swore in disbelief. 'Christ, man, come and look here! Have those two young whelps of mine joined in some sort of riot?'

Daniel joined him, staring in amazement at the scene below the office window. Marching through the narrow winding street, boots resounding metallically on the cobbles, was a disorderly column of men. Four were in hard hats and the usual pit captain's garb. The rest were stippled white from the clay dust, and two of them were astride horses, hair awry and more dishevelled than Daniel had ever seen them. He smothered a grin at the unlikely sight of Ben Killigrew and his cousin among the marching clay workers.

'We'd best let them in and see what's to do,' Charles said angrily, since it was obvious that this office was their destination. He had an inkling of their intention. He knew of the wage rises at the other pits. He knew that eventually he'd have to keep in step, or lose some of his workers...

Hal Tremayne removed his hat as he walked into the office with its plush carpet and deep leather chairs. As many as could cram inside followed the pit captain, falling silent at being in such grand surroundings. And being faced with two gentlemen instead of one made them ill-at-ease. Ben and Jude had left their horses with a street boy for a penny due, and jostled among the men. Ben was suddenly enjoying the situation, and especially his father's black looks.

'What's this all about?' Charles demanded. 'Are you spokesman, Tremayne? Make it short. I've a home to return to—'

'So have we all, Mr Killigrew, though none so fine as yours. I doubt that you've lived in a home where you can see the stars between the slates because the owner's too mean to put his hand in his pocket to pay for repairs. I doubt that you'll know what a difference an extra twopence a day means to poor men. But that's what we're asking – no, *demanding*! Twopence a day for clayworkers, a penny a day for bal maidens and kiddley boys, in line with other pits—'

Charles let out a roar that stopped him.

'Demanding, you say? Is this the way you think to extract extra wages from me, man?'

'Would you rather we went on strike, Father?' Ben's voice said lazily. Charles glowered at him.

'What in God's name are you doing with this rabble?' he snapped. 'Don't talk to me of strikes. You know nothing about such things—'

'I intend to learn! You made me one of the workers, remember? If they demand twopence a day more, then so do I. If they strike, then so do I. How do you like the sound of it?'

Ben liked the sound of it, more than he had expected. It was the first time in his life he'd enjoyed such a position of power, although he got no backing from Jude, who merely slouched against the wall and said nothing.

'So you're one of them now, are you?' Charles snorted.

'No, he's not, Mr Killigrew!' Hal Tremayne spoke up again, with mutters of agreement from the men. ''Tis our wish that your son and nephew be employed elsewhere and not at the pit. It ain't fitting. Not that they ain't done a fair day's work, and I daresay they'll ache for a week to remind them of it, but we're all of the same opinion. Employ them elsewhere and give us our fair dues, or we might just take it in our heads to work for a boss who's willing to see sense.'

Hal had never spoken so boldly to a boss before, and his eyes challenged Charles Killigrew. He seemed hardly aware of the mass of men behind him, nor the stink of them in this posh office. Right then there was only one thought in Hal's mind, to get fair dues for all. For a second, the air was thick with tension, and then Charles Killigrew bellowed with laughter.

'By God, Hal Tremayne, I knew what I was about when I made you pit captain of Clay One! You're a leader and a champion, and by all that's holy, your guts have won the day. You don't intimidate me, mind! But I've just had word of the profits—' he waved a sheaf of papers in the air, 'and I'm willing to share a little of them with good workers. All right. You've got your twopence, and the rest their penny—'

He had to pause a moment for the cheers.

'But there'll be no immediate payment,' he warned. 'When my dues come in, then the wage rise will begin. I can't pay out from empty coffers, and I can't be fairer than that, can I?'

The cheers subsided a little, but they could see they'd get no better deal. Hal stood his ground, not done yet.

'And your son and nephew?'

'It's up to them for the final word.' He looked at them both. 'Do you want to continue at the pit—?'

'No thank you!' they said together. This reply drew more cheers and laughter and relaxed the atmosphere in the office. Gradually the men began to disperse, relaying the words back to those who hadn't been able to crowd into the office. Ben and Jude remained behind. To their surprise, so did Hal.

'I've more to tell 'ee, sir,' he said gruffly. 'My good woman will be finishing working for Killigrew Clay at the end of the week.'

This time Charles was taken aback.

'Am I having mutiny from your family, Hal?' he asked. 'I took your wife for a placid woman with no discontents—'

'So she is, but she wishes to work as a seamstress, and has been offered plenty of such work, sir. It pleases her to take it on.'

'And does it please you, Hal?' Charles said suddenly.

'Aye. I've a wish to find her waiting when I get home from my shift,' he said simply.

Charles was more moved by the words than he let on, and felt a swift, surprising envy for Hal Tremayne's close-knit, loving family.

'Then so be it. Now get you gone from here, all except Jude. I want words with you,' he said grimly to his nephew.

Hal left quickly, sighing with relief that it had all gone smoothly. Ben and Daniel Gorran went out together, while Jude looked sullenly at his uncle.

'So how was your day at the works?' Charles enquired.

Jude scowled, knowing this was no idle question. 'Tipping waste into little trucks is not my idea of fun—'

'Then what is, Jude?' There was an edge to Charles' voice that Jude recognised.

'I'm not used to it, Uncle! I've no objection to working with my hands, but—' he whined.

'Good. Because you'll be taking over the gardens and stables at Killigrew House. Old Jenks is getting too feeble now, so you begin tomorrow. You'll receive a small wage, but little more than you get already for doing nothing. If the arrangement doesn't suit you, then find other accommodation.'

He was crisp and cold, daring Jude to object. It was a menial job, but if Hannah Pascoe could work as her brother's housekeeper, then her lout of a son could damn well earn his keep too. In Charles's opinion, it was a decision long overdue.

Hannah had originally said she wanted to be useful and not beholden to him, and if she had grown to resent her position, then it was just too bad. There was no love lost between them, and he had no intention of letting her act the lady in his house. That privilege was for Ben's future wife.

He heard Jude mutter his agreement, having little choice before he stamped out, banging the office door behind him in his rage. Charles leaned back in his leather chair, not displeased with the day. A lot had happened, he ruminated. Hal had got his wage increase for the men; he'd lost a good worker in Bess Tremayne; Jude was firmly under his thumb, and Ben had shown he had spirit beneath the fancy education.

He poured himself a large whisky and disregarded the lot of them. He'd been well pleased with Daniel Gorran's monthly report. Profits were good, if not spectacular, and if he held out on the wage payments a little longer, so much the better.

He was aware that he paid less than other clay owners. He'd stuck it out, knowing the day would come when he'd have to come in line with them. But if these dolts thought they'd scored over him with their puny demands, he would still have the last laugh. He'd already gained a month or two of extra twopences and pennies, and it was pennies that turned into pounds.

Charles considered himself an expert with words. He'd seen to it that his workers wouldn't expect the new rate for a while yet. It only took a bit of careful wording to give with one hand and take back with the other.

–

Ben was just thankful that the aches and pains of the day weren't to be repeated. Jude could forget that miserable day too, despite the new indignity of acting as groomsman and gardener and stable-boy for his uncle, and the irritation of asking permission to attend the Truro Whitsuntide Fair.

But permission was readily given, and Jude forgot his grievances as he stabled his own horse at a hostelry in Truro town and joined the throngs from the surrounding districts. Like him, they all headed for Boscawen Street and the Cross, and the major streets of Truro where all the stalls were set up, making the entire town into a giant street market.

Everything in the world must be on sale, Jude thought. There were toys and gingerbread and farm produce and penny dreadfuls and pilchards and live eels and cure-all medicines. A cheap John shouted his wares, reducing them shilling by shilling until the first gullible customer accepted his offer.

The music of hurdy-gurdies and tambourines mingled with the shouting and laughter of the crowds. The bright coloured dresses of the bal maidens, traditionally turned out as loudly and colourfully as they could on Fair days, were like clusters of brilliant flowers among the more sober garb of the rest.

Jude's interest flickered for a moment, then his attention was caught by the Punch and Judy stall. In other parts of the fair, serious actors and actresses spoke tragic lines from makeshift stages. Monkeys dressed in tinselled clothes chattered on sticks. Exotic birds were on sale in gilded cages. Smells of humanity, of gaudy paints and powders, vied with the smells of the river nearby...

'Are you taking up the play-acting as a change from shovelling clay, then?'

Jude heard a cheeky female voice nearby. He turned quickly, to see the bright green skirt of Celia Penry swirl away from him as her friend Morwen Tremayne dragged at her arm. But Celia's laughing face was all the spur he needed. He chased after the two bal maidens, easy to spot in their gay dresses. Morwen's was daffodil yellow, and their long hair bounced beneath their bonnets. Jude felt a surge of excitement. Maybe the Tremayne girl would keep a fellow at arm's length, but the other one...

He caught up with them and spun Celia round to face him. In such crowds, any amount of impropriety could be forgiven, and in Jude's opinion, jostling up to a pretty wench was one of the delights of the fair.

'I remember you, my pretty! Will you come and take some sweet-drink with me——?'

'Celia, you'd best stay with me,' Morwen said at once. She didn't like Jude Pascoe, nor the way he sidled up to her friend, far too close. Celia might enjoy it, but Morwen was sure Jude wasn't to be trusted. No more was the sweet-drink, that delectable honeyed drink so innocent to the taste, so potent to the senses.

Whether boiled merely with hops and a small measure of brandy to every mixture of honey and water, or with more reckless amounts of spirits, the effect was the same. The taste was often disguised by the delightful additions of cinnamon and mace and cloves, or such aromatic plants as the tops of sweet-briar or rosemary or thyme. Delicious, dangerous concoctions all, especially to a young girl coaxed into drinking more than was wise by an ardent young man...

Celia turned on her. 'Mind your business! If I want to take the sweet-drink with Jude, then so I will.'

She flounced away, with Jude following her, laughing back at Morwen's angry face.

'I'll take care of her, never fear! And if you're looking for my cousin, he's gone to see his lady-love.'

Morwen hated him even more. How could Celia be attracted to him? It was clear to Morwen that she was, and she watched as the two of them were swallowed up in the crowds. She felt ridiculously alone, and knew it was because of Jude's jeering words about Ben seeing his lady-love. That could only be Miss Jane Carrick, of course. Not until that moment did Morwen admit that her eyes had been searching for Ben's tall, powerful figure... she turned blindly, calling herself a fool, and cannoned right into someone.

'Are you going to make a habit of this, Miss Tremayne?' She heard Ben Killigrew say mockingly, as she was held hard against his chest once more. Her heart pounded in sickening, excited beats as he made no attempt to let her go, as though he liked the feel of her in his arms. Ben had decided on that long ago, and although Fair days were bohemian days, she knew this was no way for a young gentleman to behave with a lady... but to him, Morwen Tremayne wasn't a lady, she reminded herself.

'Where's Miss Carrick?' she said stiffly. 'You'd best get back to her before she sees you cavorting with a common bal maiden!'

'Why are you so damn conscious of your status, Morwen?' he countered. 'I've worked at the kiln too. I know what clayworking's about—'

She was scornful. 'For one day! I heard about you riding along with the marchers to support my Daddy too. Is that your claim to clayworking, Mr Killigrew? And don't talk to me of my status. Beside you, I don't have any, do I?'

She ranted on, half appalled at the way she spoke to the owner's son. She was angry because he made her aware of herself in her gaudy dress that had seemed so fine that morning, and which now seemed to shout loudly beside Ben's tasteful clothes. She hated him and all he stood for, because he made her dissatisfied with her lot, and she had never realised it before.

'Don't fight me, Morwen,' Ben said quietly. 'That's not what I want for us.'

She looked up into his face, her cheeks flushed with anger, her eyes that incredible blue, so beautiful they made him draw in his breath. No eyes were ever like Morwen Tremayne's...

'What you want for us?' she echoed, a catch in her voice. 'There is no "us", Mr Ben. You have your Miss finelady, and I – I shall probably marry John Penry, as befits a bal maiden who shouldn't aspire to anyone above her class. Where is she today, anyway?'

She changed the conversation while Ben was still registering the fact that there was a young man in Morwen's life, and noting the spurt of jealousy it gave him. He was tempted to shock her by saying he had delivered Jane to her lover's attic rooms, where they were probably oblivious to anything but each other by now. He managed not to say the words, partly because he didn't know how far Jane's attachment to Tom Askhew had gone, and partly because he would never betray a confidence.

Morwen knew none of this. She saw the brief blank look on Ben's handsome face, and assumed he would rather not speak of Jane to her. They weren't to be spoken of in the same breath, she thought bitterly. She wrenched herself out of his arms and away into the crowds. It was a gloriously warm, fun-packed day, but for Morwen the sun had suddenly grown cold.

–

Celia giggled. Her head swam as though a shoal of pilchards swam there. She had taken too much sweet-drink, and Jude still offered her more. Tucked away in a secluded corner of the quay with the tang of salt in the air and the brawny fishermen setting up stalls with their catch only yards away, Jude Pascoe was finding a raw pleasure in sporting with the willing little bal maiden.

She was soft and pliant beneath him, although she still resisted too many demands of his seeking hands, and teased him that if he tried force, she'd cry rape and have the constables on him in a trice. He believed her. No matter. There would be other times, and meanwhile there were other delights. One rough hand cupped her breast and he tasted its rosy peak with his tongue.

Celia ached to give in totally… but she still had enough control of her senses to be wary of this masterful rogue with the fine line in seduction, and the thrillingly wicked words he breathed against her flesh.

'You've a fine pair here, my wench,' he said thickly. 'A man could sink into 'em and lose himself for ever—'

'What a waste!' Celia burbled. Her hands clasped the tangled hair at the back of his nape, and wanted more… 'I wouldn't want to lose 'ee, Jude—'

'I'd lose myself in more than these mounds, if you'd let me.' He raised himself up to kiss the soft parted mouth, and probed its sweetness with his tongue, letting her know just how he'd like to lose himself.

Sounds of people approaching made Celia take sudden fright. She wriggled from under him, her head rocking as she did so. Jude's face was a hazy shape, and dear God, but she would have to sleep this off, Celia thought desperately. Nowhere near Jude though, or he'd have the maidenhead off her in no time, and if it was going to happen, then she was going to enjoy it!

'Course, it 'ould be different if you was my intended,' she said, a silly grin sliding over her face at the thought. Jude grinned. He had no intention of wedding anyone, least of all a wench who worked with the clay. But she needn't be aware of that.

'Would that make a difference, then?' He ran a practised finger around her lips and let her small white teeth take a nip at it.

'O' course it 'ould! Mebbe I'll find out if that's what you have in mind in a week or so, when Morwen and me take the potion to the Larnie stone.'

Her thoughts were muddled as the words ran on. Celia pooh-poohed old Zillah and her charms, but it would be dearly agreeable if it was Jude's face she saw through the stone...

'What potion?' he said softly. 'Tell me about it. If it's a charm, it can't be as charming as you!'

She giggled. His skin tasted salty, and the scent of him excited her. What harm would it do to tell him? It was all nonsense, and it was only Morwen who was really taken in by old Zillah... without thinking too much, Celia rattled on about the visit to the old woman, and what they intended to do with the potion. And Jude listened with a mounting interest.

This damn shed was no place for lying with a wench. He'd known it would probably come to nothing. But away over the moors by moonlight, when this ready wench was filled with a wise woman's potion to dull her senses... Jude's eyes gleamed at the tantalising prospect. He hauled Celia to her feet, pretending no interest.

'I'd best get you some food to counteract the sweet-drink, Celia,' he said, knowing now that he could bide his time. 'Hold on to me, and I'll take care of you.'

She clung to him gratefully, her flushed face alive with pleasure at this young gentleman's solicitude. Like a lamb to the slaughter, Jude thought jubilantly. Like a lamb to the bloody slaughter.

–

By the time Jude left for home that night, Celia Penry's charms were still on his mind. He saw a familiar figure ahead of him in the twilight.

'Hold on for me, Ben!' he called. He dug his heels into his horse's flanks. He wouldn't readily seek out his cousin, but company was always preferable to riding through the darkness alone at night. Truro Fair would be riddled with ruffians and pickpockets ready to relieve honest folk of their money.

Ben was ruffled at being kept waiting so long for Jane to appear from Tom Askhew's rooms. He had waited outside the house, his imagination seeing the two of them upstairs together. He imagined Jane in Tom's arms, flesh on flesh, bodies warm and glistening, limbs intertwined. He imagined the culmination of love, the exquisite, almost painful sensation of a man's seed flowing into a woman. He imagined every moment... and what he imagined most of all was the interpretation of love by himself and Morwen Tremayne...

When Jane finally appeared, he was highly sensitive to the warm musky scent of her, the scent of love. Frustration swept through him, making him curt with her.

'Ben, I'm sorry I kept you waiting,' Jane said in embarrassment. 'Please don't be cross—'

'I'm not,' he said shortly. 'Jealous, perhaps—'

At the look on her face, he elaborated.

'Not on your account, never fear! Merely jealous of an afternoon such as yours, while mine was just – commonplace.'

'Poor Ben,' Jane said sympathetically. 'I hope you'll find someone of your own very soon.'

Ben wondered for the hundredth time if he had already found her...

—

Now he waited for his coarse cousin to join him on the ride home, and the reek of spirits preceded Jude as he drew near.

'Did you have a good fair, cuz?' Jude drawled, his very demeanour irritating Ben as always.

What right did this cur have to enjoy the day, when until this week he'd done little to earn the Killigrew money he squandered? Ben's own homecoming had made Charles Killigrew realise how idle his nephew had become, and a good thing too.

'You enjoyed it, I see,' Ben snapped in reply. 'You've drunk enough spirits to drown an ox by the look of you—'

'And then some,' Jude laughed in agreement. 'I had a fair companion to help me, see? A pretty maid wi' long dark hair and a way of melting into a man's arms—'

Ben jerked his horse to a halt as his temper flared.

'Keep away from Morwen Tremayne, d'you hear? She's the daughter of my father's pit captain, and he'll not thank you for sporting with her—'

Jude laughed again, his voice oozing triumph at catching his cousin out.

'You give yourself away, Ben! 'Tis the wench herself that's on your mind, not your father nor hers! I've seen the way you've looked at her, and Jane Carrick had best think how to keep you in her bed at night once you're wed. If your body's with her, 'tis clear that your thoughts will be with the other one—'

He ducked quickly as Ben's fist slashed towards him, striking him on the shoulder instead of connecting with his jaw.

'Keep your filthy thoughts to yourself,' he ground out. 'But if you've been dallying with Morwen—'

'I never said 'twas her, did I?' Jude rubbed tenderly at his bruised shoulder. 'If you must know, 'twas her friend, Celia, and a pretty tale she told me about the two of 'em—'

He dug his heels in his horse's flanks and sped away, knowing Ben's curiosity would be roused. It was a mile further on before Ben caught him up and grasped at Jude's reins, pulling him to a stop. Both panted from the exertion of the gallop.

'Now then, scum, what's this tale that Morwen's friend told you?' he snapped. 'The truth, mind, or I'll wring your neck and enjoy doing it!'

''Tis the truth all right,' Jude snarled. 'Two of 'em have got some love potion from the old crone on the moors, and intend testing it on the first full moonlit night. What say we give them their moneys' worth, cuz?'

'What kind of test?' Ben hated the thought of sharing anything with this lout, but he wanted to know more…

Jude told him the tale, thinking privately that the girls would be so tipsy with the potion and the circling, they'd be ready to imagine anything. In fact, Jude was counting on it.

'And you plan to ride to the moors every night around midnight to play a game with them, do you?' Ben said grimly.

'Why not?' Jude challenged him. 'If 'tis Morwen or Celia who sees my face through the stone, it makes no difference to me. One wench is as good as another on a dark night—'

His throat was suddenly seized in Ben's powerful grip as Ben leapt at him, sliding off his own horse and pulling Jude to the ground with him.

'Get off me, bastard!' Jude croaked as stars danced in front of his eyes. 'You won't stop me, with your bloody inheritance and your Killigrew money! I've as fine a load in my breeches as you—'

He bellowed with pain as Ben's hands left his throat and made a fist into his groin. The full impact was lost as Jude slithered backwards, but it still winded him and made him fear for his wenching tackle.

'I'll be there, if you intend going through with this,' Ben said furiously. 'I'll not see one of those girls touched by you. I'll stay so close, you'll think I'm your shadow, you bastard. Now get on your horse, and get home. I'm sick of the sight of you.'

Jude smiled faintly as he climbed painfully on to his horse. He'd got his way, whether Ben realised it or not. What did Jude want with two bal maidens on the moors? One would be enough, and while Ben took care of Morwen, he'd be more than ready to have a high old time with the other one.

—

And Ben was asking himself bitterly just who he thought he was fooling, as the two of them rode silently home towards St Austell. Such noble talk to be safeguarding the honour of two bal maidens, when they might be no better than many of their kind. And what in hell's name was he contemplating, to be taking part in some heathen ritual on the moors, as though all the expensive college education his father had given him was as nothing compared to the mystic beliefs and potions of a Cornish witch.

Theirs were ancient ways… believed by the majority of the truly Cornish, such as Morwen Tremayne. And such as Ben Killigrew… he drew a deep shuddering breath, knowing that his real reason for trysting with her at the Larnie standing stone was to make sure it was Ben Killigrew's face that Morwen Tremayne glimpsed through the stone. Whatever the consequences…

Chapter Seven

'Tonight!' Celia whispered as she and Morwen parted company after their day's shift. 'I'll be waiting for you, Morwen, and don't forget the potion!'

'Of course not.' Morwen tried not to betray how her palms sweated at the thought. The time was here, the moon would be full that night, and she palpitated with nerves. Were they tampering with fate…? Would there be other, more human dangers waiting for them on the dark and mysterious moors…?

She smothered the thought. They knew the moors, and the moonlight would guide them. Zillah's potion would do the rest. Despite her fears, Morwen still tingled when she thought ahead to the magical moment when she looked through the Lamie Stone. Whose face would she see…?

–

'You're pensive tonight, Morwen,' Bess commented. 'Are you ailing? Perhaps an early night would serve you well—' Morwen tried to smile naturally at her mother, hunched over her sewing by the oil-lamp. The last thing she wanted was for Bess to fuss over her now, though she could perhaps turn the query to her advantage. She yawned, rubbing her hand lightly over her brow.

'Just a slight head-ache, Mammie,' she murmured. 'Nothing that a night's sleep won't cure.'

'Aye, 'twill do us all good,' Bess decided, starting to fold up her work. 'We'll have a hot drink and I'll shoo these others off to bed, and you can rest undisturbed, my lamb.'

'I don't want to drive you all away—' She was immediately guilty.

'There's been plenty excitement this last week,' Hal put in. 'An early night won't come amiss, and once Matthew's indoors, we'll all be as snug as bugs in our beds.'

Hal frowned as he spoke, more anxious about his son Matthew than he admitted. Something troubled Matt lately – troubled or enervated – in a way Hal didn't understand. He was a simple man who disliked under-currents, at work or at home, and there were definite undercurrents in Matt's attitude of late.

It seemed an age to Morwen before they all went to their own beds, and the cottage was finally hers. It always felt that way, when she had pulled her curtain across and the space inside it was hers alone. How wonderful to live in a house with a room for everyone, Morwen thought wistfully. Rich folk knew nothing of cramped cottages and the daily ritual of taking turns for the washing space and the privy. They knew nothing of the lack of privacy, especially for a young girl with special needs, and secrets…

Beneath her pillow was Zillah's potion. Her fingers curled around it, trembling a little. Her Mammie would like none of this, and she knew it. She listened for a long time, until the creaks of the house quietened, then she slid from her bed and listened again. There was no sound. She was still fully dressed, and in moments she had slipped away from the cottage, scorning shoes to move more stealthily in the night.

Her heart beat painfully fast. Despite the huge moon casting its light, the customary ground mist swirled about the moors. She gasped as a hand suddenly seized hers, her senses rocking until she saw Celia move towards her.

'I thought you weren't coming!' Celia said hoarsely, and her voice told Morwen they were both as scared as each other.

'I had to wait for Matt to come home,' Morwen spoke jerkily. 'We've got more people to get settled, and my Daddy doesn't come home half drunk every night so he doesn't hear a thing after nine o'clock—' She bit her lip furiously, not really meaning to sneer at Tom Penry's penchant for the drink. She knew as well as anyone that it had got worse since Celia's mother died and left him in need of forgetfulness.

'I know,' Celia said. 'Though I heard that your Matt's taking to the drink, Morwen. Folk are talking about un—'

'Our Matt?' Morwen echoed resentfully. 'What are they saying? I've heard nothing—'

'I daresay it was only gossip,' Celia said quickly. ''Tis just that he frequents the kiddleywinks in St Austell a lot, instead of jawing wi' the clayworkers, and you know how that causes talk among 'em.'

'Mebbe 'tisn't that at all. Mebbe 'tis a girl he sees, same as our Sam.' Morwen was defensive of her brother.

'Mebbe 'tis the same then,' Celia agreed, sure that it wasn't. She'd heard tales from her father, of the rough salty characters Matthew Tremayne had been associating with in St Austell. If Morwen didn't choose to believe her, it was no concern of Celia's. Besides, they had more important things on their minds that night than Matt Tremayne.

'Did it ever seem so far in daylight?' she muttered, when they had walked for what seemed like hours, and the Larnie Stone seemed as far away as ever. It loomed gaunt and ghostly in the distance. Lit by moonlight, the ground mist all around, it seemed to float on a sea of gauze.

Beyond it, the night was too dark to see the sea properly. In daylight, it glittered blue and silver. Now, it was a dim and hazily imagined shape that added to the unreality of the night. Beneath their feet, the moors were damp and cold, the soft turf spongy. Fronds of bracken snatched at their ankles like clawing fingers. They were both very afraid, and both tried not to show it.

The moors appeared wide and open in the daytime, but now they seemed to be peopled by watching shapes that were no more than bushes of gorse when they neared them, or the twisted gnarled trunk of a weathered tree leaning against the remnants of a stone wall, or a cluster of stones from a rotting derelict cottage. Neither was aware that two of the night shadows had real, living substance.

'This is a fool's errand,' Ben said savagely as he and Jude watched the two bal maidens approaching the holed stone in the moonlight. 'At best, we'll scare them half to death. At worst, they'll go screaming rape—'

'Nobody asked you to come,' Jude snapped. 'If you've no stomach for the game, I daresay I can manage the two on 'em—'

'You'll manage neither,' Ben snarled back. 'Do you understand what I'm saying—?'

'When I want a nurse-maid, I'll ask for one,' Jude retorted. 'And keep your trap shut, or the wenches will hear you before they begin their ritual.'

Ben heard him snigger, and wished himself a thousand miles from here. This whole night was a farce, and he still didn't know what he intended doing with it.

—

'It must be near to midnight, Morwen,' Celia stuttered.

'We must wait for the church chimes. The charm won't work unless we follow Zillah's instructions exactly,' Morwen said. Her palms were damp, the bottle slippery in her grasp, but her mouth was dry and it was hard to swallow. The potion would be a welcome drink…

'Listen!' Celia exclaimed.

They heard the distant clock chimes, and Morwen took the stopper from the bottle with shaking hands. She drank half the fiery liquid, then Celia did the same. Morwen's head spun, but whether from fear or excitement she wasn't sure.

'Begin circling,' she said. She thought she spoke quickly, but the words seemed to emerge with ponderous slowness. Her lips and tongue felt thickened, and not part of her.

They began circling and counting, moving on leaden feet, yet at the same time feeling peculiarly light. Morwen felt as though she skimmed the earth without feeling it beneath her. She felt disorientated from her body. She was ice and fire, drawn to the Larnie Stone like a moth to a flame, and through the hole the distant sea danced like a mirage.

If the charm failed, they would weep or laugh… if it succeeded, the thought burned in Morwen's mind that it was Ben Killigrew's face she wanted to see. Ben Killigrew, and no one else for her destiny…

'We're nearly there, Morwen,' Celia mumbled as they counted on. 'I wager it won't be our John that you see—'

Morwen felt her heartbeats quicken as the sky seemed to press down on her. The moon was huge and full, directly overhead, benign and friendly. At the rate her head spun, she doubted she would see anything by the time the twelve circles were done!

They didn't see the two shadows move towards the stone as they finished counting. Celia saw a face first, her scream loud enough to waken the dead. The face was whitened by moonlight, grinning through the hole at her, and Morwen stumbled against her friend as Celia stopped dead.

'Hold fast, my pretty,' Jude Pascoe's voice chortled at her. Morwen saw Celia pick up her skirts and run hell for leather back the way they had come, with Jude lumbering after her. Then she heard another voice, swivelled round to look straight through the Larnie Stone, and into the eyes of Ben Killigrew.

He came towards her at once, seeing the fright in her face. Her eyes were even larger than he remembered them, and he cursed himself for allowing Jude to talk him into this. He cursed the old woman on the moors, and the two gullible bal maidens for believing her tales. His anger at himself and everyone else made him curt, and he gripped her arms tightly as she swayed against him.

'The girl will be all right, Morwen. Jude's all talk. He'll give her a chase and no more—'

'You guarantee it, do you, Mr Killigrew?' Morwen said shrilly, humiliated at realising they must have somehow known about tonight, or why would they be here instead of in their comfortable beds...?

Ben wasn't at all sure of his words, and his silence made her look sharply into his face. She was suddenly struck dumb, all the anger dying away as her heart beat sickeningly fast. Her thoughts were jumbled like driftwood on a beach. Was he real or a dream? Had old Zillah's potion sent him here to torment her? She felt so strange and weightless, as though she would slide to the ground if his arms didn't hold her. She tingled all over as she felt his heartbeat, so close it seemed to merge with hers. The warmth of his skin seemed to melt with hers, and then she sensed a brief anger in him.

'Was it John Penry you saw through the stone, Morwen? Was it his face you saw first?'

Her face was tipped up to his, the long fall of black hair around her shoulders. Ben caught a handful of it and held it tight, as though to hold her captive. A wild exhilaration filled Morwen's mind. He was jealous. Ben Killigrew was jealous!

All other thoughts vanished. It seemed she could only think one thought at a time right now. Celia and Jude Pascoe... the potion and stone circling... all were diminished compared with the glorious magic of this moment. Ben Killigrew was jealous! She forgot his Miss finelady as the wonder of it possessed Morwen's mind.

'Would you care?' she taunted him. 'Did you think it would be *your* face, Ben Killigrew? Is that what you thought I wanted to see?'

He pulled her to him, furious to be playing this idiotic game. He was not inexperienced, but he was at a loss in handling this delicious young woman with the looks of an innocent and a wanton at the same time, especially since all the differences between them decreed that they should stay worlds apart.

But they were not worlds apart. They were here, beneath a great yellow moon, beside a standing stone with magic powers. A trysting-place... and this was Cornwall, where anything was possible. And ancient ways were stronger than the laws of etiquette at that moment...

He covered her mouth with his, demanding her response as though to impress on her that no other kiss could match it, before or later. Morwen felt her passion soar to meet his, her arms winding around him as though to make him hers, here on the moors beneath the moon and stars, halfway between his world and hers.

Neither knew nor cared how they sank together on to the cool mossy ground, arms still entwined, mouths still clinging, still part of each other. It was a continuation of the strange magic that possessed them both, as though the potion Morwen had taken had flowed into Ben. And the sweet torment that had existed in him since he first steadied her in St Austell town, at last found fulfillment in covering Morwen Tremayne's lovely body with his own.

'God, how I've longed to hold you like this,' he uttered, his voice husky with passion, drugged by his need of her. He felt her warm and yielding beneath him. He caressed the curves of her breasts and felt their quick response to him. He ached to cover each rosebud tip with his mouth, and he moved his hand inside her bodice with gentle exploration. Her heart throbbed beneath his fingers as the milk-white contours were exposed to him, and the longing wouldn't be eased until his mouth moved over each one and he tasted its sweetness.

Morwen's mind could only accept the new and exquisite sensations racing through her, beautiful and erotic and exciting. The sudden coolness of night air on her body, followed by the warmth of Ben's lips on her breasts... it was ice and fire again, a mingling of pleasures too acute to be put into words.

There was only the powerful knowledge sweeping through her, that this was the man she desired, wanted, loved, above all others in the world. There was only the tightening of her throat and the relaxing of her limbs as the sweet lethargy of submission coursed through her veins like warm honey.

'I feel strange, Ben, as though I'm possessed,' Morwen whispered through dry lips. His hand moved softly downwards over her flat belly, to begin a circling, palming movement that made her catch her breath with the sweetest kind of anguish. Only the thin fabric of her dress separated them, and despite its covering, Morwen felt that he must already know every intimate part of her body. She should feel shame, and yet shame was oddly absent.

She was not unaware of a man's body. Two of her brothers were young enough to have been bathed and dressed by her at different stages of their childhood. She knew the way even a small boy could experience those dreams that resulted in the almost magical erection of that small tender finger of manhood... had felt almost humble at this evidence of man's perpetuity, even in a young child...

But there was nothing of the child in Ben Killigrew's hard male need of her, and she was unafraid at knowing it. Ben was the lover she would choose if she had the choice of the whole world, and her every nerve-end was aroused, yearning to possess and be possessed. She felt those marvellous questing fingers inch upwards beneath the hem of her dress, and gloried in the knowledge that it was Ben's hands, caressing her where no other man had ever touched her. It felt so right, so gloriously right, that this night that had begun with old Zillah's potion should end with the finding of her soulmate, and in their belonging.

'I want you so much, Morwen,' Ben said thickly against her flesh. 'I've wanted you from the first moment—'

'And I you,' she murmured into his shoulder, hardly willing to speak or move, just wanting to hold this moment for ever, while she left the realms of girlhood and became a woman... Ben Killigrew's woman...

–

Out of the night came a frenzied scream, and the fragile moment was shattered like splintering glass. The two figures locked in a close embrace on the ground, froze for an instant, then broke apart, two separate entities once more.

'What in God's name was that?' Ben said harshly, wrenched from Morwen so fast that his loins ached appallingly. Before he could think properly, Morwen was leaping to her feet, still swaying from the potion and the near-seduction, but with the flush of passion already vanishing from her face as she staggered back against the granite stone.

'It was Celia!' Her voice was suddenly shrill and accusing. 'She's with that bastard cousin of yours. Is this what you planned – to separate us, and sport with us—?'

He shook her furiously, his tenderness gone. Even in his fury, he knew that where Morwen Tremayne was concerned, his feelings would always go to extremes, fury or passion...

'Don't you know the difference between Jude and me—?'

'I know the difference between love and lust!' Her eyes brimmed with sudden tears, bright and brittle and hurt in the light of the moon. Obviously it wasn't love he felt for Morwen. He saved that for his Miss Finelady from Truro. But she couldn't think of that now. There was time for that pain later. It was Celia who needed her now. She twisted out of his grasp.

'Don't follow me!' she shouted. 'If that lout has hurt Celia, I swear I'll kill you, Ben Killigrew. Don't ever come near me again, you hear?'

She tore past him, the sobs tearing at her throat. She had to hit out at someone, anyone, and she felt so guilty that she had let Celia go off alone, knowing that Jude was after her, while she and Ben... she and Ben... she swallowed the hurting lump in her throat, because if only he had once said he loved her, things would have been different. Even if it had been a lie, she had so ached to hear the words, and she hadn't even realised it until now.

He shouted after her, and she ignored him. She knew these moors better than he did. The mist had lingered, aiding her now in swallowing her up in its gauzy haze. She heard the dull thud of horses hooves, and guessed that Jude would be getting out of here as fast as he could.

And Ben too, Morwen thought bitterly. Killigrew men wouldn't need to run barefoot over the moors the way the bal maidens did...

'Morwen, is it you?' she heard a quavering voice call from a huddle of stones nearby. Morwen moved towards the sound, and dropped down when she saw the crouching figure there. She felt a sawing fear at seeing Celia's bedraggled state, hair awry, tear-stained cheeks, as unkempt as old Zillah herself. Morwen folded her in her arms and held her tight.

'What's happened?' she said huskily. 'Did he hurt you?'

She bit her lips at Celia's wild laugh, cursing herself for the stupid question. Why else would she have screamed so violently in the night?

'Yes, he hurt me, Morwen,' Celia said croakily. 'I thought it was a game at first. He'd been drinking, and he was a tease, and he was fun, and he made me feel wanted. Do 'ee know what I mean?'

Morwen nodded, for didn't she know only too well that soaring of the spirit at feeling so wanted, so needed?

'He was still funning wi' me, Morwen, and there seemed no harm in it, rolling on the ground and kissing and touching – and then he pinned me down and he was as strong as a bull, and he said we must be quick, because he didn't want his poxy cousin appearing on the scene and spoiling things—' her voice was jerky and choked. 'And then he hurt me, Morwen. He near to split me in two, making me bleed, and he didn't care. And if that's what 'tis like to lie with a man, then I'll die before I let it happen again. I'll kill myself first—'

'Celia, stop it!' Morwen snapped, as her friend's voice rose fearfully. She held Celia's hands, and wished it was

Jude Pascoe's throat she squeezed so hard. 'You know damn well it can't always be like that. There wouldn't be any babies born in the world if it was always so hateful—'

Celia jerked away from her, eyes huge and black in the pallor of her face, her lips bloodless.

'God help me, Morwen, if Jude Pascoe has put a babby in me, what will I do? My father will turn me out, and I'll be disgraced—' She finished with a small scream as Morwen slapped her face to stop the torrent of words.

'Don't even think of it, ninny! It doesn't always happen, and you were so unwilling, it's hardly likely, is it?'

She wasn't certain at all, and the horror of it was in Morwen's mind too. The potion's power was at last leaving her, and she was seeing a lot of things more clearly now. And what she saw was that somehow Ben and Jude had learned of this night, and both had had the same intent. She felt betrayed and bitter, knowing how she had so nearly succumbed to his seduction. The pain of it washed over her in waves of sheer misery.

With a great effort, Morwen pushed down the feeling. Celia was the most important one now. But for fate, it might have been her who was lying here instead of poor silly Celia, who couldn't tell a rogue from a gentleman. She hated herself for ever having felt superior to Celia, she with her pit captain father and her seamstress mother, because she hadn't been able to tell the difference either.

They held each other for a long time, until Celia's shaking subsided, and she felt able to walk home.

'Morwen,' she said huskily. 'If I'm not at the pit tomorrow, tell them I was feeling unwell today. I can pretend as much to our John and Daddy, but I may not feel able to face people—'

'Of course I'll tell them, but no one will know! It's not written on your face, Celia, and I daresay Jude Pascoe was too drunk to remember too much of what happened. By tomorrow you'll be wondering if it ever happened. Anyway,' she tried to tease her, 'you always said you'd be the first to be broken. You always had to be first in everything, didn't you?'

They made their painful way home across the moors, each knowing it would be a long while before either would forget this night. And one of them, at least, hoping desperately that it wouldn't show, on her face or anywhere else.

–

In untying his horse, Jude's fumbling fingers had loosened Ben's. The animal had wandered off, and it had taken Ben a while to find him. By the time he reached home that night, he was in a towering rage. He'd galloped back to Killigrew House in a fury, then having to give the nag a quick rub-down where it was lathering so much. Finally he stalked upstairs to find his cousin, barging into his room without knocking.

Jude was spread across his bed, still fully dressed, a lazy smile on his face. Ben strode towards him, jerking him into a half-sitting position by hooking his fingers in his collar. Jude gurgled, his face reddening as he glared at his visitor.

'What's to do?' he snarled, his eyes pig-small in the half-light. 'Finished sporting, have you?'

'I'll finish you, you little turd, if you've ruined that girl!' Ben ground out the words, surprised at his own anger. She was nothing to him, but she was Morwen's friend, and that made her important. If Morwen despised him, then he would sort that out later. For now, it was this little runt he had to deal with.

'What girl? The one wi' the knowing eyes? She was ripe for it, cuz, just like t'other one! Don't tell me you had no luck. I know a lusty look when I see it, and you've been lusting after Morwen Tremayne all right. I wonder what your pretty Jane would say to it?' he crowed, dodging sideways as Ben lunged at him.

The blow missed Jude's body, and Ben's fist sank into the bed-covers, pulling him off balance. He ended in an undignified sprawl across Jude's bed, and moved away in disgust at the reek of drink and body sweat from his cousin. Jude's guttural laugh ended in a great yawn.

'I won't be the one to tell her, Ben. I got more interesting things to do than worry about Jane Carrick's breaking heart. That's summat you and she can sort out for yourselves.'

Ben's fury mounted again, but he saw he was wasting his time. Jude was already asleep, inert across his bed, a vigorous rhythmic snoring coming from his slackly open mouth.

Ben turned abruptly and left him. And only when he reached his own room did his tight-stretched nerves begin to relax, though he couldn't forget the memory of that girl's dreadful scream, magnified by the silence of the night. If Jude had damaged her... his brain had felt like scrambled yarn ever since that moment, when he had been torn so cruelly away from Morwen by Celia's scream, but it was unravelling at last.

Now, lying between the cool sheets, with only the night sounds of the house and gardens, and the distant first-light cry of the sea-birds, his thoughts returned to Morwen, whom he had so nearly made his own that night.

He had known instinctively that it would have been the first time she had lain with a man. He had intended making it so perfect, so beautiful. Ben had lain with many others before her, and was amazed at the feelings her nearness had awoken in him. He'd wanted to love and cherish her, and he wanted to tell her so. He had wanted to show her the way to the stars. There was a life-force in him that needed her as he had needed no other in his life before.

Two people, one love. Out there, on the moonlit moors, he could have found the words, and fulfillment would have been theirs. Instead of which, Ben was frustrated and alone, and for all the advantages that his father's money could buy, he had never felt so lonely in the whole of his life.

Chapter Eight

Hal delighted in finding Bess at the cottage each day when he returned from his shift, the sewing spread around her, the clean smells of cloth and chalk about the place. He liked the change in her, away from the clay. He didn't like the change he saw in his son, Matt.

'Where do you get to these nights, our Matt?' he asked finally, when he decided the boy had had every chance to confide in his folks, the way he used to. 'John Penry was saying he'd seen nothing of 'ee lately, away from the pit, not even in the local kiddleywink.'

Hal didn't miss the colour in Matt's face at the words, nor the way he avoided his father's eyes. It was a few months since Hal had become Killigrew's Number One captain, and over a month since the march to the St Austell office. In that time, he and Matthew seemed out of step with one another.

His daughter, too, seemed taken up with secrets, Hal thought. He knew that women had thoughts of their own that a man could never understand, so he could disregard Morwen's closed-in looks a little. But if Matt had something troubling him, then the sooner it was out in the open, the better.

'Can't a body make new friends wi' out it seeming odd?' Matt countered his father's question. 'There's no rule that says clayworkers have to stick together after their shift, is there?'

'There's not,' Hal agreed keenly. 'There's no ruling that says a boy has to be civil to his father when he shows an interest in his son's doings either, but I'd prefer it in this house.'

He was aware of a sudden tension between the two of them, and then Matt rushed out with the words he'd obviously been boiling up in his mind.

'Is there any rule that says a son has to follow in his father's footsteps, Daddy? Or would a fair-minded father object to a son working at the harbour? He'd still be involved wi' the clay, and wi' other goods besides. What would be your thoughts on that?' He stopped, clearly expecting opposition.

Hal spoke evenly. 'If 'tis what you want, Matt, I'd say good luck to you, though you might make Charles Killi-grew a mite sad to think another Tremayne is deserting the clay works. But mebbe 'tis not such a bad thing. Having all your eggs in one basket is not always the best move—'

'Then I have your blessing?' Matt said at once, and Hal guessed that this was no idle query, but had been thought out already. It could be that Matt's visits to the town were no more than a wish to be near the sea that he loved, and not the suspected nightly drinking with disreputable ragtags.

'Yes, you have it,' Hal said. There was nothing more soul-destroying than for a man to be tied to a job he hated. He'd never thought Matt actually hated the clay, but he'd always known he didn't love it either. Not the way Hal did, with a fierce pride in gouging the thick wet substance from the earth and seeing it go through all its processes until it was finally loaded onto the waggons for the docks.

Hal always felt a sense of achievement in seeing the loaded waggons careering away from the works, and never mind what happened to it after that. He cared nothing for the fine tableware his family would never possess, nor the excited talk of medical products and far-reaching refinements of newsprint. His were the hands that claimed the clay from the earth, and in that Hal had his pride. If Matt couldn't feel that way, then he was best out of it.

–

Charles Killigrew made irregular visits to all his pits, especially in summer months, when the air seemed to crackle with life, with the dry scent of clay dust mingling with the wild flowers and the drone of bees. His workers were like busy swarms of bees, all touching their forelocks to him when he appeared, and Charles liked that too.

He was especially pleased with Hal Tremayne. Hal was a leader, but he still had the common touch with the rest of the clayworkers. Charles congratulated himself on his choice of Number One captain. But for the circumstances of birth, Hal would have made a good boss. Probably better than himself, Charles thought in a rare moment. Hal's temper was more even than his own…

'What ails that girl of yours, Hal?' Charles asked now. He'd been watching Morwen and her friend for some minutes, and all the sparkle seemed to have gone out of the girl for whom he had an odd fondness. 'She's not wanting to join the rest of your brood in making the break from Killigrew Clay, is she?'

He spoke jovially, but he noted the strain on Morwen's pretty face. She was only one of his workers, and they were all his minions. But she touched a spark in Charles, and it was irksome to him to see her look so troubled. Hal mistook his meaning, and began gabbing about his son Matt's reasons for leaving the clay works, until Charles brushed aside his explanations.

'Good God, man, d'you think I'd censure you for your son's ambitions? If he's unhappy working in the clay, then he should get out, and you and I both know it. It's Morwen I'm curious about. It's not like her to be so quiet!'

'That 'tis not, sir, but 'tis only girls' talk, I'm sure,' Hal smiled, though he had noticed Morwen and Celia in deep conversation many times lately, and wondered about their unusually downcast looks. He hid his concern from Charles Killigrew though. A boss wouldn't want to be bothered with a bal maiden's small discontents.

It was an understatement, for the corner where the two girls sat was more tension-filled than a stew-pot about to burst its lid. He changed the train of Charles Killigrew's thoughts by mentioning how well Bess liked her new role as seamstress.

'I'm glad,' Charles said easily. 'Though you must all be cramped to death in that small cottage of yours. When a bigger house comes vacant on the estate, I'll remember your family, Hal. A good worker deserves recognition.'

Hal was startled. Charles had never mentioned such a thing before, and to Hal it was as likely as a pig flying to the moon, but he touched his hard hat in acknowledgement and muttered his thanks. Killigrew nodded, striding off to his horse and trap.

Charles was asking himself why he had made the obscure offer. Not especially for Bess Tremayne's eyesight! Not even because he liked Hal Tremayne better than any pit captain before. He felt a fondness for the whole family, dammit, and especially he hated to see Morwen so dejected. Almost as dejected as that friend who worked alongside her. He began to feel irritable at his own feeling of responsibility towards the Tremayne family.

He'd made no demur when Matthew Tremayne had requested to leave his employ. Nor shown surprise when it was clear the boy had already made his future plans to work at Charlestown port. Charles had seen in Matt's blue eyes the longing to be free of family ties and to stand on his own feet, and he respected that. He knew the feeling. He saw it in his own son, even though Ben didn't seem too sure where he was going at the moment. But Ben was a man now, and Charles was only just realising it. So was his nephew, Jude Pascoe. The thought changed the smile on Charles's face to a scowl, and he urged his horse on over the sun-kissed moors and down the steep slopes towards St Austell.

—

The two bal maidens sitting tensely together in a corner of the linhay tried desperately to jolt each other out of the black mood they shared. Morwen spoke harshly, fear sharpening her voice.

'I've heard tell it can't happen first time, Celia. You must have counted wrongly—'

'I've not miscounted!' Celia was equally harsh. ''Tis too important to make such mistakes. Twice the flow's not come, and I know it won't come. And since I'm not in my middle-life, nor dying of the blood sickness, there's only one reason for the flow not arriving every month. You know it as well as me, Morwen.'

'I'm trying to calm you, that's all,' Morwen said, as the other girl's voice rose. 'Do you want everyone to hear about your trouble?'

She bit her lip. The trouble... that was the phrase whispered behind cupped hands when a girl got herself pregnant without a wedding-band on her finger. Morwen felt cold, knowing that Celia's trouble could only have come from one night when the moon shone full, and they had gone so recklessly to the Larnie Stone. A night filled with sweet enchantment for Morwen, until that horrendous scream that had wrenched herself and Ben Killigrew apart cleaner than a surgeon's knife.

The images of herself and Ben were out of place now. They were precious and private, but they were bitter too. She had hardly seen Ben since that night. For him, the incident was probably no more than a small diversion. The kind the rich folks had when they went slumming for a moment's excitement...

'What does it matter, when they'll all know it soon enough?' Celia lashed out. 'We both know what's wrong wi' me, Morwen, so stop pretending!'

They looked dumbly at each other, and then Celia seemed to crumple as she clutched at Morwen's arms.

'What shall I do, Morwen?' Her voice was cracked with fear. ''Twill kill my Daddy to know the shame of it!' Morwen knew that it would. Other girls had held their heads high in defiance of the shame, but a small closed community never forgot. And for all Celia's hot-eyed glances at the boys, her nerve would fail her when the shame became obvious.

'We must see Zillah,' Morwen said huskily. 'She gave us one potion, and she must give us another to put things right—'

Celia's face paled even more. 'I can't do it, Morwen. 'Tis an evil thing to take a life, however unwanted—'

'What of the brute who put the life there against your will?' Morwen said, vibrant with anger. 'Did you ask for this new life inside you? If it had been started in love, 'twould be different, but this one – if it *is* one – was begun in hate. You can't deny that, can you?'

Celia shook her head violently. Hate was all she felt whenever she thought of Jude Pascoe. She tried never to think of him at all, and that made the trouble she bore seem like a cancerous growth she had spawned by herself. It was blasphemous to think so. It was likening herself to the blessed virgin, and nothing could be more shameful when the thing that she carried came from the seed of that devil Jude.

Sometimes she felt that her head would burst with the hate she felt for him. How could she ever have fancied him, or felt excitement surge through her at his touch? The thought of that was as blasphemous to Celia as wanting to lie with a beast in a field. She shuddered, forcing herself to listen to Morwen's words.

'We have to go back to work, Celia, but think about it, please. We must see Zillah. We have no other choice. Think of it as ridding yourself of a troublesome visitor. 'Twill be little more than a speck of dust in your belly yet, hardly flesh and blood at all!'

Celia moved away from her as though in a dream. Hardly flesh and blood... but it *was* flesh and blood – hers and Jude Pascoe's. The thought of it festered and anguished in her mind like a recurring sore that would never heal. It was a mingling of his seed with hers, the crowning obscenity from a night of pain and violation, and if a living child emerged from her body it must surely be decked with horns and a cloven foot... the horror of it was a continuing nightmare...

'Celia, you ninny, look what you're about!' another bal maiden shouted angrily at her, cursing at her carelessness in the linhay as she dropped a tool on the woman's toe. 'You young wenches have your heads filled with boys and gigglings when you should be working—'

Celia bent her head to hide the stinging tears. Morwen was right. She must see Zillah. But she would wait one more day... one more week... just in case the flow would come naturally, and she didn't have to live with the fact that she would be taking a life...

If her brother John hadn't slipped and broken his leg, she would have gone to see Zillah sooner. As it happened, she was needed at home for nursing, and it assumed so much importance in her mind that even her father was surprised at this sisterly concern. Her nerves were as ragged wool, and Thomas Penry finally decided to ask his sister Ruth to take over the household duties to give his daughter a break.

'Your Aunt Ruth's been wanting to take care of us since your Ma passed on, girl,' Thomas said with rough kindness to her. ''Tis time you looked to yourself and had some funning wi' that pretty friend of yourn.'

'Is that what you want, Daddy?' Celia said huskily. She'd hardly realised the strain of these last weeks. The summer was hot, the sky a cloudless blue, and she had enjoyed none of it, because of her trouble, and her self-imposed dedication to her brother's needs.

And it had done no good, she thought bitterly. God hadn't sent down a miracle and rid her of the cancer in her womb, so she may as well do as Morwen suggested and see old Zillah before it was too late. By now, she had convinced herself that the thing inside her was a hideous growth that must be removed before it destroyed her. It was the only way she could accept the fact that she felt nauseous each morning, that her breasts were swollen and tender so that even the fabric of her dress against them felt rough and sore. She was ill. The growth would control her entire body if she didn't get rid of it. It dictated what food she ate, and how fast she could move each morning. It grew insidiously, like a vine that would ultimately strangle her unless she killed it first...

–

Morwen opened the cottage door to her friend, shocked to see the burning light in her eyes, and the fire in her cheeks.

'Will you come wi' me, Morwen?' Celia asked, her voice shaking. 'It will have to be now, while my Daddy's away fetching my aunt to look after us all—'

She didn't need to say any more. Morwen told her to stay there, not wanting her mother to see the state Celia was in, and told her parents she was off for a walk with her friend. Morwen was afraid for Celia, with that feverish look about her. She had been so reluctant to set foot in

Zillah's cottage again, yet now she seemed fanatical to get there as fast as she could. Morwen could hardly keep up with her as she sped across the moors. Only when they neared the cottage did Celia clutch Morwen's arm.

'You'll not leave me, whatever happens, will you?'

'Of course not,' Morwen said roughly. Right or wrong didn't come into it, though in past weeks, Morwen had begun to think uneasily about tampering with nature. Women had been driven mad from losing a child natu-rally. They had bled to death... she musn't let herself think of it! She must think positively, for Celia's sake. She must have the strength for both of them...

They knocked at Zillah's door, and when it opened, the remembered smells met their nostrils, pungent, aromatic, thickly nauseating. The old woman's bead-like eyes went from one white face to the other. Her gash-like mouth tightened still more.

'So one of 'ee needs more help. Which one requires the needle to pay for your funning, my pretties?'

They gasped, and Celia babbled, almost incoherently.

'Don't you have another potion, Zillah? One that will send the – the trouble away? I'll not try any other way – I'll die first – I'll not have red-hot needles thrust in me—'

'Who's told 'ee about red-hot needles?' Zillah spoke with fearsome indignation. ''Twould be done tidily without fuss, but I can see that 'ee wouldn't lie still long enough. Where's the brave maid tonight then? There was one red-hot tip that didn't frighten 'ee, that got 'ee in this state—' she cackled.

Celia was suddenly screaming. 'Will you help me or won't you? I've no one else to turn to, you old hag—'

Morwen grasped her hands and held them tight, feeling them tremble. Zillah glowered at them both, her various cats winding themselves around her legs and growling at the intruders.

'Help her, Zillah! She doesn't know what she's saying! Please mix her a potion, for God's sake. I'm afraid for her!'

Zillah studied Morwen thoughtfully, and addressed her words directly to her, as if Celia wasn't there.

'How far gone is she?' Her practised eyes swept over the shivering girl, the belly hardly rounded, but the breasts were full and heavy and would give her away to anyone who wondered…

'It was the night we went to the Larnie Stone,' Morwen couldn't stop the bitterness in her voice. Jude's treachery seemed no less than Ben's to her now. She blamed them both. Neither could she have gone to Ben for help, and Celia would as soon ask a toad for help as go to Jude Pascoe.

'Near to three months?' Zillah exclaimed. ''Tis too long to expect the potion to work well. The needle would be sharp and quick and less painful—'

'No!' Celia screamed again. 'I want the pain. I need the pain to scour myself of the guilt—'

'You need a good dose of common-sense,' Zillah said sourly. 'The deed's been done, and you're wanting rid of it. Either stop your screeching, or get away from here. I'll give 'ee a potion, but don't tell me tales of wanting pain, miss! When it begins, you'll wish you'd never spoken so rashly. Wait while I prepare it, and take half of it one hour before the rest, or you'll remember the severity of the pain all your days.'

They sat on the edge of Zillah's settle while she worked, feeling trapped like flies in a honeypot by their own actions. At last, Zillah handed Celia a small dark bottle. The girls knew this potion had lethal qualities. It could kill.

''Twill work soon after the second dose,' Zillah said crisply. 'Stuff a towel in your mouth to stop you crying out, and have another ready to catch the waste.'

Morwen felt faint for a moment, not daring to look at Celia. The waste. She wouldn't think too deeply about what they were doing, but the waste of which Zillah spoke so cruelly was a living child, however unwanted, and the thought of destroying it suddenly seemed terrible. But she knew Celia wouldn't back out now. It had been her decision in the end.

They couldn't wait to get out of the cottage, and make their plans. Each would tell her family she was staying the night with the other. They had done so often enough in the past, and no one would question it. There was a tumbledown cottage on the moors, isolated and nearly overgrown by grasses and gorse. They had to go home first and behave normally, and then make their way back to the derelict cottage. They couldn't think farther ahead than that.

By the time they were installed there, it was growing dark. Each had brought a towel as Zillah had instructed, each avoiding mention of it.

'You'd best take part of the potion—' Morwen began.

Celia held out the empty bottle.

'I couldn't wait. I've already taken it all,' she said jerkily.

'God, Celia, you know what Zillah said! The pain—'

'I don't care! I thought you'd understand—' She was stopped in mid-sentence by a searing, knife-like pain that seemed to tear her apart. She doubled up, retching and choking, and clutching at Morwen for support.

'Christ Jesus, help me!' Celia croaked, as powerful waves of pain ripped into her, intensified by the wrongly taken potion. 'Morwen, I'm so frightened. Devils are raking my body—'

She clung to Morwen, bathed in sweat, and shivering violently. Morwen's nerves felt battered to a pulp at seeing her in such agony.

'We'll have to trust Zillah, Celia, and pray that the potion won't harm you,' she said harshly. 'But you may as well have had the needle, sharp and quick, as take the stuff all at once—'

'For Christ's sake, don't lecture me now!' Celia screamed. 'Lecture the bastard who did this to me! I swear I'll never let another man touch me, Morwen.'

She threshed about, hitting her head on a stone until it bled and not noticing. The pain enveloped her, more savagely than any induced abortion, because of the double dose of the potion. When she vomited it was black and stinking, and Morwen was terrified she was going to die.

How long it lasted, neither could have said. It seemed to go on for ever, until at last Celia gave a great gasping, her teeth clenched over the towel, and there was a sudden expulsion from her body. Celia's eyes rolled, and Morwen had no choice but to put the second towel between Celia's legs to trap the bloody mess that seemed to be the stuff of which nightmares were made. Celia slumped back on the ground, breathing shallowly, and it was Morwen who had to bundle the waste inside the towel, tears burning her eyes at knowing what she did. A child, who hadn't had the chance to live…

'Is it over?' Celia's thready voice said. 'Am I rid of the trouble, Morwen?'

'Well rid, love,' Morwen said huskily. 'Lie still a while. We've plenty of time before we go home. We can take an hour or two until you get your strength back.'

They clung together for a few moments.

'We must bury it, Morwen,' she muttered. Tears were suddenly pouring down her face. 'I can't look at it, but it must be buried. We can't just leave it here, all alone—'

'All right,' Morwen said quickly, hearing the hysterical note come into Celia's voice. 'I'll dig the earth with a stone and make a mound, and say a prayer over it like any preacher would. God will take care of it, Celia.'

Celia nodded, and Morwen carried out the task, her heart beating sickly, the enormity of what she did threatening to overcome her. It was wrong, blasphemous, and she wondered if she would be damned because of it… but it was preferable to seeing Celia's brain turn at leaving this night unfinished.

At last they left the place, and made their slow, painful way home, pausing many times for Celia to catch her breath. They had to pass through Killigrew Clay Number One works, and Celia scooped up some of the pale green clay water and dribbled it into her mouth to assuage the dragging pains in her body.

'The men say it helps,' she grimaced. 'Though what ails me is a far worse pain than mere stomach gripes. Mebbe I should immerse myself in the pool, Morwen. Would it rid me of the memories as well as the pain?'

'Don't talk so wildly, Celia,' Morwen said roughly.

'This time tomorrow, you'll feel better. You're young and strong—'

'I feel like a murderer,' she muttered. 'Can't you see that, Morwen? You're meant to be so clever!'

They moved away from the clay pit, and Celia's feet dragged as though she were an old woman. Morwen was afraid for her, and prayed that tomorrow would restore Celia's usual optimism. She hated Jude Pascoe with a fierce hatred for what he had done to Celia, forcing her into tonight's actions. She hated every bastard male in the entire world at that moment, for the way they used women to gratify themselves.

By the time she had helped Celia crawl silently into her own bed, and crept away into the night and her own private corner of the Tremayne cottage, Morwen was near to weeping with fatigue and brittle nerves. She felt as old as the hills, yet no wiser than a new-born babe. And she could have wished for a less emotional simile to be churning around in her brain as she curled up beneath the cold bedcovers.

Chapter Nine

Soft warm rain fell gently over moors and towns and hamlets, a reminder that the long hot summer couldn't last for ever. Bess Tremayne glanced inside her daughter's snug bed corner, and decided to leave her curled up there a while longer. It was Sunday, and Morwen didn't often lie abed like this. For once it would do no harm, while the rest of them went to church over at Penwithick. A spot of rain never hurt anyone, and God wouldn't object to a steaming congregation any more than the preacher did.

Bess roused the rest of her family, noting that Matt was missing again, and hoping Hal wouldn't make too much of it. Matt was moving away from the family. It saddened Bess, even though she knew it was only right and proper for a boy to grow into a man and stand on his own feet.

A family should be like a tree, the roots strong but spreading outwards. Matt was hinting that he'd like to lodge in the town, to be nearer to his work at the port. It made sense, and it would give them more room at the cottage, however much Hal may oppose the idea.

When the rest of them left for church, Morwen still hadn't stirred. By then the rain had stopped, and the morning was beautiful, spangly with dew, the mist dispersing in the first pale rays of sunlight. Bess walked beside her man, her two older sons behind, the younger ones in front, slicked and polished for the day, and was well content.

In another church in St Austell, the Killigrew family gathered, making their regular appearance, though one of them fidgeted, and wished he were elsewhere on this Sunday morning.

Jude Pascoe had arranged to meet Matt Tremayne later that day. The Tremayne boy was less prissy than the rest of his family, Jude thought. Together they might be able to set up a nice little connection in contraband goods to supply to the kiddleywinks, if Matt was as agreeable to adding a bit of spice to his life, as Jude suspected.

He caught his mother's frowning glance and bellowed out the words of the hymn with the rest of them. But he wished to God he was with Matt right now, and meeting up with the old sea-salts who were far more entertaining than these religious old farts.

–

Charles's mind wasn't on the sermon that day. He was irritated at his son Ben's casual attitude towards Jane Carrick. Charles was anxious for his grandchildren to carry on the Killigrew name. It suddenly seemed more urgent since the goddamned doctor had alarmed him a few days ago, telling him his heart wasn't what it used to be, and ordering him not to rant and rage so much. What did goddamned doctors know of the clay owner's lot?

He hadn't told Ben of the doctor's warning. Ben would only fuss, and Charles wanted to give him free rein a while longer. All the same, even a little peccadillo might be something to brighten the days, if Ben couldn't manage it legally. He wasn't as short-sighted as Jane's fond Mama seemed to be where their relationship was concerned...

–

'You haven't seen Ben lately, have you, Jane?' her mother asked her that same Sunday. She found it hard to disguise her impatience. Didn't Jane see how eligible the Killigrew boy was? He was strong and handsome and rich... what more could any girl ask?

'Ben and I aren't in love with each other, Mama,' Jane said flatly, deciding the time had come to be as truthful as she dared about where her affections lay.

'Love will come, dear,' Mary Carrick said blithely, echoing Charles Killigrew's own thoughts. 'You're fond of each other, aren't you? I'm sure he thinks of no one else!'

Jane hid a smile, uncaring whether Ben thought of another girl or not. She only cared about Tom Askhew. His brashness excited her, his occasional coarseness more stimulating than she had imagined. She loved him to the exclusion of all others. And Ben – dear Ben – would understand that she couldn't marry for less than love. She turned to her mother with a winning look.

'Ask Ben to tea any time you wish, Mama! I've no objections!'

'Then so I will! What a tease you are, Jane, to make me think you don't care for one another!' Mary said fondly.

And what a fool you are, Mother dear, Jane thought gently, to listen and not to hear. She cared for Ben Killigrew, but not in the way Mary imagined. She cared for him more just lately, for helping her in seeing Tom whenever he could. She liked Ben enormously, the way she would a brother.

Ben was willing to help, but he didn't really care for deceit. It surprised him that Jane could so readily agree to it, although he saw that Tom Askhew was hardly the husband the Carricks would have chosen for their daughter.

As he listened to the interminable sermon in church that Sunday morning, his thoughts drifted towards Morwen Tremayne, as they often did nowadays. He still felt furious at the happenings of that night he'd gone with Jude to the Larnie Stone. He knew he should have gone to see Morwen again to find out if everything was well with her and her friend. He despised himself, knowing he was afraid of a rebuff – Ben Killigrew, who was never afraid of anything... and knowing the reason made him all the angrier at himself.

He had cursed himself a thousand times for accompanying Jude that night, and for not stopping the whole jaunt happening. He hated himself for witnessing the pagan ritual, and he still couldn't decide just what he felt for Morwen Tremayne. His feelings for her were more powerful than any he'd felt for a girl before...

He caught Jude's eye, and scowled at him. Each time he met his cousin's leering look, he remembered the awful screams of the Penry girl that night on the moors. He hoped to God her screams had frightened Jude off before anything had happened... no matter how he'd tried, he couldn't get anything out of his cousin, other than that the girl had been willing.

Ben knew he shouldn't leave it there, but even he never guessed at the far-reaching consequences of his cousin's gaming. He scowled at his hymn-book again, aware that he wasn't giving of his best in church that day. He wondered briefly if he should warn the dreamy-eyed Matthew Tremayne to keep away from his cousin... and then thought fervently that the whole damn Tremayne family could sort out their own problems.

–

Matt had finally made up his mind to move out of the cottage. He'd spent the night drinking and jawing with the old sea-salts who coloured his nights, and had decided he would lodge with the shipworkers and fishermen in the harbour lodging house, and he'd simply move out, leaving a note to avoid arguments.

He felt a wild freedom inside as he tramped towards home that morning. The countryside looked freshly laundered after the early rain, and he felt good to be alive. He felt a renewed urge to break away from home, and he strode jauntily in his long leather boots, as useful in his new occupation at the docks as they ever were at the clay works. He took the short cut through the pit, wanting to get everything cleared up and be away before his folks got home from church.

Suddenly he stopped dead, his heart nearly leaping clear out of his chest. He had skirted the pit, the milky green pool below him. Sunlight danced off its surface in opaque jewelled globules, and outlined the shape of something – someone – lying face down in the milky water. He could see the once-bright long dark hair, lying in dull rats' tails over the inert body...

Matt scrambled down the sloping gravel of the pit, his heart thundering in his chest. He could only think of Morwen, his sister Morwen, and he heard the blood screaming in his ears as he waded into the shallower rim of the pool. The water quickly went over the top of his boots and chilled him through, but he heeded none of it as he reached for the cold limp arm of the girl, twisting her around until he could see her face.

'Christ Almighty. Celia!' He croaked out her name, almost puking with shock and guilty relief that it wasn't Morwen after all. He stared in disbelief, remembering Celia pert and pretty and rounded enough for a man to warm towards her...

Nobody would warm to her now, Matt thought with a shudder. Her face was white-slimed from the clay slurry, her lips distorted as though with some private agony. Her eyes were wide open as though she'd walked into the clay pool deliberately, keeping her senses intact until she drowned.

Matt hauled her out of the pool. His thoughts raced jerkily. He'd have to get her away from here, before the early shift workers arrived on Monday morning. He couldn't take her home like this. It would kill her father to see his pretty Celia covered in such muck. The Tremayne cottage was nearer. He'd have to clean her up before he told Thomas Penry to come and fetch his daughter home...

Matt tried not to notice he carried a dead body in his arms. He wished he'd closed her eyes, so he wouldn't have the terrifying sensation that at any moment Celia would turn to look up at him with those staring dead eyes...

He finally stumbled through his own cottage door, kicking the door shut behind him, and thanking God that all God-fearing clayworkers were away at church.

Morwen's curtain still hung across her sleeping corner. He would lay Celia there for now. He pulled the curtain back, and the next minute he thought he was being accosted by demons.

Morwen leapt up in bed, her nerves still jangling from last night's ordeal. In an instant she took in the sight in front of her. Matthew held something in his arms. Something that dripped clay water and stank of it. Something cold and dead that was her friend Celia…

'No! Oh, God, no!' Morwen screamed, scrabbling back against the wall as though afraid to let Matt near her. 'What have you done? Matt, what have you done?'

Her screaming didn't stop, and a new shock rippled through Matt. He dumped Celia on the bed and struck Morwen hard. He'd never struck her before, and his fingermarks showed on her face in angry red weals.

'Christ, what d'you think I've done?' he shouted. 'I've just dragged the maid from the clay pool where she'd drowned, and I've brought her here for cleaning before her father sees her like this. What else d'you think I've done?'

Morwen's harsh sobbing quietened him. Of course she didn't think he'd murdered Celia. It was merely the first thing that came into her head. She knew why Celia had drowned. She should have seen the possibility last night. She shook violently.

'We must tell Thomas Penry,' she whispered through chattering teeth. 'You tell him, Matt. I'll wash Celia's face. You tell un to come and get his daughter.'

He looked at her uneasily. 'Will you be all right alone with her?'

Morwen glared at him. She needed to be alone with Celia. She needed to do some kind of penance... but she couldn't expect Matt to know or understand that!

'I'll be all right as long as I keep busy,' she stuttered. 'Just fetch her father, Matt. He has a right to be told what's happened. He'll be at the church—'

Matt turned and left her. Morwen made Celia more comfortable on the bed, resisting the appalling urge to ask her how she felt. She fetched a wash-cloth and wiped away the slime from Celia's soft mouth and pearly cheeks.

'Forgive me, Celia,' she whispered to her friend. 'I shouldn't have left you alone last night. You should have stayed here wi' me. We'd have shared the memories, Celia—'

Now Morwen had to bear them alone. She squared her shoulders as she finished her task. They had told lies, and now she would have to tell more lies. She must, to keep Celia's secret...

She flinched as a hand touched her shoulder. She turned to see her mother standing there, sadness clouding her blue eyes.

'We met our Matt, Morwen, and he told us,' Bess said quietly. 'Her Daddy will come for her soon.'

Morwen's whole body was suddenly convulsed with weeping as she threw herself into her mother's arms.

'Oh, Mammie, I should have seen this coming. She's not been herself for weeks now—'

'Hush, my lamb. How could you have known what Celia meant to do?'

Morwen swallowed, knowing she must continue to keep the secret, however tempted she was to blurt it all out at this moment. She didn't know how Celia had found the courage to die alone and in the dark, the thing she most dreaded. If Celia had that much courage, then Morwen must find her own.

Thomas Penry arrived and gathered up his daughter without saying a word. His fortitude made it all the more terrible somehow. Hal came home and spoke softly to Morwen.

'Our Matt's gone for the doctor and the constable, Morwen. They'll want to talk to you, to see if you can throw any light on why Celia should have been in the clay pool.'

For the first time, Morwen felt caution sweep over her. She took a deep breath, saying she didn't know what anyone could tell them. Celia was dead…

'Will you go to her cottage to speak with the doctor, Morwen?' Hal insisted gently. 'You saw her last, my love, and it could be important.'

Morwen's quick wits knew the importance of it more than Hal did. She nodded, and quickly made her way to the Penry cottage, suddenly nervous as she saw the doctor's cart outside. If she lied now, God must surely forgive her the wickedness of it to give Celia this last bit of dignity…

Inside the cottage, John Penry still reclined, his broken leg plastered and awkward, his frustration at such a time obvious to all. His Aunt Ruth was red eyed, but in command of the household now. The doctor was upstairs with Thomas and presumably Celia, and she could hear the low rumble of their voices. The constable asked Morwen a few keen questions, and seemed satisfied with her answers. She was then told to go upstairs to where Celia lay beneath a sheet, and Morwen had the wild urge to wrench it away from her face, because it would stifle her… she forced down the nausea the feeling induced.

The doctor asked more probing questions than the constable, but Morwen was ready for them, her mind having worked like lightning on the walk to the cottage. She was able to tell him why Celia's mind was so tormented…

'She thought she had a growth in her stomach, Doctor. She was very afraid, and wouldn't tell anyone but me. She was ashamed, as though she could be held responsible for it. She couldn't be, could she, Doctor?'

Morwen held her breath. He must have examined Celia. Did he know the truth? Could he have guessed, even before he looked at her? The thought of the cancerous growth had been an inspiration to Morwen. Celia had spoken of the pregnancy in those terms so bitterly.

'Of course not,' the doctor said at last. 'It might explain her state of mind, which can play strange tricks when it gets a fixation. If the poor girl was convinced she had a growth, then she should have come to me. Since she didn't—' He gave a small shrug, and then gave an imperceptible nod, as though satisfied that everything was in order here. Or else he had no wish to investigate further…

'I think you can send for Mrs Bagley now,' he said gently to Thomas Penry, referring to the laying-out woman. 'I won't disturb your grief any longer.'

He went downstairs and out of the house with the constable, and Celia's aunt went for Mrs Bagley at once. Thomas looked in bewilderment at Morwen, across Celia's bed.

'Our Celia thought she had a growth in her stomach, you say?' He couldn't take it in. Morwen went to him and put her arm around his shoulder.

'She didn't want to worry you, Mr Penry. If this was her choice, we all have to bear it. I loved her too—'

Her voice broke, and she felt Penry's hand stroking her hair, the way he used to stroke Celia's.

'You'm a good maid, Morwen. You'll walk behind the coffin wi' the Penrys. Celia would like that. I must get started on the making of it. '

He left her alone with Celia. Morwen went to the bed, pulling back the sheet to stare down at her friend. She looked as though she was just sleeping. As though she understood how Morwen had made everything as right as she could. Morwen's throat felt choked as she bent to kiss the cold cheek.

'I'll miss you,' she mumbled, before she fled down the stairs and out into the sunlight.

—

News of the drowning quickly reached St Austell. Ben Killigrew was away visiting the Carricks in Truro, where news filtered through more slowly. No one had thought to bother Charles Killigrew with it personally, and when he heard, he went about roaring like a bull.

'A maid in my best pit drowns herself because of a stomach growth, and nobody thinks fit to tell me!' he bellowed at his sister Hannah, who had heard the tale while out walking with her friend, Emily. Hannah answered back furiously.

'Don't talk as though you blame me for it! I'm just passing on a tid-bit of news. She was only a common bal maiden, anyway. Rough, noisy creatures, all of them—'

'She was one of my workers, you stupid, heartless bitch, and she died at one of my pits!' Charles roared back. 'That makes it my concern. What kind of owner d'you take me for, if I don't show an interest? The maid may have been poor, but nobody's deserving of a growth in the belly, nor death in a slurry pit. Sometimes your lack of humanity makes me wonder how we were ever produced by the same seed!'

Hannah went scarlet. Truth to tell, Charles couldn't exactly place the girl, but he knew that Penry was the name of one of his waggoners, and that his daughter worked at number one pit as well. Of course he was bloody well concerned! And after his evening meal, he intended going up to the cottages to see the family. No one would say Charles Killigrew was too big a man for that. His chest tightened as he stamped about, reminding him of the doctor's warning that he wasn't immortal. Slowing him up a jot, or else he'd be the next one needing a wooden overcoat.

—

Ben waited impatiently outside Tom Askhew's lodgings in Truro. It was time Jane told her parents the truth... while he waited, Askhew had another visitor, and then to Ben's surprise all three people emerged together, the man to hurry away, Jane and Tom with disturbed looks on their faces.

He knew at once that something was wrong.

'What is it?' He asked quickly.

'That man—' Jane began.

'He's one of my informants for the paper,' Tom said in his flat nasal accent. 'Not officially on the payroll, but useful at times. There's been a to-do at your father's clay works—'

'*What?*' Ben forgot his dislike of the Yorkshireman, and looked at him sharply.

'Aye. Some lass has drowned herself in one of the clay pools, I'm told. I'm off to find out more for the *Informer*. If you're going there yourself, Killigrew, I'd be obliged of a lift in your fine trap to save me the cost of hiring a nag—'

Ben disliked him even more, but dislike of Tom Askhew wasn't his prime concern right now. All he could think of was the lass who had drowned herself. All he could think of was Morwen Tremayne. His Morwen... his entire body throbbed with fear that it might be her...

'Of course I'm going there,' he snapped. 'We'll drop Jane at her house first, and you'd best tell what you know to your father, Jane. He'll want to be kept informed. I'll send Tom back with news in due course. It'll be an excuse for him to set foot in your house with a legitimate reason.'

He put the fellow in his rightful place with a touch of sarcasm, but that too was of little importance to him right now. Jane tried to hide the swift pleasure Ben's words brought, quickly hidden because it was a girl's death that was under discussion.

Why should that matter to the lovely Jane Carrick, the one Morwen Tremayne so scathingly called Miss finelady? What did it matter that Ben Killigrew's heart had stopped beating for a moment, and then raced on erratically, still not knowing which girl had drowned herself in the clay pool? If he discovered that it was Morwen... whatever Ben's feelings for her before now, they suddenly multiplied a hundredfold.

Chapter Ten

The whole day was a nightmare to Morwen. Why couldn't everyone leave her alone? It seemed as though they hounded her, either with sympathy or just plain curiosity. They were ghouls, the lot of them. People came and went, and Bess told them what she could, wanting to spare Morwen any more pain. They felt too embarrassed to call at the Penry cottage, so it was to the Tremaynes' that they came...

Out of the sea of faces during that terrible day, came one that Morwen didn't know. With sharp features and a strange accent, a notebook in his hand. With him was someone she recognised immediately, whose presence could make her heart drum, and she didn't want the feeling... not now... not any more...

'Sit down here, Mr Ben, and you too, Mr Askhew, and just ask our Morwen anything you like, while I make some tea—' Bess said in agitation.

Mr Ben! Morwen felt a surge of hysteria sweep over her. She loathed hearing the Killigrew boy addressed so grandly. Why kow-tow to him, when but for the grace of God Morwen might be in the same plight as poor Celia...? But her mother had no knowledge of that, of course...

She felt a hand cover hers. Felt its warmth, and wanted to snatch it away, hating the memories it awoke.

'How are you, Morwen?' Ben said quietly. 'I'm so sorry about your friend—'

Her voice was brittle. 'Am I expected to say I'm quite well, thank you, sir?' Her eyes stabbed with tears, her throat felt thick, but he wouldn't let her pull her hand away from his. She was as numb and frozen as Celia. Couldn't he see that?

'Morwen, this is Tom Askhew,' he ignored her words. 'He wants to put a brief account of what happened in the *Informer*. It will be a fair account, you have my word on it—'

'A fair account? Is Celia on trial then?' Morwen said shrilly. 'Why should I help to sell newspapers—?'

Ben knew he'd chosen his words badly. Truth to tell, he was overwhelmingly relieved to see Morwen alive and not beneath the muck of a clay pool. He ached to hold her close and take that haunted look away from her, but he could see it was the last thing she wanted from him. He could see the blame in her eyes, even if no one else could. He didn't understand it, but it was blatantly obvious to him.

'I'd like to see that the lass had a few kind words said about her, Miss Tremayne,' Tom Askhew said gravely. ''Tis not prying in the general sense. Will you help me put the record straight for her, so folks wouldn't think badly of her?'

Tom knew the right words to say. He saw the indecision in her eyes, and asked brief, detached questions that wouldn't distress her too much. He was clever, businesslike and sympathetic at the same time. He drew out what little Morwen was prepared to tell him without fuss, and closed his notebook before she began to feel harrassed.

He looked at Ben enquiringly. There was nothing else to do here. Reluctantly, Ben got to his feet, his face still troubled as he looked at Morwen. She hardly seemed to notice whether he was there or not. He could see that she was in severe shock, but he sensed there was something more… something Morwen kept a tightly-guarded secret. He knew it as surely as night followed day, but he had no choice but to follow Tom out of the cottage as Bess said firmly that she thought her daughter had said all there was to say.

Ben didn't want to discuss Morwen with Tom Askhew. He drove him back to Truro as fast as his horse would go, wanting to be rid of the man. He was very troubled by Morwen's attitude. Naturally she was grieving, but it was more than that. Ben had sensed the hate in her, and Morwen wasn't a hating person. He burned to find out the truth.

But first he had to get this fellow back to Truro. As silent partner in Killigrew Clay, Carrick had a right to know what had happened, and it gave Tom an excuse to enter the house in his role as newspaperman. And although it made Ben's lips tighten to think of Richard Carrick offering the fellow a glass of his best port, oblivious to the fact that he was his daughter's lover, all Ben wanted was to be rid of him.

—

While Ben went back to Truro, Charles Killigrew was already setting out to call on Thomas Penry as a good boss should. He still bristled at his sister's sneering comments on the fact, and he had nearly given her her marching orders at dinner-time. She had shouted back that her friend Emily would be happy to give her board and lodging.

'Then why don't you go there?' Charles had thundered. 'I'd willingly pay to be rid of you, whenever you care to pack your bags!'

He'd never meant it more, though the upset had started the grinding chest pains again, but he still intended calling on the Penrys, as benevolent as a father-figure at that moment.

He heard the sound of sawing wood as he neared the cottage, and smelled the dry dust in the air. Charles followed the sounds and smells. Thomas Penry was in the yard at the back, measuring and sawing, and keeping furiously busy as though his hands stopped his mind from mourning. His grief was too raw to give the boss the customary deference, but today, neither considered the fact.

''Twill be the finest coffin this side o' Truro, sir,' Thomas grunted in his exertions.

'That it will,' Charles agreed, eyeing the oblong box taking shape. 'Will you allow me to line it for you – to make it more – more—'

'Comfortable.' Thomas said. 'If 'ee've a mind to it, sir. Our Celia will lie there like a princess.'

The tinge of pride in his words made Charles's stomach. Christ, but there were times when he loathed the class distinctions that made a coffin lining of such importance to a simple man, when the cost to Killigrew was no more than a good breakfast.

'I'll see that the lining's sent here in good time,' he said briskly. 'It's a bad day for you, Thomas, and for your family.'

Thomas shook his head sadly. 'I don't understand why she didn't tell me what ailed her. She told Morwen, but then she told Morwen everything. But to be troubled about a growth in her stomach and not tell her own father—' His eyes returned to the coffin. 'Goin' to kill her anyways, o' course, if 'twere a growth, but to drown herself in the clay pool like that—'

He sawed furiously for a few minutes, sending little flurries of golden dust into the air like powdered rain.

'Funeral's on Thursday afternoon, sir, after my shift,' he went on, businesslike again.

'For God's sake, man, you'll do no shift that day,' Charles said roughly. 'You'll stay at home until the time comes. My son Ben and myself will attend Penwithick church for the burying.'

Thomas looked at him in awe. If he touched his fore-lock now, Charles felt he would strangle him. He turned away before the man could stutter his thanks. Such a small thing to do, that obviously meant so much…

'Morwen's walking behind the coffin, o' course, sir. Morwen was her best friend, see? Thank 'ee, sir—'

Charles moved out of earshot and climbed into his trap. He felt as though he'd run a mile uphill. The humility of these people stifled him at times. Thomas Penry, drunk, was as riproaring as any man, but sober, he was like a limp rag at times, like all of them. No, not quite all. Thank God for Hal Tremayne and his family, who had the guts to speak their minds when necessary and not fear the consequences.

Morwen's name had cropped up again, as though determined to weave itself into the fabric of his life. He'd heard the tale that Matt Tremayne had found the dead girl, and guessed what a shock it must have been for Morwen. He would see for himself how she fared.

Bess immediately began fussing as she saw the Killigrew trap approaching the Tremayne cottage.

'Don't get so flustered, dar,' Hal grunted. 'Give him some refreshment if there's any left, and be your natural self. The man won't eat you!'

'No sir, Mr Pit Captain!' Bess said smartly, a small smile tugging at her mouth. It was a long while since any of them had smiled. She wouldn't have dared now, if Morwen hadn't been sleeping in her bed corner, suddenly exhausted.

Hal opened the door to the pit owner and offered him a seat. Charles came straight to the point.

'A bad business, Hal, and how are your two young 'uns taking it, being most closely involved with the dead girl?'

Hal told him quickly. Charles was appalled to learn how Matt had thrust aside Morwen's bed curtain with her dead friend in his arms, and the shock of the discovery.

'I hadn't heard that bit,' Charles growled. 'The tales have got so garbled, I wasn't sure what to believe, but this is a ghastly story.'

He took the drink of tea from Bess's hands and drank deeply. Behind the bed curtain, Morwen heard the buzz of voices and recognised her employer's. She was tempted to stay where she was, but knew that her Mammie would hear the bed creakings and guess that she was awake. Her head still mazed, she slid out of bed and joined the others.

'Morwen, my dear, I'm sorry about all this!' Charles spoke awkwardly, covering the intense shock of seeing the girl look so ill and dazed.

'Thank you,' she murmured the inane reply expected of her, and hated the falseness of it. Then she looked into Charles Killigrew's eyes, and knew that he had meant it sincerely. Strange, that he of all people... she had to look away, because he suddenly reminded her too poignantly of Ben. And she didn't want to enquire too deeply how sincere Ben had been, probably coming straight from his Miss finelady in Truro with the newspaperman...

She heard a sudden choking sound, and heard her mother exclaim in alarm.

'Mr Killigrew, are you ill?' Bess cried, as he clawed at his chest. His face reddened as much with anger as pain.

'Damned blasted ticker playing me about,' he hawked between the knifing pains. 'Got some powders in my weskit pocket. Mix with water—'

He was exhausted, just giving instructions, Hal found the powders, and Bess tipped one into a mug of water. Charles closed his eyes, cursing his luck, then felt a cool hand on his brow, and a soft voice in his ear.

'Don't talk, Mr Killigrew. Don't move. Stay still and breathe gently. Think of nothing, and let the strength flow back into you.' Morwen spoke by instinct, her breath warm and sweet on his cheek as she knelt beside him. He did as he was told, marvelling at the stillness in the girl that could create such serenity in him at that moment. She was beautiful and spirited, yet she possessed a power in her that he was sure she never suspected.

He felt the cold touch of the cup against his lips, and was instructed to drink the draught. He obeyed, and thought of nothing, and at last he felt the pains subside.

'That's better,' he heard Hal say in relief. 'Your colour's coming back, sir.'

Charles opened his eyes and saw the concern of the family. He envied them their closeness. His eyes went to Morwen's with gratitude.

'I would wish to have a daughter like this one, Hal. But I've stayed long enough, and I'll be on my way—'

'Not alone,' Hal said at once. 'I'll accompany you. 'Tis no hardship to walk back from St Austell on a fine day—'

''Tis no hardship for Charles Killigrew to send you back in his trap, neither. Keep it on permanent loan, Hal. You'll need transport to visit your son in Charlestown, mebbe, and I'll not have my pit captain reporting with sore feet each day. Do me a favour and take one of my vehicles off my hands. Have you a shed for it, and room to sleep the horse?'

'I'm not sure about the rightness of it, Mr Killigrew—' Hal began.

'Take it before I expire through arguing, and take me home, man.' Charles found the talk irksome. He'd made the offer spontaneously, and he wanted no arguments.

The gift of a trap and a horse meant little to him. No more than a coffin lining. He felt a swift guilt at his own wealth that was making him so generous to these others this day.

They still had so much, he thought suddenly. There was so much love in this cottage, and at the Penry home too, where a man could make a coffin for his daughter and think the gift of a lining made it a shroud fit for a princess. They made him humble, and it wasn't a feeling Charles Killigrew liked too often.

'We thank you, Mr Killigrew,' Bess said with quiet dignity. ''Twill be put to good use here.'

Charles nodded, telling Hal shortly to see sense the way his good woman did. A daughter like Morwen and a wife like Bess. The man already had riches beyond measure.

He thought about those healing hands of Morwen's as Hal drove him home. The girl would be a wonderful wife for a young man. Passionate and temperamental when roused, calming and gentle when needed. Charles hid a smile. It was usual for a man to choose a wife, but in Morwen Tremayne's case, he guessed she would have very definite ideas of her own on that score.

By the time they reached Killigrew House, he'd told Hal ten times he meant what he said about the horse and trap. The subject was becoming tedious to him. He had a stableful of such items, and it would be one less to dispose of after his death, if Ben was so inclined.

That was it, of course, Charles thought, with sudden insight. He'd had a brief brush with death, in the guise of the Penry girl, and a sharp reminder of his own limitations. Hal had best take advantage of his mood, because no doubt by tomorrow he'd be back to his hollering self again!

He was thankful to wave Hal away and get indoors, to be met immediately by Hannah's grumblings and his son's prickly temper. Too much time with Tom Askhew hadn't sweetened Ben one little bit. He answered Ben's questions on the doings at the cottages, then stumped away after telling him they'd both be attending the bal maiden's funeral on Thursday. And ignored his sister's sniffing comment that the world must be going mad when Charles Killigrew condescended to such a thing. His mouth clamped shut. He wouldn't risk another attack on Hannah Pascoe's account. He had some hard thinking to do, and he wanted a clear head to do it.

–

Thursday was cool, the sky overcast, the sun deserting them. Celia had so loved the sun... though Morwen could no more connect bright, pretty Celia with the object inside the pale wooden box, carried by a team of awkward clayworkers, than she could understand the Killigrew mens' presence here.

It was good of them, but it wasn't fitting. The day belonged to simple folk, and Morwen felt resentment burning inside her as the walking party neared Penwithick church, and she saw Ben and Charles waiting at the porch in their sombre dark clothes. Most of those following the coffin had no special clothes for the day, and wore a hotch-potch of colours. Celia would have liked that, anyway, Morwen thought, fiercely protective.

She thought of Celia, lying inside the silk-lined coffin, and shivered. It seemed such a little time ago that Morwen had wondered how it must feel to be clothed in silk. But not like this... not like this...

Ben watched the slow, dignified progress, made even slower because of John Penry dragging his injured leg, one arm beneath a makeshift crutch. His father and Morwen Tremayne supported him. To Ben, it seemed as though Morwen completed a close-knit circle, with a noisily crying woman behind the three of them.

He saw Morwen's pallor and ached to comfort her, but she looked as though she needed no one. Charles watched her too, and remembered her gentle touch when he had needed her. An idea began formulating in his mind, even then… it had begun when Hannah had discovered he'd given the trap to the Tremaynes.

'You've given a vehicle to a clayworker? They'll all be wanting bits of the estate next. I think you've lost your senses, and the Lord only knows why I remain in this mad-house—'

'Then go!' he roared. 'I've had enough of your whining to last me a lifetime. Pack your baggage and I'll drive you to that prissy friend of yours as soon as you like. I'll pay all your dues, and it'll be worth my fortune to see you living away from this house.'

Her mouth had dropped open with shock.

'What about Jude?' she demanded.

'He can stay if he works,' Charles snapped, the upset doing him no good. 'The minute he shirks, then out he goes.'

'And who's to run the house for you? Do you think it runs itself—?'

'The cook knows how to cook, and the maids know how to skivvy,' he retorted. 'Any fool could do the minimum of work you do, and I've made my decision.'

She saw that he had. When Charles was so adamant, Hannah knew there was no point in arguing. The moon would turn blue before he'd change his mind. She glowered at him.

'I'll move out tomorrow,' she said stiffly. She didn't care, as long as he made her financially secure, and she knew the Killigrew pride wouldn't let him turn her out destitute.

She didn't care about this house any more. Let them all stew in their own juice, and see if the house could revolve without her!

—

Charles forced his thoughts back to the solemn occasion. Hannah had been gone a few days, and although he felt as though a fresh clean breath of air filled the house, the servants definitely needed someone at the helm. His eyes met Morwen's across the church, and the idea took strength. It was ludicrous, of course. She was only seventeen years old, with no social graces, except for natural ones. She wouldn't agree to it. The servants would complain... and who were they to complain, when he paid their wages? He dismissed the thought.

He began to see himself as a benefactor, rescuing her from the bal maiden's lot. And more than that. He would rescue her from constant memories of her friend, whom they were burying today. His mind was made up, and he sought out Hal Tremayne as soon as the coffin had been lowered into theground.

People were drifting away. Morwen stayed by the graveside, her long dark hair hiding her face as she threw some wild flowers onto the coffin. Ben moved towards her, determined to speak his mind, but her mother reached her first, with her two young brothers. She didn't look at him as they drew her away. She didn't need him.

—

If he'd followed her, he'd have known that Morwen didn't go straight home with her family, needing time to be alone. Ben rode back alone to Killigrew House, unsettled and frustrated, taking out his anger on his cousin Jude, as he so often did. His father hadn't got back from Penwithick yet, and he never guessed at the furore going on at the Tremayne cottage when Morwen returned from her long lonely walk across the moors.

She stared at her father in disbelief as he told her of Charles Killigrew's suggestion.

'I told un you must decide for yourself, Morwen, but 'twill be a fine chance for 'ee—'

'Our Morwen will get all posh, and talk funny like the rich folks,' Freddie chanted. 'She'll have no time for we—'

''Course she will,' Jack said scornfully. 'She'll come on visits and tell us daft things about the parties the Killigrews have—'

'That's enough,' Bess put in. 'Morwen must decide, but I agree with your Daddy, Morwen. Mr Killigrew means it kindly. He wants you to be his housekeeper, and he'd like you around the place, not forgetting how you calmed him the other day when he had his attack.'

'Besides, 'twill make more room in the cottage when our Sam gets wed,' Hal added. 'Not that you must take note of that, Morwen. 'Twas just a thought—'

She found her voice, shouting so forcefully they all stared in amazement.

'No! I won't go to the Killigrews, I won't! 'Tis the worst suggestion I ever heard, and you won't make me, none of you!'

Her heart beat wildly as she leaned against the wall, feeling hopelessly trapped, because how could they know, any of them, how she would feel to be living in the same house as Ben Killigrew, for whom her feelings were in such turmoil, and under the same roof as Jude Pascoe, who had done the terrible, unforgivable thing to her friend?

It was an impossible suggestion. Charles Killigrew should never have made it, whatever his reasons. She couldn't bear to consider it. It added to the nightmare in which she had existed ever since Celia's death. Living in the Killigrew House would be a constant reminder. She loathed Jude Pascoe, and she despised herself for ever thinking she could love Ben Killigrew, and believing for one minute that he meant the sweet whisperings to her at the Larnie Stone.

She was bitter that he had dared to attend Celia's funeral. She wondered that Jude Pascoe hadn't been there too, flaunting his part in her death. But neither of them knew of it, did they? No one knew but Morwen, and the weight of it all was beginning to crush her.

Chapter Eleven

Jude couldn't believe his luck at his mother's departure from Killigrew House. Things were looking up, despite the fact that he had to work at a menial job for his uncle. He had an unlikely new friend in Matt Tremayne, who had now moved into lodgings near the port. He'd thought Matt was going to back out of the arrangements after the upset of the bal maiden's death, but he hadn't.

A pity about the girl, Jude thought with a frown. She'd given him the runaround at Truro Fair, and played virgin with him up on the moors, with hollering fit to wake the dead. But some girls did that. They pretended the fellow was the first one, tightening themselves up, and even colouring themselves with a red wash to look like blood. He was too knowing to fall for that one!

He breathed in the tangy sea air, doubly refreshing after the tedium of the day's work for his uncle. Matt Tremayne had quickly got the scent of adventure in his veins, and together they could have some high old times. He saw Matt swaggering along now, almost the old sea-salt already, enviously watching the seamen arriving from the cargo ship, faces tanned like teak from long days in strange exotic waters, bounty slung over their shoulders in bulging packs.

'Do 'ee fancy a spell on the briny then, Matt?' Jude greeted him.

Matt grinned. 'Why not? The world must be bigger than the little bit we see around here.'

'That it is,' Jude echoed. 'Why shouldn't the two of us see some on it together?'

They laughed, not really considering it seriously as they went off to the nearest kiddleywink. They were oddly assorted companions, yet they struck a chord in one another, and Jude had long since decided that Matt was the best of all the Tremayne bunch. And far better than his snot-nosed sister, so prissy about him funning with the Penry girl. But Matt was all right, and the future was definitely looking rosier.

–

Daniel Gorran had struggled with a bad bout of influenza for several days, and had decided he could no longer see his accounting books properly through his streaming eyes. Ben Killigrew had called on him that very afternoon, and was appalled to see how the man was carrying on. The office smelled of stale breath and medication, and he told Daniel shortly that the whole place should be washed down with disinfectant to stop the germs from spreading. Influenza could kill.

'I'll see to it,' Gorran began wheezing.

'No, I'll do it,' Ben retorted. 'I'll send for someone to come in at once. Meanwhile, have you any objection to my looking through the Killigrew books, Daniel? I know my father was well satisfied, but I'd like to study them myself.'

'Do as you wish, Ben. I've every trust in you, and you'll have a more scholarly head on your shoulders than we older ones.'

He was stopped by a paroxysm of coughing and sneezing, while Ben tried not to breathe in too deeply. He'd do better to take the accountancy books away, but he knew Daniel never let them leave this office unless he took them himself. The man took himself off, saying a few days in bed would put him right, while Ben promised to get a cleaning woman in to disinfect the place, and to lock up after him. He decided to stay and supervise that all was done properly.

Truth to tell, Ben was anxious about Charles Killigrew's complacency regarding the clay profits. Morwen had been right, he thought suddenly. Rail tracks from the clay pits to Charlestown port were long overdue, and Killigrew Clay was lagging behind other pits who had already constructed them. Some of the profits should go towards rail tracks.

He was anxious about Charles too. His thoughts went off at all angles. Charles had been too quiet of late, unlike him. He'd had a violent spat with his sister, and Hannah had departed in a huff, leaving the household incomplete, but infinitely more harmonious. But something had to be done there. Ben had begun to feel that all the responsibility was perhaps too much for his father. In which case, the sooner he learned all there was to know about the financial state of Killigrew Clay, the better.

By the time Ben had studied the books for an hour, balancing figures on paper and in his head, he was even more concerned. The money wasn't there for rail tracks, and yet it should be there. Daniel Gorran should have advised Charles on the slackness of his debtors. Money was owing, and hadn't been collected. Money that was expected by the clayworkers, as Charles had promised.

Ben knew them of old. They wouldn't wait for ever for their pittances. Charles could have a strike on his hands if he wasn't careful. He was furious at Gorran's slackness. The man was getting too old for his job, and should take on a younger partner. Ben dismissed the idea of applying for it himself. He was more interested in the clay than in financial jugglings…

The sudden realisation shook him. Yes, dammit, he *was* interested in the clay. It was his heritage, as Charles had so often tried to drum into him. But he'd had to feel it for himself, and he felt it now, with a fierce determination to keep Killigrew Clay the finest in the county.

His head throbbed from studying the books, and the strong smell of disinfectant with which the cleaning woman had liberally scrubbed surfaces and floors all around him. His temples felt near to bursting, his limbs ached, and he'd do well to have an early night, to ponder over how best to put Killigrew Clay on a more secure footing, before the realisation spread through the clay-workers that their paltry pay rises were being delayed far longer than they expected.

He left Gorran's office, oddly light-headed, and was glad to find his father away from home. A light meal and a headache powder was what he needed right now, before the inevitable arguments when Ben put his spoke in the wheel. He retired to his room with the curtains drawn to think things out, snapping at Cook when she brought him his food that it was freezing in his room and he wanted a fire lit at once.

'Freezing, sir?' she asked in amazement. The day had been warm, and the sunlight still lingered.

'Are you deaf, woman?' Ben ranted. 'I want a fire in my room, and quick!'

Cook sped away, storming at the kitchen maids at the young sir's unusual behaviour. And instructing Fanny to fetch some more pepper to put in the rabbit stew for Mr Ben. If it was warming he wanted, then he was going to get it!

–

Charles was doing his rounds of the clayworks, inspecting, assessing and approving, complaining where necessary. He'd watched Morwen Tremayne for a while without her being aware of it. He'd watched the slowness of her hands in the scraping and cleaning of the clay, and how she moved with heavy steps instead of with the light tripping walk he remembered. Her eyes were still shadowed.

He'd tracked down Hal Tremayne in his pit captain's hut and asked about Morwen's reaction to being Charles's housekeeper. It had been four days since he'd made the offer. Hal looked at him squarely.

'Fact is, our Morwen's refused absolutely, sir. Near tore my head off when I mentioned it. I'm sorry, Mr Killigrew. Our Morwen's still mazed by the Penry girl's death, and can't seem to get over it.'

He was uneasy at his daughter's refusal, seeing it as a slight to the generosity of a good boss. It would suit the family too. Sam was wanting to be wed soon, and they needed the room... he said as much to Charles.

'Sam's a good worker, Hal,' Charles commented. 'Does he have ambitions to better himself?'

Hal smiled, on safer ground. 'He aims to be a pit captain, same as me!'

'Good!' Charles said briskly. 'You've no objection if I speak to Morwen myself, Hal?'

He changed the topic so smoothly, Hal blinked.

'I'll send for her, sir—'

'Don't do that. She has a will of her own, and may well turn turtle if she thinks it's me she has to see. Send your young Freddie to say you want to see her in your hut, and I'll await her here, Hal.'

The man obeyed, while Charles was asking himself impatiently why he seemed so obsessed in helping the Tremayne girl, when she didn't seem to want to be helped! He was as concerned for her as if she was his own daughter, he thought, to his surprise.

He heard Hal instruct his youngest son to go and fetch Morwen for him, and the boy scampered off in the direction of the linhay, full of importance.

'Daddy wants you in his hut, our Morwen. You'm not to dawdle, 'cos 'tis urgent.' Freddie told her.

The other bal maidens glanced at one another. All were struck by the way poor Morwen was taking her friend's death so badly.

'If yon Killigrew's been saying you've been idling, girl, just tell un 'tis not every day you bury a friend!' one said sharply. 'Got no feelings, some on 'em—'

'I'm coming, Freddie,' Morwen said swiftly, not wanting to dwell on the subject. She knew she wasn't working a quarter as well as the others any more, but God, it hurt to know how much she missed Celia.

She left the linhay's chalk-dry atmosphere. She hated passing the clay pool, hurrying across the squelching ground to the pit captain's hut. She wouldn't look at the milky green water, but her imagination tormented her.

She almost burst inside the hut, slamming the door behind her, catching her breath in the gloom of it.

'Sit down, Morwen,' Charles Killigrew said gravely.

She flinched at his voice.

'Where's my Daddy?' she demanded.

'It was I who wanted you, Morwen. I'm not a man to mince words. I want you to work for me at Killigrew House. Why are you refusing me?'

'Why me?' she countered at once, her blue eyes distant. 'Anyone could do the job, and would be glad to—'

'It's you I want,' he said bluntly. 'I'm being selfish, Morwen, because I can't forget how you helped me last week. If such an attack occurred again – which it may well do – I'd like to know you were about the place.'

He didn't see the faintest flicker in her eyes. God dammit, didn't she care if he lived or died! So be it. He could be shameless in his methods when he chose. He spoke crisply.

'I'm told your brother wants to be wed soon. Your cottage is far too small to hold all of you. I hear Sam has ambitions to be a pit captain, like your father. It's possible it could happen much earlier than with your father if a vacancy arises, and of course he'll be wanting to raise a family of his own. How would they all manage in that cottage, Morwen?'

Morwen's eyes burned with angry suspicion. Her mouth tightened, but still she said nothing.

'Work for me, Morwen,' Charles said abruptly. 'When you do, I'll move your folks into a small house I own, between here and St Austell. Your mother could do her sewing in comfort. Your brother Sam and his new wife could live in your present cottage, and a lot of people would be very much happier. Think of your day off, with your mother so near. You and she could stroll about the town like the rest of the St Austell ladies. Does it begin to sound more attractive?'

'It begins to sound like blackmail, Mr Killigrew!' Morwen blazed at him. Yet she was tempted… she hated herself for being tempted by the bait he dangled in front of her. A far juicier bait than the mere advantages he outlined. He would lift her status and that of her family in a trice, if she said the word.

'That's another name for it,' Charles agreed dryly.

'Why should you do this for us? We're nothing to you—'

He caught hold of her cold hands, gripping them tightly.

'Morwen, I've taken an interest in you, and I've no wish to see you sliding downhill into a complete nervous collapse. Any fool can see that you should get away from this place with its unhappy memories, and I'm offering you the chance. I want your sunny smile around me, and it's sadly missing. A new environment can sometimes work miracles, my dear, so why not accept one when it's offered?'

A sudden shine blurred her eyes. Celia had so wanted a miracle to happen for her. She knew what Celia would say if Morwen was daft enough to refuse this chance! She wouldn't think of anything else but the benefits to her family. She wouldn't think of seeing Ben Killigrew every single day…

'I accept.' She spoke quickly. 'If you'll do all you've said, Mr Killigrew—'

'I never break a promise, girl,' he growled, resisting the urge to hug her. Reminding himself that she was Hal Tremayne's daughter, not his. But he was not one to let the grass grow, and he spoke as quickly as she.

'I'd like you to start at once. You'll be given proper clothes, of course. A plain dress for working, and a better one when you act as hostess at my table, as my sister did—'

Morwen was overcome with fright at his words.

'I know nothing of such things! I'll let you down—'

'No, you won't! Good God, a clever girl like you can check that linen's clean and aired. You can consult with Cook on the daily menus and tell the skivvies when they've left dust on the mantels. You can use the library at Killigrew House if you're flummoxed. There's a whole section of books with simple pictures to instruct you on how a house is run! Now, does it all seem so difficult?'

'Not if 'tis as straightforward as you make it sound,' Morwen said grudgingly, but unconsciously her chin lifted, and Charles Killigrew saw it. Her pride was at stake, and here was a chance to make her Daddy proud of her too. Housekeeper at Killigrew House. The words had a ring to them.

'We'll collect your belongings, and you can return with me this afternoon. We'll inform your father at once,' Charles wouldn't let her delay the moment. 'I'll not leave this pit without you, Morwen.'

His eyes challenged her, and she smothered the sudden fright. She'd made her decision, and she wouldn't go back on it. She'd have to cope with all the other things... seeing Ben... but thankfully not seeing the hated Jude Pascoe too. In her ignorance, she assumed that he would have left the Killigrew house with his mother, and was blessedly unaware of her mistake.

By the time Charles's horse and trap clattered towards Killigrew House, Morwen Tremayne was sitting tensely by his side, her few chattels stowed beneath the hard wooden seat. She was beginning to think this day wasn't happening, that she hadn't just bid her Mammie and Daddy and brothers a tearful farewell, as though she was never going to see them again. As though the few miles between them were as vast as an ocean.

If Morwen felt disorientated, then so did Ben. His head swam, feeling several sizes too big for his skin. He shivered and burned simultaneously, and he didn't need a doctor to tell him he'd contracted the influenza that was rife in the town. His brain felt like wool, Cook's stew had scalded his throat so that he drank gallons of water to counteract it. He wasn't sure if it was still day or night, and he staggered to his window to push the curtains aside for some air.

Then he really thought he must be hallucinating. Charles's trap had just arrived, and beside his father, wraithlike and nervous, was Morwen Tremayne. She stepped down from the trap, her travelling bag in her hands. What in God's name was she doing here? He tried to call out, but he staggered against the window with a great crash, and then the floor came up and met him.

Charles rushed through the house much faster than he should, with Morwen hurrying after him, her heart thumping at seeing Ben apparently falling in an upstairs room. Charles took the stairs two at a time, bawling at her to follow, and hollering for someone to appear. Cook scuttled out from the kitchen, her eyes round and frightened at the commotion.

'Where's that goddamned nephew of mine, woman? Send him for the doctor—'

'He's gone out, sir, not wanting any dinner nor anything,' she stuttered.

'Shall I go for the doctor, sir?' Morwen said at once. 'If you'll tell me where to go—'

'No! One of the skivvies can go,' he barked out. 'See to it, Mrs Horn. Morwen Tremayne's the new housekeeper, so you may as well inform everybody to that effect, and tell one of them to be sharp and get the doctor here.'

Cook's astonished eyes turned to Morwen, then she turned abruptly to do Killigrew's bidding. Morwen felt sick at his clumsiness, and at the knowledge that Jude Pascoe was clearly still part of the household. But there was no time to think of it now. She followed Charles into Ben's room, her fingers untying her bonnet, her heart leaping to see him lying insensible on the floor.

'We'd best not move him, in case any bones are broken,' Charles said harshly.

He crouched beside his son, and without thinking, Morwen did the same, putting her cool hand on Ben's brow. She could feel that it was furnace-hot. Beads of sweat studded his forehead and lips, and he was delirious. She felt fearful for him, and knew her fears were echoed in Charles's mind. Whatever else she felt about Ben Killigrew, she could pity him now.

Any unintentional ill-wishing on Celia's account that Morwen might have done had been directed at Jude Pascoe, not at Ben. She knew it now, when his body was shaking with fever, and she felt so helpless... his restless hands seemed to be seeking comfort, and it was Morwen's hands that he grasped.

She murmured softly, hoping to calm him, while his eyes burned vacantly, and he didn't see her. She was aware of Charles getting to his feet and prowling about the room, frustrated and blaspheming at the time it took a skivvy to fetch the doctor when his son might be dying…

His words made Morwen shiver. She had seen enough of death. She willed Ben to hold on… kneeling nearer to him, her dark hair swinging across his face. As though aware of her presence through his mumblings, he reached up and caught a handful of her hair in his grasp, holding her captive by it, as he'd done once before. Morwen felt embarrassed in his strong grip, held close to his face, while his father seemed unaware of what was happening between the two of them.

At last Charles said the doctor had arrived, and somehow Ben seemed to know what was happening, and released his hold on Morwen.

'We must get the boy into bed,' the doctor snapped, annoyed at being disturbed from a good dinner, despite the fee he could expect from Charles Killigrew.

'I thought it best not to move him,' Charles said resentfully. 'He might have broken bones—'

'I never had an influenza patient yet with broken bones as a symptom,' the doctor grunted. 'With all the germs flying about, it's not surprising that Ben's got it. I've been at Daniel Gorran's bedside earlier tonight, and I gather Ben's been seeing him today. Fool of a man should have been in bed a week ago. It's a good thing this young man's fit and strong. They've had a bad epidemic of the illness over at Bodmin. They've buried a dozen or so there already.'

Chapter Twelve

Ben thought he must be still dreaming. He'd heard Morwen Tremayne's voice so often while he'd threshed about in his bed, he knew his mind must be rambling. He'd felt her soft hand on his brow, smelled the warm, musky, familiar scent of her. He'd been calmed in his nightmares, merely by her presence. Yet he'd never believed that she was real until now, when he opened his eyes for the first time without the fever of delirium clouding them.

He turned his head a fraction, and saw Morwen's slender figure as she gazed out of his window at the rain sliding down the panes. The September rains could change from damp gentle warmth to the angry lashings of coastal gales and change the beautiful rugged landscape to a spectacular holocaust of grey seas and storm-washed cliffs... his thoughts shifted direction, becoming more lucid now the fever had left him.

He wanted to feel Morwen's hand soothe his brow again... a dark shadow leaned over him. Ben registered the portly shape of Doctor Pender and felt a brief resentment that it was the doctor and not Morwen who held his wrist and peered into his eyes. What in God's name was Morwen doing here, anyway? He couldn't think that clearly yet.

'So you're back with us at last, are you, Ben?' Doctor Pender commented. 'You've your pretty nurse here to thank for pandering to you this last week, which probably saved your father from putting more strain on that dicky heart of his.'

Ben looked at him sharply. In one blunt sentence, the doctor had told Ben what he had a right to know. That Charles Killigrew wasn't invincible...

'Must he continue to stay in bed, Doctor?' Morwen said, moving towards them.

Ben tried to ignore her surprising, delightful presence, and looked directly at Doctor Pender.

'Is my father ill? How bad is his heart?'

'No worse than it should be for a man who roars like a lion and sends his blood pressure soaring at the slightest provocation,' the doctor said dryly. 'He'll outlast me if he behaves himself. Installing this young woman in the house in place of that caustic aunt of yours is a step in the right direction. A pretty face is a tonic in itself.'

Morwen's cheeks warmed as Ben glanced at her. Installed in Killigrew House, was she! Surely his father hadn't gone mad and taken himself a mistress... and if he had, then not Morwen Tremayne... Ben felt his blood surge furiously at the thought. He'd best keep calm or his temperature would be rising again. But by God, it was rising now, at the mere thought of his father and Morwen...

'I'm the new housekeeper, sir,' she said primly, her eyes daring him to think otherwise. Just as if she could read every bloody suspicious thought in his head! Ben took in the plain brown dress she wore, and knew it was so. His relief made his voice curt.

'I see. Presumably it amused my father to keep this news to himself—'

'There was no time to tell you. It was all arranged suddenly—' her cheeks burned, as she made it sound worse. She turned to the doctor, her nose in the air.

'I think I'd best leave you with your patient, Doctor.'

'And tell his father the boy's well enough to receive visitors, please, nurse. I gather a young lady's been enquiring after him,' Doctor Pender said jovially.

Morwen walked from the sick room, head held high. She knew very well how many times Jane Carrick had sent messages this past week. When all risk of infection was gone, it would be Jane sitting here with him to tease his appetite with fruit and sweets. Miss finelady... Morwen had not waited for the influenza to pass...

She bumped into a shadowy figure in the passage outside, and recoiled as usual as she encountered Jude Pascoe.

'Don't fret, I won't touch you,' Jude growled. He remembered the way she had flown at him when he'd first seen her here last week. He remembered her wildcat ways... 'I'm sent for any message to deliver to the Carricks, since I'm off to Truro on an errand.'

He scowled, thinking himself nothing but a bloody errand-boy now, while Ben languished upstairs, waited on hand and foot. It was raining too, and no one would give a tinker's cuss whether he got the bloody influenza or not... he glared at Morwen, putting on airs and graces, and her the daughter of a clayworker...

'Ask your uncle and cousin about that,' Morwen said icily, as she swept by him.

Never could she forget what a bastard he was. She hated him more, since coming here to live. He'd got away with it, and was free to do it all again, with any gullible girl like Celia. Morwen remembered her first night in Killigrew House too. Once Ben was safely settled, she heard the doctor's strict orders that no visitors must be allowed until risk of infection was past. The influenza epidemic was virulent in the county, and the rule was strictly enforced.

Morwen finally went wearily to bed in Hannah Pascoe's old room, too tired to notice the strangeness of her surroundings, or even to register that at last she had a room of her own, vast and unfamiliar. The sound of the distant sea, booming against the rocks, lulled her frayed nerves... and then she was suddenly frighteningly awake again, just as she was on the edge of sleep.

She hadn't extinguished her candle, and her eyes caught the turn of her door handle. Before she could think properly, the lumbering shape was inside and leaning on the door, the smell of drink reeking clear across the room. They looked at each other in the same petrified instant.

Jude saw the slight figure in his mother's old bed. She sat upright, her cotton nightgown taut against her breasts, tensed with fear. Her dark hair tumbled about her slender shoulders, her blue eyes suddenly darkened, her full mouth unable to stop its trembling. Jude's lustful eyes didn't question the apparition. He was too drink-hazed to care how she got here. All he saw was a luscious piece, all ready and waiting, and he lurched across the room.

All Morwen saw was the man she loathed most in the world. She watched his hands move towards his breeches belt, and saw the leer in his eyes. She had no weapon to defend herself, only her fury and the flaring candle. She grabbed the metal holder and held it menacingly. Her heart pounded as she lashed out at him in words he would understand.

'You come one step nearer, Jude Pascoe, and I'll burn the bollocks off you! If I had to swing for you, it would be a pleasure, knowing you'd never force your stinking flesh into another innocent girl's body. Do you understand me?' She saw the bewilderment pass over his drunken face. He hesitated, seeing she meant what she said. His eyes glittered.

'What's all this then?' he snarled. 'You weren't so all-fired prissy with my cousin up on the moors—'

He was guessing. Ben couldn't have confided anything in this lout... she tried to stop the shaking inside her.

'Get out,' she hissed. 'Or I'll scream rape to your uncle, and you'd soon be sent packing like your mother—'

'You little bitch!' Jude grated. 'I see your game! After bigger fish than Jude Pascoe, eh? You think Ben Killigrew's got more to offer in his breeches, do 'ee—'

She hurled the heavy candle-holder at his head. He dodged sideways and caught a glancing blow to his shoulder. The flame went out, and the room was black as pitch. Morwen could hear the thud of her own heart, staccato and wild. She heard Jude's laboured breathing as he lunged towards the bed. She slid out of it, and met his charging body with her knee, vicious and hard, ramming it into his groin as her fingernails clawed at his face. He howled with rage and pain.

'You she-devil!' he screeched. 'You'll pay for that—'

'So will you if you come near me again,' Morwen said savagely. 'I'll tell about how you raped my friend Celia on the moors, Jude Pascoe. The constable's still curious as to why she drowned herself, and he'd be very interested to know who she'd been seeing.'

She heard his heavy breathing, and smelled it, rancid and stale. But she knew she had got the better of him. He wrenched open the door and slammed it after him, and Morwen wondered that the whole house wasn't awakened by it. But perhaps they were used to Jude's lurchings in the night, which was more than she was. Morwen trembled all over, and put a heavy chair behind the door, relighting her candle with shaking hands.

How wise had she been to come here after all? It was for her family's sake… but she had overlooked how vulnerable she was. She had expected Jude Pascoe to be gone from the house, and shuddered at the thought of him coming here, clearly too stupefied to remember that his mother had gone.

Morwen vowed never to give him the satisfaction of knowing the truth about Celia's child, and was angry at even hinting something of it to him. She crawled back into bed, burying her head under the bedcovers, and wept from sheer frustration and the traumas of the day.

–

She had seen little of Jude since that night. She doubted that he remembered much of what happened, but if it was enough to make him keep his distance, then Morwen was satisfied. As she left Ben's room, she heard the front doorbell, and her heart leapt as she answered it to find Jane Carrick outside, astonished to see the clay-worker's daughter at Killigrew House. Jane remembered her manners.

'Good-day – Morwen,' she quickly recalled the name. 'I've come to see Ben – my – Mr Killigrew—' She hardly knew how to address this newly mature Morwen in the brown housekeeper's dress, her dark hair swept up from her neck, and more elegant than Jane might have expected.

'Of course, miss. Will you follow me, please? You won't have heard that I'm the new housekeeper here.'

Saying the words often might make them seem real, Morwen thought. Situations like this would make them even more real. Ushering Jane Carrick into Ben's bedroom was obviously permitted, and she saw that he was now in a chair near the window, getting some welcome fresh air. She heard Jane greet him warmly as she seated herself across the room, and thought that if she had been parted from her lover for a week, then neither influenza nor wild horses would have kept her a room's width from his arms.

Morwen turned quickly and left them alone.

While Jane looked thoughtfully at Ben, and noted the way his eyes followed the trim shape of the Tremayne girl. But after a brief reassurance as to his health, Ben brushed her enquiries aside and demanded to know if she'd heard tell of his father's heart condition.

'Not a word!' she exclaimed. 'Why should I have known and not you?'

'I merely thought he may have confided in your father, and passed any news on to you, that's all,' Ben said irritably. Inactivity was beginning to irk him, and since the doctor had left, Charles had come to see him, and pooh-poohed the idea of anything seriously wrong. Treating him like a child, Ben had fumed.

'Is it serious?' Jane was concerned. Ben grunted.

'All I could get out of Father was that he'd had a couple of turns, as he calls them. One of which was at the Tremayne cottage, where apparently Morwen played nurse so effectively it gave him the idea of asking her to be our new housekeeper, as you may have gathered! The old goat didn't think it necessary to tell his own son that there was medicine prescribed for him. Supposing the attack had occurred here, and his damnable pride had stopped him admitting it?'

His throat rasped, not quite recovered yet, and he felt a swift sympathy for Charles. Ben, too, hated admitting he was ill, but stupidity could cost Charles Killigrew his life.

Jane sympathised too, and tactfully changed the conversation. When Ben grudgingly asked after Tom Askhew, Jane hesitated, and then spoke in a rush.

'Can I tell you a secret, Ben? He had an important visitor this week, who came by train and coach especially to see Tom. His name was Sir Garside Sefton, and he wants Tom to start a newspaper in Yorkshire called the *Northern Informer*. Tom's delighted about it. He wants to go back to his roots—'

'I'm surprised you sound so pleased about it. Not fallen out with him already, have you?'

Jane laughed, her face pink. 'Of course not! When Tom goes, I shall go with him, and that's the secret you mustn't tell, Ben. Tom's ambitious, and he's known of this chance for some time now. He's got an assistant keen enough to take over in Truro when the time comes. We intend to elope when the time is right, Ben, and no one's going to stop us!'

He saw the determination in her face, more than he'd ever seen it before. At that moment, she reminded him oddly of Morwen Tremayne... the same passionate look Ben had seen in Morwen's eyes on the night at the Larnie Stone when he'd wanted her so much...

'Aren't you going to say something, Ben? You won't make me change my mind!' Jane said defensively, as he seemed to be frowning into space.

Truth was, the memory of Morwen that night, soft and pliant in his arms, was so pleasurable to him that he had to force himself to concentrate on Jane Carrick's presence at all.

'I wouldn't even try,' he said shortly.

Jane changed the conversation, burning with curiosity about Morwen Tremayne. Ben shrugged elaborately – too elaborately, Jane thought sagely.

'You know as much as me. My father dismissed my aunt, and Morwen was installed here while I was ill. That's all there is to it. I didn't know she'd been in the house a whole week until today!'

It wasn't strictly true. He had been uncannily aware of her presence. Her soft hands on his brow, her soothing voice... he saw the quirk of a smile on Jane's lips.

'She's a very pretty girl,' she teased.

'Is she?' Ben said distantly. 'I've hardly noticed.'

But they both knew that he had.

–

Charles Killigrew strode into the dining-room where Morwen was arranging the table-settings. He was well pleased with the way the girl was shaping up, and he beamed at her now.

'Set the table for four this evening, m' dear. Ben will be tired of being spoon-fed, and will be joining us for meals from now on.'

Her heart jumped. This was another hurdle for her to cross. It was a relief that when Jude Pascoe was there for meals, he rarely made conversation. She was becoming used to Charles's jovial manners, but sitting opposite Ben at every meal... she had expected to eat with the kitchen staff, but Charles wouldn't hear of it. A housekeeper was a cut above the kitchen staff. His sister had always eaten with the family, and so should Morwen Tremayne. When she didn't reply, Charles looked at her thoughtfully.

'Why not take some time off and visit your family today? There's plenty of time before dinner if you use the pony and trap. Now that the risk of influenza is past, they'll be longing to see you, Morwen.'

It was true. The disease spread so rapidly that people stayed in their own homes while an epidemic occurred, and Morwen hadn't been home since moving to Killigrew House. Her mother would be missing her, and anxious to know how she fared at the big house.

Morwen felt suddenly nostalgic for the things that were past. Her life here was luxurious compared with the simple cottage, but her roots were still there. She still felt the urge to run barefoot across the moors at times, with the rain and wind streaming through the black tangle of her hair, and to feel the sensual sting of both on her eyes and cheeks. Or to lie in the warm sun with the summer fragrance all around, squinting up at the sky and sharing secrets with Celia...

Her eyes stung, remembering. None of that was possible any more, and chasing the past was as futile as chasing rainbows.

'I'll be back in good time for dinner, Mr Killigrew,' she said in a strangled voice, and turned away from him lest he suspected she was crying.

She was glad Jude wasn't in the stables, only the young boy who helped him, and she quickly got used to the pony and trap as she went through the cobbled streets of the town and onto the wild moors towards home. It looked different now. The cottages seemed smaller, and the appalling thought was in her head before she could stop it. She had been away for six days, and already she had changed...

But this was still home, she thought fiercely, greeting neighbours who called out to her, and thought how fine the Tremaynes were becoming all of a sudden. Hal Tremayne with his own trap; Bess at her sewing instead of working the clay; and now Morwen, acting near to being a boss's daughter and every bit as elegant with her hair piled on top of her head and sitting so poised and smart. Young Matthew too, gone to work at Charlestown port... life was certainly changing for Hal Tremayne and his family.

Bess was overjoyed to see her daughter, and couldn't resist fingering the soft brown fabric of Morwen's dress as she went inside the cottage.

''Tis so good to see you, love! And how grand you be. 'Tis a fine bit o' stuff Charles Killigrew provides for his servants!'

They both laughed at the thought.

'Grand or not, 'tis good to see you again, Mammie,' Morwen said warmly, trying not to notice the poor furnishings in the cottage. Bess's hands had lost much of the redness of the bal maiden's hands, but years of exposure to wind and weather would never make them a lady's hands. Morwen felt a fierce love for her mother, and an odd stab of resentment towards Charles Killigrew, who had made her aware of such things.

'And you'll have a cup of hot chocolate and tell me about the big house. Is Mr Ben quite recovered, Morwen? They say the influenza has carried off a shocking number of folk.'

'He's well, Mammie. Though Doctor Pender said it was only his strong spirit that helped him through it.'

'Ah well. Fine folk have less stamina, I daresay,' Bess commented, 'but he's a strong young man and no mistake. Now tell me about your new life, love.'

There seemed little to tell. Ben's illness had been dominant ever since she'd moved into his house, and Morwen had felt oddly in limbo ever since. She had been blackmailed into taking the job, for her family's own good, and she could never tell them that. She felt easier when the boys came home with their father, though the younger ones were a little awed at this new Morwen with the upswept hair and the look of a lady. But Sam remarked that she'd be a fitting flower-maid to his Dora when they were wed.

'Is it arranged?' Morwen said excitedly. A wedding was just what was needed to cheer folks, however soon after Celia Penry's death. To countryfolk buryings and weddings were all a part of life, and none would think it odd to have one so soon after the other.

''Tis for early December,' Sam smiled. 'Mammie's to sew Dora's dress, and yourn too, I daresay.'

Morwen hugged her tall handsome brother, and suddenly the tiny cottage seemed a joyous place as they all talked at once. It seemed so long since Morwen had laughed, but here there was love and laughter and happiness. They were all there except Matthew, nearly complete again. And Morwen made a silent vow before she left her old home.

She would ask Charles Killigrew directly to keep his side of the bargain. Sam and his bride must have this cosy cottage as their wedding-gift, to be alone as married couples should be. He had promised her family the small house, half-way between St Austell and the clay works, a link between them all. And Morwen and her mother would stroll among the ladies of the town and be part of them...

She left the cottage in a much lighter mood. She still mourned her friend, and always would, but it was as though a ray of sunlight pierced the gloom at last. There was to be a wedding in the family, and she would be part of it.

It was a long while since springtime, but to Morwen on that early autumn evening, as she trotted the pony and trap back to Killigrew House, it was as though all the ice around her heart was beginning to thaw at last. She was coming alive again, the way she always felt with the emergence of spring after the dark days of winter. Young and alive, and renewed.

Chapter Thirteen

In the smoke-filled fug of the Blue Boar kiddleywink in St Austell, Jude Pascoe glowered into his jug of ale. He'd found a kindred spirit in Matthew Tremayne, yet now he wished he hadn't. If he didn't like the fellow so much, he could dig a grave for Matt Tremayne quicker than blinking, and get his revenge on the whole shit-bagging family at one stroke. And on the high-and-mighty Morwen Tremayne in particular. He scowled just thinking of her.

The scowl changed to a grin as Matt came into the Blue Boar. There was a change in Matt that even Jude could see. Matt was independent for the first time in his life, and he liked the feeling. When Jude spoke of opportunities across the sea, Matt liked that too, but knew better than to speak of it in his father's hearing.

'Weather's on the change, Matt,' Jude said, wiping the curve of froth from his upper lip with the back of his sleeve, and feeling the ale course through his body like liquid gold. ''Tis a pity we don't live on the north coast of the county, where the real rich pickings are when the wrecks come floating in—'

Matt felt his pulse quicken as Jude dangled the bait in front of him. His Daddy wouldn't approve, but his Daddy wouldn't get to hear of it… Matt put it out of his mind and asked when they were to practise the drill of which he knew so little as yet.

Jude laughed raucously, calling for a jug of ale for his friend, and slapping him on the back.

'Soon enough! I'll show 'ee the fine old caves where we can hide the spoils while the customs men be on the prowl, ready for collecting later and selling off to obliging landlords!'

Wrecking was a sport Matt had always thought of with derision, until Jude had made it sound like fair game. The spoils of the sea... Matt had got the taste of adventure in his veins now, egged on by the old sea-salts who frequented the waterfront. He'd heard tales of exotic places, and the golden land of America where everyone became rich. Home was still dear to Matt, but there was a whole world beyond Cornwall, and he was only just becoming aware of it...

'I thought you weren't coming today,' Jude suddenly growled. 'Drink up, and let's find some agreeable company, Matt.'

He winked, and Matt's blood quickened still more. Kitty's bawdy-house was another delight he'd been initiated into, with sweet-scented girls who made an hour or two more exciting than he'd ever imagined possible. He saw Jude laughing at him, and grinned back. For a moment he wondered what his father would think if he knew the road Matt was taking, and then determinedly put all his family out of his mind. The only thing to concern him now was which one of Kitty's pretty girls would entertain him.

–

Morwen looked at the big grandfather clock in the drawing-room at Killigrew House, satisfied that there was ample time to wash and change her dress before dinner. She had hardly been out of the brown dress since her arrival here, except for sleeping. She hadn't felt like making an effort, but tonight she did. There was going to be a wedding, and she felt seventeen again instead of a hundred years old, and she knew it would give Charles Killigrew pleasure to see her wearing the second dress he had given her, the colour of young spring buds.

She would loosen her hair and be more like the girl she used to be before the disastrous thing that had happened to Celia. Despite her pain, Morwen was too young to grieve for ever, and she was fresh and pretty in the new dress, and glowing with health from the invigorating ride down from the moors.

The neckline of the green dress was deep and rounded, its fabric caressing her curving shape. She felt the softness of her hair on her shoulders, and swept into the dining-room with a reckless feeling of belonging here. She had better hide it from Mr Killigrew, she thought, a mischievous smile on her lips, as the tall figure turned at her approach, and her heart leapt.

Ben's stormy eyes took in her changed appearance. He tossed back the drink in his hand in one gulp.

'I'm sorry. I expected to find your father here—' Morwen was furious to find herself stammering, gauche as a clayworker's daughter in the presence of her betters. A world apart from the genteel manners of Miss Jane Carrick, Miss finelady...

The silly name surged into her head, and the inverted snobbery of it seemed to separate Morwen from Ben

Killigrew more widely than anything else at that moment. Her hands felt clammy as Ben slowly studied her, as though assessing this girl giving herself airs in his father's house. Her face flooded with colour, but her chin tilted higher, and she saw the faint smile on his lips as he noted it. His voice was brusque.

'My father is feeling tired, and will take his meal in his room. I fear I've angered him, and as my dear cousin has sent a message to say he'll be missing dinner also, you'll have to make do with my company this evening, Miss Tremayne. Will you take a glass of port with me? I apologise in advance for not being in the best of humours tonight.'

He spoke with heavy sarcasm, not waiting for an answer, and Morwen guessed that it wasn't his first drink of the evening. He handed her a glass of red liquid, and their fingers touched. The contact was enough to make Morwen shiver, and she took the drink too quickly, feeling her head swim as she did so.

She wished herself anywhere but here, suddenly acutely embarrassed at this obviously unwelcome tête-à-tête. She wished herself back in her old cottage, safe and secure. She wished herself running wild with Celia on a soft summer night beneath the stars. She wished herself beside the Larnie Stone, in Ben Killigrew's arms, wanting him, and willing him to want her... lying on a mossy, sun-warmed bed of turf, with his hands and mouth bringing her sleeping senses to life... such a different Ben from the cold young man standing beside her now.

'We'll go in to dinner,' he said curtly. 'There's no point in waiting any longer.'

Morwen swallowed, wondering if he could have read the swirling thoughts in her head at that moment, and encountering his steely eyes. There was nothing soft or gentle about him now. Morwen could see the echo of Charles Killigrew in his son, and guessed that there had been a crackling argument between them.

In the dining-room, Mrs Horn told Fanny to serve the meal at once, then see to Mr Killigrew's tray. She was clearly ruffled at such a haphazard household, but later she told the housemaids it was a pleasure to see the new housekeeper transformed from a plain little duckling into a beautiful swan.

Morwen could barely touch the succulent food. Ben made her so nervous, and his attempts to be civil were so forced she wished he'd eat in silence. When they left the table to sit in comfort in the drawing-room with coffee and turkish delights, her exasperation finally overcame her embarrassment.

'You don't have to talk to me,' she said tensely. 'I know I'm only the housekeeper, and a fine dress doesn't turn a bal maiden into a lady—'

'What in God's name are you talking about?' Ben said roughly. 'It takes more than clothes to make people what they are, and it's not you that's angering me.'

'What is it then?' She spoke before she could think. It wasn't her place to question him like this, but Ben gave a short laugh as he poured more wine.

'I don't see why you shouldn't know. You're a champion for the cause, after all.'

'Now you're talking in riddles,' Morwen snapped, thinking he made fun of her. He looked directly into her eyes, and Morwen was filled with sudden warmth at the look. Her heart beat erratically, and the port wine still made her head spin.

'Not at all. Don't you remember the night you came here with your family, when you spoke up so forcefully in favour of rail tracks from the clay works to the quay? Have you forgotten it already?'

'Of course I haven't.' She had forgotten nothing of that night, especially that it was the first time she had seen Ben Killigrew with Jane Carrick, and seen how impossible it was for a clayworker's daughter to dream of a young man out of her class. Her face burned at the memory.

'Then you may as well know that my father and I have reached deadlock over it,' he said tersely. 'I agree with you entirely, Morwen. Killigrew Clay is big enough to do as other pits have done, and we're lagging behind, but Father won't see it. He's as damnably stubborn as a mule—'

'And so are you,' Morwen couldn't resist a smile at the thought of the two of them warring over this. Nor a certain uplifting feeling that she and Ben were united over the necessity for rail tracks.

'He says there's no money,' Ben went on, scowling as if he hadn't heard her. 'He says he'll be obliged to stop the wage rises to the men if we consider rail tracks, and he's so disgruntled it wouldn't surprise me if he delays them anyway. He can be contrary when he chooses. But there's money in stocks and shares, mine as well as his, and it's time he came down from his pedestal and put his pits to rights—'

Morwen heard nothing but that one phrase. Stop the wage rises to the men... they had already been delayed longer than the men expected, and there was unrest among them now... she got to her feet, the breath tight in her chest, her eyes blazing as she glared across the candlelit table at Ben Killigrew.

'You can't mean it! He wouldn't stop the wage rises. It would mean a strike, sure as night follows day, Ben! I know these men, better than you do. They trusted your father, and if he lets them down over this, he'll get no work out of them ever again. They'll go elsewhere, and Killigrew Clay will rot in hell as far as they're concerned. No boss should act like God one minute and the devil the next—'

Ben stood up too. He came round the table to her side as she swayed a little on her feet. He caught her hands tightly, seeing how her young breasts heaved in her agitation. In an instant he remembered their softness on that moonlit night on the moors. He remembered more, and wanted more.

How beautiful she looked, Ben thought. So stiff and unyielding, as though she would break in two in her anger… and yet she wasn't a woman who would break easily. She was strong, in a different way from his aunt's caustic strength. Morwen was a survivor, and he could feel it in every pore of her. Could see it in the luminous depths of her eyes, blue as the sea. Her cheeks glowed in the firelight's leaping flames. He almost envied the clayworkers at having such a champion… the thought reminded him of his indiscretion in telling her of his argument with his father. He still held her. He pulled her close.

The scent of her was in his nostrils, fragrant and young and fresh. She didn't move, and he felt a spark of anger at getting no response whatever from her. Ben Killigrew was unused to holding a frigid statue of a woman in his arms, and he wondered suddenly about the clayworker up on the moors…

'You visited home today, I believe,' he said abruptly. 'Did you visit John Penry as well?'

'Should I have done so?' she asked, her heart still drumming at his closeness, and hardly able to think it was jealousy that prompted the question.

'Why not? It would have been a courtesy to your friend's brother. But that's not why I asked, and you know it—'

'I know nothing, sir. I'm merely a clayworker's daughter.' She was deliberately wooden, and to Ben's own astonishment, he found himself shaking her.

'Dammit, Morwen, will you marry him?' he said arrogantly, and saw her chin tilt upwards again in that defensive way of hers.

'It's none of your business – sir. But if you must know, I'm not thinking of marrying John Penry nor anyone else. I'm not that fond of any man at the moment, so don't concern yourself that I'll be leaving Killigrew House the minute I've stepped into it. And – I'm sure Miss Carrick need have no worries on a young woman being in this house!'

'Why should she worry? And for God's sake stop calling me sir!' Ben said angrily. 'My name's Ben. You'll call me so.'

'Is that an order – Sir Ben?' Morwen mocked him, uncaring.

'Yes, it's an order,' he snapped. 'If you will persist in this ridiculous playacting, then I order it. And I order that you kiss me, this minute!'

Morwen gasped with fury. How dare he do this? She saw his eyes sparkle with the power he had over her. She hated him. She didn't want his touch or his kiss, or the treacherous way she knew her body would behave if he held her. Her mind would resist, but her body would betray her...

When she didn't move, he pulled her into his embrace, his mouth covering hers in a kiss that was almost brutal. And at once, Morwen knew that she had been out of his arms too long. It was where she had ached to be, and the glory of love swamped every other sensation as she felt his rough-textured cheeks against her velvety ones, and their two heartbeats felt as one. Her arms, that had stayed so rigidly by her sides, held him, and needed him.

His body was hard against hers, and she could no longer deny that wherever he touched her, it was like being caressed by a flame. He touched her and she was lost.

'Did you really expect to stay in this house and not continue what we've already begun?' Ben's voice was harsh against her mouth. She tasted his breath, breathed him, loved him with a passion to match his, delirious in the feelings he awoke in her. If this was a fever, then there was no hope of recovery, Morwen thought in ecstasy...

'What a pretty little scene, cuz!'

A new voice broke into the intimate atmosphere of the room, and Morwen jerked out of Ben's arms as though stung by a hornet as Jude Pascoe's crowing tones filled the air.

'So this is why you wanted to replace my mother with this baggage, is it, cuz? I congratulate you!'

In an instant, all the warm, beautiful feelings evaporated from Morwen's mind. In their place was humiliation, hate, shame, and more... there was guilt too, because she had sworn to despise Ben Killigrew as much as Jude for his part in the Larnie Stone disaster. She could just about forgive herself for swooning in his arms at that time, drunk by old Zillah's magic potion... she couldn't forgive herself for this sweet seduction in which she would have been so willing a partner, but for Jude's untimely arrival. Or perhaps it was fortuitous, she thought in a rage, as Ben turned on his cousin.

'Get out, you filthy-mouthed bastard!' he swore expressively. 'But you'll apologise to Morwen before you go—'

Jude laughed coarsely, his eyes on the taut nipples beneath the silky green dress. A look that made Morwen want to fling her arms defensively around her body.

'Apologise to a wench? I'll see hell freeze before that happens, cuz. But I'll not disturb you any more tonight. I just came to collect a few items. Carry on where you left off...' He grinned lewdly, backing quickly as Ben lunged across the room towards him.

Before anything happened, Morwen whirled away from them both, sickened at this scene by two so-called gentlemen. She fled upstairs to her own room, her throat tight with unshed tears. She should never have come here, knowing she was so uncontrolled by her own body. It had been for her family's sake... yet how could she leave, with all the implications of such a move? Explanations to Charles Killigrew that were impossible to make... no new home for her family, the shame of it all, the shadow over Sam's wedding...

She heard the click of her door-handle. She hadn't had time to light her candle, nor draw her cutrains. She turned swiftly, to see Ben there. Was it his turn now, to do as Jude had tried to do? Morwen thought bitterly. She backed towards the bed, fear drying her mouth. She had thought so much more of Ben. Disillusion made her throat ache anew.

He reached her and caught her up in his arms. Fury made her beat her hands against his chest. She was no milk-sop to give in without a fight, as Ben Killigrew would discover. He had scratched her cheek... she would do more than scratch his... it was a few moments before she realised that Ben's actions weren't those of seduction...

'Hush, darling, no one will harm you while I'm here. Calm yourself, Morwen, breathe softly, love. You're safe now—'

Safe? In the place she most wanted to be, here in his arms? Suddenly she was weeping silently against his chest, clinging to him as if to a lifeline. They sank to the bed together as her legs gave way, and he was smoothing her hair and rocking her as though she was a child. Then, without warning, all the secrets were spilling out of her, all the hurt and the anguish. And Ben Killigrew was the only person in the world that she could bear to tell.

'Dear God, is this true?' Ben said raggedly. 'My cousin raped your friend?'

'I swear it,' Morwen sobbed. 'Celia was too ashamed to tell anyone. But she couldn't forget, because there would have been a baby—' she rushed on, telling him everything.

'We didn't know what to do,' her voice shook. 'Old Zillah tried to help, but Celia did everything wrong. It began to turn her mind, and she called the baby a growth, because she wouldn't admit it was anything else. 'Twas

189

how I came by the idea of telling the doctor so, Ben, and how the tale got around.'

'What of the child?' The tale was horrifying enough, but he knew there was more to hear yet. Morwen drew a shuddering breath.

'The potion worked,' she said jerkily. 'She had so much pain while it – it happened. Next day she was found floating in the clay pool. I swore to keep her memory unsullied. I swore never to tell, and now I've told you!'

He felt helpless as he heard her bitter tears. It was too late for recriminations now, though he'd dearly like to make his bastard cousin pay... he said as much, and was startled at the fierceness in Morwen's voice as she looked feverishly into his eyes.

'No! He mustn't know. I couldn't bear it if he had that satisfaction. Promise me you won't reveal any of this. I'll deny everything if you do—'

He touched his mouth to hers to stop the words. He longed to crush her to him, but knew that she was in too fragile a state at that moment. She was brittle as parchment, and he guessed what a weight she had borne on her slender shoulders all these weeks.

'None shall hear of it, Morwen. It's our secret now. Just as long as my cousin makes no attempt to touch you—'

She was sure that he wouldn't, and related the happenings of her first evening in the house, leaving out her indelicate words to Jude Pascoe. Ben smiled gently.

'You're a girl after my own heart, Morwen Tremayne,' he said softly, and a sudden shivering ran through her. She knew how dangerously susceptible she was to his nearness, and he had been here long enough. She had tried to hate him, but the hate had been short-lived, and the love would last for always. But he wasn't hers to love...

'Would you please leave me now, Ben?' she said in a low voice. She was acutely aware that he had said nothing about love to her. He hadn't really commented on her remark that Jane Carrick needn't worry about Morwen being in Killigrew House.

Why should he? Jane was his true love, while Morwen would be merely a dalliance, and she did not choose to be that! She would be all or nothing to the man she loved. If Ben had already chosen his Miss finelady, then she would be nothing, and make very sure that he knew it. If she must act the prude and it broke her heart, then break it must.

'You're sure you'll be all right now?' He spoke with such tenderness her spirit faltered for a minute, but she gave a tight little smile as she nodded.

'Of course. You're all very kind, Ben. Your father treats me almost like a daughter, though it's presumptuous of me to say so. And if that makes you a kind of brother, then I'm doubly blessed and protected here.'

Ben gave a slow harsh laugh. He didn't believe for an instant that Morwen Tremayne thought of him as a brother. No woman could respond to him the way she had, and think only sisterly thoughts. He was about to speak angrily to her until he saw the desperation in her eyes, and knew that she was still wrapped up in the sad tale of her friend. For the moment, he must leave it at that, and he squeezed her hand gently before he left her.

He went downstairs to drink the cold coffee, and hardly tasted it. He stared into the dying fire, and knew he was far from averse to the girl with the dramatic hair and eyes and the body that seemed meant for his. She held an attraction that went far beyond the heady delights of the moment. He knew well enough how to sort the dross from the gold. And Morwen was pure gold, pure and lovely, and his thoughts were a mixture of sheer Cornish belief in destiny, and the impossibility of it all.

Chapter Fourteen

Sleep didn't come easily to Ben that night. As well as the disturbing things Morwen had told him, and his even more disturbing feelings for the girl, the scene with his father earlier that evening went round and round in his head.

'Where d'you think I've got money to spend on rail tracks, boy?' Charles had roared at him, when Ben had said bluntly that if they didn't move with the times, then Killigrew Clay was doomed. 'You're reacting like a hysterical female, Ben. Use your sense, and leave the thinking to those who understand clay business—'

'I thought that was what you wanted me to do, Father,' Ben said edgily, knowing he mustn't raise Charles's blood pressure too much. 'I've been trying to understand it for some time now. Even your precious little Tremayne girl made a case for rail tracks, didn't she? She riled my aunt on the subject if I remember rightly!'

'Morwen's a slip of a girl—'

'But she talks sense.' Ben hadn't meant Morwen's name to become an issue in all this. 'Listen to me, Father. Bultimore and Vine's have got rail tracks, and they're an undoubted asset. It puts up their status as a forward-looking business, and it labels us as old-fashioned for sticking to the old methods. How long do you think it will be before there are petitions from St Austell because of the way the clay waggons break up the streets and create havoc and danger to the townsfolk? You're an ostrich, Father, with your head in the sand.'

'And I suppose when you take over, the first thing you'll do is provide these rail tracks and put Killigrew Clay in the bankruptcy court,' Charles growled. 'Is that the legacy I'm leaving to you?'

'There won't be any legacy to leave if we don't act now!' Ben held his patience with a gigantic effort.

'Where's the money to come from? Tell me that!'

'You know there's enough. We both have stocks and shares to sell if need be. I'm willing to risk mine—'

'We could always delay the wage rises, of course,' Charles said sarcastically. 'Let the clayworkers have their little share in providing the luxury of rail tracks. How about that idea, Ben? If they want tracks so badly, let 'em help pay for them!'

'That's the daftest thing I've heard yet,' Ben snapped. 'You made a promise, and a Killigrew never goes back on a promise.'

'Remember those words, m' boy. Now you can tell Mrs Horn I want my dinner in my room, for you've tired me out with your arguments.'

Charles leaned back in his leather chair. Despite the heated words, he was well pleased in the way Ben was taking the clay business so much to heart. It cheered him more than his son knew. Maybe Ben saw the distinct possibility of holding the reins himself in the not too distant future, and wanted to be ready when the day came. But it wasn't due yet.

Charles's heart would give out one of these fine days, but he intended going out still roaring like a lion. It didn't do to give in to new-fangled ideas too quickly. Let the boy think he had to fight for his cause, and it would be all the dearer to him when he won. It was a philosophy Charles firmly believed in.

All Ben saw was the satisfied smile on his father's face, and stormed out of his room, feeling he'd got nowhere. If anything, he may have made matters worse. To delay the men their wage rises would be certain disaster. Only one thing was clear to him now. For better or worse, he'd staked himself firmly in Killigrew Clay's business. He was a part of it.

–

Charles was away from the house most of the next day, but by late afternoon Morwen sought him out in his study. There were two things she needed to know. One was if Charles meant to stick to his word and offer the new house to her parents. The other was about the delay in the clayworkers' wage rises. A woman didn't normally concern herself with such things, particularly a lowly bal maiden, but she was no longer a bal maiden, and it was important to her to know how things stood. She knocked at Charles's study with a fast-beating heart, and was told to come inside and close the door, for the day was cool and the house was draughty.

Morwen thought wryly that these fine folk didn't know the meaning of draughts while they had a roof over their heads that didn't let in the damp and the cold. She squared her shoulders as Charles looked up at her from his big desk, and spoke quickly.

'I wanted to ask you about the house for my family, Mr Killigrew. Our Sam's set the wedding date, and 'twill be a crush for 'em all in the cottage. I've said nothing about it, and 'twould be best if it came from you—'

Charles liked the girl's spirit. She was bold, but not too bold, and he could see the pulse beating at her throat. He smiled benignly.

'Well, m'dear, the house is vacant, and since I'm well pleased with your duties here, your father may move into it when it suits him. But you may tell your family whenever you wish, and then you'll believe it's true! Does that please you?'

'It does, Mr Killigrew!' She hesitated, wondering whether to leave it there, rather than stir up more trouble than she wanted. If she didn't know for certain that he didn't mean to delay the wage rises, or even stop them, then she needn't worry her head about it. But that was the coward's way out... and besides, Charles seemed aware that there was something more on her mind.

'Was there something else, Morwen?' Charles asked. 'I have a busy morning with these papers—'

'The wage rises, sir,' she blurted out. 'Ben – your son spoke of some delay in paying them – and of a discussion between you about rail tracks—'

Charles laughed. 'A discussion, you say? Is that how Ben described it? More like a battlefield of words, I'd say, with neither the victor—'

'And meanwhile the wage rises are put on one side, are they?' Morwen was appalled to hear her own shrill voice, but having begun, she plunged on. 'Do you have any notion of how much those pennies mean to clayworkers, Mr Killigrew? To folk who have little or nothing, they mean as much as your precious silver ornaments to you! Think on it, Mr Killigrew, when you dine off fine china, what a price the clayworkers have to pay to produce your riches. Excuse me, please. I have work to do!'

She spun round while his eyes were still widening at this tirade, but his voice stopped her.

'I'm sick of hearing about these blasted rail tracks that you and Ben seem to find so all-important,' he bellowed at her. 'I keep my men in full employment, don't I? Other pits have installed new machinery and cut man-power. Is that what you'd prefer for Killigrew Clay? It can easily be arranged—'

Morwen's eyes were filled with bitterness. 'And you'd threaten them with that, wouldn't you? You have a fine way with blackmail, Mr Killigrew.'

She ducked out of the study before he could say any more to her. The house was stifling her, and she had to get out of it. Regardless of her duties, she fetched a shawl from her room and slipped out of a back door, and used the same pony and trap as before without asking. It was a crisp afternoon, but Morwen noticed none of it as she urged the pony up over the moors towards the clay works. Her Daddy would still be working his shift, and she would find him in his pit captain's hut. Hal looked up in pleased surprise as his daughter burst in on him, but one look and he knew that this wasn't merely a social call.

–

'You're sure about all this, Morwen?' Hal said sharply, when she'd finished her garbled tale. He couldn't believe the boss would be so reckless as to stop the miniscule wage rises, or delay them even further. In other pits, such happenings had resulted in an immediate strike and then everybody suffered. And with winter coming on...

'I'm quite sure,' Morwen said unsteadily. 'Maybe I shouldn't be repeating it to you, but I felt 'twas my duty to my family. I needed your advice, Daddy, but 'tis true enough. Both Ben and his father have said so.'

'The men have a right to know of it too.' Morwen heard the simmering anger in her father's voice now. 'Who's to put food in their children's bellies if they're forced to strike? And their pride will see to it that they strike, Morwen, have no fear of it.'

'Maybe Mr Killigrew will reconsider, Daddy. He's not a heartless man—' Morwen said anxiously, remembering his kindness to her.

'And what of the son? We know nothing of his heart, girl. When he takes over, he could be ruthless. He knows none of us personally the way his father does, and he cares even less, since 'tis his ways he's trying to push on to his father from what you told me.'

'Ben's taking an interest in the works, Daddy, and rail tracks are his idea. You've always agreed with that—'

'I don't agree with the son seeing the pot of gold at the end of the rainbow, and the likes of us paying for it all,' Hal said grimly.

Morwen wondered what she had accomplished in coming here. She'd wanted her father's advice, but he seemed as dogged in his way as Charles and Ben had been in theirs.

'You won't let on that I've come here with this information, will you, Daddy?' she said awkwardly. 'My loyalty's to both of you, but it was too much to keep all to myself.' Hal smiled briefly for a moment.

'You know I'd never be so indiscreet, my love, and 'tis not my way. I'll go to Killigrew myself and demand to know why the delay in payment, and see what he has to say.'

Neither was aware that there was a small eavesdropper outside the hut. Neither saw young Freddie Tremayne skim over the damp ground, feet squelching, to catch up with the other kiddley boys sent to gather moss for ramming in nooks and crannies of the pit buildings to keep out some of the end of the year winds and rains. To be met with j eers and cat-calls for being last in the stream of small boys heading for the moors.

'Don't matter 'bout being last,' Freddie said importantly. 'Not when I know summat as you don't!'

'What could you know, Freddie snot-nosed Tremayne?' a son of Eric Leeman, the kiln worker, taunted him.

'Summat as our Morwen told my Daddy, see? 'Twill cost 'ee a ha 'penny to tell 'ee—'

He howled as the rest of them set on him, finding himself beneath a tangle of arms and legs. A circle of white clay-grimed moon-faces loomed over him and threatened to tear his breeches off and tan his arse if he didn't tell immediately what he knew. And Freddie, as always, gave in.

Morwen was glad to leave the clay pit and her Daddy's worried face, and to pay a brief visit on her mother. Twice in two days! And this time without Charles Killigrew's permission. And she didn't give a rap for it. She had news for Bess, and she related it quickly. Bess's face was astonished as she listened.

'A house for us, Morwen? Are you certain? A house with no other attached to it for warmth?'

Morwen laughed. 'Killigrew House has no other attached to it, does it, Mammie? It won't be as grand as that, mind, but 'tis a step up in the world, isn't it? You're pleased, aren't you? Mr Killigrew said that Sam and Dora could have this cottage, and 'twould be fitting for a newly-wed couple to be on their own—'

'So it would.' Bess remembered the day she and Hal had come to this very cottage, when she had been as radiant a bride as Dora would be. So long ago, yet no more than a heartbeat in time, and the love they shared still burned bright. It was right that Sam and Dora should begin in the same way, though Bess would have pangs at leaving this little cottage. But she was ever practical, and became brisk.

'Your Daddy should see Mr Killigrew about all this, Morwen—'

'I think Daddy will be seeing Mr Killigrew very soon, Mammie,' Morwen said quickly. She had no intention of saying any more about the other business. But she was reluctant to leave, and was still there, discussing curtains and bedspreads for the new house, when Hal came storming in.

'Has our Morwen told 'ee, dar?' he said at once.

Bess smiled, misunderstanding. 'Of course. Isn't it wonderful, Hal?'

His slow anger erupted in disbelief.

'Wonderful? Have you lost your senses, woman?'

He saw immediately that she didn't know all of it, and told her Morwen's news in short, staccato sentences. Bess rounded on her daughter.

'Why didn't you tell me this?'

'I – I wanted to tell you the other news, Mammie—'

'What other news?' Hal barked. 'It had best be summat good to offset all this!'

Morwen told him quickly, and heard him laugh shortly.

'Oh ah, and 'twould be a right time for we Tremaynes to move into a new house, wouldn't it? Right into a snug little house the boss puts at our disposal, so we're on easy street while the rest of the clayworkers exist as best they can on strike money from the fund!'

Bess's face whitened. 'You speak as though a strike's a certainty, Hal—'

'If the rest be true, then don't 'ee doubt it, woman,' he growled. 'And you can say goodbye to any notions of moving out o' here until 'tis all settled.'

Morwen could see the sick disappointment on her mother's face, and shared it with her.

'Mr Killigrew will find a way out of it, Daddy—'

'With his clever son talking about bringing in new machinery and throwing workers out of their jobs?' Hal was in no mood to listen to reason. 'This is the thin end o' the wedge, you'll see.'

'With rail tracks, there'll be more work in digging out and laying tracks, won't there? You always said the waggons needed replacing wi' rail tracks for the mens' safety—'

'Whose side are you on, Morwen?' Hal snapped.

Her eyes brimmed with tears. 'I'm on nobody's side!'

''Tis time you chose, then. You can't sit on both sides o' the fence at the same time—'

Morwen jumped to her feet, her voice tight with fury.

'I seem to have become the scapegoat in all this! I came here with some news for you and I wanted to make Mammie pleased about the house, and it was for our Sam and Dora too. It was because of the house that I agreed to work for Charles Killigrew! It was for all of you. You know I didn't want to go there!'

Bess and Hal glanced at one another, and Bess put her arm round Morwen's shoulder.

'Don't take on so, my lamb. When tempers have cooled, your Daddy will see that you did what you thought was right. As for the house, it was kind of Mr Killigrew, though I don't like the thought of my girl taking bribes. We'll have to see how things go on before we decide.'

'There's no decision to be made,' Hal snapped. 'I'll not be called a boss's man.'

Bess sighed, but she was more concerned right now with her daughter's distraught face.

'Tell me the truth, Morwen. Is it so awful at Killigrew House? If so, then you must come home at once. You always have a place here with us.'

Morwen swallowed. No, it wasn't awful there. She wasn't unhappy, but neither was she particularly happy, except at certain times... she wouldn't think of those now. She tried to weigh up the good and bad in seconds, while her mother waited for her answer.

She had so much at Killigrew House. Status and pride, a good home with no worries. Clothes on her back and payment enough to buy little feminine trinkets she'd never owned before. She was Miss Morwen to the kitchen staff. She slept in a large room of her own, and if the sheets weren't quite silk, then they were soft to her skin. She knew she could never return here. It was a lesson poignantly learned. You could never go back…

She hugged her mother so that she wouldn't see the truth in her eyes.

'I'm all right, Mammie,' she said huskily. 'Mr Killigrew's been very kind to me. I just wish everyone knew him like I do—'

'Everyone's going to see un in a very different light if this tale of yourn gets about,' Hal said grimly. 'We'll pray to God it stays buttoned up for the present, and comes to nothing.'

–

He discovered the futility of his prayers a few hours after Morwen had left for Killigrew House. Sam and the younger boys were indoors by then, the story told to them, and Hal was pacing the cottage floor like a cat walking on hot coals. Every nerve-end was tensed, as though he waited for he knew not what to happen.

They all became aware of the fast-growing noise outside at the same time. He and Sam reached the window together, recoiling at the jostling band of men heading for the Tremayne cottage, faces black with fury.

'Christ Almighty!' Hal didn't often blaspheme, but this visitation warranted it. The crowd was led by Gilbert Dark and the captains from Number Three and Four clay works. Hal knew instantly that somehow the story had leaked out. He threw open his cottage door before he had the indignity of having it battered down. Gil Dark roared out at him above the shouting of the clayworkers.

'Now then Hal Tremayne, it seems you be in the boss's ear-hole from your young whipper-snapper's tales. What's all this talk of rail tracks doin' the waggoners out o' their jobs, and new machinery coming in and making half the workers idle? And if Killigrew means to stop the wage rises, then we mean to stop working for un, and that's a promise!'

The bellows of approval from the others drowned out any more words, while Hal was still taking in the fact that Freddie must have heard himself and Morwen talking and got puffed up with his own importance at relaying the tale. And getting half of it wrong... the boy needed a thrashing, but that could wait. It was more urgent to calm down the men.

Gil Dark was a strike-monger. Hal could see he'd already whipped the clayworkers up into a frenzy. If the men had got so incensed on the march to town about the slowness of the wage rises, it was nothing to their fury if the money didn't appear at all.

'I know no more than the rest of you,' Hal shouted, to be immediately hollered down in disbelief.

'Why don't you bastards shut up and let my Daddy speak?' Sam roared back. 'You came here to hear him speak, so *listen*, damn you all!'

Gil Dark flapped his hands for quiet, and the shouts died to a growl as he taunted Hal and his eldest son.

'All right, boss's man. We're listening!'

Bess knew how Hal would hate the insult. Her heart beat like a drum as she heard the vibrato in Hal's normally quiet voice, and knew he'd be sick to his gut at being forced into this, when it was none of his doing. She saw how Freddie cowered at the back of the cottage, and would personally box his ears later, she thought grimly.

'I've been told nothing by Killigrew, and 'tis only rumours—' Hal was shouted down at once.

'Rumours be mighty powerful bedfellows! We want the truth on it. We want our jobs and fair pay for a fair day's graft, and you can tell Killigrew our terms or we strike—'

Roars of agreement followed.

'What good will it do to strike?' Hal was as white-hot as the rest of them now. 'Strikes never won anything, and the bosses allus come out best. Any fool knows that—'

'That be a boss's man talking, sure as eggs be eggs—'

Hal tried another tactic. 'Didn't we all agree that rail tracks would be better than waggons for shifting the clay to the port?' He had to shout to make himself heard. 'Why the sudden turnaround when 'tis suggested?'

'Nobody said nothing about jobs being lost when it happened—'

'Nobody's said nothing about it now, you daft buggers,' Hal raged, wishing his youngest son to the devil for starting all this by his innocent prattling.

'They'll not listen, Daddy,' Sam yelled in his ear.

Hal thought swiftly. They all looked to him to take command, being in charge of number one pit, and he waved his hands about for silence.

'Shall we find out the truth of it from Killigrew, then?' Shouts of approval met his words, and Hal glared around.

'Then I refuse to take sole responsibility for facing un, since you all seem set to doubt my word.'

Some of the men shifted uneasily, showing shame and embarrassment at the accusation, for of all men there, Hal Tremayne was the one most respected and trusted. Deep down, they all knew it.

'What do 'ee propose then, Hal?' Eric Leeman spoke up, knowing he'd started much of the present discontent after his own son had come running to him with Freddie Tremayne's tale.

'That we four pit captains go straight to Killigrew House tonight,' Hal rasped. 'You'll trust the four of us not to conspire against 'ee, will you? We'll find out what's to do, and report it back to you all tomorrow. Is it agreed?'

There were rumblings of ayes and nods and a few grudging cheers.

''Tis settled then. Gil Dark and Walt Pugsey from Number Three works can go in Pugsey's cart. Billy Brown from Number Four can come in the trap wi' me—'

'Oh ah, the boss's trap—'

Hal pushed his way through the crowd of clayworkers and caught the spokesman by the scruff of his neck and twisted.

'If you'd prefer to go instead of me, Leeman, just say so.' He let the man go, hearing him choke and splutter. The kiln worker backed down at the raucous jeers of his fellows, all knowing him for a loudmouth and not much else. Certainly never the type to face a boss in his own house.

'Does anyone want to change the arrangements?' Hal demanded. There was no reply. 'Then get back to your homes until there's summat to report, and try to think on the consequences of doing anything foolish.'

He marched back indoors, slamming his own door behind him. His breath came thickly, but he saw that he had his wife's approval in the plan, and Sam slapped his father on the back. Jack slunk at the bend in the stairs, his thirteen-year-old eyes fearful, and of Freddie there was no sign now.

'I'll deal with the boy when I get home,' Hal said curtly. He gave Bess a quick hug, turned and left the cottage. The men were still there, parting as Hal reappeared, and Billy Brown, the young pit captain of Number Four works, marched after him. Pugsey and Dark had gone to fetch their cart, within ten minutes the four of them were making the impromptu descent through the deepening twilight towards St Austell and Killigrew House.

Chapter Fifteen

It was late evening when the two vehicles wound their way back through the cobbled streets of the town, and into the pitch darkness of the moorland tracks, their way lit only by the swaying lantern on the Killigrew trap. They rode in silence, each mouth clamped tightly shut at Killigrew's reception of them, each mind working furiously on how to break the news to his men. They had until tomorrow morning... or thought they had...

'Good God Almighty!' Gilbert Dark broke the gloomy silence as they came to the rise in the moors leading to the flatter hill top. 'What do the gormless buggers think they'm playing at?'

Hal reined in the horse and trap alongside the humbler cart, his eyes grimly taking in the sight above them. From here, it resembled hundreds of glow-worms shimmering on the dark sky-line, but each of the four pit captains knew it was nothing so innocent.

None of the clayworkers had had any intention of returning home that night until the dispute was settled. They were encamped now, with lantern and torch flare and hooded candle, faces grotesque in the flickering lights, gaunt and wary as the pit captains neared them, crouched in the darkness and mindless of cold or damp. Gil Dark muttered uneasily.

'You'd best continue to be spokesman, Hal. You'm the best un wi' words.'

'Only if I have your backing,' Hal snapped. 'You all heard the boss, same as me. Are you all convinced I'm not in his pocket, nor ever have been?'

Three voices affirmed at once.

'Just so long as we're all agreed to let 'em have their way,' Walt Pugsey said. 'If they'm ready to strike, there's to be no stopping 'em. 'Tis their right.'

'I wouldn't be the man to try,' Hal growled, as the body of men rose at their approach, awaiting the report.

Hal tried to be as unemotional as possible, considering that emotions were tinder-dry and ready to explode at any minute.

'I don't need to tell 'ee how contrary Killigrew can be, nor how quick to rouse. He don't like his business dealings being questioned, and he don't like tales being bandied about that belong to him and his son and their accountant—'

'What's some poncey accountant to do wi' us?' The shouting began. 'Tell us about our wages and our jobs, Hal Tremayne. 'Tis what we're here to find out!'

Hal tried to shout them down.

''Tis the accountant that advises Killigrew on how the money should be spent, you dolts. There are bills to be paid, and money owing, and the advice was to hold back on the wage rises for a few weeks, that's all, until the money flows in—'

Howls of rage drowned him once more.

'What about our bills? What of the money owing to us, while the boss sits in his fine house? And what's all this talk of new machinery to put us all on the streets—?'

'There's no new machinery,' Hal bellowed. 'Nor rail tracks neither, though young Killigrew's bitterly keen to go ahead with that idea, which would benefit all on us if you'd only see it!'

He tried to be scrupulously honest about the scene at the house, with the six men hollering and bawling at one another. Charles had seemed no worse for the upset, thumping on his heavy oak desk and telling the pit captains to get out and sort out their men, which was what they were paid to do.

His eyes had sparkled with a strange mixture of anger and exhilaration when they had gone, but Ben's mouth had tightened with fury.

'That was very stupid of you, Father. They'll strike, and you know it!'

'Let them,' Charles said breezily. 'We can hold out longer than they can. I wasn't bluffing about the dues owed to us, and once they're paid, I'll be generous enough. They'll get their extra pennies and twopences, and they'll get it from the day I gave them my say-so. But let them sweat over it for a while. 'Twill prove to them who's the strongest here.'

Ben didn't like it. He would have liked it even less had he heard the outraged shouts high on the moors that night in the flaring torchlight, as the men of all four Killigrew Clay works elected to strike as from that moment.

''Twas a bad omen from the day the young Penry girl drowned herself in the clay pool,' one or two older ones muttered. 'The pit was fouled from that night.'

'We'll have none of that kind of talk,' Hal said angrily. 'You'll each report to your pit captain in the morning, when we've gone through what funds are available while the strike lasts. Now go on home, the lot of you.'

They dispersed grudgingly. While they were all together, they could ignore the coming weeks of hardship, when wives and children would suffer. The funds each pit captain had suggested long ago for times of emergency were pitifully small, but better than nothing when honour was at stake. And each man hoped fervently that the strike wouldn't last long.

–

What in God's name had possessed Morwen to go running to her father with tales? Ben thought furiously. Charles had stumped off to bed without bothering to rouse her and question her. The damage had been done, and if the autumn waggon-loads were a week or so late reaching the docks, it would make little difference to supplies of the clay blocks being shipped out, he had said stubbornly. It wouldn't be the owners who suffered in the end.

It seemed as though they continued the argument for hours, but finally Ben couldn't wait until morning to find out the truth of it. Indiscreet or not, he marched up to her room and hammered on the door. It inched open a few minutes later. From the candle-light behind Morwen, he could see the outline of her shape very clearly beneath the cambric nightgown and hastily wrapped shawl.

'What do you want? I asked Mrs Horn to tell your father I was coming to bed early with a bad head—'

Ben pushed past her into the room and closed the door behind him. Her heart beat rapidly with fear. Was he so like his cousin after all…?

'You'll have more than that by the time I've finished,' he snapped. 'Do you know what you've done?'

Morwen stared at him, realising that this was no young man bent on seduction. He looked at her with contempt, and a sick feeling washed over her. She knew at once what he'd come about. Her chin tilted in the way he often found endearing, and which now seemed to infuriate him.

'If you mean did I think it wrong to inform my daddy of the delay to the mens' wages, or even stopping them altogether, then no! I didn't think it wrong to tell him. It was his right to know, and I think you and your father are guilty of underhand business methods—'

'What do you know of business methods? A mere—'

'Go on, say it! A mere bal maiden, without a brain in her head. That's what you were thinking, isn't it?'

'No, it wasn't,' Ben snapped. 'I was about to say you're a mere girl, and should leave mens' work to the men. But after your interference today, I doubt that any of them will report for work tomorrow.'

Morwen's skin felt clammy all over. She had heard her parents speak of strikes, with dread in their voices. With a young family to feed and no money coming in, what hope of survival did they have?

'You don't know that it will come to that,' she said, her lips wooden.

'I do know it. The pit captains came here as a deputation tonight. I wonder you didn't hear the rumpus from my father's study. Yours was the spokesman, and it was obvious where the story came from, though it's got embroidered in the telling, and the men now think we're about to replace them with machinery.'

'I didn't say that! Do you think they'll strike, Ben?'

'Of course they'll strike, thanks to you!'

He turned on his heel, and horrified tears sprang to Morwen's eyes. She felt so unreal. She had taken a headache powder before she went to bed, and she felt too muzzed to deal with this tonight. And she hadn't meant any of this to happen. She had only wanted to warn her own family... she ran forward to clutch Ben's arm. She had to make him see that she'd meant none of it... her shawl slipped from her shoulders, and the words wouldn't come. He was so angry, a stranger to her. Her fingers involuntarily dug into his arm.

'I'm sorry, Ben,' she said tremulously. 'But I can't bear it if you blame me!'

He looked down at her. Her black hair tumbled around her shoulders, dark against light. Her face was white, her eyes shimmering with tears, her soft mouth trembling with shock. He gave a smothered oath and gathered her into his arms, feeling her sway against him. She was still warm from sleep, still bewildered by the swift change of events. His fury vanished like the dawn mist on the moors. He saw the long line of her throat and the pulse fluttering there. He wanted to hold her and love her...

'You'll catch cold,' his voice was husky. 'You shouldn't be out of bed.'

He scooped her up in his arms as though she was feather-light, and moved towards the bed with her. She could feel his heartbeat, as wild as her own. As he lay her down, his breath was warm on her face. Her hands were still clasped behind his head, and without thinking, she tightened them, imprisoning him to her. His mouth touched hers, as gentle as thistledown, and then more urgently, demandingly...

It was as though Morwen had held all her emotions in check since the night at the Larnie Stone, that had begun so excitingly and ended so horrifically. As though she had been made of ice since then, and now at last the sun began to shine and the ice to melt... wrong or right were words neither of them considered as they moved together, first tremulously, then more surely, in an overwhelming need for each other. The first time for Morwen... the only time that mattered to Ben...

Into Morwen's scattered thoughts came the certainty that this was so different from Celia's ordeal... it had to be different, because every touch of hands or mouth brought pleasure instead of pain, a new and exquisite delight... though there was a moment when Morwen struggled to speak, when she remembered Celia...

'Ben, don't – don't hurt me—'

'Don't be afraid, my sweet one,' he said softly against her breast. 'I won't let anything happen to you, though I must confess it would be the sweetest thing to know you carried my baby, but it won't happen, Morwen. Trust me, darling.'

His voice caressed her senses as his body caressed hers, and she didn't question how it could be that he knew so much about loving. She questioned nothing in the wonder that he was here with her, and wanted her. It was so beautiful to be wanted, so loved...

By the time Ben left her room, Morwen was drowsy with sleep once more, and a wonderful feeling of well-being. She hardly remembered how it had all come about, how the anger burning between them had somehow turned into love. It didn't matter how. If she had nothing else, she had had this one precious night...

She awoke with her head throbbing more painfully than before, and struggled to recall what had happened. The memories flooded back together. The fury in Ben's eyes at the certainty of a strike at the clay works. And the hour in his arms that followed... she lay and thought about that for a long while, and slowly Morwen's face burned, wondering in the cold morning daylight if she had been incredibly foolish.

All the loving feelings had gone, and she felt bitterly that she had become what she always despised — the servant who was a willing bed-mate for the master's son. How would he treat her this morning? How was she meant to react to him? She had been a fool, a gullible fool, for he would never want her as a wife. Not when he already had a wife promised to him!

She looked at the clock on her table, and sprang out of bed, wincing as she did so. It was late, and she should be downstairs, organising breakfast. It was too much to hope that Ben would be gone from the house. The gentry didn't usually rise so early. But to her amazement, Jude Pascoe was lounging in the dining-room, and grinning widely at her, to Morwen's annoyance.

'Looks as though there's fun and games going on, don't it, Morwen? My uncle and cuz went off at a fine rate early this morning to see what's to do at the works. Seems as if the men are striking or summat.'

Morwen looked at him coldly, saying nothing. She didn't have to talk to him. His eyes narrowed, still with that offensive grin on his face.

'Still, you'll be all right, won't you? I'd say the Tremaynes have come out of this little lot pretty well.'

'And just what's that supposed to mean?' she was provoked into snapping.

'Well, you've got a job away from the pit, haven't you? Your Matt's doing all right at the docks, and don't your Mammie take in sewing for the gentry now? A strike needn't bother the Tremaynes too much with all that money coming in!' he taunted her.

Morwen was scarlet with rage. But despite her anger, she began to realise how the clayworkers would see it – the way Jude Pascoe outlined the facts. And there was more. If her parents had moved into the little house away from the cottage, they'd have been thought even more in Charles Killigrew's pocket. As it was, this strike effectively stopped any such move. Her father would never agree to it now. And how would that affect Sam and Dora's wedding? The enormity of it all was only just beginning to dawn on her.

'Don't you have work to do?' she snapped at Jude.

'Oh ah. Me and your Matt have got some business of our own down the coast aways,' he leered. 'We're taking a job on a trawler to Falmouth way to see if there's any dock work going there. We're getting tired of the same old faces here.'

It would be good riddance to him, Morwen thought viciously, but she didn't know what her Daddy would say to Matt moving even farther away from the family. Everything was changing, she thought, in a moment of blind panic. Nothing ever stayed the same, no matter how you tried to keep things safe… she swallowed, because that kind of thinking was for children, like Freddie, and she was supposed to be a grown woman now, with responsibilities…

Charles Killigrew and his son went straight to Number One clay works. The men were on strike, but it seemed that none of them could keep away. They hung about in groups, arguing and muttering among themselves, and plenty had had tongue pie from their wives for breakfast. The pit captains were still sorting out the strike fund, and spread among all the men, it would be meagre dippings. And there was no knowing how long the deadlock would continue. There was a rumble of apprehension as the Killigrew men approached the pit.

'Where's Hal Tremayne?' Charles demanded to know.

'In his hut, Mr Killigrew, sir,' he was told sullenly.

Charles eyed them keenly.

'Are all you men agreeable to this strike?' he bellowed suddenly. 'Do you know what it means to go hungry for weeks on end, with your womenfolk belly-aching at you to return and bring home some regular money?'

'We ain't going back on our word,' the men started yelling. 'We're striking for our rights, so you go back to your fancy house and leave us to get on wi' it!'

'Father, you're doing no good here,' Ben said angrily. 'You'll have a seizure—'

'Dammit, don't tell me what to do!' Charles roared at him. 'When I want a nursemaid, I'll send for one—'

'You've already got one, haven't 'ee?' someone in the crowd jeered. 'What's young Morwen Tremayne doin' at your big house, if tain't nursemaiding 'ee? Or mebbe 'tis the pretty young sir she minds of a night—'

The man was jerked off his feet by Hal Tremayne's fist seconds before Ben himself reached him.

'I'll deal with this, Mr Ben,' Hal's eyes were cold as ice. "Tis best if you and your father go on to my cottage if 'tis words you want wi' me, and leave us to sort out our own business.'

'This is our business too, in case you've forgotten it, man!' Ben shouted back. 'We want the men to go back to work. A strike does nobody any good—'

'And we want our money, and to know what's what,' the men shouted angrily. 'If there's to be rail tracks, then let's know about it. If there's to be new machinery, then give us your promise we'll not suffer because of it—'

'You'll do the work you're paid to do, and we'll do our job of overseeing it,' Charles bellowed. 'Bosses don't have to account to you—'

He gave a sudden shout of pain as a stone struck him on the side of the head, and a trickle of blood oozed out.

'All right, you bastards, that's enough!' Hal stepped swiftly between the Killigrews and the menacing crowd of men. Sam and young Jack closed in on either side of him, and the men paused.

'Get out of here, sir, while they're hesitating,' Hal said shortly. 'I'll meet you both at the cottage. Bess will see to that cut for you.'

'For God's sake, Father, do as he says,' Ben said roughly, knowing that a cheer would go up as the Killigrew men turned tail. It was galling enough, but it was better than being set upon by this mob. He'd argued in vain against his father coming here today, and in the end had felt obliged to come with him. The two of them rode quickly to the Tremayne cottage and rapped on the door. Bess was aghast when she saw Charles's cut cheek. When they were seated, she bathed the cut with warm water and ordered the man to hold a cloth against it to stem the bleeding.

'You shouldn't have come, sir,' Bess said. ''Twas best left to the pit captains for a while, until tempers cool.'

'Who's the boss around here, woman?' Charles growled in a weak try at humour. Bess looked at him seriously.

''Tisn't a question of boss and worker now, sir. 'Tis who's going to give way first, and the men think they've had a raw deal with being made to wait for their money.'

'Is that what you think, Bess?'

She shrugged, looking at him squarely. 'A fair day's work deserves a fair day's pay. That's what I think. And they're stubborn men, sir, with as much pride as any owner.'

She dumped the bowl of water in the sink, uncomfortable at having these two fine men in her cottage so early in the day. Charles looked around him, seeing how cosy Bess had made it, and made a clumsy attempt to lighten the conversation.

'You've a pride in your home, Bess, and even more in the new house, I daresay—'

She looked at him in astonishment.

'We can't go now, sir. Surely you know that! How would it look, if we deserted our striking fellows and lived in a fine new house? Oh no, that'll all have to be postponed indefinitely—'

'But that's ridiculous—'

'No, it's not, Father,' Ben put in. 'Mrs Tremayne is quite right. A lot of things will be different now.'

'Well, the strike won't last for ever, will it? Good God, we need the clay, and you need money to live. We' re all dependent on one another in this life—'

'Try telling that to a woman who can't put food in her baby's mouth in two week's time,' Bess said caustically. 'And then remember that you could put all this right by one word, Mr Killigrew. Give the men the wage rises they've been promised.'

Ben saw his father's lips thin to a mutinous line. He wouldn't be dictated to, no matter what the consequences. If only he was in charge, he thought savagely... but right now, that likelihood was as far away as the moon, with Charles blustering as loudly as ever, and not ready to hand over the business to his son until the day he dropped.

He was sorry for Bess Tremayne, seeing the disappointment in her eyes when she'd refused to move to the new house. He respected her for it, but things could be difficult for her too. And for himself... Ben hadn't really considered Morwen's position in the Killigrew household before, but he was considering it now. It could be impossible for her... he hadn't allowed himself to think of her at all since last night, and he didn't know how the blazes he was going to face her when they got back.

She had seemed so warm and loving... but he didn't need a crystal ball to tell him that the Morwen of last night was a very different one from the one he was going to encounter when he and his father went home. He couldn't bear the thought of her scorn. He'd had a glimpse of heaven in her arms last night, and in the silent hours that followed, he'd been honest with himself. He loved Morwen Tremayne more fiercely than he'd loved anything in his life before, and the thought of her in his arms was like a drug to his senses.

Her mother was offering him some cordial, and Ben wondered if the truth was written on his face for all to see. He waited impatiently for Hal to come home, wishing himself well away from here, and wondering just how much more tangled his life and hers were going to be.

Chapter Sixteen

Morwen had made up her mind. The situation here would be impossible. Hal had told her to choose sides, and so she would. She left all the clothes she had been given in a neat pile on her bed. She left a note for Charles Killigrew with the cook. She no longer felt under any obligation to him, and he would surely understand that. Her family would have to refuse the new house now, and Morwen was free to leave Killigrew House.

But not without a pang. She looked around the pretty room, her throat thick. It had been very sweet to act the lady. She had loved this room… and it was here too, that she had found love… so much love… for such a little time.

She turned quickly, before she could falter. Her place was with the clayworkers, not here with the bosses. This strike had shown her that all too clearly. She belonged with the likes of John Penry, not with Ben Killigrew. She wouldn't have it thrown at her that she gave herself airs and graces, while her friends starved.

Some might say that she should stay, and bring in some money for her family. Well, she had too much pride, even for that. She had one week's wages to offer, and she could help Bess with the sewing for the time being. Thank God for her Mammie's skills, and for sharing them with Morwen.

And Matt too… surely he would help them all. The Tremaynes wouldn't go under. They were all survivors, every one. While Charles Killigrew and his son were riding on to Truro to discuss the matter with Charles's partner, Richard Carrick, Morwen arrived home at the cottage on foot, and dumped her few belongings on the table.

'I'm home, Mammie,' she said thickly. 'Is there still room for me?'

Her voice wavered until she saw Bess open her arms, and Morwen rushed into them. Here she was safe…

Bess looked at her searchingly. 'Are you sure you want to stay, my lamb? 'Twon't be easy—'

'I want to be with you all. I can do some of your work, Mammie, and I've brought my wages for you. It's not much, but if it'll help—'

Bess's eyes were damp as she hugged her daughter. Every penny would help from now on. She became brisk as she told Morwen to change the sheets in her bed corner, and that it would be almost like old times again. They avoided one another's eyes, because nothing would be the same again.

'Where's Daddy and the boys?' Morwen asked as she worked. 'I thought they'd all be here.'

'The pit captains will be at the works each day to see that the pits stay idle. They'll have no scabs at Killigrew Clay. Sam's gone to tell Dora the wedding may have to be postponed a week or two, and the young uns are with your Daddy, thinking 'tis all a bit of excitement.'

Morwen looked at her mother. 'How long can it last, Mammie?'

'There's no telling, love. A strike is always ugly, until somebody gives way, and we've a strong-minded boss in Mr Killigrew. He won't want to give in to his clayworkers. It becomes a matter of principle in the end.'

'Even if he gets no clay produced or shifted? How long can that go on?'

'I don't know.' Bess became edgy. 'But we can't change anything by bleating about it all morning, so if you mean to help me with the sewing, there's plenty for you to do, Morwen.'

—

Richard Carrick was stunned and alarmed by his partner's news that morning. Across his heavy lawyer's desk in Truro, he faced the Killigrew men, his face troubled.

'We could put an end to all this at once, Charles,' he said meaningly.

'Pay 'em their extras, y' mean?' Charles barked. 'Yes, we could do that, but it'll do them no harm to be without wages at all for a few weeks. They can't be allowed to dictate to us.'

'I've tried to make Father see reason,' Ben put in angrily. 'It's madness to stop clay production at this time, with winter just around the corner, and the autumn waggon-loads not yet ready to be sent to the docks. We've orders that won't be met if the strike lasts any length of time.'

'It can't last. I've told them the situation. When we get the payments due to us, they'll get theirs. It's business, boy. You know it as well as I do. If the damn fools want to strike, it'll be their loss, not ours.'

'I'm not so sure of that, Charles,' Richard said. 'We must think sensibly, and not go at it stupidly—'

'Do you think they're sensible?' Charles began to redden with anger. 'They don't want new machinery because of some crazy notion it'll put them out of jobs, when new machinery's never even been mentioned! They do want rail tracks, but Gorran's advised us not to think about that until we get a better cash situation—'

'I think we should forget Daniel Gorran's advice,' Ben said curtly. 'He's too cautious by half. We should take a risk, Father. I've told you I'm willing to sell my shares to make rail tracks viable, and I think you should do the same.'

Charles glowered at his son. 'You know nothing about the business side of things, boy—'

'I know more than you seem to think,' Ben snapped. 'I've not been wasting my time since I got home from college. I've a brain, Father, and I've been using it. Rail tracks aren't out of the question, and you're as short-sighted as Daniel Gorran if you don't see that.'

'I'm tired of hearing about bloody rail tracks!' Charles shouted, beads of perspiration beginning to dot his fore-head.

'They're not the issue here, are they?' Richard Carrick intervened hastily, although privately he wondered about that. 'What we want is to settle this strike quickly, so that no one loses face. All right, Charles, we'll give them a couple of weeks and see if they're ready to return to work with the promise of their wage rises when our dues come in. Meanwhile, a strong letter to each of our debtors is the first priority. I'll see to it at once.'

Ben got to his feet, annoyed at being made to feel young and inexperienced in business matters, when the solution was as clear as the nose on his father's face, glowing so rosily now.

'I'll call on Jane and her mother while we're here, Father. Don't bother to wait for me. I'll borrow one of the Carrick horses to get home.' He spoke shortly, wanting to be out of his father's company as soon as he could, and guessing the feeling was mutual.

He couldn't wait to be out of the stuffy chambers. The air around the Truro river was pungent, but preferable to the claustrophobic atmosphere of old men who wouldn't budge in their ways. Maybe he did have radical ideas, in wanting to give the workers what they deserved, but he was fair minded too, and it was wrong to give with one hand and take away with the other, which was what the wage delay amounted to.

He walked to the Carrick House, needing the exercise, and needing time to think. An idea was simmering in his mind. His father wouldn't like it, but there was nothing new in that. Charles seemed opposed to anything he said or did lately.

The thought of Morwen Tremayne surged into his mind, warm as summer, and he wondered about Charles's reaction to that too. About the fact that his son had lain with her and loved her, and wanted her more desperately than he'd wanted anything in his life before. And what would Morwen's father say to it? Hal Tremayne, with all the fierce pride of his class, would be just as disapproving as Charles Killigrew. To hell with the lot of them, Ben thought blazingly. Whose life was it, anyway?

He was glad to find Jane at home alone, her mother out visiting a friend for the day. Jane's eyes were sparkling, and anyone could see that she was in love. Presumably her parents knew her too well to even notice, Ben thought perversely. He had no time to say what he'd come for, before she took both his hands and drew him down besideon the sofa in the drawing-room, her face flushed.

'It's all arranged, Ben,' her voice was breathless. 'Tom's leaving Truro in two weeks' time, and I shall go with him. You promised not to tell, but when I've gone I'm trusting you to assure my parents I'm not leaving you with a broken heart! They'll be upset enough without having you on their conscience, but it's the only way, Ben. They'd never agree to a marriage between Tom and me. Father ranted about the latest articles Tom wrote, exposing the lot of the pilchard-fishermen. He just has no time for newspapermen, however right their cause—'

She stopped as Ben's grip on her hands tightened, realising that he wasn't listening any more.

'Does your Tom have the guts to print a damning article about the owners of Killigrew Clay, Jane? There's no need for him to mention your father, since few know he's a partner, and I wouldn't want to cause your mother any more distress. But something's got to be done. My father won't listen to reason, and I've thought it all out—'

'What are you talking about?' Jane said in bewilderment. 'If there's a story to be told, Tom won't balk at it, but think what you're saying, Ben. A damning article about Killigrew Clay will hurt you as well as your father. Why should you want Tom to write it, anyway? What's happened?'

He told her briefly. Her eyes widened, especially when he was obliged to say how Hal Tremayne had come to hear of it, quick in his defence of Morwen's part in it all.

'You think a lot of her, don't you, Ben? You may hide it from everyone else, but you can't hide it from me.'

'Then I won't try,' he retorted. 'But tell me if you think Tom will co-operate. If the story is exposed, it may push my father into paying the wage rises at once. Other pits will leap on the story and make offers to the Killigrew workers, and if we're not careful, we'll be left with pits and no men. Tom can hint at that too. Anything to bring Father to his senses!'

'Why don't we go and ask him?' Jane said. 'I admire you, Ben, but I don't know that I agree with your methods.'

'I think Tom will,' he stated grimly. It was the kind of story on which the *Informer* thrived, and he'd never appreciated its usefulness until now. Charles would hate to be thought a skinflint. Ben still didn't care for Tom Askhew, but he was a champion for the working-classes, and he was just the catalyst Ben needed to make his father see sense.

'He'll be at his rooms now,' Jane said quickly. 'He goes there for a bite to eat in the middle of the day.'

'Then let's waste no time,' Ben said. 'I've plenty to do this day.'

Including talking to Morwen. There were things to be settled between them, and he had to clear the air of the nonsense about Jane. She had to know that his affections were given elsewhere than to Morwen's Miss finelady... but all that must wait awhile. He was determined to put his case to Tom Askhew, although he didn't particularly relish enlisting his help.

Tom listened with narrowed eyes as Ben tersely outlined his idea.

'You take a risk, Killigrew,' the Yorkshireman said bluntly. 'Your father could cut you off without a penny, if that's the right phrase your sort uses.'

'Never mind all that,' Ben told him angrily. 'Will you print the piece, man? I didn't think you'd be lily-livered enough to refuse—'

'Neither I am,' Tom growled. 'But I'm thinking o' Jane's father, and the two of us. Carrick's a partner in Killigrew Clay, I understand, and 'twill be bad enough for Jane later on, knowing her parents' feelings. I'll print the piece and welcome, but only on the day we leave Truro, as a parting gesture—'

'And have folk say you were too yellow to stay and see the outcome?' Ben demanded.

Tom's face was furious. 'There'll be nowt like that said about me, Killigrew. I may leave the town, but the paper will continue in the same spirit I began it. I've seen to that. I've given you my word on your article, so take it or leave it.'

'I'll take it—'

'Good. Maybe 'twon't be needed, if things are settled by then, but if you're still wanting my services, then we'll rough out the piece together when you've a mind to it.'

There was nothing more to say, and Ben was glad to take his leave of the fellow. He wished Jane well of him. All he wanted now was to borrow one of the Carrick horses and be on his way home to see Morwen. To his secret annoyance, Jane's mother had returned home from her visiting, and he was obliged to be the gentleman and take lunch with her and Jane before he left.

–

The minute Ben entered Killigrew house, he heard the shrill voice of his Aunt Hannah, excitedly jabbering to his father in the drawing-room. There was no way he could avoid being seen, since the door was wide open, and nor could he miss hearing what Hannah Pascoe was saying.

'I couldn't believe my ears when Emily came rushing home with the tale going around the town, Charles. The story's come from one of your maids, so don't tell me it's false! Your clayworkers have gone on strike, and that haughty young miss has left your employ. You'll be needing a reliable housekeeper, so I've decided to swallow my pride and come back. And not before time by the look of the dust on the mantel—'

Charles's voice suddenly roared out into the room, and Ben guessed that he had been drawing breath all the while his sister had been talking.

'You'll wait until you're asked, woman, and it'll be a damn long wait, I promise you! And since you've pushed your way into my house, I might tell you that I've not seen hide nor hair of that useless son of yours since yesterday—'

'I was coming to that. Jude came to see me this morning. He and that Tremayne fellow have taken a sea-going job. I thought you'd at least be glad to know he's working.' Hannah managed to sound affronted and condemning of the entire Tremayne family at the same time. Ben strode into the room.

'Are you saying that Morwen's gone, Aunt Hannah?'

She looked sourly at her nephew, so well turned out, despite his dusty ride, compared with her scruffy son.

'You always took too much interest in that girl, Ben. Good riddance to her, I say.'

Ben ignored her, and looked directly at his father.

'Is it true?'

Charles handed him the short note Morwen had left. Ben scanned it quickly. Morwen was no scholar, but she wrote with dignity in a large childish hand:

> *You must see that I can no longer stay here, Mr Killigrew. My place is with my family. I'm sorry, for you've been kind to me. Please take good care of yourself.*

It was signed simply 'Morwen Tremayne'.

There was no mention of Ben, nor presumably any note for him. Why should there be? he thought angrily. Yet, after all they had been to one another, to leave like this... or did she think it had merely been a diversion for him? She would think that, of course. Girls of her class always did... he cursed himself for the thought, for it was a long while since he had thought of Morwen as anything but his equal. Background didn't matter. The feelings between a man and a woman did...

'You see, Ben?' Hannah said vindictively. 'Girls like that have no loyalty to their employers. I could have told your father this would happen—'

'Will you be quiet, woman?' Charles shouted at her. 'And get out of here before I throw you out. If you see your son, tell him he needn't come back either. I'm glad to be rid of you both.'

Hannah stared at him in disbelief. 'What are you saying? You need me back, Charles! This house can't run itself—'

'Whether it can or cannot, I'll not have you in it, woman! I'll hire a dozen extra servants before I let you loose in here again. Now get out of my sight before I change my mind about the allowance I send you every month.'

Hannah's mouth fell open. She and her dear friend Emily had been scratchy with one another of late, and if her brother had not been so touchy, it would have been good to slip back to the family fold again. But if he wanted to be pig-headed, then she wouldn't beg for favours. She swept towards the door, not wanting to betray how shaken and furious she felt.

'I wish you luck, Charles. From the rumours circulating in the town, I think you'll need it. They're saying that Bultimore and Vine's will be taking your men away from you, so the strike won't do you an ounce of good. When you decide to settle it, you'll have no workers left at all.'

The door slammed behind her. Charles winced, but Ben cared nothing for his aunt's temper. He'd heard it all before. She'd be more worried about her own allowance than any hardship to clayworkers, he thought drily. He was more concerned with Morwen's departure, and by the white look around his father's mouth that he noticed with sudden alarm.

'You'd best sit down, Father,' he said abruptly. 'I'll get you some brandy.'

'I don't need brandy,' Charles brushed him aside. 'The damn woman told me nothing I didn't already know.

The other owners will be quick to offer jobs to our best workers. They'll be hanging round them like vultures in a few days.'

'Then give them what they want, for God's sake!'

'I won't. Not until I'm good and ready. Carrick agrees with me now—'

'You mean you forced him to agree,' Ben said bitterly. 'You manipulate everyone, don't you, Father?'

Charles glowered at him. 'You said that to me once before, if I remember rightly. You disappoint me, Ben. I thought when you came home from college, you'd be an asset in the business, not a bloody obstacle! I thought we'd see the partnership of Killigrew Clay made doubly solid when you and Jane Carrick were wed—'

'And I thought I'd made it clear that I'm my own man, Father, and not one that you can use as your puppet. I'll marry whom I please, when I please, and it won't be to further the business. That's a promise! Now – do you want me to go and see Morwen and tell her to stop this silly nonsense and come back?'

'I do not. I admire the girl for standing firm, and so will you. The strike will be over in days. Clayworkers don't like standing idle. They'll come to their senses soon enough, and we'll not go near them for a week. Do you understand me?'

'I think my brain's working adequately enough,' Ben said sarcastically.

'Ask Mrs Horn to come in here,' Charles said next. 'She knows a good woman who'll stand in as housekeeper while we get all this sorted out. Morwen will be back here soon enough.'

It would never be soon enough, Ben thought, as he strode out to the kitchen to find the cook. Morwen had been here such a short time, and yet the house was empty without her. She had become a part of his life, and he wanted her back. He was tempted to ignore his father's wishes, and go to the Tremayne cottage immediately, but he knew that would be hot headed. It may also antagonise the Tremaynes from their fellow clayworkers.

Ben cursed the class differences that drove a wedge between him and Morwen, but he was forced to admit that they existed. Right now, Hal Tremayne wouldn't thank Ben Killigrew for coming to his cottage and persuading his daughter to leave her family. If Morwen had to choose again, Hal would lose face with his men... Ben raged inside at the frustration of it all.

He wondered if he had been so wise to approach Tom Askhew about the article in the *Informer*, and was grudgingly grateful now that he had two weeks' grace until it appeared. By then, the strike might be over. If not, then it would be surely time for more action. He pushed the unease out of his mind, and thought instead of the odd remark his aunt had made.

His cousin and Matt Tremayne were off on a sea-going job, were they? He hoped it was as innocent as it sounded, but knowing Jude he doubted it.

–

He would have been even more alarmed if he'd been able to see the two of them a week later. The trawling ship that had taken them to Falmouth had put to sea again, and Jude and Matt had money in their pockets and were looking about for more excitements. They knew nothing of any clayworkers' strike back in St Austell, and Falmouth was a hundred times livelier than Charlestown port. There were rogues and pickpockets, the scum of any waterfront, and there were colourful characters too, boasting of voyages across the Atlantic and coming home to England richer than they ever dreamed...

'There's a ship looking for hands, mateys,' they were told. 'If you're not afraid o' hard work, with a pot of gold at the end of it—'

'What d'you think, Matt? Do we cut our losses and go?'

Matt wasn't so sure. There were thousands of miles of ocean between here and America, and the tug of home was still there. Besides, how could he just go, without leaving word for his family? And there was none here, in this ill-assorted company, that he'd trust with a message to them.

'I'll need time to think on it,' he said slowly. 'I'm no seaman, Jude. I'm a pit worker—'

'There's plenty o' jobs for experienced pit-hands,' the sea-salt put in. 'What's your trade, boy? Tin or copper?'

'Clay. Tell me there's clay-pits, and I might think about it,' Matt grinned, sure that the man knew as much about America as he did, and that was nothing at all.

'There's everything in America,' another added his tuppence. 'They say the country's so big 'tis like bein' in another world. Ain't you seen the posters in town asking for pit-workers to apply for passage with a view to settling?'

'We ain't been here long enough yet,' Jude said. 'Where are these posters?'

'Along the waterfront. You can't miss 'em if you're goin' to Miss Lottie Flynn's, and that's where most young buckos make their way when they've got money jingling in their pockets!' He made a gesture they couldn't misunderstand.

'I reckon that's where we were heading, then,' Jude said. He gave Matt a sidelong glance. 'Well, Matt? Caught your fancy, has it?'

'Why not?' But Matt couldn't have said if it was the delights of Miss Lottie Flynn's establishment or the lure of the posters advertising for pit-workers across the sea that attracted him most at that moment. He'd never considered it before, but he was considering it now, just as long as he didn't have to make an immediate decision. He was still enjoying his freedom, and this town with the wide expanse of harbour and the vast array of ships in it looked a good base for a week or two. America may be another world, but so was Falmouth to Matthew Tremayne, and he wanted to enjoy this one before moving on.

Chapter Seventeen

Morwen pulled the shawl more tightly around her body. October had begun with an unexpectedly cold spell. The wind was bitter on the moors, where the mist had lingered all morning, but the atmosphere in the Tremayne cottage was so tense and uncomfortable that she was glad to be out of it. She and young Freddie were searching for sticks for the fire, and he was grumbling all the way. Finally Morwen stopped walking and shook his shoulders.

'It's no use going on at me for summat that can't be helped,' she snapped. 'I didn't start this strike, but we've all got to do what we can, and our job today is finding wood, so stop your snivelling and help me!'

'We'm gettin' close to old Zillah's cot, and you know what Mammie would say about that. You wanted to come here, I'll bet!'

Morwen sighed. All Freddie's teasing seemed to have deserted him lately, and she couldn't blame the child. Everyone was on edge, wondering what the outcome of this strike was going to be. They'd seen nothing of the bosses, and that was making the men who gathered at the pit each morning angrier than ever. They were taunted too by clayworkers from other pits, with money to spend and more so-called sense than to strike at this time of year.

'I don't want to see old Zillah—'

'Why not? Mebbe she can tell us when we'll be getting proper days again,' Freddie retorted, contrary as ever.

Truth was, Morwen hadn't set eyes on the old crone since Celia's death, and nor did she want to be reminded of that dreadful time. There would be too many things to remember, painful and beautiful, and she had closed her mind to all of it. Leaving Killigrew House had meant leaving her dreams…

'Hellfire! There she is!' Freddie nudged her hard. It was as though old Zillah's cottage had suddenly appeared like a mirage in the mist, and the old woman peered out at them from the doorway. Morwen licked her dry lips, too startled to rail at Freddie for his language.

'Come you inside, my pretties. 'Tis a bad day for wandering abroad, and old Zillah's glad of a bit o' company.'

'Don't go inside, Morwen,' Freddie whispered at once. ''Tis said she cavorts with the devil in there—'

'Don't be stupid, and don't be such a baby. I've been in there before, and no harm's come to me.'

Morwen stopped abruptly, unsure of her own words. She was too truly Cornish to disbelieve in magic, and whatever the outcome at the Larnie Stone, she couldn't deny it had been Ben Killigrew's face she had seen, and it had been the face she'd wanted to see…

Her footsteps seemed to move towards the cottage in spite of herself, and Freddie stuck close to her skirts, muttering all the way. He didn't want to admit to his sister that he was scared stiff of old Zillah, but he was.

'You've had a sad time, missie,' Zillah croaked as soon as they went inside, and the familiar cloying smells filled her nostrils. Freddie screwed up his nose, unable to hide his reaction to the place. He looked round fearfully, jumping as one of Zillah's cats curled itself around his legs.

Morwen jumped, hoping Zillah wouldn't refer to Celia in front of Freddie. The boy's ears were too long already, listening to things he shouldn't hear. But Zillah was too canny for such indiscretions.

'And now I suppose you'm wanting to know how long you'm to be scratching for firewood like old Zillah, instead of living the lady's life, is that it?'

'Let's go, Morwen,' Freddie said fearfully. Zillah looked at him, perched on the edge of her hard bench.

'Be 'ee afeared o' me, young un? There's no need. Old Zillah means 'ee no harm. Warm yourself by my fire and I'll give 'ee a bundle o' sticks to take home with 'ee. Your face is fair pinched with the cold.'

He stretched out a tentative hand to the blazing fire in the hearth, relaxing a little. Morwen was reluctant to ask any questions of the old crone, but since she had brought it up, she couldn't resist it.

'You know all about the Killigrew strike, then, Zillah. What are your thoughts on it?' she asked cagily.

Zillah cackled, thrusting a mug of dark hot chocolate into each of their hands, whether they wanted it or not.

'My thoughts are that men are fools. 'Tis women who should rule the world, then folk would get things in their proper order, like putting food in their childrens' bellies and letting them sleep warm at night. Stubborn men need the shaking of an earthquake afore they come to their senses.'

'We don't have earthquakes in Cornwall, thank goodness,' Morwen said quickly, as Freddie sat agog and fearful.

'There's more than nature that can move the earth,' Zillah said in her droning visionary voice. ''Twill take summat o' that importance to make yon Killigrew right his wrongs.'

'You agree that he's done wrong then in not paying the men their dues?' Morwen didn't really care whether old Zillah thought so or not, but she wanted to bring the talk about more ordinary matters for Freddie's sake.

'That's for him and his to discuss. Now, if you'm both warmed, I'll fetch 'ee those sticks, and I daresay your mother will be wanting 'ee back home soon. Seems like we'm in for a storm, and you'd both be best indoors out on it.'

Morwen looked out of the window. The mist had all gone now, blown by a strong wind from the sea that moaned through the bare bracken. She shivered, and thanked Zillah quickly for the bundle of sticks. Home was the best place to be when a storm got up.

It was much colder when they stepped outside the hovel. They raced back across the moors, Morwen's skirts flapping against her legs, and before they reached the Tremayne cottage, too anxious for talking, the first great spots of rain were lashing down. Bess looked up with relief, all her brood safely indoors now... all except Matthew, and she could only hope he was somewhere safe as well, and not on the boiling sea around the Cornish coast.

'We've been to see old Zillah,' Freddie said importantly, once he could get his breath. Morwen glared at him, knowing Bess's thoughts on it, but now that the fear was gone, Freddie was busy preening himself on the adventure.

'I've asked you not to go there, Morwen,' her mother said angrily. 'I know she's reputed to be harmless, but I don't want Freddie to get involved with her nonsense—'

'She said there's to be an earthquake—'

'No, she didn't—'

Morwen's defensive voice was drowned in the guffaws of laughter from Hal and her other brothers. Freddie's face was scarlet as he tried to protest that old Zillah had definitely said the earth was going to move…

'And we're all going to be millionaires by Christmas!' Hal ruffled his youngest son's hair and refused to take any of it seriously. The boy was fairying to make a good tale, and mocking him was the best way to take the heat out of Bess's reaction to visiting the old crone. 'What say we have a game of charades to pass the time—?'

'You boys can if you wish,' Bess said tartly. 'Morwen and me have work to do in the kitchen, and then we'll get to the sewing. There's pennies to be made and it seems we two are the only ones to make them at present.'

Hal's face darkened, but he'd vowed to do his utmost to keep the house harmonious, and didn't rise to the bait as his wife and daughter went to the tiny kitchen and left him and his sons to themselves.

'Well?' Bess said at once. 'Did the old woman give any indication to the length of this strike?'

Morwen stared. 'You do believe in her powers, Mammie!'

'I never said I didn't,' Bess retorted. 'Just that I didn't want any of you visiting her. Was there any hint of an end to it? I know she talks in riddles—'

Morwen shook her head. 'Nothing sensible. Only some talk of an earthquake, and different ways of making the earth move than through nature. I didn't understand it. She referred to Mr Killigrew as a stubborn man—'

'Well, it didn't take a soothsayer to tell us that!' Bess looked at her daughter, her voice softening. 'Do you miss the life there, my lamb? You took to it so sweetly—'

Morwen turned away, fighting the sudden tears and the tightening in her throat. It wasn't the house she missed…

'I'd rather be here with you,' she lied, but she didn't meet her mother's eyes as she spoke.

'Let's get these potatoes ready for the soup,' Bess said briskly. 'There's bread to dip in it, so let's be thankful for what we've got. I hope our Matt's faring as well, wherever he is. I suppose we should be glad we've one less mouth to feed in these hard times.'

Morwen guessed that her mother's thoughts were very mixed on that score. Bess missed Matthew more than she admitted, and Morwen gave her mother a quick hug.

'He'll be all right if I know our Matt,' she said huskily. 'He'll come home the fine gentleman one of these days, you'll see, Mammie!'

She didn't altogether believe it, any more than Bess did, but neither of them would admit it.

–

They would have been even more alarmed if they had heard the waves of excitement in Falmouth that night. From kiddleywink to kiddleywink the word spread like forest flames. A ship had been sighted down the coast a little way, heaving and rolling, and listing heavily to starboard as the gales pushed her nearer and nearer to the jagged black rocks. There was going to be a wrecking, and

Jude Pascoe's greedy little eyes were alight with thoughts of it.

'This is it, Matt! By the end o' the night, we'll be rich! No more grubbing about on filthy trawler decks. We can live the good life for a while.'

'What about the poor devils on the ship?'

Jude shrugged. 'They're no concern of ours. Spoils of the sea are there for the taking, and 'tis you and me who'll be in on the taking this time. Unless you're turning chicken, o' course!'

'Nobody calls me chicken,' Matt snapped.

'Then let's get some sacking to put round ourselves and be on our way. We're in for a cold wet night, but 'twill be worth it by tomorrow morning. We could even buy our passage on that ship for America you've been dreaming about,' he taunted Matt, knowing how often his thoughts had strayed in that direction.

'We could even do that,' Matt agreed, putting his uncertainty behind him. Anyway, there were enough of them now, making their way south along the coast to where the floundering ship had been sighted. The sailors would hopefully wade ashore or be able to cling to the wreckage and be saved by those on shore. He was naïve enough to believe it.

Some hours later, frozen through, and wishing himself anywhere but on a miserable stretch of moorland above the churning sea, Matt began to reverse his thoughts. He was surrounded by a vast crowd of men, women and children, all intent on watching for the first sign of merchandise bobbing about on the huge seas that crashed onto the rocks. White spume cascaded over those too impatient to wait above and already crouched on the rocky beach to claim their spoils, and finally Jude grabbed at his shoulder, pulling Matt behind him to scramble down the cliff, stiff and aching in every limb.

'Come on,' he said harshly. 'We ain't been here all night for some other buggers to take what's rightfully ours!'

'You can hardly call it that!' Matt said.

Listening to the jeers of his fellow wreckers all night, and the cheers whenever the stricken ship lurched still nearer to the churning water, he began to feel sickened by what was happening and what he knew now was inevitable. There was no intention of saving the poor wretches whose occasional cries for help could be heard in a small lull in the thundering waves. They were as doomed as their ship, and Matt would be as guilty as anyone here of leaving them to drown.

'What d'you think will happen to that fine French brandy and wine if we don't take it?' Jude demanded. 'Look around you, Matt Tremayne. We're all wreckers here, all tarred wi' the same brush, so don't put on your fine airs now. 'Tis too late for that—'

Whatever else he might have said was lost in a sudden mighty roar from the throats of the wreckers. They seemed to rise up behind him and Jude in one surging mass as the ship suddenly heaved over, creaking and gurgling as though with some hideous death rattle as it was enveloped in the foaming sea.

The wreckers almost knocked Matt down in their rush to retrieve the ship's cargo as it was unleashed from the holds. Brandishing sticks and flaring torches, they rushed to the beach and out thigh-deep into the water. Wherever they met the unfortunate sailors they crashed them about their heads, to Matt's growing horror. Survivors would tell the tale, Jude hollered in Matt's ear as the two of them were pushed and pulled with all the rest, part of them whether they wanted to be or not.

And Matt did not want to be with them. He panicked, seeing for a minute his mother's face in the greedy caricature of the hag alongside him, screaming to kill the bastards before they got ashore and roused the preventive men… his mother would disown him if she ever dreamed he could associate with scum like these, Matt thought in sickened shame…

'Look out, Matt!' Jude suddenly shouted as he floundered in the sucking waves, his hands grabbing the bottles of French brandy that slid by him and losing them just as quickly. Matt turned his head, in time to see a sailor staggering ashore, terror rolling his eyes. The sailor saw Matt at the same time, bent and grabbed a piece of rock and slammed it against Matt's head. It rocked his senses for a minute, and then he knew it was a case of survival between the two of them.

He ducked and weaved as the rock came for him again, and knew raw fear for the first time in his life. The breath was ragged and painful in his chest. It was the sailor's life or his. He grabbed at the man's throat, squeezing, pressing, feeling the pulse in his neck and almost ready to puke. He could hardly see for rain and spray and tears, and couldn't have said which was which. He was killing a man, and it burned into his conscience even as he did it…

Suddenly the sailor went down silently, his body limp in Matt's hands. Matt couldn't stop himself from falling, swallowing sea water and nearly blinded by it. It seemed an eternity before he felt strong hands hauling him off the sailor's body, to which he seemed to have become attached like a leech.

'Christ, but you nearly throttled him,' Jude said in admiration. 'I finished him off for you, Matt. I grabbed some poor bastard's knife and stuck him in the back. He won't bother anybody again.'

Matt retched, spewing into the already tainted sea. It was a nightmare and he was never going to wake up... he felt as if he must slide about in this bloodied water for ever. It was his penance... he ducked his head beneath the freezing water as though to rid himself of the sight of the wreckers and their victims, only to be dragged back to the surface again and onto the shingle beach.

'What are you trying to do?' Jude yelled in his ear. 'Have 'ee found summat worth saving down there?'

Not any more, Matt wanted to scream at him. There was only the remnants of a man who wouldn't be returning to his woman after a sojourn at sea. He felt like weeping...

'Preventers!... Preventers!...'

The words suddenly rippled through the wreckers as the shrill whistles of the Preventive Men were heard above the noise of it all.

'Bastards! Before we've had a chance to get anything worth taking,' Jude said savagely. 'Quick. Let's get away before they pin this murder on us. We won't be the only ones guilty of it this night, but they'll be looking for scapegoats once they find the bodies floating.'

Gasping and near to sobbing, Matt followed Jude up the cliff, scrabbling for footholds and near to collapsing with fear and fatigue. Was this what they all found so exhilarating? This shameful night would be a permanent scar on his mind. He would never be able to face his father again. The guilt must surely be written in letters a foot high all over him.

Once he and Jude reached the moors they crouched silently for a few moments until it seemed safe to move on, with the Preventers' activity all concentrated on the beach below. Other wreckers sped by them, some with spoils, some blaspheming at their untimely interruption. And he was one of them, thought Matt sickeningly. He was just as bad as any of them.

'I've got to get away,' he said in a wild panic. Jude's hand clamped over his mouth as they knelt panting to get their breath. Jude's voice was as harsh as Matt's, and he knew that Jude was as scared as himself.

'Ain't that what we're doing, toe-rag?'

Matt clutched at his arm, digging his fingers into the cold flesh.

'I mean right away,' he said hoarsely. 'I can't face any of my family after this, and I've no wish to be hounded by the Preventive men or sent to gaol. There's a ship bound for America, Jude, that's looking for hands. I mean to be on it, and you can come with me or not.'

'Why not?' Jude said slowly. 'I've been pissed on by my uncle and cousin for long enough. They wanted to be rid of me, and now they can be rid of me for good. I'm with 'ee, Matt!'

They sped on in the darkness, under cover of the driving rain and scudding low cloud over the moors. Matt's heart thudded wildly, but somehow it was as though his whole life had been leading up to this. He'd always been the dreamer in his family, and his yearning to be different had almost led him to disaster. He felt a gnawing pain that he might never see his parents and his brothers and his dear Morwen ever again, but it was the price he had to pay.

If he stayed, the price might be much higher, he thought grimly, remembering the face of the sailor he thought he'd killed. He had as good as killed him, he thought. The blame was shared between him and Jude, and in that they were bound together. They had to leave Cornwall and England, whatever the pangs, and as soon as possible. The ship was due to leave Falmouth in two days' time, providing the weather improved, and there would be two extra hands aboard when she sailed.

There was only one thing Matt insisted on, when he and Jude were steaming in front of a meagre fire in their lodgings a while later. He refused to simply disappear off the face of the earth without letting his family know what had happened to him, and grudgingly Jude said he may as well send his mother word as well. They arranged it cleverly.

Not until the morning the ship sailed did they give the notes in care of a coachman travelling between Falmouth and Truro. Jude had sniggered when they'd seen the coach depart.

'That'll set the cat among the pigeons,' he sneered. 'I never did like those Carricks, thinking themselves above everybody else, but Richard Carrick will feel obliged to deliver the notes. That's one thing about our so-called betters, Matt, they're sticklers for doing the right thing. We needn't bother our heads about 'em again. We're as good as on our way, boy!'

Matt's thoughts were too private to be shared with Jude just then. He had tied himself to this lout, but whatever

Jude's feelings, Matt was already missing his family, and mourning them as if they were dead. Which they might just as well be to him. And they might just as well think of him in the same way, because it was unlikely that they were destined to meet again.

–

Richard Carrick was too busy to ride to St Austell himself with the two envelopes the coachman delivered to his chambers two days later. He paid a boy a few coppers to take the notes to their destinations, one to Jude's mother at Miss Emily Ford's house, and one to Miss Morwen Tremayne, care of Killigrew House, where Matt firmly believed his sister to be still employed, and whom he had thought the best one to tell his news.

As the ship left Falmouth harbour and out into the broad expanse of water beyond, Matt looked back at the receding coastline, his heart full. What he did now he felt obliged to do, for his family's sake as much as his own. If the murder of the French sailor had been traced to him, his father would never get over the disgrace of it.

Sadly, Matt knew that he had already gone far away from them all. He didn't know how far. If he had been aware that his family was caught up in a strike at Killigrew Clay, he may have thought twice about his decision to leave. But he didn't know, any more than Jude did. Falmouth might have been as far from St Austell as America, for all that the news filtered through so slowly.

It was better that he should disappear out of their lives for ever than bring disgrace and pain to their door. But as the shores of Cornwall merged into a misty blueness, he knew he had never loved them more.

Chapter Eighteen

Richard Carrick had been unwise in his choice of messenger boy. The urchin met some skallywags and promptly forgot the two notes stuffed inside his shirt until it was too late that day to deliver them. It was several days later when they began to feel itchy against his skin, and he started out for St Austell. It mattered little to the boy. He'd had his payment, and bits of paper he couldn't read were of no consequence to him. They were for rich folk who lived in big houses like the one called Killigrew House, outside which he gawped and hesitated, before handing them in to a skivvy.

—

Inside the house a fierce argument was taking place. Ben had been to Gorran's chambers that morning to try to get Daniel Gorran to back him in the strike settlement, but though the old man sympathised with Ben's opinions, he said tersely that while Charles Killigrew's health lasted, he was the man in charge, and new-fangled ideas must wait.

'Your loyalty does you credit, but in other words, you're saying that my father has to die before progress can be made,' Ben had said bitterly.

'That's an unpleasant way of looking at it, Ben—'

'But nonetheless true,' he'd snapped. 'I can see I'll get no help from you, Daniel, and I'll bid you good-day.' He'd gone out into the crisp October morning, breathing heavily, furious with frustration. He felt at odds with everything. He and Charles constantly argued. His aunt still irritated his father by her visits to the house in the hope of being reinstated as housekeeper, and finding fault with the new one, Mrs Tilley.

And he missed Morwen more than he could say. He hadn't seen her since the strike began. His father had been adamant that neither of them should visit the works until the men's tempers had cooled, but it was getting them nowhere. He had taken one positive step though. He had been to Truro and roughed out the article with Tom Askhew. It should be appearing any time, and when it did, Ben would know that Tom and Jane had left Cornwall. More upsets to come, he thought grimly...

He strode off by way of the Killigrew Clay offices, and stopped short. A small crowd outside was being pacified by two constables. When they saw Ben they turned on him.

'There's the son, Constable! Sort it out wi' him and let's have some order in the town! We won't have ruffians disturbing our peace because of the Killigrews, however important they think they be!'

'What's happened?' Ben said, pushing through the angry crowd. As soon as he was near enough, he saw for himself. Windows had been broken and stones hurled through them. There were daubings on the walls of the offices.

'Does anyone know who did this?' Ben demanded.

'They say 'twas a gang o' clayworkers, Mr Killigrew,' one of the constables said. 'Came here early this morning and smashed up the place—'

''Twill be our homes next if you don't sort out your own affairs, Killigrew,' the crowd became menacing, and the constables puffed themselves up and moved closer.

'Do you think we like this any more than you do?' Ben said angrily.

'Ah, but 'tain't your home that's wrecked, be it, sir?'

'Nor yours,' Ben retorted. He turned to the constables. 'I'll send someone to board up the windows before any more vandalism's done, if you'll stand guard in the meantime.'

'I think 'tis a wise move, sir,' one of them said meaningly. The onlookers didn't look too savoury themselves, and Ben guessed that there'd be few fittings left in the offices if these rogues were let loose. Ben nodded and pushed his way through, more alarmed than he showed.

This was the beginning, and the clayworkers must be getting desperate. It was sheer folly to let the strike continue with no communication between the two sides. He rode home in a fury, his horse lathering by the time he reached Killigrew House. He slid off the animal's back and marched into the house.

His father stood by the window in the drawing-room, his back stooped. He had become oddly shrunk of late, despite being a powerfully made man. Ben ignored the alarm he felt on that account. There were more urgent things to be sorted out. Before he could tell Charles about the offices, his father turned, holding out two grubby notes for Ben to see.

'Read these,' Charles said harshly. 'The envelopes were so tattered they were almost in shreds, and the paper's none too sweet. One's meant for your aunt, the other for Morwen Tremayne.'

It was only the mention of her name that stopped Ben impatiently discarding the notes. He took them and read them quickly. He was glad to see the back of his cousin, but he guessed what Matt Tremayne's departure would mean to his family. In that instant he knew what he had to do.

'I'll take the note to Morwen myself, Father—'

'You will not!' Charles snapped. 'You know my views on going there just yet. Give them time to sweat—'

'Freeze is more likely,' Ben said angrily. 'Do you know what they've done today? They've broken windows in our offices and daubed the walls—'

'What?' Charles roared. 'The bastards! This calls for an extra week before we meet them—'

'No, it does not.' Ben glared back. 'I shall take this note to Morwen, and I'll talk to the men. Short of locking me up, you won't stop me. This farce has gone on long enough. Since I understand family feeling, which you apparently do not, I'll pass on Jude's note to my aunt too, though as far as I'm concerned, it's good riddance to him.'

Charles's face was puce with rage, but Ben didn't stop to see it any longer. He wasn't a child to be treated as such. The days when his father could dictate to him were over.

He stopped only to saddle a fresh horse, and rode to Miss Ford's house, slipping the note through the letter-box. Now for the Tremayne cottage, Ben thought grimly, and wondered just what kind of reception he would receive there.

Hal was striving in vain to quieten a meeting of his clay-workers. Number One pit was oddly still without the trundle of the little waggons to the sky-tips. The kilns were silent, and the only fires were those around which the clayworkers huddled in blankets to keep out the cold and damp, grudgingly listening to their pit captain.

'You're fools if you think violence will get you anywhere,' Hal had to shout above the din. 'It was madness to go to Killigrew's offices and smash windows. Someone will end up being killed—'

'What of our families being killed wi' no food in their bellies and no warmth in their cottages? Killigrew's the murderer, and the bastard stays smugly in his big house while the likes of us starve—' they hollered back.

'We'll send a deputation—' Hal tried again.

'We don't want no more talking. We want our dues! Can 'ee give us they, Hal Tremayne?'

'My Daddy's not God!' Sam intervened angrily.

'No, but he's a boss's man,' some began to chant.

'If he were that, would he be standing here wi' us all in this weather?' Sam shouted back. 'He'd be warmin' himself by his own fire, and we've little enough o' that. We send our children to gather sticks, same as the rest on 'ee.'

'All right, Sam, we may as well let them go home. They'll not see sense—' Hal muttered wearily.

'No more will Charles Killigrew,' Sam snapped. 'Why isn't he here to sort this out? Groups of them are talking of going to Bultimore and Vine's. Did you know they're offering free ale at the kiddleywink for all Killigrew's men who'll go to a meeting to talk over terms? I don't know

254

how many have gone already, but 'twon't be long before they do. They can't hold out. The strike pittance won't help the large families, and you know what they're like. When they've had money, they've spent it. None of them are savers—'

A commotion near the gate momentarily stopped the growling discontent among the men. Freddie Tremayne came running towards them, his blue eyes wide with alarm. He gasped to get his breath as the words tumbled out.

'Daddy, you'm to come home quick. Mr Ben Killigrew's there wi' a note for our Morwen, and when she read it she fell about crying, and so did Mammie, and they won't tell me what 'tis all about, but said I had to come and get you and Sam and our Jack, and to say 'tis urgent.'

At mention of Ben Killigrew's name the clayworkers moved in a body behind the Tremayne men. They raced over the moors to the cottage, where the clayworkers stayed silently outside until they knew what was to do. Ben's horse was tethered to a post, so it was clear he was still there.

Hal went to his wife's side. Her face was red and filled with pain, and he saw that she and Morwen had been crying.

'What is it, dar?' he said harshly.

Bess's throat was thick. ''Tis our Matt, Hal. He's gone across the sea to America. He left from Falmouth three days ago wi' that cousin of Ben's, and he sent us a note. 'Tis all we have of him now, Hal—'

She began weeping again, the silent tears running down her face, more awful to him than violent sobbing.

255

He folded her to his chest, not yet ready to see any note. He heard young Freddie begin to wail, and Jack was sniffing loudly, finding it hard to be a man at that moment. Morwen went to comfort Sam, who looked as stricken as any of them, and Ben could only stand by helplessly, hating himself for being the one to bring even more sorrow to them.

It was Morwen he wanted to hold, to comfort, but after the first shock of seeing him when her heart had leapt in her chest, she had seemed as aloof as on that first day he'd seen her in St Austell town, and had his first brief contact with her in his arms.

He ached to have her there now, to be alone with her and say all the things he wanted her to know. But this wasn't the time. These moments belonged to her family, and he felt very much the interloper. They were the strong ones, Ben thought suddenly. They supported and comforted each other, while he and his father, who were supposed to be so superior, were more often at each others' throats. It was ironic and poignant at the same time.

'I'm sorry to bring you such news, Hal,' he said awkwardly. 'Perhaps you'd like me to leave now—'

Hal turned from Bess at once. Even now, part of his mind could be with his workers, Ben thought humbly, as it became obvious that personal problems must be put aside. Hal spoke gruffly.

'The men are outside, Ben. It'll make things worse if you don't say a few words to them. They're in an aggressive mood because your father hasn't come to the works—'

'I know that. I've seen our offices this morning, and I've every intention of speaking to them,' Ben said curtly.

Suddenly he couldn't bear to be in this little cottage. He'd seen it filled with so much love, and today it oozed sorrow. He wanted to be away from it. But he couldn't leave Morwen like this.

'My father asked me to speak to you, Morwen,' he invented quickly. 'Perhaps we could meet somewhere else a little later. I've intruded here long enough.'

He didn't dare to suggest meeting at the Larnie Stone. It was too far distant on such a day, but it would have been a sweet trysting-place... but Morwen would be in no mood to think of such things. She said that if Charles wished Ben to speak to her, then she would be walking over to the churchyard where Celia was buried, since it was her day to visit her friend's grave. She would meet him inside Penwithick church.

His eyes met hers. As if there was a sudden telepathy between them Ben knew instantly that Morwen intended telling her friend that the hated Jude Pascoe was gone for good... or was he going as mad as the old woman on the moors for letting his imagination run away with him? He nodded to her abruptly before going out of the cottage to face the clayworkers.

—

'What's to do, Killigrew?' they shouted at once. 'Has your father come to his senses?'

Ben looked at them coldly. 'My visit has nothing to do with the strike. It's a personal matter for the Tremaynes. If Hal Tremayne wants to tell you, then it's his place to do so—'

'The whelp's as stubborn as his father,' the shout went up. 'They sit on their arses in that big house o' theirs, and

257

care nothing about us. We can all starve. I say we take Bultimore and Vine's offer, men. Take the free ale and take the jobs they'm offering!'

Ben's voice was drowned in the cheers that echoed round the men. Several of them bent to pick up stones, and threw them at him. He dodged as one of them grazed his cheek, and waved his arms frantically; knowing he'd made an appalling mistake. He'd been caught out by his own emotions inside the Tremayne cottage, and now he was paying for it.

There was no stopping the stampede of clayworkers away from the row of cottages. From the direction they took, Ben guessed they were making for the rival pit. He had failed miserably. He stumbled away from the cottage, not wanting the Tremaynes to see his humiliation. His senses were reeling as he straddled his horse and galloped off across the moors.

For the moment he was too upset to remember his meeting with Morwen. But after half an hour's hard riding, she was the only sane thing in his mind, and finally he turned back towards Penwithick. Once he reached the church he tied up his steaming horse and went inside the old stone building.

It was dark inside, and he couldn't see anyone at first. He couldn't blame her if she'd decided not to come, Ben thought bitterly. She'd probably witnessed the whole scene outside her cottage, and thought he'd gone home like a dog with its tail between his legs.

'Ben.'

His heart stopped beating for a moment as he heard her soft voice from one of the high-backed pews. He caught sight of her long black hair as the shawl slipped away from it as she rose to meet him.

'What was the message from your father?'

She paused, looking at him mutely for a moment, her eyes still swollen from the tears shed over Matt, and he covered the distance between them in long strides. Pride held her taut until he pulled her swiftly into his arms, and then she was soft against him. All the way here he had agonized over the right words. And now there was only one thing he could say.

'There was no message, and you know it! God, Morwen, I've missed you so,' he spoke roughly against her hair. 'I've missed you—'

'Have you? You haven't been near me—'

'You know the reason for that! It's been impossible, and you made it plain that you wanted to be with your family. It would have made things worse if the clayworkers had seen us together in that way—'

She looked up at him, her mouth trembling a little, the colour warm in her cheeks. She wouldn't give him an inch.

'In what way, Ben?'

'Do I have to spell it out for you—?'

'I think you do,' Morwen said gravely. 'I'm a mere bal maiden, a clayworker's daughter, sir, and I don't have your education—'

He held her fiercely, bending her backwards and holding her head in his hand to kiss her mouth and to feel its swift response to him. He thanked God for it.

'You have everything I ever want or need,' he said. 'You have my heart.'

Morwen drew in her breath, wondering if this was really happening... she still couldn't quite believe he was here... and then the memory of what had brought him here this day rushed into her mind. How could she have forgotten it so soon! Her eyes misted over, and her face burned.

'Ben, I must go home. My mother's distraught over Matt's leaving, and I mustn't stay away too long. She'll need me.'

'I need you too. You know that, don't you?'

She had to ask. 'And – and your Miss Jane Carrick?'

Ben smiled gently. 'Miss finelady, you mean? Would it surprise you to know that she's going to marry someone else very soon, and move right away from here, my Morwen? I can't tell you any more than that, but it's another secret you and I share.'

Morwen's blood sang at his words. There was something else she needed to say.

'Did you guess why I came here today?'

'To tell Celia that Jude had gone for good,' he said calmly.

'And you didn't think I was crazy?'

He touched her mouth with his finger. 'Why should I? I'm as Cornish as you are, and there are some things only we understand. You had to come here, to make Celia content.'

Between any other two people the conversation might have seemed totally illogical, but Morwen knew he understood her completely, and now at last she felt as though her heart brimmed over with love for him.

'You know we can say nothing about our feelings until this damn strike's settled?' Ben went on. Her face whitened again.

'I'd forgotten! How could I have forgotten?' In an instant the barrier was there between them. He the owner, she the champion of the clayworkers. She wriggled out of his arms. 'Have you any brilliant ideas for putting an end to it?'

'None that my father will agree to,' he said caustically. 'Sometimes I wonder if we're of the same stock, we think so differently. He's the most obstinate man in the world. I think it will take a miracle to shake him.'

'Or an earthquake,' Morwen said with a shiver.

'You're cold, my love. Let me take you home, or at least part of the way.'

He didn't say that it was best that they weren't seen on horseback together, but he didn't need to. They left Penwithick church and she sat in front of him on his horse. As they rode, her hair streamed against his face, and suddenly Morwen put her hand against his cheek.

'You're hurt, Ben. There's blood on your face.'

He'd hardly noticed the sting of it before.

'It's nothing,' he said brusquely, forcing a laugh. 'Maybe you scratched me the way I scratched you with my pin that first day. Do you remember? When I said I had branded you?'

'I remember,' she said softly.

She said no more about it, but she was perfectly sure she hadn't been responsible for the cut on his face. She asked to be put down a fair way from the cottage. The mist was swirling again, conveniently hiding them from prying eyes. Ben kissed her swiftly. Morwen clung to him, and the moment was sweet.

'Trust me, my darling. I'll do all I can to get this thing settled,' he promised. Then he was gone, his horse's hoofbeats soon muffled by the sodden October ground.

—

Ben had every intention of declaring his love for Morwen Tremayne to his father the instant he got home. Charles Killigrew should know that he couldn't mark out his son's life from infancy, and both Ben and Jane had minds of their own, and would love whom they chose. He stormed into the drawing-room, to stop at once on seeing Richard and Mary Carrick there. Richard's face was ashen, while Mary continued weeping even more noisily the minute she saw Ben. He knew immediately...

'Have you seen this rag?' Charles shouted at his son, thrusting a copy of the *Informer* under Ben's nose. 'The fellow's gone too far this time! Calling me a strike-monger, and practically inviting Bultimore and Vine's to take our clayworkers away from us, and promising to print leaflets for the men to inform them of better working conditions at other pits! It's libel, that's what it is! I'll have Askhew's guts for this—'

'No, you won't, Father,' Ben said as calmly as he could. 'I helped Tom compose the article. It was my idea about the leaflets too. If you won't give the men their dues, then they have every right to go where they get fair pay for their work.'

Charles's jaw dropped in a fury. 'Have I got mutiny in my own house now?' he shouted.

'Not mutiny. Just a wish to see the strike over, and to be fair—'

'I'm sorry, Charles, but we didn't come here just to listen to your arguments,' Richard said sharply. 'Mary's in a state of shock, and I hardly know how to tell you, my boy—'

'If you're going to tell me that Jane's eloped with Tom Askhew, and that they're to be married in Yorkshire where he's starting another newspaper called the *Northern Informer*, then you don't need to,' Ben rounded on him. 'And if the three of you had taken the least notice of Jane and me all these years, you'd have known that we only cared for one another like brother and sister, so please don't be upset on my account! We have more important matters to think about—'

'More important than my daughter's future?' Mary Carrick suddenly screamed at him. 'How can you be so heartless, Ben? I can't believe what I'm hearing—'

'Do you mean you knew what was being planned by Jane and this – this newspaper muckraker?' Richard demanded.

'I've said so. I also knew that this article in the *Informer* was the only way to make you all see the strike the way decent people will see it. When the facts are known to them, they'll think the clayworkers very hard done by, and it will be Killigrew Clay that loses face, unless you make amends right now. Give them their wage rises and their rail tracks and Tom's successor has promised to print a follow-up article that will exonerate Charles Killigrew from being such a skinflint, and make folk respect him again!'

'I'll tell you all one thing!' Richard Carrick shouted. 'You Killigrews take so much on yourselves that in future you can deal with everything. All the decisions will be yours and I wash my hands of them. I'll see that it's all legally drawn up. Just send me my dividends each quarter and do what you like with the damn clay works!'

Mary's ragged sniffling was the only sound in the brief silence that followed. Then, as he expected, Ben saw his father's face darken with rage. He waited for the tirade, but it never came. Instead, Charles suddenly clawed at his throat as if unable to breathe. His massive shoulders seemed to crumble and his eyes glazed as he slumped to the floor.

Chapter Nineteen

Kitchen gossip spread quickly through the town. It soon became common knowledge that Charles Killigrew had suffered a stroke, leaving him partially paralysed and bed-bound, only able to mumble gibberish, and with one side of his face and body hideously contorted.

'They say he cries like a baby the whole time, and has ordered every mirror in his bedroom to be taken out,' the story got more embroidered with every telling.

'He were always a vain un—'

'But a fine figure of a man, for all his bawling,' some said fairly. 'He'll not want to see the shadow of himself. They say the son's in a terrible state as well, and Mrs Tilley could hear a woman screaming in the drawing-room long afore the old man collapsed.'

'Ah, I heard that too. Seems like his young lady's gone off to marry some newspaper chap, and her folks had come to tell young Mr Ben. 'Course, when all the excitement happened, he had to forget all that and see to his father, and the others went off back to Truro, no doubt sorry for bringing all this extra trouble on the Killigrews.'

The town sages shook their heads dourly.

''Tis a bad time for 'em. Money don't make merriment, do it? What wi' the strike an' all, we'm best off in our own small cots, neighbours!'

It hadn't taken long for the news about Charles Killigrew to reach the clayworkers, and on a miserable wet morning the men at Number One pit were grouped around Hal Tremayne, even more uncertain of their future. Until the clayworkers arrived, the only daily movement at the pit was in the stables, where the stable-lads had been allowed to feed and exercise the waggon horses, the pit captains deciding it was no fault of the animals that all work had ceased.

'I know as little as you,' Hal told them tersely. 'It's several days since he was taken ill, and the tale's got so garbled, there's no knowing what condition the boss is in—'

'We know what condition we'm in, Hal Tremayne! And if Killigrew's not in his right mind, then you'd best see the son, and get some sense out on him, afore we all starve!'

The mutters of agreement dispelled any brief sympathy the clayworkers had for Charles's plight. At least Killigrew would be suffering in warmth and comfort, while they eked out their existence in their miserable hovels. Hal couldn't blame them for their resentment.

'Do you wish me to go to see Ben Killigrew?' he demanded. ''Tis hardly the time to badger the man—'

''Tis exactly the time!' The shouts went up. 'If he's less sharp than usual, then so much the better. Push him to the limit, Tremayne. You owe it to all on us!'

He looked around the gaunt grim faces, seeing the desperation in some, and the anger in others. At that moment, Charles Killigrew's stroke meant little to them. It changed nothing, and they wanted action. Already, six men had signed on with Bultimore and Vine's and would be in danger of being thrown out of their cottages when Killigrew found out they were working at the rival pit.

Why hadn't they listened to him and shown some sense? Hal thought savagely. The cottages were tied to Killigrew Clay. They were all tied to Charles Killigrew, and those that scabbed by taking work at other pits might gain a few shillings, but stood to lose their homes, mean as they were.

He'd seen the leaflets flooding the district, in the kiddleywinks and pinned to trees and cottage doors. He'd set Jack and Freddie to collecting them and burning them, but it was too late to stop more discontent among the men. The Penry men were two who had been tempted away, and Thomas Penry had informed Hal bitterly that he and his son had nothing but bad memories of Number One pit, where they saw their pretty Celia in the milky pool every idle day... Hal couldn't blame them for wanting to leave.

But he didn't relish being spokesman for the strikers, and felt acutely embarrassed to go to Killigrew House and speak to Ben about money matters at such a time. A man had a right to die with some dignity without being harassed about business matters...

The sound of wheezing chests and racking coughs stopped his thoughts at once. What in God's name was he thinking about? Nobody said Charles Killigrew was going to die, and these men depended on him. The clayworkers were in more danger of dying from pneumonia and bronchial troubles if they didn't soon get some warmth and nourishment for themselves and their families.

'I'll go to Killigrew House today,' Hal said abruptly. ''Twill take some time, so my advice to you all is to go back to your homes and keep as warm as you can. I'll send word as soon as there's anything to report.'

'And tell Killigrew we ain't moving none of his clay blocks until we get our dues!'

Hal pushed through them. It was a waste of time coming here every morning, but it was a way of holding the men together, of keeping some kind of daily routine, so that complete lethargy didn't add to the anger and frustration they all felt. This last development alternately maddened them and gave them a spark of hope, and they didn't bother to hide the reason for it.

Some said quite bluntly that if Killigrew died, maybe the young owner would be more sympathetic, and openly wished it would happen... others said more cynically that all Killigrews were tarred with the same brush, and that once Ben Killigrew was in charge, he'd be as greedy as his father...

Hal stormed into his own cottage, his face tense and set. Bess and Morwen looked up from their sewing, busy as always, and the fact that his womenfolk were the only ones earning any coppers for the family shamed him as a man.

'I'm to go to Killigrew House,' he said shortly. 'The men insist on it, and nothing less will satisfy them. They want the truth about Charles Killigrew, and they want their money—'

''Tis a bad time, Hal,' Bess exclaimed. 'You can't expect a favourable reception with the poor man lying ill—'

'Tis hardly a favourable reception I get from the men every morning,' he snapped. 'There's no help for it. I'll talk to Ben and see what's to be done.'

'I'm coming with you, Daddy.' Morwen threw aside her sewing, her face defiant. 'I've not been able to get Mr Killigrew out of my mind since I heard about his collapse. He was good to me for all his devious methods, and I – I've a fondness for him. Please don't try to stop me.'

Hal looked at her bright eyes and determined chin, and gave a small sigh. Stopping his wilful daughter when her mind was made up was like trying to stop the tide. He saw the colour in her cheeks and wondered suspiciously for a moment if it was only Charles Killigrew for whom his girl had a fondness. It had better be... any other notions would be foolish indeed.

He reassured himself with the thought that Ben Killigrew would be doubly distraught at present, if reports of his young lady leaving him for another were true. He would be in no mood to take kindly to a clayworker's daughter giving him soft looks. He gave a brief nod as Bess said quickly that she had no objection to Morwen visiting Charles Killigrew. She added that she thought he might welcome it, since he had been calmed before by Morwen's presence.

Morwen's heart beat faster as she got ready to leave with Hal in the Killigrew trap. It was a shock to see some of the clayworkers outside the cottage when they left, running behind the trap to be sure Hal Tremayne was really on his way to see the boss. They had always trusted him implicitly, but trust, like their weekly pay envelope, seemed a thing of the past these days.

Morwen was truly anxious about Ben's father. A stroke could be a cruel affliction, leaving a strong man as weak as a baby, disfigured and helpless, while his brain remained aware of all the humiliation he suffered. To some men, the indignity would be harder to bear than the illness itself, and Morwen was sure it would be so with Charles Killigrew. Her heart ached for him, and nothing the clay-workers said or did could change that.

And nothing could dispel the sudden glow at the thought of seeing Ben again. They hadn't met since being together at Penwithick church, when their love for each other had been too strong to withhold any longer. No one knew it but themselves, and it was a secret she cherished.

'There's no telling how we'll find Mr Killigrew, Morwen. If you feel 'tis too much for you, 'tis not too late to change your mind about coming—' Hal said gently when they had ridden in silence through the mud-churned tracks for a mile or two.

'I'm not afraid to face sickness, Daddy. I just hate to think of anyone in pain. If it was a perfect world, there'd be no more suffering—'

She spoke quickly, guilty that her thoughts had been far from Charles Killigrew at that moment. They had been with Ben, and the sweet young love that surged through her veins whenever she thought of him. They had been transporting her to a heaven of her own, shared only with one man... her breath came more sharply in her chest, wanting him with a great wave of longing.

Needing his strength and his love, and remembering the ecstasy she had known in his arms on one perfect night... if it was wrong to be thinking such thoughts when his father lay ill, possibly dying, it was just as impossible to dismiss them, when every turn of the wheels through the clinging mud brought her nearer to him…

She heard her father give a short laugh.

'I doubt if a perfect world will happen in my lifetime or yours, my dear.'

She refrained from answering, for how could she say she had already had a glimpse of hers, when Hal was so obviously full of concern for the men in his charge? Morwen's heart ached for him too, for her family and all the others. And then her thoughts turned to her brother Matthew as the trap lurched along, rocking so badly she would surely be bruised all over by the time they reached Killigrew House.

'Daddy, do you think we shall ever see our Matt again?' she said sadly. They had discussed him for hours, and got nowhere in understanding him. Bess mourned the loss of her son, but came the nearest to knowing his wish to be something different… she'd known it too, and accomplished her own modest desire at last. Matt had presumably found his way that much sooner than she had.

'I doubt it,' Hal grunted. 'Unless you've a mind to travel to America as well, and break your mother's heart twice over, Morwen!'

'I have not! I don't agree with the way our Matt went, but don't condemn him for wanting to make his own life, Daddy. We can't all be copies of each other,' she said pointedly.

'Mebbe not, but I've a pride in our Sam I can't deny, and the rest of 'ee too, Morwen. Our Matt – well, mebbe one bad apple in a sackful ain't too bad to some folk—'

'Don't say that! He's still our Matt, and nothing can alter that—' she said heatedly, hating to hear him so bitter. 'Matt's not wicked!'

'And nothing alters the fact that he went off wi' that prize wastrel Jude Pascoe, and I've my own suspicions about that young un,' Hal retorted. 'But we've enough to think on without fretting over things we can't change, Morwen. So unless you want to greet Charles Killigrew with a stormy face, we'd best talk of other things or stay silent.'

She bit her tongue hard and turned away from her father's set face. He spoke of change as if it only happened to others, but they had all changed. Time changed everything and everyone. She felt older than he did if he couldn't see that. She felt much older than her seventeen years. Girls matured quickly when they began work in a clay pit at a tender age. They were ready for marriage and child-bearing and widowhood before the fine ladies of the towns had discovered how to crook their little fingers at tea parties. Morwen was ready for love and for Ben Killigrew...

Thinking of fine ladies reminded her immediately of Jane Carrick, and Morwen wished her luck with her new life. She would probably need it, but Morwen still envied her, because it was a life she had chosen. She had heard the gossips gleefully discussing it all, and of its effect on the young Killigrew boy. They thought he'd got his comeuppance, and it must be galling for him to know folk believed him to be thrown aside for a brash, hard-talking Yorkshireman, when he was happy for Jane and Tom.

How sweet it would be to tell the world that it had never been Jane Carrick that Ben Killigrew loved, but

Morwen Tremayne, the daughter of his father's Number One pit captain… and that was where the fantasy ended, for it was hardly likely to happen so flamboyantly, if it happened at all.

As the trap entered the imposing gates of Killigrew House, and the solid stone-built building came into view, Morwen felt an appalling depression settle over her, as dire as a premonition. Was she mad, to think she could ever be accepted as anything but a housekeeper here? Her heart thudded painfully as her father grunted that they had best knock at the kitchen door for admittance, unconsciously reminding her even more clearly of her place.

–

Cook was pleased to see her, falling on her neck and confiding in her ear that the new housekeeper was a bit of a trial, but preferable to Hannah Pascoe for all that! Morwen laughed at her blunt words.

'You are a tease, Mrs Horn!' she said huskily. 'But tell us quickly. How is Mr Killigrew? We've heard such tales—'

'I've no doubt,' Cook said dryly. 'But 'tis pitiful to see un, my dear. The poor man can't speak without dribbling, and he's that vexed at his disability. He'll be that glad to see 'ee, though. Like a little ray of sunshine you'll be to un!'

'And – and Mr Ben? How is he through all this?' she asked hesitantly, feeling it a reasonable query. Mrs Horn sniffed.

'Well, if he's got a broken heart, he's hiding it mighty well, that's all I can say! Mebbe he's too taken on wi' his father's trouble, but what wi' all that, and callers to the house, and unsigned letters arriving calling Mr Killigrew terrible names on account of this here strike, well 'tis no wonder he can't spare a thought for himself. But my guess is that he's not as upset over Miss Carrick as his father would like him to be!'

'So the newspaper piece we heard about had an effect?' Hal broke into the woman's chatter. Mrs Horn looked at him, annoyed for a moment at being diverted, then rushed on again.

'That it did, Hal Tremayne. Did 'ee see it? We've a copy in the kitchen—'

'Later, perhaps. We've come to see Mr Killigrew if we can. Will you ask Mr Ben if he's well enough, please?'

Mrs Horn gave her usual sniff. ''Tain't my place. I'll send for Mrs Tilley, and she can pass on the message to Mr Ben, if you'll wait a minute.'

Morwen could have smiled at her dogged insistence on keeping her rightful place, as she sent one of the skivvies scuttling off to find the housekeeper. But she was impatient to see the invalid for herself, and even more impatient to see Ben.

Mrs Tilley appeared a little later, smiling pleasantly enough, and saying that the doctor was with Mr Killigrew, but that they could go upstairs if they wished.

Morwen's heart pounded as they entered the sick room. The doctor was just snapping his case shut after his daily examination of the patient. Ben leaned over the bed, wiping the spittle from his father's chin. The doctor looked keenly at the two visitors.

'Please don't tire him. It's good for him to see new faces, despite the fact that he says he wants no one to see him looking like an ape! But he knows you both, and the young lady will be good for him. She's a calming influence. I'll call again tomorrow, Ben. Don't bother to see me out. Good-day to you all.'

Hal moved awkwardly towards the bed. How in God's name was he going to put the clayworker's case to this pathetic lump of a man? The face was twisted sideways, one eye drawn down like the corner of his mouth, the flesh beneath his jowl sagging like a chicken's crop. He felt a deep sorrow for the man... and then remembered that it was Ben he'd come to petition, not his father. Though how could he do that in the circumstances...? Ben looked weary to the bone with worry, yet Hal knew he had better take some results back to his men or there'd be more stone-throwing, and maybe worse...

Morwen pushed past him to go to Charles's bedside, ignoring them all, even Ben. He was there and he was whole, while the sight of this poor wreck of a man made her want to weep. She caught hold of his useless hand, and saw his watery eyes gladden at seeing her there.

'I'm so sorry, Mr Killigrew,' she whispered. 'If there's anything I can do for you, please tell me.'

He attempted to speak, but it emerged as a guttural choking sound, accompanied by bubbles of spittle. Morwen gently wiped them away with the cloth Ben silently handed her. Killigrew's eyes rolled, and his other hand waved towards Ben.

'He wants to talk to you,' Ben's voice was harsh with anguish at seeing his father like this. Whatever their differences, he would never wish this on any man, let alone one that he loved.

Morwen saw Ben fetch a black writing block and thick chalk. He placed the chalk in Charles's hand and held the block in position. It was painful to watch his struggle to form words with his left hand, and he finally sank back, his eyes full of fury and exhaustion at performing such a small task. He had written only one word, and it was for Morwen.

'Stay.' She read slowly. 'You want me to stay here a while, Mr Killigrew?'

Ben finished the sentence he was unable to speak.

'My father wants you to stay in this house, Morwen,' he said tensely. 'I know how you helped him when he was taken ill at your cottage, and I know how you helped me.' He avoided her eyes, lest Hal saw the blaze of love he wouldn't be able to hide.

A sick feeling washed over Morwen, not understanding Ben's reason. All she heard was Ben telling her his father needed her as a nurse, to help him and his son as she had done before.

It seemed to Morwen in those heightened moments that he was as good as telling her they should forget all that had happened at Penwithick church... maybe now, when he could so nearly be the new young owner of Killigrew Clay, he truly did regret confessing that he loved a clayworker's daughter...

'Morwen?' She heard Ben's voice, more urgently now. She forced herself to look at him, unable to believe that her surmising was true, her senses too numbed to think otherwise.

'I'm not sure if I can—' she began thickly.

'You must make up your own mind, my love,' Hal put in swiftly. 'If 'tis the men you're worried about, they can't object to your staying here as Mr Killigrew's nurse, and I know your Mammie would wish it.'

She felt as though she was screaming inside. Did no one understand that it wasn't what other people thought that mattered? It was only Ben... only Ben... and Charles Killigrew. At his croaking sounds, she turned her wounded eyes towards him.

'Stay,' he managed to make the first intelligible word since his collapse, and his eyes closed with the simple joy of it. Charles Killigrew, whose forte was roaring like a bull, had managed to say one word.

'Your clothes are still here, Morwen, and your room still ready for you,' Ben went on. 'It would mean so much to us both. You'll not be here as housekeeper, but as friend and nurse.'

Friend and nurse... it was so much less than she wanted. It was the difference between an ant hill and a mountain, and she felt as choked as Charles Killigrew at hearing the polite request from Ben's lips. Oh, she knew he couldn't have begged her as a lover... but if she was everything to him as he'd professed, he could have given some sign, some recognition...

As it was, she heard herself agreeing woodenly, and it was as though all her dreams were dying as she saw the relief in Ben's eyes. He wanted a nurse for his father, and he had got one, Morwen thought savagely. She was disturbed enough to believe it was all he wanted of her. Distraught enough to wonder if he was even having second thoughts about Jane Carrick going off to marry Tom Askhew. She couldn't think clearly about anything any more.

She heard her father address Ben in a low, urgent voice.

'Can we talk privately, Ben? There are matters I must discuss with you.'

The clayworkers' strike... how futile it all seemed to Morwen at that moment as she saw the two men leave the room, and she was left with the pale shadow of the man of whom she had once been so much in awe. He had always seemed so god-like... but there was nothing god-like about any of the Killigrew men, Morwen thought with a bitter irony. They were just men, with feet of clay, like the substance they gouged from the earth. And they didn't even do that for themselves. What fools the rest of them were, to dance to their tune...

Chapter Twenty

High up on the moors a few nights later, the kiddley-wink landlords were vainly trying to turn out some of their bawdiest clientele, even though there were still a few more hours' drinking time left to them. But the kiddleywinks had become so rowdy of late, even the landlords were prepared to forgo the extra coppers from late-night drinking rather than risk their establishments being wrecked.

Few of the clayworkers from the Killigrew pits frequented them now, needing their strike dues for more basic necessities than drink. The men from other pits were more fortunate, and frequent battles broke out among those for and against Killigrew's men. But the few who had already taken the enticement to work at Bultimore and Vine's were the most reckless spenders of all. Much of the nightly talk was of the clay strike and Charles Killigrew's affliction, and there were plenty who thought he'd got what he deserved for being such a skinflint.

'Ah well, me boys, I ain't troubling my head about un no more,' declared Thomas Penry, slurring the words as smoothly as spreading warm honey on hot bread. 'Me and my family gave un good service, and more than most men. We gave un our Celia besides. Don't none on 'ee forget that. Killigrew's Number One pool claimed our Celia, and left her choked wi' slurry and muck, and no man has the right to expect such a sacrifice—'

His voice became thick and choked, and his son John growled at him to be quiet, because they'd heard it all before, and no amount of talk was going to bring Celia back.

'Don't 'ee be shutting your daddy up, young John,' one of the older clayworkers reprimanded him. 'We all know the cost o' bringing clay from the earth, and you and your daddy paid more'n most—'

'I don't need to be told,' John muttered. ''Tis just that there's no sense in blaming Charles Killigrew for what happened to our Celia, and talking about her all the time ain't going to bring her back.'

'I can't be shutting her out neither, our John,' Thomas became more and more belligerent. 'Your memory seems a mite shorter than mine, and if I've got to blame somebody, then I blame Killigrew. 'Twas his pit, and if 'tweren't there, my girl wouldn't have been able to drown herself in it!'

Rumbles of agreement at his simple logic drowned out John Penry's exasperated reply. His father had brooded too long over Celia, even to refusing to go to the works in sight of the still, milky pool of late, which was one reason he'd leaped at the offer to work at another pit. As though the pools at Bultimore and Vine's were preferable to Killigrew's... in all honesty John had to admit that to the Penry men they were.

Even he, not so given to fancifying as his father, had sometimes imagined he could see his sister floating to the surface in her strange milky green shroud... he shuddered at the very thought of it. The drink was getting him addle-brained tonight even though it was still only mid-evening, but thankfully the talk was changing direction again, and Charles Killigrew was getting the brunt of it once more.

'The autumn loads be still stacked in the linhays,' Thomas Penry grunted. 'Killigrew has only himself to blame if he don't get 'em to the port for shipping. His clay blocks may be the finest, but they'll do no good to man nor beast lying idle up there—'

'Mebbe we should see to shifting 'em ourselves,' one of the others sniggered. 'Pile 'em on one of the waggons and take 'em to the port. There's allus a ship's crew willing to pay for a load o' clay blocks, whether 'tis sent by fair means or foul, and 'twouldn't be the first load to arrive by moonlight—'

'And 'twould just serve yon Killigrew right! What say we load up a waggon, me boys, and make a few shillin' for ourselves?'

''Tain't such a good idea—' John began uneasily, to be shouted down by his father, who also hadn't thought it such a good idea until his son put it into words. But Thomas was having no son of his playing the coward when all around him were liking the sound of the notion, and it would also be one in the eye for Mr high-and-mighty Killigrew!

'Do 'ee know the lay-out o' Killigrew's Number One works, Thomas Penry?' a swarthy clayworker from Bultimore and Vine's asked baldly. 'Be there waggon horses stabled there, or do we borrow landlord's dray horses—?'

'You take no horses o' mine,' the landlord bellowed at once. 'And the sooner you get out of here, the better. Do your planning elsewhere, and let me hear none on it.'

''Tis no matter. There's farmers' nags to be found—'

'There's Killigrew stables at Number One works,' Thomas said shortly. 'We don't need to go rustling. How many are game for it then? To load up a waggon and get it to Charlestown port for selling to the first bidder, and the shillings to be shared among they that do the work?'

There were half a dozen willing takers, belching noisily and ready for any excitement. They had the recklessness of an evening's drinking inside them, and a sudden desire to avenge the lot of the striking clayworkers by taking Killigrew's clay to the port, and do themselves a bit of good at the same time. They were all in agreement, and lurched out into the night on unsteady legs, red-faced and determined.

By the time they arrived at Killigrew Clay Number One pit, the moon was full above, the clay pool eerily still and beautiful, the sky-tips glinting in the moonlight with the mineral waste deposits. It was a different world at night, silent and strange, but the rip-roaring clayworkers had no time for pondering on its charms.

They relied on Thomas Penry to lead the way to the stables, where the stable-boys had gone home for the night, and where the horses moved restlessly at this disturbance. Thomas knew them all by name, and calmed them gently, while John pointed out the shed where the heavy waggons were housed. It took a short while to harness up the horses to one of the waggons, and lead them towards the linhay where the clay blocks were stacked.

'Two horses will serve our purpose this night,' Thomas declared. 'We'll take just enough blocks to make it worth our while, and we ain't bothering to bring the waggon back!'

There was agreement all round at that.

'None on us had best be afraid o' doing women's work. We'll load up as fast as possible, and get back to our beds.' Thomas took command. 'There's no bal maidens here to show a pretty leg in the lifting, so let's get started, me boys.'

They were all clay men, and even if they didn't do the lowly bal maidens' work, they were used to handling the blocks. Stacking them on the waggon was done without care or thought for neatness, for the lure of some extra shillings for the night's work was suddenly doubly exciting. They lumbered about the squelching ground, sometimes laughing as they bumped into each other; sometimes cursing as their feet stuck fast and sent them sprawling off balance.

'Don't waste time loading it too full,' Thomas shouted again. 'We want room for the six on us, unless any of 'ee want to run alongside!'

'If you'm riding, then so be we, Thomas Penry!' the swarthy man growled. 'Half a load will bring some shillings, but a few more blocks won't hurt, and we can all squash up.'

The load looked precarious. It needed the solidity of a full load to keep the blocks tight together, but the men were quickly tiring of the work. Their bellies were full of ale, their heads muzzed. They fumbled with ropes and then fell gladly onto the waggon as it was decided that they had done enough.

Thomas took the reins, ignoring his son's offer to be lead driver. This was Thomas's waggon. Despite the fact that he no longer worked for Killigrew Clay, he felt the swell of pride inside him that he'd always felt, driving his clay waggon through St Austell town.

He flexed his muscles. If the drink had made him feel weak as a kitten and more ready for sleep than hollering through the streets of St Austell, it was all forgotten now. Thomas had been given a less prestigious job than a waggoner at Bultimore and Vine's, but here and now he was master of his team once more.

His voice suddenly hollered out into the night, startling clay men and horses alike. The horses leapt into action as Thomas jerked the reins and gave his commands; the men fell backwards in a tumbling heap on the hard wooden floor of the waggon.

'Here we go, me buggers! The waggons are rolling, and nothin' had best stop 'em until we reach Charlestown port! Hold on to your bellies!'

'There's only one waggon, Daddy!' John yelled in his ear, alarmed as he saw his father standing with legs spread wide to keep his balance, and heard the note of elation in his voice. He had the look of a Roman charioteer, of which John had heard tell... or of a man possessed...

The horses had been too long idle in the stables. The welcome night air met their nostrils; they heard the familiar sound of Thomas Penry's voice; they followed their well-trodden route with the weight of the clay-blocks behind them, and if Thomas had got the bit between his teeth with exhilaration, then so had the horses.

They galloped on through the mire, not giving the wheels time to sink fast. The waggon rocked from side to side, the clayworkers clung on fearfully as Thomas shouted at them to hold fast, and they'd get this load down to the port faster than any rail tracks.

The horses' hooves began to slip as they reached the cobblestones of the town, and the waggon lurched as the animals seemed oblivious to Thomas's commands. The men's raucous comments changed to shouts of alarm as the few townsfolk on the streets at night screamed abuse at the frightening sight of a clay waggon thundering through.

With six men aboard, and one hollering like a demon, some thought fearfully that it must be a spectral waggon and not real at all... a thought that sent them scurrying indoors as fast as they could.

'For Christ's sake, man, you'll have us all killed if you go through at this rate. Slow 'em down—'

Thomas wrestled with the reins, desperately trying to control the slavering horses. John fared no better than he did, and their combined weight could do little to stop the runaways. The usual pace through the narrow hilly streets was slow and careful, not this breakneck speed with the waggon almost touching the crowded buildings on either side...

'I can't slow 'em if they've no mind to be stopped!' Thomas roared. 'The bastards have a will of their own, and they've been cooped up too long in stables—'

The waggon gave a gigantic shudder as its back corner caught the side of a house, and the load of clay blocks shifted.

–

Morwen had never asked about the outcome of her father's meeting with Ben in Charles Killigrew's study. Her time was completely occupied from that moment, caring for Charles, who was pathetically attached to her, and wanted her near him as much as possible.

She and Ben met at meal-times, and occasionally across his father's bed, but Morwen was aware of the strain between them. It was a few days later when it became apparent that Charles's condition had improved a little, and Ben visibly relaxed. The doctor said it could be a long drawn-out recovery, or quite rapid – or not at all. But it seemed as though speech was returning slightly, and the stiffness in his face was less marked.

'It means a great deal to my father to have you here, Morwen.' Ben was mightily relieved at Charles's improvement. He and Morwen still sat at either end of the long dining table after dinner that evening, and it seemed to her as though a chasm yawned between them. She felt the sting of tears on her lashes and tried not to show them.

'Does it? I'm glad to be of use to you both. 'Tis little else I can do, since my place as housekeeper has been taken over, and there's no use for bal maidens at present—'

Ben's eyes were deep-hued as he looked at her.

'Don't talk of returning to such servile jobs, Morwen,' he said roughly. 'You know I want better for you.'

'I don't know anything,' her voice was low and passionate. 'One minute I'm a seamstress like my mother, because 'tis the only way we can earn a few pennies for the family. The next I'm a nurse. I don't know who I am any more—'

He came swiftly around the table, his arm sliding around her taut shoulders.

'You're my love, and always will be, Morwen,' Ben said in a husky voice. 'You know it without my putting it in words.'

But what did it mean? She needed the words. She longed to hear him say he wanted her with him always, not as his father's nurse, but as his wife... Ben Killigrew's wife... her soft mouth trembled, both at the glory of the thought, and the unlikelihood of it ever happening. The Killigrews didn't marry the daughters of pit captains, and it was folly to think otherwise. It was a thought Morwen constantly drummed into her head.

She looked away before she had the humiliation of seeing in his face that he would never want her as a wife, part of him. Only as his love... once, those words would have meant everything, but she had discovered she wanted more. Not just the trappings of Ben's more elegant world, but his name, and the right to share his life.

Instead of her dream, she was left with the nightmare of being in this house and seeing him day after day. Avoiding too much close contact with him, because she could no longer bear to know it was leading nowhere. And she had the added nightmare of caring for Charles Killigrew, and had to constantly steel herself at the tasks she had to do for him, since he would have no one else.

Doctor Pender called her a born nurse... it was meant to flatter her, but to Morwen it put her even more severely in her place. She was born to serve, in one capacity or another, and the free spirit in her rebelled bitterly, even while she tended Charles with tenderness and pity.

As if to emphasise the difference in their status, Ben straightened abruptly as Mrs Tilley rushed into the room all afluster, with only the briefest of knocks. Her eyes darted from side to side, and Morwen knew without telling that she had some disaster to report.

'What is it, Mrs Tilley?' Ben said in annoyance, not so sensitive to the woman's mien as Morwen.

'Sir, there's been a terrible accident in the town. A boy's been sent to tell 'ee, but he's so near to fainting that Cook's making him sit with his head between his knees. It's to do with a clay waggon—'

'Oh, my God!' Morwen leapt to her feet, every nerve-end on fire. Ben was already on his way to the kitchen to get the story out of the boy. Morwen raced after him, her heart hammering with fear.

'Order my horse to be brought to the front of the house, Mrs Tilley,' Ben shouted back at the woman.

'Two horses, please,' Morwen insisted. 'I'm going too—'

She didn't wait for any objection, but rushed into the kitchen behind Ben, where Cook was holding a glass of water to a young boy's lips. He was the colour of the clay.

'Tell me what happened, boy,' Ben said harshly. 'As quickly as you can.'

The pale lips seemed to move with agonising slowness, but when the boy began to speak the words poured out in a torrent. His terrified eyes rolled all the while.

'Some clayworkers brought a waggon-load of clay through the town, and they say the horses bolted since they were bein' driven too fast. When it got to the corner of Nott's bakery, the waggon struck the wall, and the driver couldn't straighten un. The horses went right through the front of the bakery, and they'm both needing to be slaughtered.'

He gulped, swallowing down the bile.

'Did you see all this?' Ben asked. He prayed it was just a tale, coloured in the telling. The boy nodded vigorously.

'I were in bed, but I live nearby, and 'twere a noise like demons. Then there was the crash, and the squealing and yellin', and when me Daddy called me to come and inform 'ee, sir, 'twas a terrible sight to see. Me Daddy said the horses be crushed, and so were some o' the men, wi' the waggon pushin' em further into the bakery, and the clay flying everywhere—'

'I think we've heard enough,' Ben said quickly. 'Let the boy stay as long as he wishes, Mrs Horn, then send him home in the trap. Miss Morwen had best stay here too—'

'No! I'm coming with you,' she said. 'There are men there needing comfort, and the doctor will have enough on his hands.'

Ben didn't argue. There was no time. His place was at the scene of the accident, however harrowing. God knew how it had happened, and why a clay waggon was being driven through St Austell town at such a time was something else that needing thrashing out. But not now. Not yet.

Mrs Tilley had brought their outdoor coats, and they shrugged into them quickly. Morwen had a great dread of what she would see, but she could never have stayed behind. Thank God Charles Killigrew would be sleeping by now, having had his nightly sleeping-draught. At least he was spared the immediate news of the disaster, she thought grimly.

They sped away on the waiting horses and tied them up at the nearest stabling yard, walking the rest of the way.

'We Killigrews may not be too popular right now, Morwen,' Ben said bitterly. 'Anything could happen after this outrage, and at least we won't get our horses stoned if they're safely stabled.'

Morwen's mouth was dry. Was he hinting that they themselves might be stoned? It was so unfair. This was none of their doing, nor of Charles Killigrew's. But incensed townspeople would not consider any of that tonight...

They were aware of the accident long before they approached the scene. There were people running everywhere, and garbled tales were excitedly bandied about. A great pall of white-grey dust hung over the town, and the stench of burning was on the air. Burning wood, burning flesh...

'Poor old Nott was at his ovens when it happened,' a passer-by shouted at them. 'They say he were crushed at once by the horses, and they toppled straight onto the ovens and set the place ablaze. The waggoners followed 'em, and the waggon's already burning merrily. There's naught but stinking black flesh down there now, and 'tis one lot o' clay that Charles Killigrew won't benefit from!'

Morwen felt the urge to retch at the gleeful words, and forced the feeling down, thankful that Ben hadn't been recognised by the man. The two of them pushed their way through the gawping townsfolk to where the remnants of the Killigrew Clay waggon was stuck at a ludicrous angle through the shop front, fiercely ablaze.

The smell was appalling, clogging the nostrils, turning the stomach. The smoke stung the eyes, the heat drying them. Morwen choked and gagged, feeling Ben grip her arm tightly. Workers tried desperately to get near to the flames, but were instantly beaten back. Morwen guessed that the boy's tale of the horses needing to be slaughtered was quite unnecessary now. Surely nothing could survive in there. She felt the sobs, tight in her chest, and was too horrified to cry.

'Does anyone know who the men were?' Ben shouted to the crowd. The men would have families, would need to be identified. Morwen couldn't believe that any of her family were involved, but it was always possible... it made her ragged with fear.

''Tis the Killigrew boy!' The shout went up, and a new fear shivered through Morwen as the crowd seemed to turn their fury onto Ben. ''Tis all due to the bloody Killigrews that poor old Nott's a charred crisp!'

'What be 'ee goin' to do about it, Killigrew?'

Someone threw a stone, grazing the side of Ben's cheek.

'I've got more sense than to think violence will help matters!' Ben shouted. 'I'm here to help, in any way I can—'

'There's no one can help poor Nott, nor they others in the waggon—'

'Ben, I must know who they were!' The sobs were suddenly tight in Morwen's chest. No amount of blame could bring back the clayworkers that were dead. She had to know if any of them belonged to her... Sam or Jack or her Daddy... the thought was unbelievable, but she knew how aroused the men were. They were wild enough to insist on a token delivery of clay, claiming the dues for themselves. She'd heard of it happening before...

The constables were suddenly thrusting through the crowd, shouting for order and for space to let the doctor through. He had been tending a sick child when told of the accident, and was furious with himself for being so tardy on the scene. Doctor Pender saw Morwen's white face and beckoned her forward.

'Do you have the stomach to see if we've anyone to save in there, girl?' he asked roughly. 'A woman thinks she heard cries a while back, and now the worst of the flames have gone, will you assist me if need be? It won't be pleasant—'

'I'll help,' she said at once, her mouth so dry the words would hardly emerge. She saw Ben talking rapidly to the constables, and they managed to get a little quiet among the angry mob, shouting that Ben Killigrew had something to say. She moved towards the charred waggon, steaming from the buckets of water thrown on it. She was near to fainting, but she had to know. She had to know.

Behind her, she heard Ben roaring well enough to do his father credit that if there was compensation to pay, then Killigrew Clay would pay it, even though the cost of it might well finish them. The strike would have been all for nothing then, for the entire lot of them would be out of work.

She heard his voice rise above his critics as he said he would call for a town meeting as soon as the damage could be ascertained, and until then, they had best go back to their homes, stop acting like ghouls and let the helpers get on with their task.

He was authoritative enough to be obeyed. Morwen sensed the dwindle of voices as she and Doctor Pender picked their way through the stinking wreckage, along with the constables, the firefighters, and those who had genuinely come to help. Her breath was tight in her chest, both from the choking smoke and the fear... she clambered through what had once been the frontage of Nott's bakery into the dusty gloom inside.

'Christ!' she heard the doctor blaspheme softly. 'Don't look here, Morwen. There's no help for these, nor any chance of telling who they were.'

'Over here, Doctor!' one of the constables called. 'I think the man's dead, but there's another beneath un who may not be. 'Tis hard to tell—'

Morwen followed in the doctor's footsteps, trying not to look at the tangled carnage of men and horses. The acrid stink of burning and the soft sweet lingering smell of old Nott's loaves were in horrible contrast. And then she stumbled against something soft at her feet, where the constable was kneeling with a lantern. She looked down and screamed.

'Oh God. Oh, dear God—' the words were torn from her lips, and then she felt Ben's hands gripping her shoulders.

Doctor Pender was bending over the two crushed men. One older, one younger, both horribly mutilated, their faces more grotesque than Charles Killigrew's...

'Both dead,' the doctor snapped. 'Nothing to be done. At least someone can identify them—'

'I know them!' Morwen's voice shook. 'Their names are Thomas and John Penry. They used to work at Number One pit. 'Tis Celia's Daddy and brother. Oh, I can't bear it, I can't—'

Ben's hand struck her cheek hard as her voice became distracted. First Celia, now Thomas and John... John Penry, who had loved her in his gentle way...

'Take her home, Ben,' Doctor Penry said harshly. 'Get her out of this before I have another patient to deal with tomorrow. I was forgetting she would know these people so well.'

It was so ironic right now... had the doctor thought she was a young lady, like Jane Carrick, because she had been so often in the Killigrew house? Once, she might have preened herself. Once, before this terrible night when poor John Penry was one of the victims of the Killigrew strike. Morwen wept silently, mourning them all.

Chapter Twenty-One

Somehow they got through the menacing crowd. Ben roared all the way, his arm protectively around Morwen's shoulders. It was as though the spirit of his father was in him, and Charles Killigrew's authority was rarely disputed.

'I'll speak to you at noon tomorrow in the market square,' he bellowed above the noise. 'The constables have my word on it. I can do no more until then, and I'd thank you to let us pass.'

The townsfolk parted to let them through, muttering all the while. Morwen was still numb with shock, unable to think of anything but the poor crushed bodies of the clay men, who had been as familiar to her as her own family. Sobs choked her throat as they hastened away, and she almost fell across the back of her horse as she and Ben reached the tethered animals.

Before she could get her jumbled thoughts together, Ben had jumped up behind her, holding her fast, and digging his heels into the horse's side. The two horses had been tied together, and his own followed obediently as they headed for home.

Morwen leaned against Ben, hardly knowing that she did so, merely grateful for his strength and warmth. Without it, she felt as though she would crumble into a spongy mass, like those others... the thought began a deep silent weeping inside her, racking her body that Ben held close to him. He felt the sorrow in her, and ached for her, even through his fury at the night's recklessness and needless tragedy.

'I can say nothing to comfort you, my love,' he said harshly, never feeling so helpless as at that moment. 'All I can say is that they can't have suffered long. It would have been over in seconds, long before anyone had a chance to help them—'

Whether he spoke truly or not, he didn't know. It was all he could think of to say to her. Her reply was bitter.

'They needn't have suffered at all! If it wasn't for this senseless, cruel strike—'

'Are you putting the blame on me for that?' Ben said, angry at the thought. 'God knows I've tried to calm things at the pit when I could, but I'm ruled by my father as much as anyone. At least, I have been, until now.'

Morwen jerked her head up to look at him in the gloom of evening. There was a grim note in his voice. She couldn't see him clearly as they rode, only the outline of his face, strong and handsome and determined, and at any other time, infinitely dear to her. But she couldn't even think of that now.

'Until now?'

Ben gave a short harsh laugh that jarred into her pain.

'I think the time has come for my father and I to have a reckoning over Killigrew Clay. I want you to say as little as possible about tonight's happenings for the time being, Morwen. The household staff will want to know the details, and you'll be obliged to tell them, but impress on them that my father mustn't be distressed by hearing of it yet—'

She stared at his dark silhouette.

'You talk as though you'll be elsewhere,' she said suspiciously.

'So I shall. Don't ask questions of me right now, Morwen.' Suddenly she could feel the tension in him, and her anger died. This was Ben, whom she loved, and it was obvious that he was going through hell. The weight of Killigrew Clay was lying very heavily on his shoulders now, and the clayworkers' reaction to tonight's disaster was still unknown. It would be very ugly. She swallowed dryly, but he couldn't leave her like this. They were nearing Killigrew House now, and she clutched at his arms.

'Ben, tell me what you're going to do, please! And – and don't do anything foolish. Too much blood has been spilled already. I couldn't bear it if anything happened to you—'

She stopped. It wasn't the time or the place for themselves. She wondered sorrowfully if there would ever be a time. But now they were inside the gates of Ben's home, and for a moment they were safe. As though the same thought struck him too, Ben twisted her to him as the horse trotted towards the stables.

She was warm in his arms, and his mouth was on hers, his fingers tangling in her hair as he held her captive. She felt the rapid beat of his heart against her body, and knew that whatever else happened, this much was theirs. These precious moments, this silent avowal of love. She felt it and knew it, as surely as if old Zillah on the moors had decreed it. Together they were strong. Together they would survive anything.

'I have to fetch something from my wall safe, and then I must leave, Morwen,' Ben spoke softly against her lips. 'Trust me, my love. See that my father thinks I've gone out early in the morning, for I'll not be back until then. I mean to speak with him at the first opportunity, and before I go to the town meeting. Don't alarm him if I don't see him as early as usual.'

She pulled slightly away from him. 'You mean to be out all night? Ben, you'll be in no condition to face the town—'

'Trust me,' he said again, with that edge to his voice she knew well by now. The Killigrew edge...

She bit her lip and stayed silent. She had no idea what he planned, but she believed in him implicitly. Briefly, he held her close once more, and she knew she would trust him with her life. She said no more as they went quietly into the house and he went to his own room.

He didn't take long, not even bothering to change his clothes, and she went back to the stables with him until he rode off again into the night. For a few moments, Morwen stood still, breathing in the night air, the saltiness of the distant shore and the damp sweetness of the grasses mingling. It was all so calm and beautiful, ethereally drenched in moonlight... and the scene she had left behind her that evening was so terrible by contrast...

But Ben was right. There was nothing to be done for those who had died, and if something good could emerge from this tragedy, then it would recompense in some small way. How Ben hoped to achieve anything, she had no idea, but his determination to salvage what he could gave her a strange hope.

It was all she had for the moment. She squared her shoulders and turned to go inside, prepared to answer all the questions hurled at her with as much dignity as she could. She would follow Ben's instructions. This much she could do to help.

—

Ben rode hard for Truro. The plans were only half formed in his mind, but they became clearer with every mile he rode. First, he must see Richard Carrick, inform the man of tonight's accident and of Ben's promise to hold the town meeting. Then he had other things to discuss with Carrick, and from their last uncomfortable meeting, Ben prayed that the man would agree to everything he suggested. He was counting on it.

By the time he arrived at the Carrick house, Jane's parents were about to go to bed, and he was shown into the drawing-room by a very wary housekeeper, relieved that the loud knocking on the door at this late hour was by the young Killigrew boy and not some vagabond.

'Ben! By all that's holy, what's wrong? Is your father worse?' Richard exclaimed at once, eyeing Ben's unusually dishevelled appearance with dismay. Ben had completely forgotten how he must look, dirty and smoke-grimed, with the stench of the burning waggon still clinging to him. Mrs Carrick had risen to her feet, alarm in her eyes, putting a delicate hand to her nose.

'It's nothing to do with my father,' he said abruptly. 'At least, only indirectly, which is why I must see you, Carrick, and I apologise for the ungodly hour, but emergencies don't take account of such things—'

'Emergencies, by God! You'd best take some brandy and tell me what's to do, Ben.'

'I'll leave you men to discuss your business—' his wife said stiffly. She had still not forgiven Jane for eloping with the newspaperman, despite a letter from some titled northern gentleman praising Tom Askhew's ability, claiming that he had a part in their departure and inviting Mary and Richard to stay at his elegant country home at their convenience.

Neither had she forgiven Ben for apparently knowing of her daughter's plans, and ruining her own.

'I'd rather you stayed to listen, Mrs Carrick,' Ben said, to her surprise. 'I've much to say, and you may as well hear it all at first-hand, since I'm sure Richard will relate it to you later.' He dispensed with formality, and drank the brandy Carrick handed him at one gulp, needing its fiery sting to his belly.

'Go on, Ben,' the other man said quickly.

'There's been a terrible accident in St Austell.' He spoke bluntly and concisely, refusing to lessen the impact for the lady's benefit. In fact, he intended to shock, and pausing only for Mary to gasp, he went on ruthlessly.

'Some of the Killigrew clayworkers who left our employ took a Killigrew waggon and loaded it with clay blocks. They were probably drunk, and by all accounts they careered through the town at a furious rate. They crashed through Nott's bakery, killing the baker, all six clayworkers and the horses. By the time I was informed and reached the scene, it was as though an earthquake had occurred. The waggon and the bakery were in flames, the weight of it all had crushed the horses and the men. The stench of burning animal and human flesh was appalling—'

Mary Carrick gave a low moan, scrabbling for her smelling-salts and sinking on to a chair, her bosom heaving with distress. Richard's face was an angry red as he began to fan his wife, and turned on his visitor.

'Just wait a moment, young Ben! Do you have to be so graphic in your description? What you've told us is ghastly enough, but you could temper it a little—'

'No, sir, I could not! I meant it to sicken you both to your stomachs, the way it sickened me. You're part owner of Killigrew Clay, even though you're content to sit here in your fine house and keep away from the business dealings. But it's time you knew about the hardships of the clayworkers, and what far-reaching effects this bloody strike is leading us to—'

Richard leapt to his feet.

'I begin to curse the day I ever went into partnership with your father, Ben! I told you recently I wanted to know as little of it as possible,' he shouted. 'The two of you act like gods over the damn works – begging your pardon, my dear – and now that Jane's no longer part of your plans, I'd dearly like to be rid of any involvement with you!'

'I couldn't agree more,' Ben said rapidly. 'It's one of the reasons I've come here tonight. I intend to buy you out, Carrick.'

For a minute, Richard Carrick stared at him, and then gave a short laugh.

'Now just you hold on, young fellow. Have you any idea what Killigrew Clay is worth? It's one thing for me to want to be rid of you, but you're still wet behind the ears when it comes to business, and I've no intention of letting go of my half for a pittance, however attractive it may sound—'

Ben smiled pleasantly.

'You forget that I studied business methods at college in London, Richard. You also forget that I acquainted myself very fully with Daniel Gorran's accountancy of Killigrew Clay when I first came home to Cornwall. I'm not the dullard you seem to think I am. I can tell you the value of the works in exact figures, and I assure you that I also have sufficient investments to more than cover your half of the partnership. Maybe these will convince you.'

He thrust his hand inside his coat and pulled out a bundle of share certificates, keeping a few of them back. He tossed them onto a table. Richard Carrick picked them up curiously, his expression changing to astonishment as his legal mind saw the value and implication of the investments.

'Does your father have any notion that you're such a wealthy young man?' Richard said at last.

'No more than you did. He knew I had a few shares, but he merely thought them trifling, and never bothered to find out if I had a business head on my shoulders or not. I didn't realise their true value myself until tonight.' He spoke meaningly. 'Well, sir? I'm willing to leave these shares in your keeping to buy you out of Killigrew Clay, if you'll give me a note to that effect to show to my father in the morning. You'll agree that there are sufficient funds there.'

'More than enough, though not for much else,' Richard said. He looked keenly at Ben. 'You're shrewder than any of us thought, I'll give you that. So your father knows nothing of this visit here tonight? Nor of the accident, I wager, by the look of you. I presume you've ridden straight here?'

'My father is sedated as usual for the night,' Ben said shortly. 'He'll be told in the morning, and by then I want your note in my hand. Give me your answer, for I've more to do this night yet.'

'Be rid of the partnership, Richard!' Mary Carrick put in shrilly. 'The Killigrews have proved themselves a ruthless family, and I want to be disassociated from them!'

He wished it too, yet there was a surge of admiration in Richard as he looked at Ben almost covetously. He had never felt a weaker man, seeing the boy's defiant look. He envied Charles his son at that moment, and knew he could never hope to be like either of them.

'I've had a long friendship with your father, Ben,' he said slowly. 'I would wish to be still his friend, but in the interests of Killigrew Clay, I'll agree to sell my half to you.'

Ben gave an audible sigh of relief. He needed control of the clay works, and this was the first step. Leaving Killigrew Clay in the hands of old men, one weak, the other an invalid, was certain to lead to more disaster. He held out his hand to Richard Carrick, who grasped it firmly. Richard turned away to write his note, while Mary looked at Ben with open dislike, where once she had adored him.

'You don't even think to ask after Jane!' she said in annoyance. Ben just managed not to explode with anger at the petulant remark. He was openly sarcastic in his reply.

'My time has been too occupied with seeing the effects of an accident, Mrs Carrick, and to thinking what can be done about it! But since I have a moment, then how is Jane? Well, I hope?'

'Do you really care?' Mary burst out. 'She's well enough, I'm told, if you call being married to that – that Yorkshireman a life suited to my daughter!'

'If they love each other as I believe they do, then she is more than suited,' Ben retorted.

He turned from her, sick that she could be so shallow, when more important matters were at stake. Though no doubt Mary Carrick thought him an opportunist for pressing this night's meeting with her husband. It was not his intention to appear that way, but having secured his note, and handed over the shares to Richard Carrick's safe keeping, Ben wasted no more time with them. His next move was none of their business, anyway, and would probably only have damned him even more in Mrs Carrick's eyes.

Before he left, however, he begged the use of a guest room to wash and tidy himself, a request that was agreed to unwillingly. It should partly redeem him in the lady's eyes, Ben thought humourlessly, with her dogged attention to etiquette. He washed away the smell of smoke from his skin, smoothed his hair, and brushed off as much dust as he could from his clothes. He needed to be presentable in the next hours. He made his escape gladly from Jane's home, where he'd once spent so much time in other days.

He knew the address of the house in Truro that he now sought, though he hadn't frequented it. It was discreetly hidden in a side street, and he remembered the coded knock on the door, given to him by a wag at his London college, surprised that Ben hadn't discovered it for himself, being so close to home.

The door opened, and he entered, giving the friend's name, and then his own. George Foggerty was a member of various gaming establishments across the country like this one, and his name held good for entrance. Ben went at once into a different world, of softly-lit rooms with plush red furnishings; of gentlemen busily intent on their own pursuits and barely looking up when a newcomer entered; of heaped notes and silver coins and IOU's tossed into the centres of tables with a carelessness that said their owners were prepared to win or lose considerable amounts by the throw of a dice or turn of a card.

It was just what Ben had anticipated, and all the old skills that had proved so lucrative in the past were about to be put to the test. He had never been a compulsive gambler, but his erstwhile college friends had known him for a damned lucky one. He counted on that too.

He hadn't been back in the county often enough in past years for these gentlemen to know him, and he was thankful not to recognise any of them. Not that it really mattered a damn to him. He was here for a purpose, and unconsciously his fingers flexed themselves as he saw the sidelong smirks from one to another, as if wondering how this young whippersnapper expected to beat such regular gamblers as themselves. And anxious to see whether he had enough funds to make a game worth their while. If not, they'd soon have him out of here... Perriman's wasn't a club for the chicken-bellied...

Several hours later, the smiles were gone, and the gentlemen all knew they had underestimated the talents of the newcomer. The air was thick with cigar smoke, the faces tense, the untidy piles of money and notes all heaped in front of Ben Killigrew. He'd gambled with money and the few shares he still had left, and it had paid off handsomely. But it still wasn't enough. He'd done his calculations in Gorran's chambers, and knew what he needed.

'Who's brave enough to gamble for higher stakes?' he said boldly. 'One throw of the dice or one turn of the cards, highest number the winner in either case. Who'll risk it?'

'I've had enough for one night,' growled one large gentleman.

'And I——' agreed another, and another.

'What's your stake, Killigrew?' A hard-eyed man of obvious prosperity said. Ben hid a smile, guessing he would be the one. He had the look that Ben had seen so often in the London gaming houses, unable to resist a challenge, no matter how risky, greedy to the last, and with ample resources to cover large losses. Ben was well pleased with his surmise.

Instead of pushing all his winnings to the centre of the table as the man clearly expected, Ben drew out a folded piece of paper from his pocket, and opened it out for the man to see Richard Carrick's writing and signature. All would know Carrick's name in Truro, a most respected lawyer, and know that the note was authentic.

'This represents a half-share in Killigrew Clay,' Ben said calmly. 'You may not know the name of it so well in Truro, but Carrick was my father's partner, and has now signed over his half of the partnership to me. I'm prepared to stake this note against your matching one. You'll see the amount it represents.'

It was the biggest gamble of the night. If the man refused, Ben doubted that any others would take him up.

If he agreed, then Ben could lose everything he'd gained so far this night. The gamble could be a disaster... but it was a risk he was prepared to take. He needed to double his advantage before he faced his father. The man stared at Ben's unflinching eyes, and then gave a raucous laugh.

'I'll take you on, Killigrew! No man can continue to have the luck of the devil, and that's what you've had, by God! We'll have witnesses for this transaction. Steward, bring pen and paper, and let's make it legal. There's plenty here will be happy to see me avenge their losses tonight!'

Ben smiled more coolly than he felt. If the bragging was meant to undermine his self-confidence, he'd heard it all before. Let them all think he had beginners' luck, but he knew every trick of eye movement and trembling fingers, every sleight of hand and bead of sweat on the forehead. They were novices compared to some of the gamblers he'd met in London, but this last wager was the biggest of his life, and he too was beginning to feel the strain, and the clamminess in his hands that he didn't want.

'Bring me some powder and a towel, Steward,' he ordered, once his opponent's note was signed and witnessed. The other guffawed, clearly seeing this as a sign of Ben's unnerving, but it was merely a precaution, and one that was regularly practised by those experienced city men who had taught Ben his expertise. But powder and a towel were brought to him forthwith, and the gambler was obliged to wait until Ben was ready.

'What will it be?' he asked the hard-eyed man. 'You have the choice. Cards or dice. One turn or one throw only, remember.'

He looked at the man unwaveringly, letting a flicker dilate his eyes as the man chose cards. Immediately, he changed his mind and called for dice instead, just as Ben had anticipated.

'No more change of mind allowed,' the Steward of the house declared. 'Dice it is. Gentlemen, will you please agree that this is a new pair, with the seal unbroken?'

He brought forward a sealed box, at which the opponent waved his hands impatiently.

'All right, man, we can all see that you know the procedure. Now, let's get on with it. I'm anxious to become the new half-owner in this clay works!' He spoke arrogantly, as though the idea of it was a novelty to him.

The Steward broke the seal on the box, and tipped out the two dice in front of Ben's rival. As he was the challenger, it was his privilege to throw first. The gentlemen remaining in the club crowded round, half of them eager to see Jervis Penhaligon teach this young upstart a lesson, the other half just as eager to see Ben Killigrew wipe the complacent smile off the old reprobate's face, and give them some satisfaction for the times he'd taken their money from them.

Penhaligon rubbed his fingers together to make them supple, and threw the dice into the centre of the table. A six and a five. He scowled, amid the cheering of the watching crowd. He'd have hoped for a clean sweep to make certain of his victory, but he drew deeply on his cigar, unable to believe that his young opponent could have any more luck than he'd already had that evening. He could well stand the loss, but that wasn't what mattered...

He watched intently as Ben picked up the dice, weighing them in his hands and feeling their coolness change to warmth against his skin. The time he took began to unnerve his opponent now. He could see it in the quick drawing on the cigar, but Ben wouldn't be hurried. There was no sound in the room but the shallow breathing of the waiting crowd and the click of the dice in Ben's cupped hands.

And then he let them go, spinning them across the table, while the watchers craned and stretched to watch their progress. One dice rolled quickly, to end face up with six black spots clearly visible on the white surface. A small cheer went up. The other dice teetered momentarily as if undecided which way to fall, and then dropped with painful slowness to make a perfect pair of sixes.

Amid the deafening applause, Ben smiled in satisfaction at his rival, unable to disguise the relief in his eyes. He extended his hand, thankful that none had guessed how his heart had pounded sickeningly in that final moment.

'A fair win, sir, wouldn't you say? And let no one deny that Jervis Penhaligon was a worthy opponent!' Ben said generously.

The man's eyes flashed for a moment, and then he laughed, acknowledging the gamesmanship in Ben's words and gesture, and quick to respond to it with a strong handshake.

'A fair win indeed, boy,' he agreed. 'And if you ever consider another kind of partnership, I can think of no better ally on the gaming table!'

'Thank you, sir, but I think I know when to stop,' Ben commented. 'Now, if you'll all excuse me, I'd like to settle things with the Steward.'

He could hardly believe his good fortune. This night, which had begun so appallingly with the accident in St

Austell, had turned into one of unbelievable luck. He wasn't insensible to the sorrow of that accident, nor to the fact that there was still a great reckoning to come. But out of it had come the chance and the guts to do something he'd hardly dared to think about.

As he rode away from Truro and headed for home in the pre-dawn hours of the morning, with a pale pink-gold light already streaking the deep curtain of the sky, he still couldn't believe he'd done it. Yet here was Penhaligon's note safely inside his coat, along with Richard Carrick's note signing over the half-partnership of Killigrew Clay to him. He had doubled the value of Richard's share in one reckless venture.

There were also the shares he'd held onto at the gaming house, and all the money he'd won besides. Unknown to his father, Ben had been quietly rich before, but now he had power as well as riches, and this had become the strangest night of his life.

Despite the trauma of the accident, the exhilaration of what he'd already accomplished and the soaring realisation of all he could achieve in the future was more intoxicating to his senses than wine. At that moment, Ben truly felt as though he held the world in the palm of his hand.

Chapter Twenty-Two

Exhaustion overtook him long before he reached Killigrew House, and he didn't remember stabling the horse or stumbling upstairs and falling across his bed without even removing his clothes. He knew no more until Morwen was shaking him gently, and he awoke to a blindingly bright morning, and the vague realisation that it was the beginning of a new era in Killigrew Clay. He was still drugged with sleep, not too sure what that new era entailed...

'Are you all right, Ben?' Morwen said. 'Your father's been asking for you. I can't make many more excuses to him. The doctor's due soon, and he's sure to tell your father about the accident. You must tell him first, Ben!'

Memory rocked his brain. He sat up so fast that his head spun, but there was no time to waste in lying abed. He had to speak with Charles, and there was a town meeting at noon. He mustn't be late for that, and by then, he must have something definite to say to the townsfolk. He was determined on that.

'Ask Mrs Tilley to send me some washing water, will you, Morwen? I look like a rag-tag. And tell my father I'll be with him in half an hour.'

She was bursting with impatience and curiosity.

'Ben, what happened? Aren't you going to tell me where you went last night? You look terrible, but there's such a strange light in your eyes. Oh, please tell me!'

Not yet. He had to see his father first. Then he would tell Morwen Tremayne everything she needed to know...

'Later,' he promised. 'Are you going to delay me still further by standing there like a defiant chick? Do as I asked, there's a love.'

She flounced out, thinking his words condescending, while Ben smiled at her stiffly retreating back. Just as he'd seen her that first day in St Austell, when he'd so enjoyed the feel of her in his arms. It seemed so long ago now. A long time since he'd not loved Morwen Tremayne. He wondered now if there had ever been such a time...

He heard the knock on his door, and Mrs Tilley came herself with a jug of hot water to fill his washing bowl. He must have been dreaming, and he had no time for that...

'We're all very sorry about the accident, Mr Killigrew,' the housekeeper said fussily. ''Twill be a terrible blow to your father to hear of it—'

'He hasn't been told yet, has he?' Ben said sharply.

The woman shook her head indignantly.

'Miss Morwen was most particular that no one should say anything to un. Most insistent she were—'

'Good. Thank you, Mrs Tilley. That will be all.'

She went out reluctantly, clearly wanting to hear more about the accident, but Ben wanted to speak with no one but his father. His head was clear. He recalled everything that had happened since first hearing of the waggon crash in St Austell, and he was his own master now. Charles must be made to realise it, and more. Ben intended being master of Killigrew Clay.

He was ready in less than half an hour. He went into Charles's bedroom. In his pocket were the spoils from last night, the barter that would make him king. The brief remorse was quickly smothered. In his place, he knew that Charles would do exactly the same. Charles had built an empire, and wouldn't want it to crumble because of incompetency.

Ben went quickly to Charles's bedside as the old man tried to mouth some words of greeting. The words still resembled gibberish for much of the time, and Charles still looked frail and twisted. Despite his pity, the sight of him strengthened Ben's resolve. He caught at Charles's trembling hand.

'I'm sorry I'm so late, Father,' he said steadily. 'I have a lot to tell you. Will you listen patiently and try not to get upset?'

Charles nodded, a look of suspicion in his eyes. Ben plunged in, telling him as calmly as possible of yesterday's accident. He heard the choking noise in Charles's throat as he tried to comment, and wiped the bubbling saliva from his chin as it dribbled down. He went on, telling him everything in a flat monotone, while Charles watched him unflinchingly. That cold watery stare was unnerving, but the presence of the notes in Ben's pocket reassured him. He had to go on.

'I went to Truro to inform Richard Carrick, Father. He had a right to know. Your partner had a right to know.' He repeated the words slowly, as though to a child. He saw Charles give a small nod, his throat working as though to speak, but the words remained unformed. Ben gripped his hand more tightly.

'Father, Richard is no longer your partner. He has lost interest in Killigrew Clay, and although he wants to remain your friend, he and his wife are embarrassed to keep on the business interest because Jane and I will not marry each other. Do you understand what I'm saying? Richard was prepared to sell his half of Killigrew Clay, and he has sold it to me. I had my own investments to buy him out, and I am now your legal partner.'

He waited for Charles's reaction before going on. His father's eyes seemed to dart from side to side as if unable to comprehend, but from the hard squeeze on Ben's hand, he was quite sure Charles understood. Was the old devil pretending to be more infirm than he really was? Ben wondered for a second, but there was no way of knowing for certain.

'Father, it's not enough. I need to have total control of Killigrew Clay. The clayworkers must have someone at their head who's capable of immediate action on this strike. You have to sign the business over to me entirely. I beg you to do this—'

'How dare you suggest such a thing while your father lies so ill! I never heard anything so underhand in my life! I always thought you were too good to be true, Nephew!'

The shrill voice of his Aunt Hannah made Ben whirl round in a rage. He hadn't heard her come into the room, and nor had she needed to be announced, being part of the family. She arrived at Killigrew House whenever she chose, knowing full well that if she waited for invitations, she would wait for ever. Ben glared at her furiously.

'And how dare you interrupt like this, Aunt!' he snapped.

'Why should I not visit my brother in his time of need?'

'He doesn't need you and never did,' Ben said harshly. 'And since we have important matters to discuss, I'd be obliged if you would leave this room until we've finished. If Father wishes to see you later, then you may return.'

Her answer was to sit firmly in the window seat, arms folded. Ben glared at her for a minute, then turned back to Charles, ignoring her completely.

'Have you understood all I've said, Father?' he asked Charles urgently. Charles nodded, his mouth working painfully.

'Not – an imbecile – yet!' he managed.

'Good. Then you'll know I speak for the good of Killigrew Clay, and not for personal power.' He heard his aunt snort in the background, and knew his words were not the entire truth. Personal power was suddenly very sweet, but only for the future of Killigrew Clay and its continued prosperity. He went on.

'Father, I don't want to wait for my inheritance. I want total control of the works now—'

Hannah jumped to her feet, outraged.

'What are you saying now? You'll give the man a seizure, forcing him into these wicked agreements. I've been wrong about you all this time! You're ten times more devious than my Jude—'

'Aunt, will you please shut up!' Ben rounded on her wildly. 'Otherwise, I shall forcibly put you outside this room.'

Her mouth dropped open. This was certainly a different Ben from the one she had always known, the Ben she'd thought so prissy with his college ways compared with Jude's brashness...

A nervous-looking Mrs Tilley announced the doctor's arrival, and Ben guessed that the fuss could be heard all over the house. Doctor Pender looked from one flushed face to another, and put his own interpretation on it.

'You'll have told your father about the accident, then,' he said briefly.

'And that's another thing,' Hannah put in angrily. 'Those awful waggons are a danger to townsfolk. I've always said so—'

A strangled roar from the bed made them all pause for a moment as Charles managed a pathetic attempt at his old style.

'Get – out – woman!'

Doctor Pender took charge. 'I think it would be best while I examine my patient,' he told her. 'I'll call you when he's ready to see you again.'

She had no option but to obey, and stamped outside in a fury. Ben guessed that she wouldn't move far, but he cared little for her movements. There were more pressing problems.

'Doctor, it's essential I speak with my father. Can your examination wait a short while? I shall also need a witness, and I would prefer you to my aunt.'

'Very well,' the doctor said, a little mystified. 'You're paying the bill, young man.'

The words were truer than the doctor knew, and Ben quickly outlined what he had already told his father, seeing the doctor's eyes widen a little. Had he appeared so lily-livered that none of them expected him to take such action? Ben thought angrily. He turned back to Charles.

'Father, when I said I didn't want to wait for my inheritance, I wasn't asking you to give me everything. I've bought out Richard Carrick, and I want to buy you out too.'

Charles sucked in his breath, and once again Ben wiped away the spittle at his mouth. Then, slowly, he drew out the two notes from his pocket, and held them up for Charles to see.

'This is from Richard Carrick, signing his half of Killigrew Clay over to me on payment of shares to the correct value. This other note is from a gentleman called Jervis Penhaligon, promising to pay me the same amount. I'm offering this second sum to you, Father, to buy your half of Killigrew Clay and put the entire works in my safe keeping.'

'Dear God!' Ben heard the doctor exclaim, as Charles struggled to follow all that was being said. 'Forgive my asking, Ben, but just how did you come by this vast amount of capital? Investment Shares, and promissory notes from gentlemen?'

Ben gave a tight smile.

'I came by them both in the same way,' he said dryly. 'It wasn't only my education that flourished in London. I also learned how to gamble for high stakes, and there were never higher stakes than this—'

Hannah Pascoe rushed into the room, and had clearly been hovering outside all the while, as Ben had suspected.

'So this is how low you've sunk, Ben Killigrew! You had the gall to censure my son, and you nothing but a common gambler! Your father will never do as you say. He's got more sense, despite his addled brain—'

A strange new noise was coming from the bed, stopping her flow of words. Ben looked sharply at his father, where Doctor Pender was already bending over him. But it was no new seizure racking the old man. Incredulously, Ben saw that Charles was laughing, his poor twisted face a grotesque mask, but still laughing for all that. His hands waved wildly, gesturing towards the paper and pen beside his bed.

'Well – done!' Charles ground out. 'Boy's – got – guts! I'll – sign – paper—'

'You're a fool, Charles Killigrew!' Hannah shouted. 'You'll live to regret this—'

Ben smiled sweetly at her. 'If you're worried about your continuing allowance, Aunt, it will go on as before – providing, of course, I don't hear that my name has been blackened by any defamatory tales about me. Do I make myself clear?'

He could see by her face that it was crystal clear. She was as beholden to him now as she had been to Charles. She may hate it, but without their patronage she was penniless. She gave a furious nod before she strode out, speechless for once. Ben spoke to the doctor.

'I'll write the note for my father, and I'd be obliged if you would witness his signature, and then I'll inform Daniel Gorran of the new arrangements, and put everything in the hands of our family solicitors.'

He looked down at Charles, feeling a great lump in his throat now that it was all settled. Charles had founded Killigrew Clay, and built it up from nothing. It had been his dream... Ben squeezed his father's hand hard, and leaned towards him.

'You have my pledge that I'll do my best for Killigrew Clay,' he said huskily. 'I'll make it the best pit in Cornwall!'

Charles's eyes watered, whether with tears of relief or just the damnable ailment that made him so helpless, Ben wasn't sure. But he became briskly efficient and saw to the business dealings between them all. Time was running on, and he still had much to do that day. He had had very little sleep, but sleep could come later…

–

By the time he'd been to town and back on the necessary errands and was preparing to leave again for the meeting in the market square, Morwen was sitting with his father. He had given her the brief gist of what had been happening, and it still stunned her. She could hardly take it all in, but it appeared that Ben Killigrew was now the owner of Killigrew Clay, and as such, his status had changed. She was pleased for him, of course… but for herself…?

She must have been looking vaguely into space, when she felt the touch of Charles's hand on her shoulder. She looked up quickly, but he wasn't in any distress.

'Go – with – Ben,' he said in his laboured way. 'Be – with – him.'

He had talked enough for one day, and the hand fell away from her shoulder as Ben came into the room. Morwen felt her face flush, unsure what Charles meant. But Ben was very sure.

'I agree with Father, Morwen. I want you with me at the town meeting,' he said quietly. 'Mrs Tilley will sit with him for the rest of the day—'

'The rest of the day?' Morwen echoed.

'Once the town meeting's over, they'll know I'm the new owner, and the clayworkers must be informed just as quickly. I want to call a meeting at the works, and try to end this damn strike once and for all. Will you come with me, Morwen?'

She felt her throat tighten. 'Is it my place to be with you now? People will be sure to resent it. I'm still Hal Tremayne's daughter, Ben—'

'I know exactly who you are. You're also in my employ now, and I'm ordering your attendance, woman!' He made an attempt to be jocular, and Morwen gave the ghost of a smile as Charles chuckled. It amused him... but Ben's words were enough to turn her stomach all the same. Her chin lifted.

'Of course I'll accompany you, sir,' she said gravely.

'Then let's be on our way. It's nearing noon, and it wouldn't do for me to be late. Mrs Tilley will be with you directly, Father.' He spoke briskly.

'Good – luck—' Charles croaked.

–

Ben realised he needed some luck when he faced the jostling crowd at the town meeting. The day was cold, but it hadn't stopped everyone turning out to hear what young Killigrew intended doing for poor old Nott, who had suddenly assumed heroic status in their eyes; and for the foolish clayworkers who, after all, hadn't asked to die...

Ben took a quick look round, and thanked God that he had the wherewithal to make some amends. He had never really appreciated the usefulness of money until now. He had always had an ample allowance from Charles, but now he realised the power it gave him when he had control of his own destiny at last.

He thanked God too, for the presence of the constables, who pressed back the crowd as they surged forward when he and Morwen stood on the stone steps of the market square, and he tried to call for quiet.

'What's the girl got to do wi' this?' A few angry shouts came from the crowd. ''Tain't her business—'

'Morwen Tremayne is the daughter of my top pit captain,' Ben shouted back. 'She has every right to know what's to be done for the clayworkers who died—'

'*Your* pit captain, is it? Be 'ee taking over now that your Daddy's lyin' ill and helpless, Ben Killigrew? Do he know it, I wonder?'

The man was shushed by those nearest him, but the catcalls went on and on... Ben was frequently shouted down by the fierce arguments among the crowd as to the priorities of the meeting.

'It don't matter about that! What's to be done for poor old Nott, eh? He didn't get no fancy doctorin' like Charles Killigrew, and who's to pay for the funeral? We want to see justice done, Killigrew—'

Morwen's heart hammered at the onslaught on Ben, with every new accusation bringing more angry abuse. She couldn't guess how he was feeling. He stood tall and proud, and she felt a surge of love for him, facing this angry mob with courage and patience. But his patience wouldn't last much longer. He had his father's temper, and it was about to erupt.

'If you noisy buggers will keep quiet for five minutes, I'll tell you exactly what I intend to do about the situation!'

Ben's voice suddenly roared out above the tumult, and to all of them, it was Charles Killigrew's voice to the life. It was Charles Killigrew's style and, incredibly to Morwen, they all fell silent, shifting uncomfortably from foot to foot in the cold damp afternoon.

'That's better!' Ben's voice rang with authority. His eyes were cold as steel as he looked around the crowd. 'Firstly, for the benefit of those who think I'm play-acting here, I am now the sole and legal owner of Killigrew Clay, and for any who doubt that, you may call on Messrs Grey and Boswell, where the legal documents are being drawn up right now.'

There were murmurs among the crowd at this, and Morwen could see that none doubted what they were being told. This was a different Ben from any that even she knew...

'Secondly, I want justice done every bit as much as the rest of you,' he went on coldly. 'And although it was no fault of mine that the accident took place—' he had to pause for some jeering that was quickly suppressed, 'I will take full responsibility, since it was a Killigrew clay waggon that was involved. Mr Nott will have a respectable funeral, and so will the clayworkers. The bakery will be rebuilt as soon as possible.'

The mood of the crowd changed. Ben was quickly becoming their champion now. Morwen could see it and feel it, and the relief of it was overwhelming, though how Ben could hope to pay for all this, she didn't know. His next words made her gasp.

'I see no need to prolong this meeting much longer, but I want to say one final thing. Now that Killigrew Clay is under my control, I propose to end the twice-yearly movement of clay waggons through the streets of St Austell. As soon as I can make the arrangements, I intend to build rail tracks to take my clay to Charlestown port—'

Anything else he said was drowned out in a great burst of cheering. Hats were tossed in the air, and people pressed forward to shake his hand. Ben Killigrew was the hero of the hour…

—

Mingling among the crowd were groups of young kiddley boys from the Killigrew clay works. Sent by the clay-workers to see what was happening about the accident, or just arriving out of plain curiosity to a new bit of excitement to brighten the dull idle days, they had their own views on Ben Killigrew's words as they raced back over the moors to report on the town meeting to any who would listen.

'My Daddy says if the boss builds rail tracks, there'll be even less work—'

'Ben Killigrew's a snot-nose, just like his father. We'll get no wage dues out of un now—'

''Twill throw more on us out o'work, 'specially if he's payin' for some old fool's buryin'. What's it matter to a dead un if he gets a fine buryin' or not?'

''Tis all show, just to keep in well wi' the townsfolk. Bosses don't care about we! Old Thomas Penry 'ould rather have a few extra pennies to put food in his belly than a fine box to bury un in!'

''Tis too late for un now. My Daddy says he had his fun and his ale in the few weeks he worked at Bult's and Vine's—'

'And look where it got un. Burned to a frazzle and squashed like rotten turnips. They say his brains were all spewing out of his head when they found un, and they couldn't even see John Penry's arms and legs, where they was all mixed up wi' the horses' guts—'

They panted on over the moors, adding more and more gory scenes to what they knew, and what they had gleaned in the town. When they reached the crown of the hill, they dispersed, each with his own garbled tale to tell, adding even more fuel to the flames of an already incensed striking body of clayworkers.

–

If Ben had been aware of this, he would undoubtedly have gone immediately to Killigrew Clay to organise the clayworkers' meeting. As it was, by the time the constables managed to clear the market square of people, and he'd had his hand shaken so many times that it throbbed, he felt badly in need of a breathing space. So much had happened so fast, and his throat was hoarse from shouting. He spoke quickly.

'We'll go round to the solicitor's chambers before we do anything else, Morwen. I want to be sure everything is going ahead, and Philip Grey will give us a welcome hot drink. I'm so parched I could drink an ocean.'

'I'm not surprised.' She spoke almost shyly. People still milled about, and she looked up at him with shining eyes. 'Ben, you were magnificent. I was so proud—'

She stopped. Should she be saying these things? She was so conscious of his position now, so damnably conscious...

He squeezed her hand, but he was unable to comment, as yet another matron came forward to gushingly compliment him on his diplomacy, and to express pleasure that poor dear Mr Nott wouldn't be entirely forgotten.

'Next thing, they'll be constructing a wooden seat in his memory,' Ben whispered in her ear as they finally made their way through the busy streets towards Messrs Grey and Boswell's chambers, aided by the constables.

Morwen felt as though she moved in a dream. None of this seemed real. She was suddenly swept up into a world she didn't know, of legal negotiations, and the staggering knowledge that Ben had done all this by his own shrewd thinking.

Going to Richard Carrick, and banking on the fact that the Carricks would be glad to be rid of any association with the Killigrews now. And the next, unbelievable step, to her, of risking everything he'd won on a throw of the dice. She had heard the full story by now, and it only underlined the fact that she didn't really know Ben Killigrew at all.

Had she ever known him? Or was he just a fantasy in her mind? One that she loved so much that she would die for him... he had told her he loved her too, and she had believed him. But that was a different Ben, not this somehow lonely figure who now owned an empire...

Morwen shivered as they entered the solicitors' chambers, and here again, she was out of her depth as the men spoke of the legal details she could never hope to understand. Everything served to put her at a distance from the Ben she loved. Everything made him seem even further out of reach, as remote as the stars that she could never hope to touch.

Chapter Twenty-Three

Freddie Tremayne hurtled in through the door of the cottage, his legs still running as he was caught up by his father.

'Be 'ee trying to scare the daylights out on us, boy?' Hal said shortly. His good humour was not so noticeable of late, as the clay strike was seemingly endless.

Freddie squealed to be put down, his eyes round with excitement as Bess remonstrated with her man to stop being so hard on the child. But Freddie had no time to be affronted. He had news to tell.

'Some o' the other kiddley boys be saying Ben Killigrew's told the town that he's the new boss o' Killigrew Clay. Our Morwen were there with un, all fancy-like in the market square, and Ben Killigrew's saying we'll get our dues, and he'll build rail tracks, and there was cheering and clapping—'

He stopped for breath as his brothers leapt to their feet to quiz the boy.

'You'm fancyin' again, our Freddie,' sniggered Jack. 'Or else the kiddley boys were funnin' with 'ee—'

'Our Morwen was with Ben Killigrew in the market square while he gave out such news?' Bess exclaimed. She frowned, for it was hardly the girl's place...

'The girl's more Killigrew than Tremayne these days,' growled Sam.

'Be quiet, all on 'ee,' Hal said tersely. 'We've more important things to think on than our Morwen's doings at the moment. Are you sure o' this, Freddie? 'Tis not more of your fancyin' like Jack says?'

'Ask 'em for yourself, Daddy! They'm all running about, telling folk! And Ben Killigrew said as how he were givin' old Nott a fine send-off, and one for the clayworkers who got crushed an' all—'

Bess clutched Hal's arm.

'Oh Hal, do 'ee think 'tis all true?'

His voice was more caustic than his wife's.

'If 'tis, then 'tis we who should have been told first, not the townsfolk. What's it to do with them? 'Tis we who've been living on scratchings all these weeks, while they grow fat in the town—'

Bess shook his arm with impatience.

'How can you be so stubborn? What does it matter who was told first? If Ben Killigrew means to put things straight, that's all that matters—'

'Tell that to the clayworkers, dar,' he retorted. 'I've no doubt they'll be here in their numbers soon, demanding to know why the posh folk get preference over we!'

As though to reinforce his words, they heard the rumpus beginning outside, the running feet over the marshy ground, the shouting and hollering, the demands to know if Hal Tremayne had been in on this report they were hearing from their kiddley boys…

'You see, Mammie?' Sam said tensely, backing his father as always. 'Daddy was right. The mens' mood is as sparky as a tinder-box. It takes next to nothing to set them off—'

Jack and Freddie were bobbing up and down by the window, their faces filled with alarm.

'Why do they allus come here?' Jack said resentfully. ''Tain't our fault we had a strike, nor that the Penrys got themselves killed! 'Tain't our fault that our Morwen be more Killigrew than Tremayne, neither—'

'That's the second time I've heard that today, and I'll not hear it again,' Hal snapped. 'I'll try and calm them until we hear something official. I've no doubt Ben will be here soon, if he's any sense, and if there's anything in the tale.'

He was more disturbed than he showed, feeling like the rest of them that if any changes were to be made in the running of Killigrew Clay, then they had a right to know of it. But he trod a fine line. If he swayed too much towards the men's feelings, there could well be a new riot and a rush to the town to create more havoc. If he showed himself in too much sympathy with the bosses, he risked the safety of himself and his family. He knew it only too well.

When he opened the cottage door, he was met by a sea of angry faces. The other pit captains were among the clayworkers, the kiddley boys swelled up with importance at having been to town and got the information.

'You'll have heard the news from your boy, Hal Tremayne!' Gil Dark shouted at once. 'When's young Killigrew taking time off from his fine friends to come and tell we properly? When do we get our dues?'

His words prompted a loud chanting. It was all they cared about, and Hal couldn't blame them. The money was desperately needed by families entirely dependent on Killigrew Clay for food and warmth. They asked for little else, and it was hopeless to try to quieten them for a full five minutes as they hurled abuse at Hal, at Ben and Charles Killigrew, and at Hal's own daughter.

'Yours be a fine family, Hal Tremayne!' The jeer went up. 'Yon Matt's gone for a sailor, your missus be too good for the bal maiden's work, and your Morwen's as toffee-nosed as they Killigrews by now! Do 'ee still have time to care what happens to we—?'

Hal was slow to anger, but when the abuse became personal to his own family, he showed that he could roar with the best of them. His voice rose above the din now.

'You stupid, short-sighted buggers! Instead of coming here like a crowd of sheep, why don't you listen to your own children and think what good can come o' this? If Ben Killigrew's the new owner o' Killigrew Clay, it means one o' two things. Either Charles Killigrew is dead, or the young un's showing what he's made of, and taken control. If he means to pay us our dues and build the rail tracks we need, then we'll all be in profit!'

'Ah. *If* he does all they things!' the shouts went up again after the brief pause.

'If we give un a chance to tell us, we'll all be as wise as he!' Hal shouted back.

'Where is he, then? Why ain't he here, doling out the pennies—?' The anger spilled out again.

Gil Dark pushed forward, flapping his hands about for quiet. He turned to Hal, his face stormy.

'All right, Hal Tremayne. Now I'll tell 'ee what the rest on us think! Either we see the Killigrew boy and hear what's what, or we smash up his bloody offices like we started afore, and then we'll start on his bloody mansion—'

Roars of approval followed his words, and Sam whispered quickly in Hal's ear.

When the bellows died down, Hal spoke out again, his voice becoming hoarse.

'Listen to me a minute, you hot-headed fools! I say we put a time limit on it. Ben Killigrew should be here to tell us, and we'm all agreed on that. But we don't know all the facts yet. If Charles Killigrew's dead, the boy will be distraught, and no man who ever lost a loved one can deny him that!' He waited for the few jeers that followed, and had a ready answer for the complaints that Ben hadn't been too distraught to call a town meeting.

'We've all heard what happened with the clay waggon. He had to settle the townsfolk first or they'd have lynched him—'

'Ah, and we'll be doin' the lynching if we don't hear from un soon!' The roars went up again, but now Gil Dark and the other pit captains stood solidly beside Hal, and this time it was Gil who tried to placate them.

'Hal Tremayne's talking sense now, you buggers. Listen to un, can't 'ee? We'll give the Killigrew boy until nightfall. If he don't appear, 'twon't be only Nott's bakery that's burning in St Austell town tonight! And that's a promise I'll keep with the rest on 'ee.'

—

Morwen and Ben finally left the solicitor's chambers, thankfully breathing the cool fresh afternoon air after the stuffiness inside. Ben decided they should return to Killigrew House to tell his father that all had gone well, and that the solicitor would be calling on him soon with more papers to sign.

'We'd best have a bite of food as well,' Ben said. 'And then I must visit the works, call the pit captains together, and convince them that the strike must end.'

'Don't leave me behind, Ben. I want to come too. I want to see my family.' Her voice was jerky, the events of the past hours suddenly too enormous to comprehend.

She bit her lip. Everything seemed unreal, and it was as though the family life she had once known belonged to someone else. Perhaps it did. She was no longer the same Morwen who had run wild across the moors with Celia Penry, hair flying, eyes glowing, dreaming of young men who would sweep them up in their arms and love them... love them... it was all a dream... and nothing ever stayed the same...

'I can't stop you,' Ben said. 'But I don't anticipate a great welcome from the clayworkers until they've heard me out, and I've discovered that they're none too keen on listening. They prefer action to words.'

He was polite, the strain telling on him too, and she knew that his thoughts were not solely with her. He had too much at stake, and he must be exhausted. He'd had so little sleep... Morwen pushed down her brief resentment. There would be time for themselves later... though she didn't dare guess at the future. Not any more.

She couldn't guess at how Ben was going to fulfil all his promises, but the solicitor had been so impressed with what Ben was telling him, that Morwen presumed all was well. She hadn't realised he had such a business brain, and the figures quietly being discussed in the solicitor's chambers were more staggering than she had ever dreamed about. It divided them even more…

'Your father will be anxious to know the town meeting went well,' she said quickly, smothering the swift misery.

'It went better than I expected,' he admitted now, able to smile properly for the first time in a long while. It felt strange to smile, to think that at last he began to see daylight, as though at the end of a long dark tunnel. He had plans… and at last he was able to utilise those plans. He was no longer reliant on his father, no longer the courtesy figure at the works. Ben Killigrew *was* Killigrew Clay. It was a good and heady feeling, the feeling of power. And he had the substantial amount of ready money he'd won at the dice table last night. He had more than power…

They spoke little on the ride back to the house, and once there, Ben went immediately to see his father, while Morwen told the household staff what had been happening. They were agog, but when they knew that the young man with the forceful ways was taking charge, the fact wasn't entirely unwelcome. A household without an able master was like a ship without its captain, and it was obvious to all that Charles Killigrew would never again be the man he was.

'Can you serve us some food as quickly as possible, Mrs Horn?' Morwen said, while they were digesting her words. 'We have to be away again very soon.'

Cook looked at her keenly.

'You mind and look after yourself, my dear,' she said kindly. 'You'm extra pale today, and 'tis all a strain on a young maid, the caring for a sick man, and attending town meetings, let alone the terrible sights at poor old Nott's bakery last night! You take a rest after your meal, and let

Mr Ben see to his own business. We'll see to Mr Killigrew's needs—'

Morwen shook her head almost feverishly.

'Thank you, Mrs Horn, but I have to go to the clay works with – with Ben. My family is too much involved in all this for me to stay behind. I'd never be easy in my mind if I wasn't there, but I'm grateful for your concern.'

She hurried out before the cook and housekeeper saw the shine of tears in her eyes at the rough kindness. When would there be an end to it all? When would there be time for dreaming again…?

'Will you come and see Father for a few minutes, Morwen?' she heard Ben's voice. 'He likes to see for himself that you're still part of the household. You calm him better than anyone.'

She looked up to see him watching her from the top of the curving staircase, and composed herself. She mustn't crack now. She intended being at the clay works today at Ben's side, at her family's side.

The thoughts were a muddle in her mind, and she gave up trying to sort them out, and went to sit with Charles for a short while until their meal was ready. Ben was right. There was a softening in the old man's eyes whenever she was around. She held his hand, and told him gently what he must already know from Ben, that all had gone well, and that the townsfolk were reassured. She told him more. She told him how splendid Ben had been, how proud Charles would have been of him… the hand holding hers squeezed gently.

'Were – you – proud?' he asked in his quavering voice.

She felt her face grow warm. Yet what did it matter if Charles knew? Perhaps he already knew. He might lie here, as useless as a lump of his own untreated clay, but the brain was still active enough to think, to sense emotions, to guess at feelings...

'I was proud,' she said softly. 'So proud of him!'

Impulsively, she leaned forward and did something she would never have dared do when Charles was strong and whole. She kissed his twisted cheek, her soft dark hair falling forward to tease his skin, the scent of her a swift delight to his nostrils. A small smile curved the good side of his mouth as she moved back in sudden embarrassment. He still held onto her hand.

'You – and – Ben,' he said weakly. 'You – and – Ben.'

His eyes closed, and he had drifted off to sleep as he was wont to do without warning. Morwen looked down at him, and the stinging behind her eyelids again was a poignant pain. She left him sleeping, but his words echoed in her head like a sweetly recurring tune.

–

They left for the works in the late afternoon. This time they rode in the Killigrew trap, for the sky had darkened and a light rain had cooled the day. As they climbed the steep hillside towards the moors, the mist clung to the slopes in ghostly wisps, yet to Morwen there was nothing sinister about it.

This was familiarity. Behind her the grey huddle of St Austell town, and beyond that the distant sea; beneath the horse's hooves was the spongy moorland, spangled with wild flowers that blossomed even in winter; the tangle of bracken, the fronds of yarrow, the glory of yellow gorse; humble cottages and lowlier hovels, with curls of smoke winding towards the sky from their chimneys; the few tall shafts of the tin mines, the more prosperous clay pits, with their milky pools and glittering sky-tips; the standing stones…

Morwen was suddenly aware that her breathing had quickened, and that Ben had called the horse to stop. He was watching her face, and slowly he leaned towards her, his arms around her in a protective circle, his mouth warming hers. Skin touching skin, breaths mingling; all the longing and the needing was instantly there, when Morwen had been so heartbreakingly afraid it would never happen again…

'We'll spare a little time for ourselves, Morwen,' he said huskily. 'And there's only one place where I can tell you all that I want to say.'

She nodded wordlessly. Ben jerked the horse to a trotting pace, and the trap took them across the moors to where the Larnie Stone loomed up out of the mist. The rain still fell softly, but neither heeded it as Ben helped her down from the trap, and they moved towards the magical stone together.

Ben held her in his arms and bent to kiss her lips. They were in a perfect, silent world, enveloped in the gauzy half-light, oblivious to anything but each other for long, sweet moments. Moments stolen out of time…

'You don't know how jealous I felt when I thought it might be John Penry's face you saw through the stone, my Morwen,' Ben said, when he released her mouth at last, still holding her close. Morwen drew a shuddering breath.

'And now he's dead, and so is Celia,' she said tremulously. 'So much has changed since that night when we foolishly took old Zillah's potion, Ben. John and his father crushed in that terrible accident, and Celia drowning. My

335

brother and your cousin gone over the sea, your poor father so ill. Everything's changed so since the spring—'

Ben tipped up her face to meet his.

'Spring will come again, my darling, and few things stay the same. Only one thing – and that's my love for you. Even that changes – it deepens with every hour, and that's what I wanted to tell you, here at this trysting-place. I wanted you to be sure of it. I want you to marry me, Morwen.' He suddenly held her even tighter, and his heartbeats drummed against hers. 'Oh God, I love you so much it hurts. I can't bear to think of anything else coming between us.'

'I love you too, Ben!' She said the sweet words, loving the sound of them, loving him. She was delirious with joy, and even a sudden sharp gust of cold wind that whipped her hair across their faces couldn't spoil it. He held her for long moments before he led her back to the waiting trap and helped her inside it, his voice still husky with passion as he said that they were foolish to stand there in the rain, and at this rate they'd be going to a burying instead of a wedding!

His words dazzled her. He meant it. She knew he meant it, and yet she couldn't think beyond the moment. Ben Killigrew wanted to marry her… and the fact would throw more cats among more pigeons than anything else that had happened. Ben Killigrew was now a boss, and bosses didn't marry clayworkers' daughters… but she wouldn't think of that! She would only think that he loved her and wanted her for his wife, and it was the most beautiful thought of her entire existence.

They rode back towards the clay works, his arm still around her. It was as though the brief pause at the Larnie

Stone had unleashed all the words they had been unable to say to one another all these past weeks. Too many other happenings had kept them from themselves, but now at last the future beckoned, no longer something to fear...

–

Morwen didn't notice the exact moment when Ben's arm was no longer around her, or when his mood subtly changed. The nearer they got to the clay works, the quieter he became, and the more aware she was of the unusual number of men and boys about in the cold damp air.

Ones and twos became small groups and then larger ones. Some carried flaring torches as the daylight faded, and the mutterings among them when they realised who was in the smart trap became more menacing. There were shouts and accusations, a few bawdy remarks that made Morwen's face flame, some vicious jibes, several stones thrown... they quickly became surrounded.

'I see we're too late,' Ben said savagely. 'News of a sort has obviously reached them before us. Damn their eyes. We should have got here sooner.'

Instead of diverting to the Larnie Stone. Instead of lingering closer to heaven than anything Morwen had known on this earth... she imagined the thought buzzing in Ben's mind, and her stomach seemed to knot up inside her.

'There's my Daddy!' She gasped out the words, as she saw Hal and her brothers near Number One works. She felt unutterable relief at seeing them, even though their faces looked so grim and set. Hal had decided they could no longer stay in the cottage waiting for nightfall, so nearly upon them now, and if any rally was to begin at Number One works as the others had decreed, then he must be there too, to try and drum some sense into their angry heads.

'Sit still, Morwen,' Ben ordered, as the men began ranting for their dues and giving no one a chance to speak. Hal pushed his way through them as Ben jerked the horse to a stop. He ignored Morwen as she shrank back in the trap. This was mens' work.

''Tis well that you've come here,' Hal said grimly. 'We're due explanations as well as our wages, and if there'd been any more delay, your offices in the town would have been fired.'

Ben's fury rose, but there was no time to waste in temperament. He stood up in the trap, where the men could all see him. He didn't deny his fear at the gaunt, torchlit faces in front of him. He felt like a lone sheep among a pack of wolves. If they didn't like what he said, they would be after his blood.

'What's to do wi' your father, Ben Killigrew?' a single jeer went up. 'Be the old bugger alive or dead?'

Ben's fear died away. Again, he thanked God that luck had been on his side last night, and above the din, his voice was as resounding as Charles Killigrew's used to be...

'The old bugger's still breathing, and he's still got enough sense to know he can't run Killigrew Clay from a sick bed, which is why he's signed it all over to me—'

''Tis true, then! And what do 'ee intend doin' for we?'

'The boy's still in his cradle,' snarled one or two. 'What do he know about clayworking? One day's work were all he put in, and thought he were crippled—'

'We'll get no dues out of this un! Cornin' here in his fancy trap—'

'And wi' his fancy woman! Hal Tremayne's daughter's gone up in the world since poor John Penry went courtin' her. She'll not be cryin' that he's squashed to a pulp—' Sneers were added to the bitter resentment in the shouting.

Morwen's head spun at the vicious words, her eyes stinging with tears. They were blind fools, the lot of them, and if they had seen what had remained of John Penry as she had done, they couldn't be so cruel... she flinched as her father's voice rang out above the rest.

'No man here calls my daughter a fancy woman!' he roared. 'And the next shit-bag who stops Ben Killigrew saying what he's come to say can have my fist in their guts. Shut up, the lot of 'ee, and let the boy have his say.'

Ben's eyes were dark with rage, his face a tight mask as he clipped out the words. He'd dearly like to tell the lot of them to go to hell, for their stupidity and their shaming of the girl he loved. But that wasn't his purpose. There was clay to be shifted, and prosperity for all, if they would only listen...

'Killigrew Clay now belongs to me,' he spoke coldly and savagely. 'What happens here in the future depends on my say-so, so think very hard on that for a minute! You know of the accident in the town. The men who stole my waggon and my horses and my clay will be given a decent burying, even though I'm the loser by their foolishness.'

Above the mutterings, he went on loudly.

'All the same, they were good men, and didn't deserve to die. I want to be fair. The blame for it all is this bloody strike, and it's time it was ended—'

'There's only one way we'll work your clay, Killigrew!' the shouts went up. 'Give us the dues your father owes us—'

'Your wage rises will be paid to you from the day you return to work.' Ben bellowed out. 'If that's tomorrow, then I'll see to it that a token amount is brought to each works in the morning, the rest of it being paid out with the next pay envelope. There's money waiting for you, and there's clay waiting to be sent to the port, and I want this strike ended right now! It could be the last time we use clay waggons to take the blocks through St Austell town. I intend building rail tracks as soon as possible. It will increase our efficiency and we'll all benefit, and no one will be thrown out of work. That's my pledge to you. Do I have your promise to return to work tomorrow and help make Killigrew Clay the best pit in Cornwall?'

After a brief, startled silence, it was like a stampede. The small trap was in danger of being as crushed as the clay waggon as the men surged forward, the suspicious faces suddenly alive again. Cheers and stamping alarmed the horse, and Ben had to grasp its reins firmly, while Hal and the pit captains tried to control the men. The relief was too great. Ben still kept calm, but Morwen was weak at the outcome.

'Get back to your homes now,' Hal shouted harshly. 'And show hands all those who'll report for work in the morning.'

Every hand rose, and at last they began to disperse, congratulating themselves. Tomorrow they would have full bellies again. Tomorrow was suddenly beautiful.

Ben sat down abruptly, feeling as though he'd run a hundred miles. The fight was over, and he'd won. Let the clayworkers think they were the victors, which they were, in a way. They'd got their wage rises... but he'd got his works in production again, and that was the important thing. It didn't matter who had won.

'Will you bring Morwen to the cottage for a while, Ben?' Hal said abruptly. 'Her mother will want to see her.'

There was an odd constraint between them. They were on the same side, but now that the fight was over, neither could forget the slight to Morwen's name. She felt humiliated as she remembered the jeers tossed her way. She'd heard the mutters in the crowd that she acted more like a Killigrew than a Tremayne now, and in the clayworkers' angry mood it would be a betrayal.

They couldn't know how dearly she would like to change her name to that of Killigrew. To be Ben's wife... how would they view that! She glanced at his hard, carved features in the early evening twilight, and wondered if it would ever happen. He had shown a new authority in his dealings with the clayworkers. She had seen the ambition in him.

Would he still want a clayworker's daughter for his wife? He had said so, but that was before he had got a surging crowd of men roaring their approval for their new boss. Ben Killigrew was really somebody now, and everyone for miles around would soon know it.

They reached the cottage, and her menfolk were there almost as quickly. The trap was stopped every few yards by one or another who wanted to shake Ben Killigrew's hand, or to tip his cap at the new young boss who was going to make Killigrew Clay the best pit in Cornwall. The words would be music to their ears. Why then should Morwen feel so cold inside? So uncertain of anything, as though the earth was shifting beneath her feet...

And then she shivered again, suddenly remembering old Zillah's strange words. It wasn't an earthquake that had occurred in St Austell town when the clay waggon had crashed through Nott's bakery, but the effects had been just as devastating.

Chapter Twenty-Four

When they reached the cottage, Morwen was immediately enveloped in the old familiar atmosphere, and now the celebrations began. Ben drank fruit cordial with them as though it was the best French champagne, but there was more to be discussed yet.

'My father offered your family a small house, Hal, and for Sam to take on this cottage—'

'If you'm thinking 'tis unwise for us to be moving out just yet, I'll understand,' Hal said quickly.

Bess gave a small sigh. She dearly wished to move into the house nearer the town. It was Bess's dream...

Ben didn't look at Morwen, yet she sensed that his words were for her as much as her father and brother. She still felt oddly disorientated when she should feel so secure, here, among her family, and everyone she loved most.

'That's not what I think. I want you to move to the house, Hal, and I'm offering more. I want a manager for Killigrew Clay, to oversee all the works. There will still be some resentment towards me and I need someone I can trust who's respected by the men, and you're the one for it. If Sam will take over from you as pit captain of Number One works, then that job is his—'

There was no doubt the cottage became a more jubilant place than for many weeks past. Only one face still found it hard to smile. Not until now had Morwen realised the full potential of Ben's power, and the ability to manipulate mens' lives... what he was telling them was wonderful, of course... they all laughed and cried and said how wonderful it all was...

'We hardly need say we agree to it, Ben.' Hal's voice was thick as cream, and Bess's eyes shone. Sam said that'd he'd best get over to see Dora and arrange the new wedding date as quickly as possible.

'Though I'm not sure how the men will take it all,' Hal was bound to comment. ''Twill need some delicacy to make sure it don't sound like a reward for summat—'

'I'll be at the works in the morning to explain my reasons,' Ben promised. 'And Sam's wedding will soon make people forget the dark days that are past.'

For the first time, he looked full into Morwen's beautiful eyes and then back at her father. She felt the sudden pounding in her heart, the leaping hope in her veins as she heard an unusual tremor in Ben's voice as he went on.

'I'm sorry for what was said about Morwen. She didn't deserve it, though they were partially right if they think she's more Killigrew than Tremayne. That's what I want her to be, Hal. I want Morwen to be my wife, and I'm asking – begging – for your permission for it.'

He had never begged any man before, but at the unexpected look of doubt on Hal Tremayne's face, he would beg on his knees if he had to. He saw Sam frown... but then he heard Morwen's sudden indrawn breath and saw the blaze of happiness on her face as she moved quickly to his side.

His arm went around her, knowing fiercely that he would keep her there and defend his right to love her against any opposition. Ben Killigrew had everything he ever wanted, but without Morwen it was nothing…

Freddie began jumping up and down with excitement as no one spoke for a few seconds.

'Our Morwen's going to marry Ben Killigrew! Can I tell em all, Daddy! 'Twill be one in the eye for em—'

''Tain't such a rattlin' good idea as all that!' Sam objected. 'She's still a babby apart from all else – and you'd best keep your trap shut, our Freddie, until Daddy's had summat to say on it.'

'I ain't sure I want to be related to no Killigrew, neither,' Jack was sullen, the mood of the strike still too recent to welcome this new development in their fortunes.

'Morwen, have you thought carefully about this?' Bess said quietly, seeing the joy fast fading from her daughter's eyes at her brothers' reception of Ben's words.

'What does your father say to it, Ben?' Hal was more forceful. 'There's no – no reason for this sudden request, is there?' He couldn't hide the swift look of suspicion, nor stop his eyes raking Morwen's slender shape, tensed now with unbridled fury as she almost pushed past Ben to glower at her father.

Her eyes were brilliant jewels, her face fiery with colour, but when Ben murmured to her to keep calm, it was like telling the sea not to ebb and flow each day…

'You shame me worse than any of those louts at the clay works! You think because I'm young I'm incapable of feelings, of loving. And you think there's some bad reason for Ben wanting to marry me, Daddy! Can't you understand that we love each other? We've loved each other for a long time – for *all* time! I thought you'd know all about that, Mammie – and you too, Sam. You and Dora know what it means to be kept apart when all you want is to be together—'

Her voice choked and shook. Ben stood behind her, his hands firm on her shoulders as though to support her, but she needed no physical support. Despite the emotion charging through her, she was strong, and the shifting earth beneath her feet no longer moved. She had a purpose, and her belief in it was insuperable. If clay dues were worth fighting for, then so was love… so was love.

'We're not trying to block 'ee, Morwen,' Hal said, more moved by her impassioned words than he had expected. 'Just to talk it out, the way we always have—'

She blazed at him. 'What's to talk out, Daddy? Ben has been honest with you. He wants to marry me, and I – oh, Daddy, I want to marry him too! It's everything I want.' She swallowed hard, her soft mouth trembling, and turned to her mother.

'Don't 'ee think that if Celia was old enough for dyin', then I'm old enough for marryin', Mammie?' Her voice was thick, the pain of that terrible day vivid in her mind.

She saw Bess's eyes mist with tears, and now she did need Ben's arms, and they held her tight.

'Don't damn us completely, Hal,' Ben said harshly. 'As to what my father thinks – I've said nothing to him yet, but you know how fond he is of Morwen—'

'Bein' fond is different to having a bal maiden for a daughter!' Sam was still doggedly aggressive.

'Do you think she's not good enough for me, Sam?' Ben demanded.

'No, I bloody don't think that!' Sam said angrily, falling into the trap. 'Our Morwen's good enough for anybody, even a bloody Killigrew—'

'Sam, we'll have less of that kind of talk, please,' Bess said sharply, stunned at the way this day was turning out. One minute filled with joy, the next plunging them all into arguments over what should be a happy announcement.

Bess could think for herself, and it was clear as moonlight that these two young ones loved each other. She saw the echo of herself and Hal in every glance, every gesture. Love crossed all the barriers...

'Put it another way, then. You think I'm too good for Morwen, is that it?' Ben went on relentlessly, his eyes firmly fixed on Sam's face.

'O' course I don't think that!' Sam blustered now. 'I think you'm a fine un wi' words, Ben Killigrew—'

Morwen snapped at him. 'Words! Words! I'm tired of all these words! Why are you so against us, Sam? I thought you of all people would be happy for us! You'll have your new job, and you and Dora will have the cottage—'

'If 'twas just me to consider, then I might be happy for 'ee, Morwen. But 'tis what other folk'll think—' Sam was less easy in his talk now, irritated that Ben's taunts had made the younger boys snigger, and that he'd come off worse.

'What do I care about other folks' thoughts! Why does no one listen? 'Tis what Ben and me think that counts. Ben and me who want to be married—'

'And so we shall be.' Ben said furiously. 'Have no fear of that, any of you! I don't know how long it will take to make this stubborn family see sense, but no one will come between us, and as long as Morwen and me both know it, I don't give a cuss what other folk think either!'

The sniggering died away, the boys looking at Hal uncertainly. This Ben Killigrew was somebody to look up to as much as their Daddy, and they all knew it. If they had always thought of him as just Charles Killigrew's poncey son, come home from his London college to poke fun at his clodhopping clayworkers, they saw him differently now.

'I'll tell you something else,' Morwen's voice still shook with rage. 'I believe Charles Killigrew already knows! In his poor slow way, he told me so. I didn't understand it then, but he said to me "You and Ben", and he was telling me he knew, and giving us his blessing. He knows, Daddy, and he'll not stand in our way.'

She saw her parents exchange a glance, and Bess gave a small nod. Hal took a deep breath and spoke more calmly.

'Then neither will we. But I entreat 'ee to wait awhile before letting it be public knowledge, that's all. Folk have too much to think on already, so give 'em time to get used to the new way o' things. 'Twill be shock enough to know we'm moving out, and all the other bits you've told us today, Ben. And if 'ee think we've been hard on 'ee both, 'tis only because we love our Morwen, and want what's best for her, but I think we can all see that she already knows what that is—'

He said no more as Morwen gave a cry, and rushed to hug him and Bess, and it was as if Hal saw for the first time how beautiful his daughter was, and knew that it was Ben Killigrew who made her beautiful.

As always, the family took Hal's lead, if grudgingly on the older boys' part, for there were plans to be made, and young Freddie was threatened with all kinds of deprivations if he dared say one word of what had gone on here today.

Morwen marvelled at how quickly the mood changed again once the opposition was gone, and gradually the gaiety and effervescence of the Tremaynes drew Ben into their circle. At last the boys lost most of their resentment, and it was a cottage filled once more with love…

But they couldn't remain much longer. Charles would be anxious to know of the day's happenings, and as well as happy plans, there were more sombre ones too. Buryings had to be arranged before weddings, and it was only fit and proper that a few weeks should pass between the Penry send-off, and Sam and Dora's marriage. Sam went off to Penwithick and brought Dora back before Morwen and Ben left for Killigrew House, and the wedding was planned immediately after the turn of the year.

'A new year and a new beginning for all of us, Morwen,' Ben said softly, as they finally left the cottage. One hand held the horse's reins, the other clasped Morwen's, fingers entwined. 'If we have little time for ourselves in the busy weeks ahead, my love, always remember that I love you more than life. And long before spring comes again—'

'I'm almost afraid to hear you say it, Ben,' Morwen whispered. 'I'm afraid I'm still dreaming—'

He leaned across and kissed her willing mouth. The tingling excitement of his touch raced through her veins, so long denied, so very wanted…

'You're not dreaming, love. Before the early blossom decks the trees, you'll be mistress of Killigrew House. How does it sound to you?' He spoke teasingly, to hide the surge of passion he felt. God knew he wanted her now. He needed her, ached for her. She filled his mind and inflamed his body. She was everything and more to him. He wondered if she had any idea of just how much he loved her...

He yearned to show her, to relive that one rapturous night when he had lain with her and made her irrevocably his. The ultimate in loving between a man and a woman... but he wanted it for all time, which was why he was prepared to wait, to know a restraint that was unusual to him, and all the more wondrous when he knew Morwen was his for the taking.

But he was learning more about himself, and he didn't merely want to take. He wanted no hasty fusion of bodies that might mean guilty glances and the womanly fears that had made Celia Penry drown herself... he wanted more than that for Morwen. And with the odd little Cornish perception they both shared, he felt that she knew it without the telling.

'It sounds strange and wonderful,' she answered him in a breathless voice, her fingers curling more tightly around his. 'I'll be so proud to be your wife, Ben, to hold my head up high in the town—'

'No more than me,' he said huskily, because it was as though she had read his thoughts and given him the answer he wanted. She could wait too, because they had the rest of their lives to be together. Ben was confident that his father would welcome Morwen Tremayne as his daughter. He had looked on her that way for a long time now... but meanwhile they must tell no one but Charles Killigrew and Morwen's family. Ben saw the sense of Hal's words. The clayworkers had enough to take in for the present.

–

Six weeks later, the scene at Killigrew Clay works was very different from the barren silence of the strike. The old year had gone, and with it all the uncertainty, the anger, the hardship. Killigrew Clay was once again in full production. The clay waggons had taken their loads to Charlestown port, with more care than of old in view of the recent tragedy; at all the pits there was music in the familiar drone of the beam engines; the scraping of clay blocks; the rattling of the small trucks back and forth to the sky-tips; the good-natured banter of clay men and bal maidens and kiddley boys.

There was the glow from the fire-hole and the heat from the kilns to warm the day; the welcome sight of digging out for the rail tracks, already under way as Ben Killigrew had promised, with great approval from the town. The clayworkers had their extra pennies jingling in their pockets every hand-out day, and though none particularly wished Charles Killigrew ill, all were agreed that it had been a good day when young Mr Ben took over.

They even approved the way he'd elevated the Tremayne men so deservedly, and with more diplomacy than they knew. Ben had chosen his words with care the morning they had all returned to work, and slightly denigrated himself in favour of Hal Tremayne's greater knowledge of the way the clay pits operated.

'I know you won't want a dunderhead squelching about the works,' he'd said bluntly. 'I think you'd much

351

prefer one of your own to be giving direct orders when necessary. Do you approve of Hal Tremayne as my works manager, and Sam the new pit captain of Number One pit? If there are any sensible objections, let's have them now, and we'll talk them out.'

There were none, nor any when Ben went on to say he'd be needing his new manager close at hand to the offices. Which was why he'd offered Hal and his family a house to rent near the town, and that Sam was free to take over the cottage if he wanted it. He made it all sound perfectly natural, and the clayworkers took it so. They were plain-speaking men, and appreciated a plain-speaking boss.

After the talk was finished, Sam Tremayne's eyes glinted with approval as Ben made to leave Number One pit.

'Like I said, Ben, you've a way wi' words. If you'll tip me the wink when the time's right for it, I'll drop a few hints as to you and our Morwen, so it won't come as such a shock to 'em — if 'twould be of use. They'll take it better from me.'

'I'll do that, Sam, and I thank you for the suggestion,' Ben smiled, knowing the two were on good terms at last.

And in the end, the telling had gone smoothly. Sam discovered a diplomacy to rival his future brother-in-law's, so that by the time the date for the second wedding was official, the clayworkers were saying belligerently that there was no reason why Morwen Tremayne shouldn't marry Ben Killigrew. She was a fine maid, and good enough for any man, and Ben Killigrew should be thankful she'd accepted him...

The weeks had been busy ones. The Tremaynes had moved into the new house, and Bess looked nearly as young and lovely as her daughter with all the pleasure it gave her. Sam and Dora had spent some time at the cottage, changing it to their own taste, and playing make-believe wedded bliss until it became the real thing... there had been a letter from Matt to make Bess laugh and cry, but she couldn't deny her wayward son his freedom, when he seemed to be so hopeful and happy, still certain that America was a golden land of opportunity, even if he was still with Jude Pascoe. The two of them had found work and lodgings at some great dock, and had seemingly settled.

Charles Killigrew had improved dramatically, and Ben wondered uneasily if he was going to regret selling out to his son, but happily he did not. He was more than content to take a back seat now, under no illusions from Doctor Pender that if he resumed his old ways, the next attack might well be his last.

And he had much to live for now. As he tried vainly to tidy his hair for the second, and most important wedding he'd been allowed to attend recently, Charles smiled with satisfaction at his reflection in the mirror. Thank God his speech was intelligible again, and he was no longer the gargoyle he'd hated so much. He was still Charles Killigrew, if only the figurehead now of Killigrew Clay, and he could still appreciate his son's lovely bride, and envy him a little...

'Ready, Father?' Ben came into the bedroom, and Charles sighed through his smile, remembering the vigorous young sprig he himself had once been. It was like seeing his own youthful image as Ben stood beside him… but today wasn't a day for wishful dreams. He looked quizzically at his son and shook his head slowly as a thought occurred to him.

'I wonder why you wasted all that money in buying me out, Ben. Killigrew Clay would all have been yours one day—'

Ben laughed. 'I know. But I may never have felt it was really mine the way I do now, Father, with the same pride in ownership. The clayworkers sense the way I feel too, and that's worth as much to me as any inheritance.'

Charles smiled more thoughtfully. 'You've really grown up, my boy. It's a longer journey than people realise to grow from a child to a man.'

Ben helped Charles to his feet.

'But you'll admit I was right to choose my own wife, Father? You wouldn't want anyone else for me but Morwen?'

'Would it have done any good if I had?' Charles said dryly.

'None at all!'

'Good. For she's the only one to match you,' he chuckled.

–

The words remained in Ben's head as they drove to Penwithick church. They could have chosen a more imposing church, but this was Morwen's choice, and he was in complete agreement with it. This was where they had first pledged themselves; where Celia had been brought for burying; where it was peaceful and cool and a fitting place for a man to wed the woman he loved, without pomp and with the simplest ceremony, their loved ones around them.

Ben turned as the rustling among the congregation told him Morwen had arrived. He turned, his throat full with love and pride as she walked slowly with her father to stand beside him. She was ethereally beautiful in a pale coloured dress, a posy on her head and carrying a sheaf of wild flowers. On anyone else it might have seemed humble trappings. On Morwen it looked spectacularly beautiful by its simplicity. Her long lustrous black hair framed her lovely face, her eyes seeing only him, love glowing in them as she took his hand, and the preacher began the words that would bind them together for all time.

From then on, the day became a haze for them both. The exchange of vows, the kiss to seal the marriage, smiles and tears and happiness spilling over... leaving the sheaf of wild flowers in the churchyard for Celia... the jaunt back to the the new Tremayne house in traps and carriages, to exclaim over Bess's home-making and the fine spread she had laid on for her daughter's wedding. No Killigrew spread this, but homely fare, baked lovingly by the bride's mother, as tradition decreed.

There were few guests outside the family. Hannah Pascoe had been sent a courtesy invitation and declined, to everyone's relief. Doctor Pender attended, and escorted Charles home afterwards, so the newly married couple could travel back alone.

It seemed but a minute, it seemed like years, before Ben and Morwen were at last leaving her family's house with their good wishes echoing behind them. By now it was late in the evening, and as the carriage rumbled through the wide gates of Killigrew House, Morwen looked at the large mellow stone building as though she saw it for the first time.

No longer in awe of it, but seeing a friendly, welcoming house, lights shining behind the gleaming, faceted windows. Home from this day on… she had lived there for some while, but never in the same capacity. Never as Ben Killigrew's wife…

They went straight to the new bedroom specially prepared for them, where a fire burned welcomingly in the hearth. Ben threw off his topcoat and gently untied the strings of Morwen's soft woollen cloak before he took her in his arms.

'Welcome home, Morwen Killigrew,' he said softly. 'It's time to stop laying ghosts.'

She laughed, tipping her face towards him. He could always read her mind…

'Even if they're comfortable ghosts?' she said huskily.

He drew her close. 'Ghosts are of the past, darling. I prefer to look ahead to our life together, and in time to some adorable babies to delight us both and appease my father. You know he won't be easy in his mind until he sees the future of Killigrew Clay assured by his grandson, don't you?' he added teasingly.

She loved him too much to be embarrassed.

'And when do you propose to begin all this?' Daringly, she teased him back, her eyes glowing in the firelight, her mouth a promise of desire, her arms holding him, wanting him…

Ben scooped her up in his arms. She could feel the maleness in him and the arrogance that had the power to thrill and excite her. He lay her on the new wide bed and began to slowly unfasten the buttons on the wedding dress, pausing between each one to kiss her nose, her mouth, her throat; and then his lips followed the trail of soft white flesh his fingers exposed. She heard the raggedness of his breathing, and knew that the time for teasing was over.

'God, I love you so much,' he murmured against the sweet warmth of her. 'So much—'

'And I you, Ben,' Morwen whispered. 'So much. I never knew such love existed until now.'

Somehow Ben discarded his clothing, not wanting to let her go for a moment, as though even now she might be an illusion, a dream he'd imagined for so long... but now at last he lay with her, his body covering hers, and she was real. She was here in his arms, she was part of him, and he of her... there was nothing else in the world but the sweet tingling joy of belonging, of knowing that pleasure was given and received in equal measure, in love that was limitless... and time ceased to have meaning for them as physical love for each other took them to the height of all sensation.

'I've wanted you like this, my Morwen,' Ben whispered against her mouth. 'I've ached to fall asleep with you beside me, and to wake up with you still next to me, and to know that we'll always belong together.'

'You and I have always belonged, Ben. I've known it in the heart of me, even if I haven't always admitted it. We can't deny what's destined for us.'

He looked into her lovely face, the face of love that only he would see, and saw the sudden exquisite change of expression as his seed flowed into her. They were truly one in those moments, and together they would begin a new dynasty. She clung to him, and there were no more words.

The Cornish Clay Sagas

Killigrew Clay
Clay Country
Family Ties
Family Shadows
Primmy's Daughter
White Rivers
September Morning
A Brighter Tomorrow